Penhally

Southern Classics Series

M. E. Bradford, Editor

Southern Classics Series

M. E. Bradford, Series Editor

Penhally

CAROLINE GORDON

with an Introduction by M. E. Bradford

J. S. Sanders & Company

NASHVILLE

Library of Congress Catalog Card Number:
91-62456

ISBN: 1-879941-03-1

Published in the United States by
J. S. Sanders & Company
P. O. Box 50331
Nashville, Tennessee 37205

Distributed to the trade by
National Book Network
4720-A Boston Way
Lanham, Maryland 20706

1991 printing
Manufactured in the United States of America

To

the memory of

Charles Nicholas Meriwether

of Woodstock

and to that one of his great grandsons

who best exemplifies the ancient virtues

Robert Emmet Meriwether

Introduction

Of the major Southern novelists of the twentieth century, Caroline Gordon has been the most neglected. She is perhaps the least appreciated of the critically and artistically important American writers who have contributed directly to the development of their chosen form. Yet before her death in 1981 she had become an acknowledged master of the craft of fiction—especially among other artists of her own stature. The explanation of this reception, combined with a certain *succès d'estime*, has several components, most notably as regards politics, religion and a certain relentlessness of vision in treating deeply painful subjects. But a major part of the story of her undervaluation has been the unavailability of her books, particularly her first five novels, which are the foundation of her achievement. This third printing of *Penhally* is designed to remedy some of that omission and to allow those who teach and read Southern literature—who cherish it—to have access to the book with which Miss Gordon's career began.

Penhally is a dynastic novel and another Southern book where place is almost the protagonist, a conjunction of place with a particular set of people. Penhally belongs to the Llewellyns only so long as they are possessed by it. The practice of entailing family property is a way of perpetuating this relationship. It is a premise of this work that, separated from the plantation, the influence of the Llewellyns disappears and that there can be no location to deserve that name without the proprietary stewardship of the family situated there, making *that earth* fruitful. Penhally becomes available in Caroline Gordon's rendering of the life of the Llewellyns as it is lived there: an action performed in a particular setting, belonging to it with a certain passionate exclusivity. This story is of four generations in interaction with a specific house and holding—a mixed heritage, flawed from its beginnings by both too much and too little of the personal, private spirit which insists on the primacy of selfhood. Thus the narrative in three parts contained in *Penhally* is tragic, concerning the noble enterprise of family continuity brought to ruin by an invisible weakness closely related to Llewellyn virtues—an action symbolized in the novel by the fate of the big sugar tree growing near the great house where the theme of Llewellyn is unfolded.

Penhally is actually Caroline Gordon's third novel, the first two not having satisfied her own sense of the requirements of her craft. She worked on this book for at least three years; and the labor of its production was painful and exacting—in the midst of a busy life as wife and mother, and advisor to literary friends. For she had so much history and so many people to bring together within the compass of one volume—*her* people and *their* history, as lived out along the southern border of Kentucky just above Clarksville, Tennessee.

Caroline's ancestors, the Meriwethers, Barkers and Fergusons inhabited a small insular world all their own into which the first of them had arrived in the second decade of the previous century, coming out from Virginia to occupy a grant of several thousand acres. There they built substantial houses at Woodstock, Oakland, Fairfield, Eupedon, Meriville, Summertrees, Cloverlands, Glenburny and The Mill, grew tobacco, and amused one another in a great matrix of sociability, celebration and common memories. Usually the inhabitants of this "Black Patch" (the "dark fired" tobacco region) married one another. Ministers, teachers and relations from Virginia were the only newcomers who found places in their magic circle. One such teacher and clergyman was James Maury Morris Gordon, Caroline's father. He had married Nancy Minor Meriwether of Merry Mont, where the novelist was born on October 6, 1895. Almost all of the Meriwether experience important to the work of Caroline Gordon occurred before she was born. Yet it is also true that when she turned her imagination away from this particular Kentucky microcosm her works exhibit less of that certainty of language and dramatic pacing which we associate with her best fiction.

Penhally is an artistic recreation/transformation of the central materials from the history of "the Meriwether connection." The book is dedicated to Charles Nicholas Meriwether, Caroline Gordon's great-great-grandfather, who dispensed legendary hospitality at Woodstock; and to the adventurous Robert Emmet Meriwether, his grandson and Caroline's favorite uncle. Although paragons and larger-than-life, they are normative figures whose grace and gallantry *preside* over the life imitated in Miss Gordon's artistic invention. Indeed, they are its formal predicate. Nicholas Allard Llewellyn, whose decision not to divide the rich lands of Penhally with his brother Ralph, sets the action of this novel into motion, recalls Nicholas Douglas Meriwether, the bachelor brother of Charles Nicholas. Ralph reminds us of the munificent elder brother himself. John Llewellyn, nephew of Nicholas and the heir who enacts his will through the generations, resembles Douglas Meriwether, who married Caroline [Carrie] Ferguson Meriwether and became Caroline Gordon's grandfather. And Lucy Llewellyn shares much in common with Miss Carrie, long the proprietress of Merry Mont.

This list of comparisons could be extended. So the story told by the Kentucky novelist is one which in a certain sense accounts for the history of her own place and time, even though the last third of the novel, the resolution of its action, is an invention out of whole cloth and gives form to the completed narrative such as history rarely provides. It is a form which speaks to the flaw inherent in the Llewellyns' design to live their own way, even when the context around them has collapsed, leaving them confronted by a social revolution and a subsistence economy which frustrate their cultural intentions.

Old Nicholas Llewellyn states as plainly as possible the practical conditions of the family enterprise: that they "might have holdings sufficient to maintain them as they had maintained themselves in Virginia." Yet the ends served by these practical arrangements were larger than they might suggest—indeed, were as large as they might be. For as Chance at the novel's end still understands, "there is something about entailing property. It made a man feel that he was not really the owner, or at least that he had heavy obligations to his successor." His great-uncle Nicholas had maintained almost the same concept in explaining to the leaders of his community gathered at Gloversville (Clarksville, Tennessee) why he stood aside from the great conflict of the War Between the States: "Land is responsibility. When a man's got land he isn't free to follow any fool uprising that comes along. He's got people dependent on him. Women and children. Niggers. . . ." It is a corporate idea of family and stewardship which Nicholas has installed at Penhally. But he has given to it a very exclusive, private cast. Which is part of what is wrong with the enterprise that is Llewellyn, once he controls it. For he is even more "intent on having his own way" than Ralph is in his plan for dividing the property.

Moreover, if what Llewellyn signifies is somewhat private when we first encounter it, that meaning is further narrowed as the novel unfolds until it involves the absolute rejection of family and all social bonds in fratricide: the total alienation of self from the nearest human connections, the otherness of Cain. The action moves from too private (putting family ahead of everything), to even more private (putting self first, as with the father of Nick and Chance) to isolation (excluding all human relations, the land of Nod). In a rage at how his brother has destroyed him by selling Penhally, Chance, the other grandson of John Llewellyn, kills Nick Llewellyn the banker, a man who sees the plantation as nothing more than property which can be converted into cash. Once deprived of his source of meaning, his way of life, Chance attacks his attacker. His fury and despair are comments on the entire action of the novel which preceded this tragic resolution— comments on the effort toward at least a restricted sort of familial oneness, amity and responsibility. In one sense, Chance is the last of the magnanimous proprietors who "had felt themselves more a part of the whole," rather than isolated agents. In the quarrel between the elder Nicholas Llewellyn and his brother Ralph the seeds of this ruin had been sown: in the division between two partial truths, neither of which could sustain a healthy society without its antithesis. Or if not with these brothers, earlier, in the handiwork of their father, Francis Llewellyn, who had carved Penhally out of the raw materials of wilderness, home (says Chance, as he regards the Llewellyn graveyard) to "all the people who had lived and died and been buried on this hill [who] had come into being through the stirrings of this one man's pride."

For those who know the history of the plantation novel from John Pendleton Kennedy and William Gilmore Simms to William Faulkner and Stark Young, there is a temptation to demonize Ralph Llewellyn, the formal antagonist in the plotting of *Penhally*. Yet, he is no selfish beast. Indeed Frederick P. W. McDowell is quite correct in arguing that "Miss Gordon respects his principle of devotion to country and heritage as much as she respects Nicholas' devotion to the soil." Ralph as Jeffersonian *is*, of course, oblivious to the protections against family ruin and dispersal which go with keeping a great property intact. He is a sanguine man who always expects things to work out. Yet it is Ralph who, out of brotherly love, defers to this brother and withdraws from Penhally rather than dispute with Nicholas, either in person or in court, the issue of their father's intentions regarding an entail of his property. Furthermore, when war breaks out, he has a full sense of his larger responsibilities to his culture if Mayfield (his home) and Penhally are to continue. Certainly he overextends himself in giving a horse and gear to all local boys who join Confederate service. But it becomes him that he goes down with the South. His manners comport well with his feckless charm and openhanded generosity; and he is aware of others (especially his children) as individuals, showing regard for those beneath him and leaving everyone room for a private life. That attitude is behind his little speech to his brother (about how "a man likes to live in his own house") with which the complication begins.

Llewellyn as family needs both Nicholas *and* Ralph to survive. One in full dominion over the other is nemesis. Which is a fact we will not recognize clearly until John Llewellyn comes to preside at

Penhally, before he has made a half-hearted marriage for the sake
of family continuity—a marriage which is misery both to himself
and his wife Lucy, his uncle Ralph's daughter. Lucy lost her fiancé
Kenneth Llewellyn because he is "practical," and John has lost
Alice Blair for the same reason. Yet the son of John and Lucy,
Frank Llewellyn, throws his life away by sleeping with (and then
marrying) his cousin Faneuil, who betrays him and brings about
his suicide. For her sake, he has given up Penhally, father and
mother. All of which amounts to both an endorsement of the
romantic view of marriage and, at the same time, a warning
against the destruction it can bring, if love is given to those who
exhibit "bad blood" (i.e., selfishness, greed, vanity or lust). John
and Lucy have been foolish to abandon their son at nineteen
because an adventuress deceived him.

Part II of *Penhally* is dominated by the formal traditionalism of
John Llewellyn, who has returned home after heroic service in the
War Between the States. Even before he turns to Lucy for shelter
he is a man broken in spirit and certainly a lesser figure than his
wife. A quiet gentleman with a transitional occupation, his
grandson remembers, he "had never regarded himself as owning
a stick or stone of Penhally." He is a man who asked himself
whenever "he made any changes in the place or cut down a piece
of timber or anything if it would be all right," reflecting on his
own conduct "as if he were appealing to the verdict of somebody
else." John Llewellyn is virtuously disinterested, with no big
gestures hidden beneath his restrained, often amused, exterior.
His grandson can't get even that far—though Chance is not
entirely to blame for what happens before his place as the keeper
of Llewellyn has been taken from him: until Penhally "no longer
has meaning in terms of society as a whole" and then ceases to
exist except as a club for wealthy "foreigners." Outside forces, of
course, have much to do with the corruption of Penhally and its
environs, but the family is not altogether at the mercy of these
powers. Nick is really like his predecessor and great-uncle, "set
on having his own way." Only when both Penhally and his place
there are gone does Chance kill Nick. For his act has defied the
Llewellyns and their home. The novel begins in the effort to

sustain family, but comes to the opposite conclusion—an irony rendered not only in the murder but also in the strained dispersal of the Penhally inhabitants and in Nick's hollow claim that he has acted only to benefit the family.

But even fratricide cannot make Part III of *Penhally* as vivid and interesting as Parts I and II. This modern afterword is a comment on the declension of the culture of Kentucky in the 1920's which inherited that other Kentucky made by their ancestors. No hero was present to check the erosion, no cultural unity strong enough to pull all of the Llewellyns in one direction. In the action of *Penhally* that loss of meaning is the proper consequence of decisions made by independent and stubborn men and women: decisions reflecting not only pride but also myopia. Little is left for Nick and Chance to decide, once their ancestors are finished.

At the end a Southern expatriate, a wealthy aesthete attempting to gratify the whims of his spoiled and beautiful wife, concludes the narrative of the Llewellyns. Or is the formal cause of that resolution. Nick has sold away his patrimony almost by accident because of Joan Parish's impulse to purchase whatever catches her fancy. The patriarchate is thus negated and cannot once again exist except by a conscious decision of the entire culture, supported by the independent freeholders who define it. Such a possibility the Agrarians wrote about in *I'll Take My Stand*. That not enough of their fellow Southerners were ready to listen should surprise no one who has read *Penhally* with care.

Because it begins classically in the midst of a story, because it contains so many characters and is told from so many points of view, *Penhally* is not an easy book to read. But its effect is certainly accumulative, brought into focus by the violence of its conclusion. According to Andrew Lytle, "The central meaning of the book is its complexity, striking like alternating current, back and forth among the characters, the situation, the historic changes." And indeed *Penhally* is, on one level, a summary of the central moments of Southern history, a microcosm of larger patterns moving from frontier to secession to defeat and its ruinous aftermath, once the region has been absorbed into the process of refounding the Republic "on a sound business basis." William Stuckey has argued that "the book is arranged and the action is managed so that the wisdom of the old way is plainly manifest." Events are kept in perspective, but not with an artificial indifference as to how they are resolved. And if an episodic structure is sometimes confusing it is also true, as Rose Ann C. Fraistat contends, that "it makes history ever present."

Penhally is an exceptionally good first novel and an introduction to the rest of Miss Gordon's fiction. Almost all of the themes which appear in her later novels are first sounded here. In her beginning she had discovered the locus of her very Southern vision of modernity. Her mentor, Ford Madox Ford, her husband, Allen Tate, and her editor, Maxwell Perkins, had all given useful advice. But at the end of this nurturing the novelist followed her own disposition, even to the point of keeping her title which referred to a place and not a person—as in *Bleak House* or *Mansfield Park*. Writing fiction *was* difficult for Caroline Gordon because of the rigor of her craft and the honest, detailed particularity of her vision of the perennial subject, man in all his hope and pride and fear. *Penhally* is a painfully honest account of what happened to one part of the South and of how certain residents of Todd County, Kentucky contributed to the destruction of their world: about the individual, the family and the relation of the two that is civilized and, over time, able to nurture both in a continuity of the living with the dead and the yet unborn. The book set her career in motion, and after its appearance she doubted herself as an artist only as modesty and truth-to-self required. Which turned out to be not too often. Though *Penhally* is not Miss Gordon's finest work, after sixty years it continues to hold its place among the classic accounts of the Southern experience. It is a pleasure to see it once more into print.

Irving, Texas   M. E. BRADFORD

Penhally

Part I

1

1826.

The shadows that laced the gravelled walk shifted and
broke and flowed away beneath his boot soles like water.
He plunged through them as a horse plunges through a shallow stream. Passing the big sugar tree he tapped it smartly
with his cane. It must be rotten at the heart by this time,
though it did not sound hollow. It had been an old tree
when little Sister Georgina—dead twenty years ago in August,
1807—no, 1808—made her doll's playhouse between its
roots, out of bits of broken china and the white pebbles that
lay at the bottom of the spring. The trees grew too close in
here. Any wind storm might send them crashing down on
the roof. Mister Piper would not come for love or money,
in August, when people were having their cisterns cleaned.
The big sugar tree would have to go, and the big poplar,
and the young oak. There would be a vista then, from the
dining-room windows of the house clean through to the big
road. He turned to look back over the lawn—a woman was
crying.

He called to her under his breath, twice: "Shut up. . . .
You fool wench. . . . Shut up. . . ." He would have cried
out, but he knew that his voice would not carry. The lilac
bushes would deaden the sound, and there was a privet hedge
beyond the lilac walk, every bush as tall as a tree. Too many
trees, all around the house. There had been from the time
it was first built. It had been built on its lawn in among the
virgin forest trees. He had seen those trees first as a child
coming with his parents from the old place in Virginia, there
to Kentucky. The old place in Virginia had been like that, a
long gray house, set in the middle of an oak grove. It was

fated that a house should be built like that. Even Brother
Ralph—who had broken up the family with his new-fangled
ideas, building for his bride a house of red brick, the doors
and windows painted white—even Brother Ralph had built
his house on a lawn with around it, already growing, twenty-
three oaks, not one with a trunk smaller than a man's body;
and as early as last spring Sister Maria had set out a double
row of jonquils on either side of the brick walk. They were
leaving to-day and sleeping in the new red house to-night.
Fifteen miles away. In the old days families lived together.
Three . . . four . . . under one roof. There had been
Uncle Will and Aunt Georgina and her mother, Aunt Charlotte and Uncle Ralph's widow, Aunt Lucy and all their
children—Jamie, Sally, who was married to Mister Barnes,
the twins—all the children . . . all of them, when he was a
boy, living there at Penhally.

"Brother" Ralph had said that day at dinner: *"A man
likes to live in his own house."*

But he, Nicholas, not looking up from his plate, had answered only: "There are six rooms in the west wing, sir."

"I shall leave my servants here as long as Ma lives,"
Ralph said then.

"I have plenty of servants to take care of my stepmother,"
he had told Ralph.

*"And I do not think we need to make any division of the
property as long as Ma lives."*

Ralph had said that as if no one else had spoken.

The knife Nicholas had thrown down had cut his plate
neatly in half; his chair fell backward as he leaped to his
feet.

"Sir!" he had exclaimed, and hammered on the table with
his clenched fists, "I do not want your servants or your plate
or your money. I would be obliged if you would take everything that is yours off my place. . . . Now . . . to-day . . ."

In the hall he had struck with the heavy, knobbed end of his cane at the open door of the old mahogany secretary. Then, with the heat of the outside air that suddenly enveloped him, the crying that for the last day and night had tormented them all had come to him again from the Quarter.

My house. . . . He had never, upon his word, thought of it as *his* house before this day. But he was his father's eldest son. The house was his, and the land, the original six thousand acres and the Robbins tract which his father had bought just before he died. The big road was the line. All the woods opposite Mayfield were his. Ralph would have to look at them every day; he should not have the use of them. He, Nicholas, would build a cabin by the gate, put a negro there, with orders to shoot . . . any cow or hog . . . *anything* that came through that fence. . . .

"The big road," he said aloud, "the big road'll be the line. Let him cross it!"

He pushed a low-hanging poplar branch aside and came out on to open ground. The cabins lay before him, white, dancing blurs in the heat that shimmered over the ravine. Shielding his eyes with his hand, he stared down at them, trying to see which house the crying came from. It stood out before him gradually, less white than the others, immobile under the drooping branches of the willow tree. Some one, a lean man in a straw hat, sat at the near end of the porch, his shoulders hunched over, his clasped hands swinging between his knees. The gray blot at his feet was a dog—or a child. But it was a woman who was crying.

He plunged down the path, faster than he had run through the lilac walk, faster, he thought, than he had ever run before in his whole life. The heat seemed to rise up about him in waves. He moved his hands sharply up and down and felt that he pushed the waves before him. The pounding in his left temple was so loud now that it shut out the woman's voice. It was not the pounding in his temples, though, that would kill him. His father, and his grandfather before him, had died of apoplexy, suffocated, the doctor said. . . . They had eaten too much red meat, drunk too much whiskey. . . . He suddenly saw his father, a tall, stooped man in a suit of gray homespun, standing book in hand under the poplar tree. . . . *"Nunc te, Bacche, canam,"* he said, smiling, and bending took the glass from the boy's hand. . . .

He brought up beside the porch, panting. "What's the matter here?" he said. "What's all this infernal noise? I can hear you clear up at the house."

The very old negro man sitting on the end of the porch raised his head slowly and stared. He was so old that the whites of his eyes were almost blue; the faint purplish ring that encircled the milky-brown iris was wavering and ragged. "It's Vi'let, Marstuh," he said. "She's weepin' over partin' from Reuben."

The child on the ground rolled over on its back, whining. The old man prodded it gently with his bare big toe. "Hush up now," he said. "Hush up; ain't no time for *you* to be cryin'."

Nicholas walked slowly up the steps. Halting in the doorway he peered into the half-dark of the cabin. There seemed at first to be nobody in the room. The wailing had ceased, and nothing moved except the sunlight that flickered through the one window. He saw the woman's feet first, brown and motionless in the rectangle of quivering light, then his eye, growing accustomed to the gloom, travelled up the huge mound of her body to the head flung sharply back against the footboard of the bed. Leaning over her he shook her roughly by the shoulder.

"Vi'let!" he said. "What's the matter, Vi'let?"

Her head dropped forward on her breast. She fell against the footboard and lay in a limp heap, her arms and legs sprawling. From the doorway the old man said softly: "She done prostrate herself, cryin' all day and all night."

"God sakes!" Nicholas said. "Where are all the women?"

"Sis Siny up at de house. Sis Maria she out in de fiel'. Emma stay here all night, but she lit out come daylight. She say she can't stand it. Dey all say dey can't stand it. Can't none of um stand it but me. I stays with her and gives her watah. Ev'ry houah I gives her watah."

Nicholas caught the woman by the shoulders. Her yellow bandanna slipped from her head and fell to the floor; he trampled it under his boot heel. "Take her feet, Uncle Ben," he said. "I'll take her head."

Together they lifted her slowly onto the great high bed. The old man whimpered as they laid her down. "I done wrench my back, Marstuh," he said. "I done wrench my back bad. Sis Vi'let's a mighty big woman."

Nicholas took out his handkerchief and wiped the beads of sweat from his forehead, then he wiped his fingers, drawing the cloth delicately over the hollows between the tendons.

"I never could stand to hear a woman crying," he said.

He looked down at the bed. "By Gad, Uncle Ben," he said, "she's going to have a baby."

The old man chuckled. "Lawd, Marstuh, if dat ain't jus' lak you. Sis Siny say it gwine come any day now."

Nicholas stood staring down at her. This, he thought, was what people meant when they talked about negroes turning pale. This woman was pale. Her face everywhere was the same, even, light brown, except just beneath the eyes where the flesh shaded to a dull purple. The muscles under her jaw were slack, the outline of the whole face blurred, heavier than he remembered it.

"She can't go to Mayfield like this," he said. "She'll have to stay here now till it's over."

The old man spat into the cold ashes of the hearth. "Dat's

what I been tellin' her. Dat's what I been tellin' all uv'um. 'Whut you want to go to Mayfiel' fer?' I ask her yistiddy. 'Don't you know de joltin' uh dat wagin' gwine sholy bring you into labor?' "

The woman groaned and sat up, folding her hands heavily over her swollen belly. "I aches in heah," she said. "I aches in heah mightily."

The old man tiptoed to the bed and leaned over her. "Whut kind uv bisness is you up to?" he inquired. "Whut kind uv woman is you anyway—wantin' to have a baby in de middle uv de big road?"

She struck at him feebly with her right hand. "Marstuh," she said, "make this ol' man go 'way fum heah. Ever'body know how mischeevous he is. He done sit heah all day long pesterin' me. Thoo all my trouble he done sit heah pesterin' me."

She spoke dreamily, in a thin, reedy voice. The last words came so faintly that Nicholas had to bend over her to catch them. It occurred to him that she might be dying. He lifted her hand. It was hot and dry, like the hand of a person wasted by fever. He patted her shoulder gently. "Don't you worry, Vi'let," he said. "You can go to Mayfield. Soon as your baby is born you can go to Mayfield."

She began to cry, not with the wailing of the afternoon, but softly, with a rush of tears. "Ol' Miss won't let me go," she said. "She won't nevah heah to me goin'."

"I'll tell her you're going," Nicholas said. "I'll tell her this afternoon."

The enormous tears still continued to force themselves between the pregnant woman's closed eyelids. She murmured: "Ol' Miss don't heah what anybody say. She don't have no undahstandin' . . ."

Nicholas left the bed and strode up and down the little room. "Good God Almighty!" he said. "Women crying!

That's all I hear. Women crying. All night long and all day long. They want to run me crazy. That's what they want. They want to run me plumb crazy!"

He came to a standstill before the window. If Ralph had stayed here where he belonged there would not have been any talk about Violet's going to Mayfield. When his father had come across the mountains he had brought with him besides forty negroes of his own, four broad wives from other plantations. He had bought Ellen and Siny from Cousin Richard Crenfrew and Martha and Mary from the Blairs, and when Cousin Tom wouldn't sell Dicey he had left John at Kinloch. There had never been any talk in those days of separating wives from husbands. But the trouble was that Ma was half blind and perfectly helpless. She would not have anybody else but Violet around her. What were they going to do? You couldn't reason with her. Her brain had softened. She would just cry and say: "Don't take Violet! Don't take Violet!"

But everything was breaking up nowadays. The country was in the hands of New England manufacturers—men who gave no thought to its true interests. The tariff of abominations, as they called it, made it almost impossible to feed and clothe your negroes. There had been meetings of protest in Augusta, in Philadelphia. But what did they amount to? His people had left Virginia because everything was breaking up there. Now everything was breaking up here. The women might very well cry and keep on crying. They would be the first to feel it if the roofs of the old places fell about their heads.

He approached the bed and leaned over the woman.

"You want to run me crazy?" he shouted. "You want to run me plumb crazy?"

Her eyelids fluttered open, then fell shut again.

"No, Marstuh," she said in her reedy voice.

Through his muttering a sound made itself heard, gradually. Men's voices on the path outside the cabin. He was aware now that they had been going on for some time.

Looking out, he saw Ralph and Reuben walking slowly between the whitewashed trunks of the sugar trees—Ralph, bulky, in his buff waistcoat and blue tailed coat, with silver buttons, brown-haired and blue-eyed, in the sunlight, Reuben, the lanky, tall nigger, the husband of the woman who was moaning behind him—uneasy and rubbing one calf on the other.

He stepped from the porch. Midway of the path Ralph stopped, holding out his hand.

"Brother Nick," he said, "I've come to say good-by."

He stood, smiling, his eyes fixed on Nicholas' face. The hand that he extended shook a little. Nicholas, looking down, saw its shadow wavering on the hard-beaten path, and thrust his own hands into his breeches' pockets.

"Don't come good-byin' me," he said. "You've got every woman on the place squallin' like a catamount, and then you come meechin' good-by at me."

Ralph bowed and, stepping out of the path, walked toward the cabin. The riding crop that hung from his wrist slapped Nicholas' legs as he passed; he did not look back. Walking toward the cabin he called:

"Vi'let, here's Reuben."

Nicholas heard his own voice screaming—as shrill and high as a woman's. "I won't have him here," it said. "You can't leave your damn niggers on me. I won't *have* him!"

Ralph stopped short between the whitewashed trunks of two trees and turned so that his florid face with the blue, intent eyes came slowly into view. "He's not my negro," he said. "I gave him his freedom this morning. You can send him away if you don't want him here."

He had turned again. Where his broad slow-moving back

had been there were only the ridged, white trunks of the
sugar trees. Nicholas stood staring. The white trunks of
the trees merged into one white bar that danced against the
scarlets and mauves and pinks of the petunia beds.

The Quarter stretched before him like a village street.
The cabins were whitewashed; there were flower beds
amongst them—against the whitewashed fence that ran
along the back yard of the house—pink and red hollyhocks;
bleeding hearts, dark red; ragged robins; scarlet salvia. . . .
He could remember their building the first cabin. It had
been Mammy's and Uncle John's . . . the one under the big
sycamore tree at the head of the slope. He could remember
playing about it whilst it was being built. Mammy had sat
under the tree nursing Georgina and shouting at the men
whilst they nailed on the shingles. He had been a little boy
of about eight—thirty odd years ago. They had stayed at
old Doctor Crenfrew's whilst the site for the house was
being selected. He could remember his father and mother
arguing about it, she wanting a southern exposure, but he
wanting it a hundred yards down the other side of the slope
to be near the big spring.

They had come driving the wagons over the Old Wilderness Trail, he sitting beside Ben Davenport, the overseer,
sometimes all day, for over a month. Once Ben stopped the
mules and got down because the dogs had treed a coon. It
had been raining and the trunk of the persimmon tree was so
slippery that Ben had hardly been able to get up it.

They had started building in the spring and it had been
nearly time for frost before the last cabin had been finished.
That was the one nearest at hand, on the right. There had
been a big celebration when the Quarter was finished. Old
Doctor Crenfrew had furnished five hogs for the barbecue,
and the dancing and singing had gone on till daybreak, long
after he had been in bed. Mammy had taken him down to

the pits after supper to watch Sam baste the carcasses where they lay on the iron bars over the flames. Sam knew how to barbecue. There had never been any one like him.

But that had been nothing to the celebration when the house had been ready to move into. Every room had been full of candles and when he had walked around in the yard the house had seemed to blaze. They had had fiddlers from Hopkinsville sitting amongst their own nigger fiddlers, but Ben Allard had been the best of them all. He had kept going till he fiddled the last guest out. They had sat down forty-seven to supper, all people staying in the house; company had come to the dance from seven counties; there had been a hundred buggies hitched to the racks and oaks and maples. Mammy had told him that they had made enough trifle and floating island for sixty people, but it had been all gone by the first table. Doctor Crenfrew had been found, black stock, long-tailed coat and all, lying in the big rose-clump at the end of the porch. They had brought up two barrels of whiskey, besides the wine and other beverages.

A party of gentlemen had ridden the bounds of the land a few days afterward with his father. There had been old Doctor Crenfrew and his two sons, his own uncle, Robert Allard, and one or two others. He, a boy of nine or ten, had ridden with them. They had ridden down the Church Hill Road as far as the tavern—three miles. They had turned to the south there and had taken a trail through the woods till they had come to a clearing on West Fork, Watson's Mill. They had spread the dinner there, on a big flat rock above the mill. Mrs. Watson had sent out blackberries and cream and hot biscuits for dessert. After dinner they had started uphill through the woods again. The big sycamore that marked the boundary there and was mentioned in the deeds had since been blasted by lightning. They had come back by the big road that ran along Crenfrew land and had reached

the clearing just as candles were being lit. The house had
been built in a clearing by a man who had lived there only
a year and then had moved West. He remembered hearing
his father say that not more than twenty acres had been
cleared when he settled there. He himself remembered perfectly when many of the fields were being cleared. Dick, his
foster-brother, and another little darky had been detailed to
keep the varmints out of the crops. Squirrels had been a
great nuisance, though they operated in the cornfield mostly
when ros'n ears were ripe. He had stayed with Dick down
in the wheatfield all day long sometimes, keeping an eye on
the deer that every now and then poked their heads out of
the deep woods. And every evening, just after sundown, he
and Dick made the rounds of the big field, the dogs yapping
at their heels, to scare the coons away. . . . They had not
had much of the land in cultivation then, but he had at least
a third of it in wheat and corn and tobacco now, and he was
clearing more land all the time. The sixty-acre field at the
back of the house was in tobacco this year; next year he
would have it in clover. It didn't do to keep land in tobacco
year after year. That was the way they had worn the land
out in Virginia.

Originally Penhally had consisted of a square block with
a big hall running through it. On each side of the halls there
were two enormous rooms. Behind the house, but separated
from it, were the kitchen, the laundry, the smokehouse and
all the other outbuildings; behind them the stable lot and the
carriage-houses. To the east there was the great orchard
whose trees were now in full bearing; along the west ran
an avenue of cedars; along the brick wall leading to the porch
were great clumps of flags. As time had gone on they had
added two wings, one on each side of the house, and an L
in the back. The west wing was built when Charlotte and
Jeems were married. They had gone to Arkansas to live by

now. Ralph could perfectly well have lived there if he had not had his nonsensical idea of a house of his own, and, after all, the west wing would have been a house of his own. For the express purpose of giving their inhabitants privacy and a sense of independence, neither of the wings was joined to the main house. For the same reason Ma was isolated in the east wing. She was the mother of neither Ralph himself nor of Nicholas, having been his father's fourth wife. She sat by the window all day in the big room of the wing. She knew nobody now; there was no use in going to see her; so she sat by the window and killed flies, waited on by the girl Violet, who was now in labor, but who when she was well took care of her like a baby.

Most of the furniture and gear *was* Ralph's. His mother had been a rich woman and had brought her furniture with her from Virginia on her marriage. Some of it had come from England. What was the sense of Ralph's leaving all that stuff? It was his idea to leave everything just as it was until their step-mother died. But what was the use of that to an old woman with softening of the brain who never left her one room?

Ralph had to be a lady's man even to his step-mother. He was the kind of man the ladies all admired, though Nicholas thought that he would be better off if he had a little more horse sense. He himself stood six feet in his stockings, which was quite enough for any proper man. Ralph ate too much; he was already too heavy for his age. He would turn out like Cousin Jimmy Crenfrew, who was so fat he never left his chair. He himself would never put on flesh. He was as lean as a rake and dark. All the Llewellyns—his father's people—were lean and dark. But Ralph was a regular Crenfrew, like his mother—people who were always digging their graves with their teeth.

Lean, dark and with eyes that appeared large because of

the narrowness of his features and were suddenly suffused with rage, he struck at the head of a hollyhock violently with his cane and set off toward the stable lot. He called convulsedly: "Townsend . . . Townsend . . .," his voice echoing away amongst the buildings.

He was going to tell the head stable-man to have wagons put in readiness to take his brother's furniture off the place.

2

Civil War.

The great room was clean swept and bare, its west windows so shadowed by the poplar branches that it was cool, even in August. As Miss Nannie crossed the threshold she stopped and sighed. The last time she had been in that room she had been making wrappers for old Mrs. Llewellyn—three with black stripes on a gray ground and one white, with a black pin stripe. That would be all of thirty years ago. Mister Ralph was now over sixty and Mister Nicholas must be well up in his seventies, but you would never think it. He had not put on flesh like Mister Ralph. His face was as keen as a hawk's and even the white locks in his brown hair were fresh, like old silver.

The negro girl laid the bundle of calico that she had been carrying on the table.

"I heard my mammy tell," she said, "how ol' Miss used to set in that there very chair. Right by the window. All day long. Killing flies . . ."

"That was after her brain softened," Miss Nannie said. "I can remember when this room was the chamber. The loom set right over there in that corner. Old Mrs. Llewellyn kept three, four women spinning all the time. By sun and candle light . . ."

She crossed the room, and dragging the huge, split-bottomed rocking-chair into a far corner, turned it up against the wall. Then she drew a low rocker up to the window and seated herself with her work-basket open upon her knees. From the top of the basket she took a folded length of cloth and handed it to the girl.

"You can begin tearing the goods now, Mally," she said. "Don't tear 'em any wider than this piece."

The slim yellow girl held the material up to the light, laughing.

"Lawd, Miss Nannie," she said, "these skirts is gwine be mighty narrow."

Miss Nannie leaned forward and inspected a length of the cloth. The black bombazine of her crinoline spread itself round her. In bending down, her silver spectacles slipped to the end of her nose. She was a plain woman and supported herself by taking in sewing, but she wore winter and summer stiffly flounced bombazine trimmed with narrow turkey-red braid, and sat down at the first table. She was a perfect repository of knowledge of all the marriages of the whole Llewellyn-Crenfrew connection and their issue. They used to say that to sit with Miss Nannie was to hear things about your grandfather that the old man himself had never known.

She said: "Can't help it. Miss Jessie told me to make 'em just wide enough for the chillun to step over the fence."

Mally bent over the table, still laughing.

"Have to fly ovuh," she said. "Can't no nigger step ovuh the fence in these heah skirts."

Miss Nannie rummaged in the depths of her basket. She expressed with a sigh of satisfaction her pleasure that she had been moved from the hotter, darker room in which she had hitherto worked. "But it's damp," she said. "Can't help but be damp, with these old walls. . . . Mally, when them boys of Miss Charlotte's coming from Arkansas?"

The young yellow girl said that she hadn't ever seen Miss Charlotte. Was she Marse Nicholas' or Marse Ralph's sister? . . .

Miss Nannie said that she was neither. But she was closer kin to Mister Nicholas than she was to Mister Ralph. They might as well have been brother and sister. They had the same blood. Exactly the same blood. Her mother had been an Allard and his mother had been an Allard and their fathers, Llewellyns, both of them, were double first-cousins. Howsomever they said that Mister Nicholas had wanted to marry his cousin Charlotte. . . . But she married Mister Jeems. Some said she had made a mistake; she didn't know. Mister Jeems was said to be distracted, but Mister Nicholas was so curious that he might as well be. There was little to choose between them in her opinion. . . . She remembered Miss Charlotte very well when she was a young girl. Pretty as a picture and with a nice way about her, too. Well, she was dead now. . . .

They said Mister Jeems and the two boys were coming to live at Penhally. Miss Jessie would be as good as a mother to those children. It was lucky for Mister Jeems. He couldn't look after himself, let alone two half-grown boys. One of them must be pretty near a young man by this time.

She found at last the piece of work she had on hand—a man's nightshirt with collars and cuffs bound in turkey-red braid like that on her own dress. She said that that night-shirt was big enough for two or three Mister Nicholases. She had cut it by the same pattern she had used for Mister Ralph.

"Lawd, Miss Nannie," Mally said, "Marstuh sholy wouldn't thank you for that."

Miss Nannie dexterously flattened a loop of braid against the cream-colored cloth.

"I sewed for Mister Ralph Llewellyn the first fall he moved into his new house, and I've sewed for them every fall since. I'm certainly not going to stop sewing for him at my time of life just to please Mister Nicholas."

"Naw'm," the girl said pacifically. "We all said that when Marse Ralph's wife had her paralysis then would have been the time for Marse Nicholas to make it up. But he didn't." She said she had heard that Marse Ralph's wife couldn't even hold a knife and fork to cut up her own victuals.

"She's got rheumatism," Miss Nannie said. "She can't hold a needle, but she ain't paralyzed. She walks all over that yard and she knows everything that goes on on that place. She's a mighty fine housekeeper, Miss Maria Llewellyn is, and a mighty fine woman."

Mally seated herself on the floor at the seamstress' feet and began sewing two lengths of the calico cloth together. "Ol' Miss was paralyzed toward the last so they had to h'ist her in and out that chaih and feed her outa a cup, just like a baby," she said.

Miss Nannie's enormous, flashing shears snipped the end of a thread. She laid them down on the window-sill with a little clatter. "Well," she observed, "she was a very fortunate woman. A very fortunate woman, I always say. Who'd a h'isted her in and out a chair, I want to know, and fed her outa a cup like a baby if she'd stayed a widow?"

Mally settled herself with her back against the wall and took up her sewing again.

"They say that the las' time ol' Marstuh turned out as a widower he drove his high-steppin' hosses all over this county, callin' on the ladies." He had driven all over that county and Christian County too till at last he had selected his fourth wife, who was a widow called Barnhart, with very little property. "Drove up to the front door with a buggy load of white trash, Mammy said," the girl concluded.

"Don't talk to me," Miss Nannie said. "My grandpappy lived adjoinin' ol' man Elkins—that was her father—for twenty years. And he was a plain man, used to take his shoes off after supper and set in his bar' feet. Many a time

I've walked up that path and seen him settin' thar in his bar' feet, talkin' to Mister Llewellyn. Had the same manners for rich and poor, old man Elkins had. Set with anybody in his bar' feet."

The negro girl stirred lazily and stretched herself.

"Miss Jessie tole me to take some cake and wine out in the front yahd at foah o'clock," she said.

Miss Nannie leaned her head out of the window and looked up at the small patch of blue sky visible through the trees, which grew thick on this side of the house. "It ain't four o'clock yet," she said, "it ain't four o'clock by any manner of means. See how short the shadows are." She pushed her spectacles up to look at the girl with her green-mottled eyes.

"You favor Julia a lot," she said. "Was she your mother?"

"Naw'm. That was Mammy's sister. Violet was my mammy. The one that used to wait on ol' Miss."

"She belonged to the Crenfrews, didn't she? Wasn't your father Reuben? The one Mister Ralph gave his freedom to?"

"Mammy always told it that she was the cause of Marstuh and Marse Ralph quoiling," Mally said. "They done quoil several times and the last time they quoil was over the prop'ty. But the first time was over my mammy."

"Is that so?" Miss Nannie said. "I never heard that before."

Mally straightened her slim shoulders with some arrogance.

"Yes, ma'am," she said, "they quoil over my mammy. As you say, my mammy and my pappy belonged to Mister Ralph. They was Crenfrews . . ." Mister Ralph's mother, she said, had brought them both with her from Virginia. The girl's father, Reuben, had later been Mister Ralph's body-servant and her mother had waited on ol' Miss Llewellyn. When she had heard that Mister Ralph had built him a house for his

bride, Miss Maria, she started in cryin' and she cried all day
and all night. She cried all day and all night till the other
niggers ran off and left her. Marster came down to the cabin
himself. He had said that Violet could go to Mayfield with
her husband but Marse Ralph would not take Reuben to
Mayfield because he had given him his liberty.

"I reckon," Miss Nannie said, "your pappy felt pretty
funny being the only free nigger around here."

"Lawd," Mally said, "my pappy wasn't nevuh no free nigger! He didn't pay no 'tention to neither one of them. He
knowed their blood was up." Her pappy, she said, had taken
to the woods. He had stayed there seven or eight days and
all the time Violet was weeping in the cabin and the old half-
blind, paralyzed woman weeping in the house. He had stayed
in a cave in the deep woods and he had come to Violet's cabin
on the second day to tell them where he was. After that a
little boy had gone out every evening to take him food.
Nicholas meanwhile had gone almost distracted. At last he
took a dog and hunted through the woods till he had found
Reuben and told him he could stay on the place. "But Pappy," the girl finished, "had to work in the field after that
'cause Marstuh would hit at him with his cane and cuss him
every time he caught him roun' the house."

Miss Nannie let her sewing fall on her lap and stared out
of the window. The flags that grew in great tangled beds
all around this side of the house were unsightly. The old
lady's doing. She was a great hand to plant flowers, sticking them in anywhere, no matter how they looked. She had
worked for years trying to get flowers on this side of the
house. But the shade was too dense for anything but flags,
and they'd grow if you threw them down on a pile of dirt.
. . . For as long as she could remember people had said that
they didn't know what would happen if Mister Ralph and
Mister Nicholas Llewellyn ever met. Sometimes when she

could not sleep at night she pictured the meeting. She saw them walking toward each other along a dusty road. In summer usually, sometimes in moonlight. They walked toward each other, people somewhere looking on, until Mister Ralph stopped and holding out his hand seemed to ask a question. Then Mister Nicholas stomped and cursed and struck at the flowers that grew along the side of the road with his cane, but Mister Ralph only bowed and walked away. . . . She picked up her needle again and setting the last tiny stitch in the red braid, looked down at Mally. A pretty piece of sass she was, and light. Too light to have around the house if it was her, but of course Miss Jessie Blair knew her own business better than other people could. . . . And Mister Ralph never had been back on the place since? she asked.

Mally leaned on the window-sill and pointed through a vista in the shrubbery to a blasted sycamore tree a hundred yards from the big gate. "He come ridin' up the big road with some gentlemen as far as that ol' dead tree," she said, "and Marstuh walked out and cussed 'em and they all turned 'round and rode back to Mayfield. Some said Marse Ralph come to see 'bout settlin' up the prop'ty but Marstuh cussed him, so he had to go back to Mayfield."

Miss Nannie's eyes, roving over the lawn, fell on the inert figure in the shadow of the big poplar tree. "Hush," she said, "he'll hear you."

Mally laughed. "Marstuh don't heah nothin' when he's nappin' like that," she said.

And indeed Nicholas, dozing in his rocking-chair under the poplar tree, his julep-glass beside him on the gray millstone—a little nigger boy brought him every half hour while he perceived him to be awake a fresh julep and was at liberty to play in the intervals—Nicholas heard their voices only as a confused murmur that rose sometimes above the rustling of the leaves, sank sometimes beneath it. When they ceased—

Mally had gone in search of Miss Jessie—he sat up suddenly, pulled his waistcoat down and buttoned it, and retied his stock. He looked up at the gray house and his hand, which had slid toward his watch pocket, dropped to his lap. He knew that it was four o'clock; the light of the sun was even with the house face, the shadow of the poplar tree just touched the flat stone sunk at the foot of the steps. By five o'clock the shadow would have mounted to the second-story windows; by half-past five the whole house would lie in the tree's gigantic shadow.

He glanced toward the wing and was startled to see a shadow on the grass, between the syringa bush and the little sugar tree, a woman's head and shoulders elongated and wavering in the late afternoon sunshine. It gave him a little turn because in his half-awakened condition he had thought it the shadow of his step-mother that he had so often seen in the same place. But it was only Miss Nannie, who had put her work aside and was leaning out over the window-sill to enjoy the cool of the evening.

"Horse face," Nicholas thought, and wondered for the hundredth time if the white even teeth that flashed between her pale lips were really her own, and if they were not how she had ever gotten enough money together to buy herself a set of store teeth.

He lifted his glass and drained the few remaining drops, then broke the mint stalks into little pieces and chewed them. The flat millstone on which the glasses stood had been there longer than he could remember; dropped there on its way to the mill and there it had lain ever since. His father before him had used it as a table. Strange how that one memory of his father persisted over all others, the tall gray man stooping under the shadow of the poplar boughs to lay his hand on the boy's head. What was it he had said? Some Greek or Latin saying. He had used to remember that too, but it slipped his mind these days. His father sat under the trees all day long in summer reading Plato, a little negro standing behind his chair to keep the flies off. His father had been a good classical scholar. He had been sent back to Edinboro' as a young man to be educated, and started on the voyage home with a Scotch wife. But she died at sea, and the widower married his, Nicholas', mother, Nancy Allard, of Virginia, the following spring. The old gentleman had met her while he was visiting some of the kin. But Ralph's mother, Lucinda Crenfrew, had been the beauty and the heiress. Something of a hoyden, too. They said her black mammy had to call her down from a cherry tree to receive the old gentleman's addresses. He was old by that time, to be marrying his third wife, but he had lived to marry a fourth time, and doubtless would have married again if that wife had not outlived him.

Nancy Allard, Lucinda Crenfrew, Mary Barnhart, not to mention the Scotch wife whose name he couldn't remember. His father had done enough marrying. No wonder he, Nicholas, had remained single. . . . Ellen; that was the Scotchwoman's name, not Annie, but Ellen Laurie.

He hummed a few bars of the song under his breath. When he was a young man his voice was a round and pleasing baritone. He had sung many an evening away in the old parlor and everybody sitting around glad to listen. He had been a good dancer, too, the minuette, the gavotte, the Virginia reel; he had known all the figures. . . . Ralph had built a ballroom at Mayfield for his grandchildren to dance in, he said. And he kept a fiddler, old Mister McLaughlin. The fiddling and dancing sometimes went on all night. People passing had seen lights burning and heard music at three and four o'clock in the morning. He was constantly giving himself the airs of the head of a family. When young Cave Maynor went distracted at the university, from too much ap-

plication to his studies—there was some talk of putting him
in the lunatic asylum—Ralph had written to ask him to make
Mayfield his home. Before he, Nicholas, had had a chance
to invite him to live at Penhally! . . .

Somebody had told him the portrait of Lucinda Crenfrew
hung over the mantel in the ballroom. In a crimson velvet
gown, he remembered, with a rose in her hair, half her face
covered by a fan. The fingers that held the fan against her
lips were too slim and too pointed to look like real fingers,
but he had always thought that the eyes in the portrait were
like Ralph's. . . . Well, Ralph had the forty thousand dollars she had brought his father. He had bought Mayfield
land with part of it, and the bottom land along West Fork.
The plate and furniture, the servants that had been hers remained at the old place. He had sent them all off—the silver
service that had been her wedding present from her father,
the six chairs that she had brought with her from Virginia,
the mahogany tester, the secretary, the little rosewood writ-
ing-desk—he had had them all, together with Vi'let and her
seven children, loaded into a wagon and driven to Mayfield.
Reuben he had not been able to return to his master; because
Reuben for the moment had taken to the woods. He had,
however, sent down to Mayfield, besides the five children of
Vi'let and Reuben, Vi'let's two children by Albert. They had
all come back in the evening of that same day, all, that is, except the picture of Lucinda Crenfrew. . . .

Emerging from the shade of the lilac walk there seemed
to swim toward him a company of women. Miss Nannie and
Miss Jessie, who had kept house for him since the death of
his step-mother. Behind them came the girl Mally, leaning
back and smiling, balancing the broad silver tray. They took
tiny steps, like pigeons. Their skirts were enormous, like
balloons.

Crossing the grass by the great solitary syringa bush they

came to the dusty worn circle on the lawn which was in summer the house place. Miss Nannie was very erect in her
black bombazine, but Miss Jessie, who was so complicatedly,
through so many strains, his cousin, that hardly even Miss
Nannie could have disentangled the relationship, stooped
slightly in her white-dotted muslin. Miss Jessie must be rising sixty-seven by now. But she had no gray in the smooth
bands of brown hair that framed her face and she seemed to
Nicholas still to have the complexion of a young girl.

He rose and went to meet them, and taking the folded
white damask cloth from over the thin, sprigged china on
the tray the girl carried, spread it on the millstone table.

"Miss Jessie's mighty finicky," he said. "Has to have a
tablecloth even when she's eating watermelon outdoors."

He smiled as he looked down into Miss Nannie's eyes.
They were a queer greenish gray, mottled, like the sides of
a trout. There was a gleam in them that puzzled him. He
was always aware when he was in her presence that he was
an object of speculation. He had never known quite why,
and had finally decided that it was merely because he, at sev-
enty odd, was still the eligible bachelor of the neighborhood,
while she was an old maid who made her living by taking in
sewing. The idea of marrying Miss Nannie amused him so
that he had to bend over to conceal a smile. Taking his pocket
handkerchief out he dusted the cane bottom of her chair carefully before he would allow her to sit down in it. "These
chickens have no regyard for you ladies," he said. "They
keep dusting themselves here all day long till the chairs aren't
fit to sit down in."

Cousin Jessie glanced at the dominecker hen that was settling herself impudently at that moment in one of the bare,
dusty holes that ringed Nicholas' chair.

"If Annie would keep the little gate shut they couldn't ever
get through," she said. Her voice was low, faintly plain-

tive. It came to them hardly above a whisper. There was a
story that a stranger hearing Miss Jessie speak suddenly at
a party had sprung forward with a glass of wine, thinking
she was about to faint. She had come out on a visit from
Virginia forty years ago and, finding the old lady bedridden,
had stayed, at first to look after her, and then to keep house.
But during all those years she and Nicholas had never sat
down once alone to dinner. There had always been company
in the house.

Seating herself now beside the table she lifted the napkin
which lay folded over the warm tea cakes, and set wineglasses
and the small flowered plates on the gray millstone.

Nicholas lifted his frosted glass. "Perhaps Miss Nannie
will drink a julep with me," he said.

Miss Nannie's white teeth flashed briefly. "I thank you,
no, Mister Llewellyn," she said. "Whiskey flies straight to
my head."

Mister Nicholas Llewellyn, she reflected, was not in any
way as attractive a man as his brother. He was too long and
lean, for one thing, as brown as a nigger from sitting outdoors all summer long. And it was a wonder to everybody
the way he kept himself clean-shaved, for all the world like a
hog about to be killed. A beard, or even a mustache, would
help his looks considerably. But he would never have his
brother's manners, not if he lived to be a hundred. There was
something about the way Mister Ralph Llewellyn bowed before ladies or children—she had seen him bow in just the
same way before his daughter, and a spoiled little hussy *she*
was—there was something about it that stayed in your mind.
Gal*lant*, that's what it was. Of course he had the advantage
of his brother in figure. He was a fine figure of a man,
whilst Mister Nicholas was as lean as a sapling. And yet,
even at his great age, Nicholas was not in the least stooped,
and when he was dressed up for a dining, standing tall before

the hearth, with the long tail of his coat parted behind him, and the seals of his fob gleaming below his black satin waistcoat, and his long trousers strapped beneath the instep and his brown hair gleaming with its silver locks . . . well, you couldn't say he did not look a fine figure of a man, too. But he neglected himself and would doubtless keep on getting leaner, the way he drank whiskey all day long and sat out in the sun. As for the nights . . . Miss Nannie abruptly drew a veil of maidenly modesty over Mister Nicholas' nights. They were no concern of hers, and she thanked God they weren't. But how Miss Jessie Blair, a lady born and bred in old Virginia, could stand the goings on . . . No wonder old Lady Llewellyn had moved into the wing.

"You're late this year, Miss Nannie," he was saying. "You were here last year when we were making blackberry wine, and the blackberry wine is a month old to-day, ain't it, Cousin?"

"I stayed at Mister Ralph's longer than I thought I would," Miss Nannie said. "Miss Thyra was there this week. She came up with me as far as Sycamore."

Nicholas laughed. "Then she'll be here next week," he said. "Thyra never can stay long at Sycamore. She can't put up with Willy's free niggers."

"She'll be here in a week or so, cert'n'y," Cousin Jessie observed. "I hope the late tomatoes are in by that time. Thyra does love those yellow tomatoes . . ."

"Let's see," Nicholas said, "she was here two weeks from to-morrow last year . . . on my birthday. We had yellow tomatoes for supper and ros'n ears, the last ros'n ears, but the tomatoes had been in for several weeks before she came . . ." Behind his calculations his mind played with persistent curiosity about the house from which Miss Nannie and Thyra had come that day, driven by Edward in a light buckboard, the roan mare, Sally, no doubt, between the shafts. He knew

what Ralph's house looked like—he had driven by it one day
on his way to Gloversville—a square red-brick house, with a
white portico and deep galleries on either side, covered with
Virginia creeper, and turned sidewise from the road. In
the centre of the meadow below the house there was a large
round pond. To the left of the pond there was a kind of
plateau. The racetrack was on the plateau, and on the right,
between the pond and the racetrack, were the stables, long
wooden sheds, half-hidden behind clumps of sumac. Ralph
liked having the stables there under his nose, no doubt, liked
having the horses and all the activities that centred about the
horses there where he could look down on them. He had
always liked fooling with horses better than anything else.
Well, he had bred some good horses. He, Nicholas, had
seen his filly, Anne of Geierstein, beat Colonel Winn's Di-
omed colt in a match race on the Bledsoe Creek track, and
had cheered with the rest. . . . Ralph had had to give up
riding, though, somebody had told him. He could not buy
or breed a horse that would carry his weight. He must have
taken on a great deal of late years. . . . He had sat his
mare, Colette's filly, she was, and sired by his own Gunpowder, easily enough the last time Nicholas had seen him.
That had been twenty years ago. He had ridden in at the
gate early one morning, between Robert Allard and old Doctor Crenfrew. The filly, catching sight of some horses she
knew in the pasture across the road, had whinnied a little, and
Nicholas looking down from the porch had seen Ralph staring up at him through the branches of the sycamore, the same
sycamore that now stood, blasted, by the gate. It was bad
luck, they said, to look at the new moon through the leaves.
It had, perhaps, been bad luck for him to see Ralph's face
through those sycamore leaves, new leaves they had been,
with the faint white down still on them. He had known at
once what the three men wanted. Ralph, though he would

make no open claim for it, regarded part of the Penhally tract as his. He had said once that their father, who had died suddenly of apoplexy under the very poplar tree beside which Nicholas now sat, had intended him to have half the land, whereas Nicholas was quite certain that his father had intended him, as the eldest son, to inherit all the land. It was true that there was no entail, but his father, though he spent his time mooning over books, had had sound ideas on such subjects. Ralph, brought up in the West, did not understand these things, and would not be instructed. The money that had come into the family with Ralph's mother was, no doubt, his: he had turned it over to him quick enough. But the land was Llewellyn land. His father had come out here and bought land in order that his family might have holdings sufficient to maintain them as they had maintained themselves in the old days in Virginia. He intended to hang on to it as long as he lived, and when he died he'd see to it that it wasn't parcelled out in hundred-acre tracts among Ralph's children and grandchildren. Land was no good to anybody that way. You might as well give it to the first beggar who came along the road.

Miss Nannie was looking at him. "I reckon Mister Jeems and the children'll be here next week," she said.

"I don't know, Madam," he said. "I don't know. Bro' Jeems never takes the trouble to inform me of his movements. . . ." He had gotten up and walked down the drive toward the three men. The other two, Robert Allard and Doctor Crenfrew, had kept back in the shadow of the sycamore, but Ralph had ridden toward him. He had not made any motion to get down off his horse or to shake hands. "Brother Nicholas," he said, "I have asked these gentlemen, whom everybody in the neighborhood knows to be men of honor, to come with me here to-day to see you about settling up our property."

He had not known until he tried to speak how angry he was. His throat had gone dry; he had had to put his hand up and press it against the base of his throat a moment before any words would come out. "Our property?" he had said. "*Our* property? Damn you, get off my land!"

Ralph had sat very still a moment, staring at him, before he wheeled his horse and rode back to the men in the shadows. Nicholas, walking back up the drive, had heard through the crunching of his own boot soles on gravel Ralph's words to those men:

"I am sorry, gentlemen. My brother Nicholas is not himself to-day. We will have to postpone our business."

The three of them had ridden out of the gate then and down the big road. . . . Ten years ago they had come near meeting face to face. . . . At the Aytoun sale, Nicholas, pushing his way through the crowd, had come up suddenly against Ralph, standing beside old Doctor Crenfrew. The old doctor had evidently been asking Ralph to ride somewhere with him, in the back country, probably, behind Penhally—for Nicholas, before he turned away, had heard Ralph say, in a voice so loud that nobody around him could help hearing: "I cannot go there with you, sir. I have not set foot on Penhally land these twenty years."

That was not true, though Nicholas, for whose benefit the words were probably said, could well believe that Ralph did not know that he, Nicholas, had been aware of his sole visit to the home of his birth. It had been during the great cold wave ten or twelve years before when an epidemic hitherto unknown had struck nearly all the horseflesh of those parts. It was supposed to have been brought in by horses imported from England—a pest, the main features of which were that the knees and hocks went puffy and then that the whites of the eyes turned scarlet, the temperature rising until the beast got over it or died. That it was probably English in origin seemed to be proved by the fact that English horses were relatively immune from it, as they would be if it came from their own country or if they had had it when young—but even English-born horses were only relatively immune. And after a month, during which the epidemic had been the occasion of endless conversations and losses, the famous thoroughbred stallion with the white star on his forehead and the white off forefoot, which their father had imported from England in the year before his death—even the famous Gunpowder, the pride of Townsend, who had charge of all the Penhally horseflesh, and the envy of every one owning anything on four legs for fifty miles round . . . even Gunpowder began to swell on his off foreleg.

And Ralph had the reputation of being the best man for dealing with the disease of any one within two hundred miles! . . . Nicholas knew—for nothing else was talked of in those days—that Ralph, setting himself boldly up against Craven, Nimrod, Hawley and all the great thoroughbred breeders of the day, announced that the proper treatment of the disease was the retention of the infected beast sheeted up in the warmest possible stables, its feeding on the most heating foods, even to the administration of small but repeated doses of alcohol—whereas the English experts advocated exceptionally well-aired stables, cold mashes and frequent drenchings, but certainly after the publication of Ralph's much-discussed letter in the *Christian County Sentinel,* the disease had seemed to be on the downgrade, at any rate in such stables as adopted Ralph's advice.

Townsend, already aging a little, with an expression of panic and his eyes starting out of his head, had come in the early morning to the breakfast-table to announce that Gunpowder's knee was puffy, and the first idea that had run through Nicholas' head was that Ralph should be sent for. But when Townsend had begged that that very course should be taken he had dismissed him with a "God damn you, Townsend, go on about your business!"

Toward midday Townsend, who was actually gibbering, had begged Nicholas to go down to the stable. There was no doubt that the horse was sick; his eyes were already lightly filmed with pink; he was shivering and the skin of his ears burned your palms. He had recommended the negro to sheet him very heavily and to give him a feed of warm boiled corn. But Townsend was already off on a flood of implorings to be allowed to send for Ralph. Nicholas had raised his cane, but had then swung round on his heel without a word. He hoped that his silence would be taken as permission, for give the permission himself he could not.

It was a horrible thing to see a great and usually fiery beast reduced to moping and shivering, and Nicholas could not but regard the animal as half belonging to Ralph. It had been the purchase of their father, no doubt with partly Crenfrew money. Penhally might have been Ralph's. home if he had not chosen to take himself off with his wife, and Nicholas had already made the gesture of sending off to his brother a great part of the furniture and gear. The very trouble between them was not that Ralph desired part of the property, but that Ralph refused to share it all between them; *Brother,* the fool had said, *a man likes to live in his own house. . . .*

Well, then, the horse being half Ralph's, let him come and look at his own property. Nothing in the world would have dragged from Nicholas the permission to send for his half-brother. He would have let the poor beast die rather. Yet he could not bring himself to refuse the permission. And he was pretty sure that Townsend with his maniacal affection for the stallion would take the matter into his own hands and take the chance of punishment.

So when, toward midnight, he had looked out of his bed-room window he had seen that the doorway of the stable was an orange oblong with the elongated shadows of men passing against the light. He had gone down; the cold night had been very dark; he had kept in the shadows until, peering in through the stable-door he could see, brightly illuminated, the hunting-crop, the high-collared riding-cloak and the tall, bulky figure of his brother. The features were hidden by the shadow of the collar, the lantern doubtless being on the floor. He was pointing with the handle of the crop to a large rotted aperture in the backboards of the stable.

"Fill this with sacking," his clear voice had come. "Cover the whole back of the stall with blankets. Hang blankets all round it on ropes. Like curtains, you understand? Like curtains."

Those were the last words of Ralph's that he had ever heard, and it had been the last time he had seen his form. And he imagined that no one else knew that he had either seen or heard, so that the memory was one he hugged to himself and luxuriated in.

"I think, Miss Nannie, I will go in," Cousin Jessie said. "It is a little chilly now the sun is down. Cousin, will you ring?"

Nicholas struck with the ferule of his cane the broken gong that lay against the base of the millstone. As he followed the ladies across the lawn it occurred to him that Ralph would have to set foot on Penhally land one day . . . to lay foot on it when they brought him there for burial.

3

Nicholas paused when he came to the brick walk and took from his waistcoat pocket the old-fashioned silver chronometer, as large as a good-sized turnip, that he had inherited from his father. Five o'clock: he would have time to pay Jeems a little visit before supper. He took the path that

slanted across the lower half of the yard, past the "office,"
and climbing the stile into the orchard, walked between the
laden boughs toward the corner of the enclosure where
Jeems' "shop" was. The two-room brick building that they
called the shop had been built years ago—when Jeems first
came back from abroad—to house his experiments, but lately
Jeems had taken to sleeping there. He rarely came to the
house now, except for meals. It distressed Cousin Jessie.
She felt that he ought to maintain some connection with the
life about him. "I'm afraid he'll go *plumb* distracted," she
kept saying. "What's to keep him from going plumb distracted if he doesn't even come to meals on time?" What,
indeed, Nicholas thought, and smiled to himself at the idea
of Jeems coming to meals on time.

He could see now through the apple trees the irregular
sloping roof of the shop, rising above its tangle of vines and
weeds. This unkempt acre had been Jeems' dominion ever
since he could remember. He had not been back from Arkansas any time, yet it was already taking on its old look.
He would never allow any of the weeds to be cut, denied, in
fact, their existence. No such thing as a weed," he would
say, and he would point out that the fruit of the wild potato
vine that farmers nowadays grubbed up as a pest had saved
many an early settler from starvation. Jeems, though he
could hardly, as Miss Jessie maintained, distinguish fried
chicken from smothered, was full of theories about diet. He
believed, for instance, that the whole population could maintain itself indefinitely on the flesh of the mussels that were
found in great beds along the banks of the tributaries of the
Mississippi-Missouri River system. Nicholas found it interesting to speculate about these things. He had actually had
scallops from these mussels cooked and brought to the table
in great steaming platters. But nobody would eat them. Not
even Jeeems, who sat throughout the meal in his usual silent

abstraction. Coffee made from soy beans had been another of Jeems' suggestions. That, too, had fallen flat.

Nicholas stopped at the fence which encircled the small plot. Between him and the shop the jimson weeds grew in orderly rows. He observed them with interest. Jeems had told him that the flies which hovered over them laid the eggs that developed into tobacco worms. The nectar of the jimson weed was their favorite tipple. Jeems was making some experiment with them now, using nicotine as a poison. He had hopes of depreciating next year's crop of worms. It seemed a sensible plan to Nicholas. Something would have to be done sooner or later about the tobacco worms. No question but that they were increasing. They had not had pests like that in the old days. He could remember as a boy walking over whole fields of tobacco and not finding more than a dozen worms, whereas nowadays it took every little nigger on the place to keep the crop wormed.

He turned in at the little, sagging gate. "Jeems!" he called loudly, "Jeems, what you doing?"

The white-haired man who was stooping over the scales in the dark room did not stir. Aleck, the tall thin negro who had been Jeems' body servant when he was a boy at Penhally and all through his years of wandering, came softly to the door. "Marse Jeems is weighin'," he said in an undertone.

Nicholas sat down in the one creaky rocking-chair that the porch afforded. Sitting there he commanded a vista: the whole orchard, the peach and plum and pear trees, at least—the apples were on the other side of the house where they had a northern exposure—slanting away, only slightly up-hill to where a stake-and-rider fence marked the boundary of the sixty-acre field. Albert Owens, the young overseer, was stooping around in there now, examining one tobacco plant after another, in order to convince himself that he had

been right in deciding it was not yet time to cut! Nicholas
smiled, glancing about the orchard. He could walk through
that field with his eyes shut, touching a leaf here and there
and tell whether it was time to cut the tobacco. Well, experience counted for something. He had been at it now for
fifty years, no, more like sixty. He had begun walking over
the fields to notice the crops when he was a small boy. And
he had kept up the practice all his life, no matter how good
an overseer he had.

He reflected upon the seasons. He remembered clearly the
year 1826, when there had been snow upon the ground every
month but one. There had been few unseasonable years
though, after that, in this part of the country. He had heard
an old man say that that was always the way in newly cleared
country. It was as if Nature, observing how hard man had
to work to clear the land, encouraged him after it was cleared
so that he might not take his hand from the plow. There
had hardly been a year since his father settled in this country when you couldn't make a good crop; of tobacco, at least
—they had early had to give up the culture of cotton. One
bad season, indeed, he recalled. There had been a spring
drought, followed by a good tobacco season. Everybody in
the country had got his tobacco set out, then came a drought
that lasted till frost. Tilman Pruitt, a young farmer of the
community, had gone mad over the drought. He had come
up into the yard where old Mister Llewellyn sat, book in
hand, under the poplar tree, day after day, to announce: "It
ain't goin' to rain no more, this year, Mister Llewellyn." He
had made the announcement one day with particular finality,
adding with a derisive smile that he had laid his crop by. He
had, indeed, taken to his bed—before his tobacco was knee
high!—and he had remained there all through July, August,
September and October. He had been right, too. It hadn't
rained again until the last of October. Tilman had been a

little cracked always after that, but he had a great reputation over the country as a weather prophet.

Jeems was standing in the doorway.

"Well," Nicholas said in the hearty tone in which he always addressed his cousin—as if he were making it up to him for being unfortunate, although, he reflected, no man in the world was more contented, *happier,* really, than Jeems, who always did exactly as he pleased, and never even considered what other people might think about it. "Well," he asked, "how you getting along to-day?"

Jeems was silent, rubbing his thin hands and staring vaguely out over the orchard. Nicholas was not perturbed. He had observed that Jeems often did not answer a question until some minutes after it had been asked. He always heard it sooner or later and answered it carefully; that was one of the reasons why he disliked being in company. The necessity of carrying on conversation galled him. He often talked, though, for hours with Nicholas here at the shop. Nicholas turned around and peered into the dim room. He could see that the pan on the scales was heaped with a fine grayish powder, the results, he supposed, of the latest experiment. That great pile of bones that had been whitening over by the sinkhole all summer, the great glass jars of acid that Jeems had procured at great expense from Memphis and had had brought out from town in specially constructed straw-lined barrels, all these had gone to make that little heap of gray powder. He wondered how much of it there was on hand, not enough, probably, to scatter over an acre. Still, it would be interesting to see the results, on an acre, even a half acre. He would have that little piece of ground back of the office plowed and harrowed—no, not harrowed. Jeems said it would be better to put the fertilizer on right after you plowed and then harrow it in. He would have it put in order immediately anyhow, under Jeems' direction, and they would see what happened. That they would get results, he did not doubt. Everybody knew what stable-manure did for land. It stood to reason that the decomposed bones of animals would put life back in it. It was a problem, though, to get enough bones to do any good. Even when you could persuade people to give you or sell you a quantity of bones—they thought, as a rule, that you were crazy—there was still the problem of hauling them great distances, and the niggers hated it. They would tell you all sorts of lies to get out of hauling the bones. He had heard a young nigger laughing around the stable: "Marster and Marse Jeems going round the country and collecting old dead cyarcases. They gwine turn buzzard if they don't watch out." It was all right to have your own niggers laughing at you—or your own kinfolks—on your own place. It was different, though, when you were living among strangers, as Jeems had lived, for six, no, seven, years in Arkansas.

Jeems had left the threshold and was sitting down on the edge of the porch. He seemed entirely oblivious of Nicholas' presence, leaning back against the post, his eyes closed, his clasped hands swinging between his long, thin legs.

Nicholas regarded him indulgently. Jeems was better educated than he was. He had remained at the University of Virginia four years and then had gone abroad to study. He had not taken to the classics, though, as his uncle, Nicholas' father, had hoped he would. He had studied mathematics, physics and chemistry and when he returned from his stay abroad he had set up a laboratory, first in one of the unused wings of the house and later in this same building here in the orchard. It was strange that Jeems should take to science the way he had. There had been a few good classical scholars in the family, one, at least, to a generation, but there had never before been a man of science. Jeems had a good many correspondents, men of science, abroad, in England, mostly,

one or two in Germany. As a young man he had been great
friends with Thomas Jefferson of Virginia. They discussed
Continental plants that they thought could be introduced into
this country with profit. It would have been better, Nicholas reflected, if Tom Jefferson had confined himself to science, instead of setting the whole country agog with his half-
baked political theories. Virginia, indeed, was in a parlous
state. A man could not, actually, entail his property on his
own children's children! That was one reason why his grandfather, Robert Llewellyn, had approved of his son's coming
West. Virginia, he said, was breaking up under their eyes; it
would be better to leave and settle in a new country.

He was glad he had Jeems and his two boys—Robert was
a limb; anybody could see that with half an eye, but the older
one, John, might have something to him—he was glad, anyhow, that they were all here at Penhally. It was not advis-
able for boys as young as that—the older one couldn't be
much over nineteen—to be in the care of a person as absent-
minded and erratic as Jeems. They had actually had difficulty
in locating the fellow for his wife's funeral! Mammy Sarah
had reported that, groaning. The people in the neighborhood
had joined together in a search party at the last minute and
had found Jeems taking his usual morning walk along the
usual road. It was, of course, the very place where they
might have expected to find him—if they had thought of his
being in the mood for a walk on that particular morning.
. . . Well, the world wagged on, though people died, like
Charlotte. She must have hated dying away from home and
all her kin, but Jeems would never have thought of that.
He had not made a very good husband. She might better
have taken him, Nicholas. He had never been able to see
why she had preferred Jeems to him, as a matter of fact!
Jeems, even as a young man, had not been handsomer or
more of a ladies' man, and he had no inheritance except a lot

of wild land in Arkansas that nobody knew anything about.
. . . They had had a good time here at Penhally when they
were all young, the Crenfrew twins, Dolly and Fanny, Charlotte, Aleck Woodford, Willy, Jeems and himself. They had
all been in love with Charlotte at one time or another. Aleck
had been desperate over her, all one summer . . . and he
himself had lain, face down, in the sweet fern along the
path there, for *hours* one night weeping over her refusal
to marry him. He tried to recall the emotion of that night,
but could remember only how he had despised himself when
he got up for the tears that kept streaming down his cheeks.
. . . It all seemed very long ago. . . .

Jeems was looking about him, indignantly, as if roused
from sleep. "Bro' Nick," he said, "can you not do something to restrain the young people of this house?"

"Why?" Nicholas asked lazily. "They been bothering
you?"

"They walk round and round in the orchard. A young
woman and her escort walk round and round in the orchard.
Surely they can find some other place to walk."

"Which ones is it?"

"It is your nephew, Charles, I believe," Jeems said irritably. "Charles and a young kinswoman whose name I do
not know."

"That's Alice Blair," Nicholas said. "Yes, most likely it's
Charley and Alice Blair."

Charles, Ralph's only son, spent half of his time at Penhally, in spite of the fact that his father and his uncle were
on bad terms. A handsome, indolent scapegrace, with his father's blue, intense gaze and his mother's bright coloring, he
was a great favorite with Miss Jessie, with all the ladies. It
would be Charles walking in the orchard with Alice. He had
been courting her all the summer. The girl had come out from
Virginia in the early spring on a visit, much as Miss Jessie

herself had come out forty years ago. She would marry one
of the young men who clustered around her—Charles, more
than likely. He was, no doubt, the best catch as far as property went, though Ruffin Woodford, who, at twenty-four,
managed a thousand acres for his invalid father, was, in
Nicholas' opinion, a more estimable young man. Charles had
been raised too soft. What had become of that good old
custom of sending the sons of the family to the field occasionally? He could remember hoeing many a day till noon,
right along with the niggers. True, it had been usually his
own choice; he wanted Dick, his foster-brother, to finish his
task early so they could have the rest of the day to go fish-
ing. But it had given him a taste for the soil that had endured all his life. Charles, likely, did not know the feel of
a hoe in his hand. Most of his time, according to report,
was spent in the stables—he was, indeed, a good hand with
horses, as his father was before him—and in gaming in town,
or even in Louisville.

He rose and stood looking down at Jeems. "I'll tell 'em
you've got the whole place mined with gunpowder," he said.
"I'll tell 'em it's likely to blow up any minute."

Jeems made a gesture of annoyance. "Tell them anything,"
he said, "so long as I am spared their presence. I find them
singularly annoying."

Nicholas swung down from the porch. He had caught
sight of Albert Owens striding across the orchard. It occurred to him that Jeems would find Albert, too, singularly
annoying; he had better forestall him. He waved his hand
cheerfully at Jeems as he started up the path. "Better be
getting ready for supper," he said. "It's almost time."

Albert Owens saw him coming and stood still between two
apple trees. The blue grass that that year covered all of the
orchard except the enclosure around the shop reached above
his knees and was speckled here and there with daisies. He

flicked with his whip at a bright yellow butterfly. A well-set-up young man in his early thirties, his handsome, heavy face nearly always wore a worried look. The Penhally place, he often said, was too much for one man to oversee, but he would have died sooner than divide his duties with any other man.

Nicholas spoke affably as he came abreast of him. "Well, Albert, you goin' to begin cuttin' to-morrow?"

"I don't know," Albert said. "What do you think of the weather?"

Nicholas squinted over the tops of the trees at the one cloud, tinged now with lavender and gold, that was visible on the horizon. "I don't see much rain in that sky," he observed. Albert never believed that any weather could hold. If it was fair he thought that it would be changing, and if it rained when rain was needed, it could never hold out to do any good. He was walking along beside his employer now, still scowling.

"When we fire this year," he said abruptly, "I'm goin' to try wet sawdust. Strikes me you goin' to get mighty dry leaf this time. . . ."

If the leaf was dry, Nicholas reflected, he would be responsible in some mysterious way for its dryness, whereas if it turned out well it would be the result of Albert's skill and foresight. A good man, though, Albert, one of the best overseers in the whole country. . . . He looked about the orchard. The light that struck patterns across the grass was greenish gold, filtered through heavy drooping boughs. There was already in the air the smell of ripening apples. Some time, in the next few weeks, he must have them get the cider-presses out and give them a good going over. It would be fall soon. The season had already turned. Because he was feeling unusually well and in good spirits he said mischievously:

"I was over at Fairfields yesterday. Mister Ruffin has got some mighty fine hay in that bottom next to the woods. Clover and timothy."

"He most always has good hay," Albert said moodily. "I don't like the way he does it, though. I never did like that way of doing it."

Nicholas nodded. "I know," he said. "You always track in it when the snow's on the ground. Well, that's a good way too. . . ." They had come to the stile. He climbed over, leaving Albert on the other side. When he had gone a little way toward the house he turned around and called to the overseer: "You goin' to the Quarter? . . . Well, I wish you'd tell Uncle Ben to come up after supper and bring his fiddle. . . ." It had just occurred to him that there were more young people than usual staying in the house. They might as well have a dance that night.

4

"If you think it won't rain," Alice said, "I'd hate to get wet."

She had reined her horse in, though, and sat looking down the slope toward the spring. John examined her face with interest. They all said she was so lovely. He did not think, really, that she was as pretty as his cousin Lucy, Charley's sister. Lucy would be considered a beauty anywhere. She had regular features, big blue eyes, bright golden brown hair. Alice's hair was ash blond, her eyes—immense gray eyes with heavy, dark lashes; did she put something on them to darken them?—were too large for her face and her mouth was too small for beauty. "Cat-faced," Cousin Thyra called it. She had a way of twisting her hands together when she was excited; she was doing that now. . . . "Law," Cousin Thyra had said, "she don't need to be any prettier. She's

got all the young men in the family crazy about her now."
Charley, who was known as a philanderer, was in love with
her. Lucy said that he was making a fool of himself. While
Alice Blair was walking in the yard with Ruffin after supper
last night the folks sitting on the porch had been talking
about her: Cousin Thyra, Aunt Jessie, and Lucy. They all
thought that she was a flirt, that she was leading Charles on
when all the time she was engaged to marry some man in
Virginia. Lucy, he knew, thought that. The two girls did
not seem to confide much in each other. Well, he thought
that was not strange. If he, for instance, were in love, he
would certainly not confide in his brother, Robert. He would
do, in fact, everything that he could do to keep Robert from
knowing about it. Not that it would do any good. Robert
could ferret out anything. . . . He glanced up at the cloud
which was gathering in the west. "It won't rain before
night," he said.

They left the horses and took the path that led through
drooping pine boughs down toward the spring. It was little
travelled. Pine cones and brown broken needles were everywhere thick upon it. Last year's layer crackled faintly under
their feet, but the dark mass beneath was sodden and unmoved.

They had come to the spring. She was kneeling beside the
rock wall that had been built up, breast high, around the pool
to gulp the icy water. A tremor ran through her body. She
raised a wet, glistening face. "Aren't you going to drink?"
she asked.

"I'm not thirsty now," he said.

He sat down with his back against one of the sycamore
trees that overhung the spring. The light that struck through
the trees all about them was flickering and very bright, as
the sun's rays are before a rain. They lay on the surface of
the pool in a quivering, luminous pattern. Sitting there on

the ledge he could look down, through the shifting layers of light and shade, straight into the depths of the pool. The water was clear; green really, but the dead leaves at the bottom gave it a grayish look. In one corner where there were no leaves the spring bubbled up through swaying wreaths of bright green gelatinous moss. It was a small rill, hardly large enough, it seemed, to form the volume of water that spilled over the ledge and ran in a broad shallow stream through the rocky basin of the ravine.

Alice was seating herself beside him on the ledge. She had taken her hat off and flung it on the ground. The skirt of her black riding habit fell to one side in a long trail. She pushed at her bright hair with fingers that were still damp. "I'm glad you brought me here," she said. "It's a lovely place."

"It's the biggest spring anywhere around here," he said; "the biggest spring in the whole country, I reckon. It was here when folks first began to settle this country." His uncle Nick had told him how he had first seen it as a boy of eight when they drove up over the hill. One of the negroes, looking down and seeing the tops of the cottonwoods, had shouted out that there must be water in that ravine. The men of the party and the eight-year-old Nicholas had run pell mell down the slope to fall on their knees beside the water. Nick got down on his knees and lapped like a dog, he was so thirsty. The men nearly died laughing at him.

"Did they settle around here on account of the spring?" she asked.

"I don't know," he said vaguely. "I reckon they did. I reckon they had to look out for water wherever they settled."

His eyes dwelt on the bright green mint that grew thickly in the shallow bed of the ravine. His thought followed the stream in its wanderings. It flowed, he knew, through the length of the Penhally land and the Fairfields woods, crossed the big road in front of the Sycamore house and dipped into a sink hole on Cousin Rufus Llewellyn's place. After that it flowed underground for miles, to emerge in a deeper stream that ran tortuously through the bottoms to empty into Little West Fork, which was an arm of Red River. It had, too, innumerable tributaries. The little branch that flowed from the spring behind the Penhally house was one, the shallow, bright stream that came from the mouth of Crenfrew's Cave was another. And he had heard his uncle Nick identify a stream twenty miles away as part of the same system. That stream emptied into Red River, which emptied into the Cumberland, which, in turn, emptied into the Mississippi. And at Cairo, Illinois, the Mississippi met the Ohio and flowed with it toward the gulf. They said that you could see the two rivers flowing side by side for a time, the one tawny yellow, the other greenish black. He himself might go down the river in the fall, when they loaded the tobacco on a flatboat for New Orleans. The old gentleman had suggested it. He was getting too old to go, he said; he would be glad to send somebody in his place. Albert, the overseer, was a good man, but he had no judgment, no judgment at all. . . . Some change in the shifting pattern of light and shade made him look up. The cloud that had been gathering back of the woods lay right over the tops of the trees now. As they watched, a streak of lightning zigzagged across the sky and great drops spattered into the cold water of the spring.

Alice was standing up. He took her arm and they hurried up the steep path to emerge panting on the wagon road. A few yards away Flora and the gray four-year-old were whinnying and pawing the bark from the trunks of saplings. Alice laughed. "I always get excited, too, before a storm," she said.

He took a step forward. "We ought to get out of here," he said. His words were drowned in a rattling clap of thunder. He shouted: "It's dangerous . . . to be in the woods . . ." The wind was rising. It tore through the woods in great gusts. The saplings were bent double before it. The horses were suddenly invisible in the midst of the hard, driving rain. He put his hands tentwise to his forehead and was able to locate a spreading network of black branches, the fallen tree that he remembered to have noticed beside the road. They struggled toward it against the wind.

Alice resisted when he sought to draw her in under the branches. He caught her by the shoulders and thrust her under the tree's slanting trunk, then climbed in after her. The network of branches was suddenly black against sheet lightning. He put one arm about Alice's shoulders, then caught both her wrists in his other hand and held them prisoner against his breast. "Shut your eyes," he commanded.

She obeyed, drawing a long, shuddering breath. They leaned back against one of the great branches. The boughs over their heads broke the downpour so that it fell on them with comparative gentleness. They were drenched, but they were not pelted as they had been a few minutes before. Outside the shelter the rain beat down monotonously, a crystal curtain that hung in heavy, straight lines or swayed occasionally before the driving wind. At least half an inch of water must have fallen, John calculated. He followed it in his thoughts over the farm. The corn had been needing rain, but a gulley washer did more harm than good. Corn could take a lot of beating down, but this rain would tear it up by the roots. And it would injure the tobacco. . . . Her hands were tense in his, but their touch was soft as a moth's wing. He had not known that hands could be so delicate to the touch. . . .

She was drawing her hand away. "We can go now, can't we?" she asked.

The rain had, indeed, slackened. And the wind was dying as suddenly as it had risen. She was wringing out her long skirt, laughing and saying that they would probably have to walk home. The horses would have broken away.

"No," he said. "They'd stand. Horses are afraid to move around during a storm."

She continued to talk, vivaciously, still laughing as they made their way through the drenched undergrowth to where the horses still stood. He observed the play of her lashes and the bright color that came and went in her cheeks, but he was not listening to what she said. Through a rift in the undergrowth he had caught sight of the river bottom below. The sun glinted on water where ordinarily were the tops of trees. He could make out the tip of a cedar tree that he thought must mark the opposite bank . . . or perhaps that tree was completely submerged. . . . It would be at least seven miles to go around by the woods road. If he had been by himself, he could have tried to get across. . . .

They rode forward, the horses splashing up to their knees. The back water was yellow, laced with foam and broken, black twigs. When they came opposite the line of willows that marked the bank John reined in.

"I reckon we'll have to go back to Sycamore and spend the night," he said.

"Oh, . . ." she said, "don't let's go back!"

He watched the water eddying around the great, white trunk of a cottonwood. He had climbed that tree only a few days ago, to fix a creek swing in the top. The lowest branches that were now lashed by the current must have been at least fifteen feet from the ground then. . . .

She had ridden closer and was laying her hand on his arm. "Please . . ." she said. "Please, let's don't go back!"

He turned around and looked at her. "You think you could swim that horse across here?" he asked.

She nodded. Her eyes were enormous in her pointed face, almost black. The little hand was tightening its pressure on his arm. "I know I can," she said.

He laughed and leaning forward caught hold of her bridle rein. "Stay right with me, then," he said.

They rode around the willows and out from the shelving bank toward the deep water. The horses arched their necks and stepped cautiously, already aware of danger. The current struck the gray first and lifted him off his feet. He plunged crazily right and left. The girl was sawing on his mouth with that flimsy bit. If it broke, or if she lost her head, they were gone. . . . He had no business trying this with a girl. . . . They would all say that. . . . He leaned far out of his saddle and gripped the gray's rein nearer the bit. His face was almost touching hers. He shouted at her:

"Keep him in the ford. . . . For *God's sake* . . . You've got to keep him in the ford! . . ."

She was speaking, in a low voice, but peremptorily: "Let him go. . . . I can manage him."

He released his hold and settled back in his saddle. Flora was off her feet too, now, but swimming as easily as if she were in a pond. She would get across, all right . . . but the gray was green. . . . Alice was the only woman who ever rode him. . . . She seemed cool enough now. If she would just let him have his head and sit tight. . . . But the current was strong along here. . . .

It was swirling over the pommel of his saddle now. . . . And a second ago a great riven branch of some tree had swept past them. . . . Flora's ears were laid back. The muscles in her neck stood out in ridges. . . . It was all she could do to keep her head against this current. . . .

He turned and met the gray's dark, straining glance. He was not making any headway. . . . It would be all over if they were swept past the ford. . . . The bank below there was covered with thick undergrowth. . . . There would be no chance of getting out. . . .

He shouted above the rushing of the current: "Bear upstream more. . . . Pull him upstream, hard . . ."

She had heard and understood. Her face, white and very small, came slowly toward him as she swung the horse around. The gelding understood too. He had left a great trough there in the water when he plunged forward. . . . Flora was swimming in his wake. . . . He watched the water fall away from her sleek shoulders, then realized with a start that for several seconds now she had not been swimming. . . . The gelding had come to a standstill under the cottonwood tree. . . . Alice, swaying in the saddle, had reached forward and caught hold of a limb of the tree. She had turned around to look back over the rushing water. She was laughing and her eyes shone.

"I thought there for a minute that we weren't going to get through," she said.

5

Charles let the branch that he had been holding swing to behind him. They were out of sight of the house now, though the wild-plum thicket was only a few yards from the orchard fence. He went swiftly up to Alice and took both her hands in his.

"I don't see what that young fool was thinking of," he said. "You might have been drowned."

She stood still in the middle of the path, not resisting the pressure of his hands on hers, yet yielding nothing. Her eyes were bent down. He knew, though, the expression they would have if she looked up. An open candid gaze that was almost a stare. She would look at him like that, almost without expression, and he would punctuate a love speech with a laugh. "Well, all right, I *won't* make love to you, then," but in a minute she would make the familiar play with her lashes and the whole manœuvre would be repeated again.

He shook her hands, a little roughly.

"A negro man and two mules were drowned in that ford," he said. "A fine teamster and two young mules. Swept the mules right up against that cottonwood tree and stunned 'em, and the man was drowned trying to get to their heads."

He had been drawing her along the path as he spoke, and now they had reached the open place that was in the heart of the thicket. Rain rushing down from the hill above had left the ground dark with moisture, but the leaves over their heads were quite dry. Not even a cloudburst such as they had just had could penetrate through that thick roof of twisted vines and boughs. It had always been like that in here. He realized suddenly that he had wanted for a long time to show her this place, and that now he was showing it to her when he was out of humor. Out of humor? And no wonder. He had been at the parlor windows all afternoon, watching the thunder clouds roll up to form a black lowering mass over the drive. The lightning had been terrible. One of the great oak trees on the lower lawn had been struck; the trunk had been cloven as neatly as one quarters an apple. They had walked down to look at it after the storm was over. It was then that he had looked up to see Alice and John approaching between the blown, wet branches that overhung the drive. Her riding habit was wet, her hair was streaming down her back. She was laughing. They had both come up, laughing like idiots, to where everybody stood around the great splintered oak.

He had not realized until that minute how uneasy he had been about her all afternoon. He had told himself, of course, that they would have seen the storm rising before they left Sycamore. But he had known all along that young John

would not have any more sense than to ride into a storm.
That was just what they had done. If even then they had
had the gumption to turn back! But they were not content
with risking being struck by lightning any minute. They had
to cross the creek when it was in flood. He became suddenly
very angry. Young John might content himself with risking
his own neck. He had no business dragging Alice through
floods—raging floods; the water, they said, had actually come
up as far as the second creek bottom. He himself could not
remember when it had ever been so high, though Uncle Nick
said that at least once in his time it had licked the steps of
the miller's house—and mounted on that scatter-brained
gray! They had no business to allow a woman on that horse.
He had behaved well enough, it turned out, but there was no
telling what might have happened. Horse and rider might
have been swept down the stream and drowned. His heart
contracted as he saw Alice's small, white face, upturned,
floating, between wreaths of hair . . . under the bridge by
the mill . . . people standing, staring down. . . .

She was detaching her wrist from his grasp, delicately,
but with unmistakable intention. "I didn't think about that"
was what she had said, smiling.

He stood still in the path, absorbed in contemplating her
gesture. "I'm in love," he told himself with pain. "Gad, I
really am in love this time."

She had sat down on a fallen tree that lay across one end
of the little clearing. He went over and sat down beside her.
Between them on the tree trunk there was a space as wide
as both his hands. The bark of the tree was rough and gray-
green, heavily ridged, with white, worn places showing
through here and there. Innumerable ants ran up and down
in the ridges. The backs of some of them shone blue-green

in the slanting rays of the sun. The ruffles of her skirt were
stirring. She had turned so that she faced him.

"I never swam a horse before," she said. "It was wonderful. Charles, it was really wonderful . . ." She went on
to tell what an exciting time she and John had had crossing
the ford. There had been a moment when she had thought
they were not going to get across. She could already feel
herself being swept downstream, and then the gray's hindquarters had doubled under him, "almost as if he were taking
a fence," and they had shot forward into smoother water.
He watched her face as she talked, but he kept his mind to
what she was saying with difficulty. The anger was all gone
out of him. She had done that with one gesture of the hand
that lay now in the space between them that had been vacant.
Her hand was white and thin. He wondered why she wore
no rings. Her people were very poor, he knew. Her father
had run through with a handsome property, he had heard,
in an incredibly short period, but for well-born women there
was always jewelry, handed down from mother to daughter.
It pleased him, though, that she wore no rings. His mother
would give him the emerald that had been her mother's for
their engagement ring . . . and the square cameo. . . . He
had told his father last night that they were going to be
married. Or rather his father had asked him about it. It
had happened that they two had been alone on the porch after
supper. They had sat there silent a long while until his
father, knocking the ashes from his pipe, had said, smiling:
"Well, son, Alice Blair going to have you?"

"I expect so," he had said, and had added that they might
be married in September, or October, of that year.

"October," the old man had said, musing. "October's the
turn of the year," and then, "Have you thought where you
going to live?"

He had said then that there was a grove of trees on the

lower end of the place—it fronted the old post road and had the creek at its back—a grove mostly of oaks, with a few magnificent elms and beeches scattered through it, that would make a good site for a house. His father had said that he had left those trees there, thinking that some day a house would be built on that little hill. There was a fine spring, not three hundred yards from the highest spot in the grove. The land lay well, too, around that eminence, and the creek bottoms brought fine corn. There would be some difficulty though, in finding sites for the outbuildings. They would have to be built, some of them at least, on sloping land.

"But you can get around that," he had said. "No question but that's the place for the house."

The matter had not been mentioned again, but he had thought of the hill ever since as already peopled. The house should be tall, statelier than Mayfield or Penhally, a porch with square white columns running across the front, deep latticed galleries on either side of the long L that should run back twice the length of the main building. He knew just the place in the grove where it should stand, far enough back from the brow of the hill to allow a wide sweep of lawn in front. Four of the handsomest oaks should be preserved to sentinel it at each corner, but many of the trees would have to be felled. It would be, though, a place of deep shade, cool in summer and sheltered by the trees from the winter winds. She would perhaps have a flower garden on the eastern exposure, and in the rear, slanting down toward the spring much as they did at Penhally, would be the outbuildings and the Quarter. . . . They would have to decide soon on which negroes they would take. His father had said that he intended to give them as bridal presents three negro men. Two of them, Jake and Oliver, were not over thirty years old, as sound, each of them, as a dollar. Bascom, old Uncle Isom's son, was a delicate negro and must be well over middle age by this time, but he was an expert blacksmith; could, in fact, turn his hand to almost anything; Charles would do well to take him in lieu of a younger negro. The old gentleman had said also that he would present the ladies' maid that he had bought in New Orleans last year to Alice. She could also have her pick of any two of the younger house servants. . . .

She had gotten up and was moving about in the small, open space that was circumscribed by the black trunks of the plum trees. She had stopped where a butterfly, opening and closing his wings, clung to a broken bough. He walked over and stood beside her. The butterfly's wings were pale green, edged with black; in the outer corner of each wing there was a large, fawn-shaped dot. The veinings that ran across the wings to converge at the body were silken and glistening, the whole design miraculously exact, conventionalized like the pictures that young ladies paint on glass or on the silk covers of albums.

She was turning her head a little to smile up at him. Her eyes in this cool, shadowed light were impenetrable. He could feel against his shoulder the light fabric of her dress shaken by her breathing. He resisted the impulse to lay his hand on her bare arm that curved along the branch between them. He knew that he could not bear it if she made again that minute gesture of aversion. He was suddenly seized with panic at the thought that he might, after all, never possess her. He would have then this desire to endure indefinitely. . . .

She was putting her hand up to touch his cheek. Her gaze was questioning and bright. He drew her to him and kissed her.

"Don't play with me, Alice," he said. "I can't stand it."

6

"Cousin Jess," John said.

Cousin Jessie was so absorbed in contemplation of the table that she did not hear him until he had called her twice. She raised an abstracted gaze, and then, seeming to think that he had been answered, bent to rearrange the roses that filled an enormous lustre bowl in the centre of the table.

"Those Tennessee Belles grow in such loose clusters," she murmured, "but the George Fourth roses are too dark, at night, don't you think?" She straightened up and clapped her hands sharply. "George," she said to the half-grown negro boy who stuck his head through the swinging door, "George, run out in the garden and cut some more roses. Right smart roses . . . You hear?"

John advanced into the room. Standing beside his cousin he surveyed the supper table. His eye, roving the length of the shining board, past the multitude of shallow glass dishes filled with sliced tomatoes and cucumbers, the round glass bowls set on slender stems filled with preserves and jelly, the smoking, covered tureens of gumbo, butter beans, corn, creamed potatoes or cimlins, past the immense, glistening ham whose topside was stuck with cloves and crusted with cinnamon, came to rest on the double stack of plates at the foot of the table. He had not known that there would be so many people to sit down to supper. Fifteen or sixteen, no, more like twenty. The stack of plates would reach breast high when the old gentleman sat down.

He moved a dish of mint jelly gently backward and forward until the whole mound began to oscillate. "Cousin Jess," he said, "let *me* sit by Alice Blair."

Cousin Jessie leaned forward and took the dish out of his hand, matter-of-factly, as one puts articles out of a baby's reach.

"Well, you'll have to have Ellen on the other side of you then," she said.

John made a face. "Why?" he asked.

"I d'know," she said; and then firmly, "That's the way I always do. You ask the other boys. The one that sits by the pretty girls has to have Ellen on the other side." She took a handful of roses from the basket which George was holding for her and thrust them among the roses in the great bowl. "G'long, honey," she said, "and see if everybody's ready for supper."

John did not move. "They're all on the porch," he said, "except Pa." He cast a glance at the steaming platter, heaped with chickens, which George was setting down at the head of the table. "Cousin Jess," he said, "is it true that Cousin Willy Crenfrew eats three chickens at a meal?"

"I certainly hope he won't," Cousin Jessie said absently. "I didn't tell Mandy to fix but eight."

She took the bell out of George's hand and rang it vigorously. John repressed a smile as he watched her. It would have made no difference, he reflected, if George had been ringing the bell at top speed, spinning around like a whirling dervish as he sometimes did, until he fell exhausted in the shrubbery. Cousin Jess would come right along and take the bell out of his hand. She had an energy that contrasted oddly with her tired voice. She seemed always on the point of doing something for you, better, of course, than you could do it for yourself.

As if materialized by the sound of the bell two ladies and a very fat gentleman had appeared in the doorway, Uncle Nick walking behind them. They were all four gravitating toward the old folks' end of the table. Ruffin Woodford, Charles' sister Lucy, Charles himself, Tom Crenfrew, John's brother Robert—all the young fry had seated themselves as near as possible to Cousin Jessie. Four lank youngsters con-

tended noiselessly for a moment as to which should sit at her
right hand and then subsided into the first seat they could
find under the dark look of inquiry which the old gentleman
suddenly bent upon them. John stood his ground until Alice
and Ellen Crenfrew were seated, one on his either hand,
then directing a comical look at Cousin Jessie, he bent so-
licitously over long-nosed, red-haired Ellen Crenfrew and
asked her how all the folks at Sycamore were.

She replied that they were all well except Aunt Drusilla.
"One of those summer colds," she said. "You know how
they hang on . . . with old people . . ."

Her voice, trailing off into silence, left the statement hanging in the air between them. But conversation with Ellen
was always like that. She could never forget that nose of
hers long enough to finish a sentence. He kept his eyes on
his plate, realizing that she had suddenly become conscious
of how ugly he thought she was. It was Cousin Jessie's
fault, always making young men sit beside the girl and dance
with her. She ought to leave her alone, or with the older
people, where she was really happier. . . . Charles had
slipped into the seat on the other side of Alice, of course.
He might have saved himself the trouble of asking to sit
beside her. It did not matter, though. He *was* sitting beside
her. He could hear her light, even breathing. The frill that
was on the shoulder of her dress brushed his arm. She was
turning slowly toward him, smiling. He remembered suddenly that he ought to inquire after her health. "I hope you
aren't tired," he said politely.

She laughed and said something; it *sounded* like "I could
dance all night," but Charles bent toward her at that moment. She had turned away before John could answer.

Across the table Robert was writhing with suppressed
laughter. It was, apparently, the presence at his side of
George, the house boy, that convulsed him. George, proffer-

ing his tray at just the right angle, his face perfectly impassive, yet managed in some secret way to acknowledge that the situation was humorous. Some tomfool joke that they had between them. Robert was like that, with niggers . . . poor white people too. . . . That was how the Roder woman had come to take them for poor white folks. The incident that he had thought forgotten rose sullenly in his memory. . . . Years ago it had been, before their mother died. They had run away from home to play in the branch that was just below the Roder cabin. At noon Robert had had the idea of getting something to eat from the people in the cabin. "Cold biscuits or something like that," he had said. "Cold biscuits are good with salt on them."

The woman hoeing in the field had looked at them curiously as they clambered up the bank. Robert had gone right over to speak to her. "Please, ma'am," he said, "kin we git something to eat here? We come fu'ther than we aimed to, and we didn't bring no lunch."

Hearing him speak, John had wanted to turn and run down the road. He had made himself stand still, had forced his eyes to meet those of the woman. Those eyes, in the deep shadow of the slat sunbonnet, had been at first startled, then merely curious, but the woman's voice, when she spoke, was listless, indifferent even. "M'ria," she had called, hardly raising her voice, "here's some chillun say they want something to eat."

The rocker's squeaking had stopped abruptly. An enormous woman in a blue Mother Hubbard came slowly around the corner of the porch and stood surveying them. "Lawd, Abby," she said suddenly and smiled, "I thought they wuz some white trash come beggin'. Them's the chillun of that crazy Mister Llewellyn lives up the road," and smiling again, "Come in, chillun, I'll fix you a snack."

Inside the cabin she had set a pan of cold biscuits and a

jar of blackberry jam before them, on a red-and-white checked cloth. He had been ravenous, but Mammy's voice kept sounding in his ears: "Don't never eat nothin' off poor white folks. Ain't no tellin' what they'll give you. Stew up a lot of flies in the jam soon as not." He had wondered, as a child, why Mammy hated poor white folks so, and how they were different from other people. He had thought once, when he was much younger, that they were distinguished from other people, people like himself and his family, by odors, the mixture of odors that was yet somehow one distinct odor, that was always associated in his mind with their dwellings, just as negroes—even Mammy—had a distinct body odor. He had learned better than that. Cousin Fanny Crenfrew, out from Little Rock to spend the day, had stopped on the threshold of the boys' bedroom, wrinkling her nose fastidiously. "Good *heavens,* child," she had said, "this place smells exactly like poor white folks. It'll have to have a thorough cleaning."

The poor white woman had sat rocking to watch them eat; the snuff stick that she had laid on the table while she was setting out the dishes depended from the corner of her mouth; a tiny drop of ambeer worked its way downward over her slightly bulging cheek. She regarded them complacently. "I hear your ma is mighty po'ly. It's a good thing now y'all got that ol' colored woman to look after you." Then with a faint, evil smile, "I seen your pa goin' up over the hill a little while ago. Abby and me been tellin' Ed he oughta drug that cow a heap further off'n what he did, but Ed he laughed and said he didn't want to give the old gentleman no more trouble 'n was necess'ry. . . . Does your pa ever take y'all with him when he's goin' round over the country huntin' up them dead critters?"

There had been silence in the cabin, broken only by the steady chop-chop of the hoe outside. He put a spoonful of

jam on the last piece of biscuit, ate it slowly, then slid down
from his chair. "We're much obliged," he had said, "for the
jam . . . and everything. Good day."

"Good day," the woman said, and rose from her chair, still
smiling, to accompany them to the door. Robert had stood
by honorably while John unfastened the twine latch and
slipped it back into place, then they ran at full speed down
the dusty road. The consciousness of the moment died gradually in the rhythm of their pounding feet. They were ready
to go back to the dam they had been building by the time
they reached the bridge. They had worked all afternoon,
swiftly, not talking, avoiding each other's eyes. Going home
across the fields in the twilight Robert had said suddenly:
"If that nasty old poor white woman ever comes in our yard
I'm going to shoot her, straight through the head."

"Stomp on her," he had said; "stomp her right down into
the dirt. That's what we ought to do to her."

The slim dark boy on Robert's right was leaning forward
to inquire if he could not come up to Fairfields to shoot doves
one day next week. "You've never been to Fairfields, have
you?" he said. It was strange to them to think that he had
never been to Fairfields . . . or to Cabin Row . . . or to
Glenburnie. "We must go over to Glenburnie one day before
the summer's gone," somebody said every now and then.
Before the summer was over he would have re-visited all the
roads and all the places that he remembered as a child. They
thought that all these places and people were new to him and
strange, but they had always existed somewhere in his memory. Mayfield was a cool, dark hall smelling of lavender and
sweet fern; Sycamore was white columns on a high hill; a
sloping stretch of sward, covered with bright fallen elm
leaves was for a long time the only memory he had of Penhally, but now that he was here he knew that he had had
always somewhere in his memory the outline of the sloping
gray roof and the shadow of the poplar tree.

The dark boy's name was Llewellyn Woodford. And there was Woodford Llewellyn and Llewellyn Llewellyn. Llewellyn turning on itself and still Llewellyn, but never Llewellyn as he had known it before. Llewellyn. The name had belonged to him in Arkansas, to him, to his father, his mother, to Robert. "Is Mister Llewellyn around the house?" the strange man asked, and the name was in his mouth, distinct, indivisible, a name that could belong to nobody but his father.

Yesterday Cousin Thyra, getting out of the buggy, had thrown back her veil to look at him out of malicious, sparkling eyes. "Well," she had demanded, "have you clean forgotten me? What's my name?"

"You're Cousin Thyra," he had stammered; "Cousin Thyra Llewellyn." And Cousin Thyra had laughed before she swept into the house. "I don't blame the boy," she had said. "I reckon he thinks everybody in this country is named Llewellyn."

He caught his breath sharply. His father was standing in the doorway. A tall, stooped, preternaturally thin old man, he wore a coat that was bottle-green in some places, in others merely frayed. His long, white hair floated to his shoulders. He turned a blue, childlike stare on the company; then his eye brightened as he caught sight of his foster brother.

"What are all these people doing here, Nick?" he asked in a high, querulous voice.

John half rose from his seat, then fell back. Aleck, the slim negro youth who was his father's body-servant, had reached the old man's side in one noiseless bound. He was piloting him now to the seat that had been left vacant at Uncle Nick's right hand. Uncle Nick himself had stood up to greet his cousin. The smile that illuminated his dark features was cordial and unembarrassed.

"Just some company for supper, Bro' Jeems," he said. "Most of 'em are kinfolks."

7

Nicholas finished carving the last slice of ham and sent George scurrying around the table to replenish the plates. He lifted the glass of whiskey that had just been set before him and drained it at one gulp, then leaning back in his chair he surveyed the company. Cousin Thyra and Willy Crenfrew were having an argument about John Brown, the man who had made the raid on Harper's Ferry last year—no, year before last. Nicholas, already in a pleasant glow from the whiskey that he had taken, went at once to Cousin Thyra's rescue.

"It'd been a sin and a shame," he said tartly, "if they *hadn't* hanged him."

Cousin Willy did not answer: his mouth was too full. His sister, Virginia, leaned forward to fix mournful eyes on Nicholas. "But, Cousin," she said, "the man was only doing his duty as he saw it."

Her eyes were light brown, ringed like an owl's. He contemplated them for a moment without speaking. As far back as he could remember, the sight of her had annoyed him. Well, she would come into none of his property! Levelling his carving knife at her he said loudly:

"Trying to do his duty! . . . Trying to commit treason, madam!"

Virginia was already fluttering into speech, but he looked away from her at Cousin Thyra, two down on his right. Here was one woman with no nonsense about her. Owning nothing but her snuff-box, round, shaped like a bull, she travelled from house to house, staying as long as it pleased her. She was with the Crenfrews now at Sycamore. She would be coming to Penhally soon and they would play cards under the trees.

Next her was young John, Jeems' son, Charlotte's first-born. This was a fellow to have the looking after of property. Charlotte had had more sense than any of them. It didn't matter who a man's father was so his mother had some sense. He had taken the boy half round Penhally that afternoon and, asking questions of the overseer, John had shown he had more sense about farming in his little finger than Ralph had in his whole body.

And he was a regular Llewellyn. He had the Allard wide, heavy mouth of his grandmother, and the low forehead; otherwise, except that he was fair, he was like enough to himself. Lean, nervous, tall, with enough space between his eyes for some sense. . . . Here at least was one of them that wasn't a fool.

He felt himself coming pleasurably out of his lethargy, and with his carving knife still levelled at Virginia Crenfrew he repeated loudly:

"Trying to commit treason. That was what he was trying to do. A lot of people think they're doing their duty when they go round the country interfering with their neighbors' business. Firing on a sleeping town, hauling respectable citizens out of their beds at night, stealing property! The man was a scoundrel and deserved the hanging he got . . ."

Cousin Jessie sat quiet, until the knife came safely to rest, missing by a quarter of an inch the ruin of the Wedgwood plate which was one of the half dozen that had descended to her from her grandmother Leyton, then breathing a short prayer of thanksgiving—she was a very religious woman and spent a great deal of time in prayer—she said with a little laugh:

"I thought that what poor Lewis Washington said was very amusing. He told that Captain—whatever his name was—that if he wanted his servants he'd have to go and find them. They were off at a barbecue or something, and there wasn't a negro on the place when John Brown came to rescue them."

Nicholas menaced the company again, this time with the carving fork. "Rescue," he demanded, "what was he going to rescue 'em from? Where would the negroes go if they were free? What would they do? That's what I'd like to know. Willy here has a lot of free niggers on his place, but what good are they? He couldn't give 'em away. Nobody else would have 'em."

Cousin Willy shook his head. "Don't believe in slavery," he said, and helped himself to half of a broiled chicken from the platter which George proffered.

"No," Cousin Virginia said, "I don't either. You can't imagine what a satisfaction it is to me to go to bed at night knowing that there isn't a soul born in slavery on our place."

"There are at least ten," Nicholas said. "Aunt Ida isn't dead yet, is she? Or Virgil or old Jim or Tom Allard?"

Her gaze wavered before his and fell to her plate. "You know what I mean, Cousin," she said.

"Don't know what anybody means," Nicholas observed, "except by what they say." He began carving more ham and sent George scurrying around the table again. Willy and Virginia, he reflected, were the softest-headed ninnies in the whole connection. The old doctor, from whom they got all their nonsense, would be disgusted if he could see them. A wrong-headed man, the old doctor, and eccentric, but no fool, like these two. Freed all his slaves, the old doctor had, one morning in October. Three years ago. Got them all up to the house and broke the news to them. "You're free now," he told them. "There are papers in the house to prove it. You can stay here and work for me if you want to or you can go somewhere else." They were still shillyshallying about it, though. Nobody else in the country would have the Sycamore niggers on his place. . . . A man had a right to do what he wanted to with his own property, no doubt, within certain limits. The old doctor had meant well with *his* eccentric ideas, but he had certainly played the devil with his children. Here was Virginia, at forty, corresponding with Northern abolitionists, and Willy, at forty-five, growing roses instead of tobacco. An acre of roses he must have on that slope toward the woods. . . . No, a man didn't have a right to free his slaves when his neighbors all around him owned slaves. It upset the whole community and played the devil generally. . . . He looked up over the rampart of roses to where Lucy sat beside the young Virginian, Kenneth Llewellyn. "Well, Lucy," he said, and raised his voice so that it carried over the hum of conversation, "how's everybody at your pa's?"

Leaning back in his chair he waited, pleasantly alert, for her answer. He always enjoyed introducing his brother's name into conversation like that. It made people jump. They hardly ever knew how to take it, their assumption being usually that he chose to forget that he had ever had a brother, while the attitude that he really took was that the brother, whose existence he perfectly recognized, was no more to him than a casual acquaintance.

But Lucy did not jump. Turning so that she faced him she called down the table in a clear voice:

"Pa isn't a bit well, Uncle Nick. He had another heart attack last week. Cousin Ben wanted him to stay in bed, but he wouldn't."

There was all at once about the table a rush of light, fluttering talk that rose and died away as rapidly as the twittering of birds. Cousin Virginia's high, reedy voice was left, saying:

"I can't think you're right about that, Thyra. If you knew what I know . . ."

Nicholas stared down at the square of white table cloth visible between a tall preserve dish and the base of the enormous lustre bowl. The cloth, where it was not shadowed by the roses' stems, was covered with minute, interlacing figures that glistened in the candle light, some flower or leaf probably . . . no, shamrock. Table linen like this was made in Ireland, he had heard. With the prongs of his fork he traced a sprawling four-leaf clover beside his plate, fluted the edges and filled each leaf with dots. . . . Ralph would probably die before he did. These huge, hearty men went off suddenly. They were always unsound; room for too many diseases inside all that bulk. A thin, wiry fellow, like himself, on the other hand, was likely to hang on a long time. To eat sparingly and drink copiously, that was the recipe for a long life. Willy, here, reversed the formula, drank nothing but water and ate thirteen slices of ham for supper. He wouldn't last many more years, digging his grave now with his teeth, like all the Crenfrews. Prodigious eaters, all of them, suffering tortures from dyspepsia to the last day of their lives. The old doctor, toward the end, had had a curious ashy pallor under the red veins of his face. He turned to Willy:

"What's that?" he said; "what's that you're saying?"

"I said," Willy repeated, "that I think he'll live to regret it."

Nicholas realized suddenly that he was talking about Ralph. "What's he done now?" he demanded.

"Air you getting deaf?" Willy inquired. "I told you he'd divided the property up between the children."

"Between the children?" Nicholas said. "He could not for the moment take in what was being said.

"That young lady gets five hundred acres. He's thinking of building her a house in that grove of trees where the overseer's cabin is."

"What's he building her a house for? Does she have to have a house all to herself?"

Cousin Willy chuckled. "She's got to have a house for her husband. She and Kenneth air going to be married, I reckon." He shook his head at George, who approached him just then with a bowl of floating island. "No, thank you," he said, "I've had enough." His hands folded on his stomach, a faint regurgitation rising now and then to his lips, he leaned back in his chair, at liberty now for conversation. "None of those Virginia Llewellyns have any land these days," he said. "They *have* to come out here to get wives."

Nicholas reflected that Willy and Virginia kept in touch with the elder branch of the family through Fanny and Dolly Blair, who had visited at Sycamore last year. "What's become of all their land?" he said. "They used to have more land than anybody in the country."

"Well, they haven't got it now. Cousin Richard has the home place, with four hundred acres left, this boy tells me, and he's the youngest of four sons."

"So Ralph's going to set him up to housekeeping," Nicholas said irritably. "What's the matter with them? Why don't they hold on to their land?"

Cousin Willy arched his almost invisible eyebrows. "Niggers," he said. "The niggers have eaten 'em out of house and home. They don't raise any tobacco to speak of, or any cotton, just corn to feed to the hogs to feed back to the niggers."

"It's that Jefferson," Nicholas told him, "Thomas Jefferson and his fool ideas." He clenched his fist and shook it at Willy. "It's men like him," he said passionately, "that have ruined this country, and damn fools like Ralph, following in their tracks, are throwing away what little was left . . ."

But Willy did not answer. He was familiar with Nicholas' political views. He was looking down the table now to where the young people sat. "I declare," he said meditatively, "Lucy certainly has turned out to be a pretty young lady."

Nicholas surveyed his niece, Lucy, with disfavor. "Shows too much white in her eye," he said. It was really, he thought, that the whole eye seemed to be full of dancing light. He had seen horses look like that. Too *much* spirit. If she was set on marrying this impecunious young man she would probably go right ahead and do it. He understood that she was used to having her own way. "Madge Wildfire," Willy called her. Considerable of a hoyden she must be yet. When Rufus Crenfrew wired up the gates on the woods road that led through his place to Ellengowan the girl had jumped her pony over the gates and kept on going through just as she had always done. She was rotten spoiled, no doubt. . . .

Ralph had divided his property among his two children; the girl inherited equally with the son! . . . Ralph was sixty-one. They would all be begging before he was in his grave. Charles was an indolent young scapegrace. A thousand acres of land, a thousand dollars, either would run through his hands like water. . . . If a man had a race track in his front yard and stables swarming with jockeys he couldn't expect his son to take an interest in anything but horses. Ralph had brought him up with expensive tastes, but the money to gratify those tastes he would leave to female heirs. . . . Young John was rising slowly from the table. Where his lean, fresh-colored face had been Robert's profile showed for a moment brown and sharp against Alice Blair's bare pink shoulder. . . . She was making a fool of him, probably, as she did of all the young men. A smart boy, Robert, quick and intelligent, but erratic, like his father, and irresponsible. Given Ralph's opportunities he would make as big a fool of himself as Ralph had done. John was different. . . . It didn't matter, though, he thought suddenly, *what* John was like. . . .

All around him people were rising. He rose, too, and followed them out of the dining-room. He was aware that

Cousin Thyra had laid her hand on his arm—or perhaps he had offered her his arm. He took three steps down the hall, then at the parlor door he halted with a peremptory sweep of his free arm. "Come in here," he said, "come in here, all of you!"

Lucy, with Kenneth Llewellyn beside her, was at the front door, about to step out on the porch. She turned and stood staring at her uncle a moment, then walked sedately into the parlor and seated herself on a chair near the window. Kenneth stood beside her. Cousin Thyra, who at Nicholas' first words had disengaged her arm, entered the room arm in arm with Cousin Virginia and Alice Blair, Cousin Willy a few paces behind them. The three ladies sat down on the old brocaded sofa. Cousin Willy, as if unwilling to be left alone, drew a chair up beside them and sat solemnly contemplating the third button of his snuff-colored waistcoat. There was complete silence in the room until Cousin Thyra, unfolding her little flowered fan, said:

"It's quite agreeable sitting indoors to-night, isn't it? Alice, hadn't you better go out on the porch and tell those boys to come in here? Boys," she added, with a pleasant smile, "are such vipers. They always have to be told everything twice."

Alice got up. "What do you suppose he wants with all of us, Cousin Thyra?" she asked.

Cousin Thyra glanced at Nicholas. "He's going to raise some kind of Cain," she said. "I can tell that by looking at him, but I d'know what it can be."

Alice Blair had not gotten as far as the threshold before young John's face showed in the doorway. Robert and Ruffin and half a dozen of the young fry filed in behind them. They were all getting over there in the corner by the window. Young John stood irresolute in the centre of the room until he saw that Alice was sitting down again on the sofa, when he turned back into the corner with the other boys. She had him on the string now too, it seemed. Well, she didn't much blame the poor boys. Alice had a come-hither eye, like her paternal aunt, Ellie Blair. Ellie had had all the boys in the Green Springs neighborhood quarrelling over her from the time she first came on the carpet, at an indecently early age. . . . She bent her head and took from a pocket of her gown—all her gowns were provided with capacious pockets—a silver snuffbox with an enamelled top, and inserting a pinch of snuff in her left nostril, leaned back on the sofa, her head a little to one side, her eyes closed. To-morrow she would send a boy on a horse to Sycamore for the carpet bag which she had left packed on the top of· her trunk, in the bedroom which was always called "Cousin Thyra's." Now that she was at Penhally she might as well make a visit. She had a sudden, agreeable vision of herself and Nicholas sitting out under the trees in the late afternoon, the sun's rays striking through the poplar leaves, a decanter flanked with glasses between them on the millstone table. . . . The sneeze for which she had been waiting sent a pleasant tremor through her huge body. She opened her eyes and saw that Nicholas had dragged the little rosewood table out into the middle of the room. He sat there now, writing something on a long sheet of foolscap. His pen, driving rapidly across the page, made great spluttering blots. When this happened he stopped and with a muttered oath gave the sheet of paper to a little negro, who dusted it with sand and held it a moment before the candle flame before returning it to the table.

"He's writing his will!" Cousin Thyra thought suddenly. "That's exactly what he's doing!"

She sat up and glanced about her, her little, bright, pig's eyes twinkling. It had just occurred to her that she was the only person in the room who might not reasonably expect to

inherit something from Nicholas. Jessie, there, if she survived him, ought to get something handsome, putting up with
his crotchets, as she had, for over forty years. Charles and
Lucy Mayfield were, of course, his nearest kin, after his
brother, Ralph. . . . But if he left anything to them it would
look like he was acknowledging that he had been wrong in
the quarrel he and Ralph had had over the property. . . .
And Charles, with his love for fast horses and his gambling
habits, was not the kind of young fellow to take the old
gentleman's eye anyway—even if he had not been his father's
son. . . . He was more likely to leave the bulk of his property to Jeems, who was, after all, his double first cousin, but
Jeems was crazy, crazy as a March hare. . . .

Nicholas was on his feet, the pen still in his hand. "Here,
Willy," he said, "and you there, Kenneth Llewellyn, I'd be
obliged if you'd witness this." As they came forward and
bent over the table he raised his head and looked at John.
"I've left all my property to you, sir," he said, "but you
needn't think you can make ducks and drakes of it after I'm
gone. I've entailed it on your children. That ought to keep
some of you out of the poorhouse for a while."

Charles, laughing all over his face, was clapping young
John on the shoulder and saying that he was a lucky fellow.
Young John stood staring. He was slow, like all the Allards.
It had gotten through his head, though, what Nicholas was
talking about. Sweat had broken out on his forehead. His
mouth was slightly open. He had the Allard mouth and forehead, but he had room enough between his eyes for some
sense, and he had a Llewellyn chin. . . . Alice Blair was
sitting there staring at the old man, too, as if she could not
take in what he had said.

In the silence that held all the room Cousin Thyra's agreeable, throaty chuckle sounded. She was thinking that Alice
Blair was going to have a hard time now, choosing between
those two boys!

8

It was so dark in the garden that at first Alice could hardly tell the shadow of the branches from the pools of water that stood here and there on the paths. She stopped beside the round bench that was built around the beech tree. "Shall we sit here?" she asked.

John did not let go of her arm. "Yes," he said, "so they'll be sure to see your white dress and come out here."

She laughed. "I'd have worn my black dress this last night if I'd thought about it," she said.

"Did you think about its being the last night?" he asked.

She brushed his arm lightly with her finger tips. "You know I did," she said.

They walked around to the other side of the bench and sat down. The shadow of the great beech trunk was a thick black shaft that slanted across half the enclosure, but the rest of the garden was drenched in the light that came from the windows. From the cover of the shadow she regarded the house. They must have lighted every candle on the place to-night. The chandelier in the parlor was like a great soft moon hovering over the dancers. They were forming a Virginia reel now, the old gentleman leading off with Miss Jessie. That nigger Ruffin had brought over from Fairfields certainly could play. *Miss Jessie's comin' down the lane!* He was holding his fiddle at arm's length, shaking his head from side to side, while he rolled the words out at the top of his lungs. It was a wonder that the old gentleman didn't call him down, but he seemed delighted with the hubbub. He was going down the line now. His coat tails spread out behind him like a fan as he spun each of his partners half the length of the room and back to her place. He was nimble for his age and he had a smooth, gliding step, a certain elegance in his dancing that young men didn't have these

days. . . . The house would be empty to-morrow night, and
dark, perhaps for a long time. They would all be gone to-
morrow night: Charles, John, Ruffin, Woodford—they would
all be gone to war. . . .

Somebody had told Charles that the bishop was in town.
He had wanted to ride in and bring him out to Penhally to
marry them that night! They had been sitting on the little
side porch just before supper. He had got up and walked
halfway to the rack where his horse was hitched. He had
pretended not to hear the first time she called him. She had
had to call low—it was just before supper, with everybody
assembled on the front porch. . . . She had been thinking
of her mother. Her mother and Ellie Sloan, in the dark
back parlor at home. Her mother's face, white between the
two dark wings of her hair, against the ragged gray velvet
of the old sofa. The crisp voice and the little laugh: "Ellie
Sloan, you eighteen years old and not engaged! Now you
go on up to Richmond next week and don't you come back
here till you're engaged or you're no niece of mine . . ."
Ellie Sloan had married a man from Philadelphia, but not
until she was twenty-four. . . . They sent you out here expecting you to make a good marriage! On the face of it, John
was the better match of the two. But the old gentleman was
likely to make half a dozen more wills before he died. . . .
John would never be able to fend for himself if he were cut
off. He was too shy, too *haughty*. . . . The lean face and
that one bright, falling lock of hair! . . . His father was
poor as a church mouse and crazy. . . . Her own father and
mother had made Josephine's marriage. . . . They had been
delighted when Talbot Lowe first began waiting on her.
They had flattered him and put up with all his high and
mighty airs, but now that Josephine was left—a *grass* widow,
Mammy called it—with two little children they spoke of her,
even addressed her, with veiled impatience, as if she ought

somehow to have known better. . . . She would *die* rather
than live at home on sufferance as Josephine did. . . . The
Scotts hadn't even invited her to their Christmas ball. . . .

John's profile was sharp as a hawk's against the lighted
windows. He sat, hunched forward, his clenched hands
swinging between his knees. He was not wearing his uniform even on this last night. She was glad that he wasn't.
Everything would be the same up to the moment of his going
away. She tried to imagine what it would be like after he
was gone, but she could not do it. They had these hours—
there would be two or three hours yet before they would
even have to think of saying good-by. . . .

She leaned back against the trunk of the tree. Her hands
had been clasped in her lap. She unclasped them, and holding them out before her flexed and unflexed them until she
could feel her whole strength in her finger tips. There had
come over her suddenly the feeling that she often had when
she was with John, not contentment so much as exhilaration,
the faint exhilaration that comes from complete well-being,
like walking through deep leaves down a hillside in clear
weather. It had been like that the first time that they had
been together. She remembered looking down when they
were halfway through the ford to see the yellow water swirling about her waist with much the same leap of the heart.
That feeling had not been all excitement; it had been partly
joy.

John, on the bench beside her, was moving restlessly.
"Don't do that," he said.

She looked down at her hands that were white, even in
the shadow. White hands flexing and unflexing in the dark.
He could not contemplate her hands unmoved. He could not
bear to be made conscious of any part of her body. He wanted her on this last night to remain undefined, formless, not
herself really. She felt that she must not stir or lift a finger,

must not tilt back her head or utter a word that would lin-
ger in his memory. . . . But it is because he wants to forget me, she told herself. He wants that more than he loves
me. . . .

She laid her hand on his arm. "Do you remember the
time we swam the ford?" she asked.

He nodded coolly. "Perfectly. Do you?"

"I've never forgotten," she said. "I've never forgotten
any of it."

It was true. She had never forgotten. That day she and
John had ridden from Sycamore to Penhally through a cloudburst and across a flooded creek. She had had no intention
of returning to Penhally for another week at least, but a little negro had brought her a note from Charles, saying that
he expected to be up there all that week and asking her to
come back if she could arrange it. She had mentioned at
the dinner table that she had had a note—she had given the
impression that it was from Cousin Jessie—suggesting that
she come home—Penhally, she thought with a start, was more
home than any other place!—and John, at the other end of
the table, had spoken up quietly, saying that he was going to
ride there that day and would be glad to escort her. She did
not remember having noticed John before. It had actually
been several minutes before she was able to place him among
the young fry who were always swarming about that house
as the brown, lean boy who was reputed to be the old gentleman's favorite!

Cousin Virginia had been delighted not to have to get the
carriage out, Leopard and Logan having been driven all of
twelve miles yesterday in the trip to and from Fairfields.
The young people, she said, might just as well ride to Penhally; the horses would have to be gotten home one way or
another. . . .

John got up and followed her, dog-like and silent, when

she left the dining-room or walked around in the yard.
Charles had remonstrated with her: "Why don't you let the
kid alone? What do you want to make a fool out of him
for?"

That night she had slipped out of the house . . . to meet
John. . . . The branches of the hemlock trees sweeping to
the ground had made a black, impenetrable spot on the lawn.
The place was so dark they could not even see each other's
faces. . . . She had put up her hand several times to touch
his face, trying to ascertain what expression went with the
words he was saying. . . . She might have told him then
that she had promised to marry Charles. She had not done
it. . . . But they had not talked much. She could not remember now one word that they had said. They had just sat
there with their arms about each other . . . until some birds
stirring in the branches over the lawn reminded them that
night was wearing on. . . .

Now his arm was along the back of the bench. He was
leaning toward her, his dark face hovering over hers. With
his arm there he had her penned, as it were, into a corner.
He had the lighted house at his back. Although his face was
so close to hers, she could barely distinguish his features.
But her own face was mercilessly exposed to the light. She
had the feeling, for the first time since she had known him,
that he was examining her, dispassionately, trying to make
up his mind what sort of woman she was. Deliberately she
made her eyes opaque, assumed a smile and then felt the
smile break in the trembling of her lips. That he should be
doing this on the last night when there was so little time, so
few, few hours that they could be together! . . . The yellow oblong of light that had been against his shoulder was
blotted out now. A man was standing in the doorway looking out over the garden: Charles had said that he would
come after her if she stayed too long in the garden . . .

Charles. . . . He must have seen Charles kiss her yesterday. He had come out of the hall as they stood there on the
latticed porch. . . . The doorway was an oblong of yellow
light again. The man had stepped aside. Down on the walk?

She drew back into the shadow of the tree. "Somebody's
coming," she whispered.

He stood up. They stepped softly over the thick black
shaft that was the trunk of the beech tree, over the network
of thin shadows that were its branches until they reached
one of the box hedges that quartered the garden. They slipped
past a pillar of box, into still blacker shadow. A low iron
seat was fixed there, between two statues. He drew her
down on to it, beside him. She pressed her body against his.
Her hands went up to lock behind his neck. He was whispering something. She took her hand from behind his neck
and pressed it against his lips. "You know I love you," she
said.

9

August, 1861.

"The camp?" the man said. "It's about a quarter of a mile
from here. Right by Sedley's Spring. You know Sedley's
Spring?"

Nicholas shook his head. "No," he said, "I come from
over the line."

The man stepped through the gate and pointed down the
road. "Well," he said, "you ride along a piece till you come
to that big gum tree on the left. Don't take no right-hand
turns at all. But when you git to that gum tree you turn
in on that little wagin road and just ride on down toward the
river. You can't miss it. You'll hear 'em hollerin' long before you git thar." He looked at John. "This young feller
jinin' the cavalry?" he asked.

"Looks that way," Nicholas said. He glanced absently
past the man's knee at the heavy green leaves that thrust here

and there through the fence. "Mighty pretty tobacco you got there," he said.

The man spat into the dust and then rubbed his foot over the spittle. "Needs rain," he said. He still looked at John, smiling slyly. "Reckon you'll see some fightin' before long, Mister. They say them soldiers aim to ride to Hopkinsville to-night to jine Gen'l Tilghman."

John smiled back at him. "I reckon they do," he said, and contracted his knee a little so that Flora bounded suddenly forward.

"Well," Nicholas said, "I'm much obliged to you."

"Good evening, sir," the man said, "and good luck to you, young gentleman."

John, riding ahead at a fox trot, turned and waved his hand. He wondered why the man had suddenly called him "young gentleman" when it had been "young feller" only a minute before. . . . It was because he was going to the war. It was because he was going to join the cavalry. . . .

If you want to have a good time, jine the cavalree . . .
If you want to have a good time, jine the cavalree . . .

Charles had been humming that when he came up on the porch, in his new gray uniform, his sword dangling at his side. He had stood there on the steps, looking at them and smiling. But that had been before that night Alice slipped out of the house! . . . Cousin Thyra, in the shade of the vines at the far end of the porch, had spoken up in her deep voice:

"Well, Charles, I see you've jined."

The sun had glinted on Charles' spurs as he walked around the rocking-chairs to sit down beside Alice. She had taken the cream-colored felt hat that he carried under his arm away from him. "It's too pretty for a man," she had said. "You ought to give it to me."

They had gotten up after a little and had walked away together over the lawn, to hunt for a peacock feather to put in the band of Charles' hat. . . .

Flora was racking. He leaned forward a little and laid his hand on her neck and she slowed down into a fox trot. She had the smoothest fox trot of any horse on the place. He mustn't let her keep at it too long, though, in this heat. "You'll go rackin' that mar' around all over the country and bring her back here plumb ruint," Townsend had said. What an old liar Townsend was! And conceited! He thought nobody in the world knew anything about horses except him— and Uncle Ralph. It was too bad that Uncle Ralph hadn't taken Townsend with him when he went off to live at Mayfield. He had thought, for a while, that Townsend did belong to Mayfield; he was always going on so about "when me and Marse Ralph had charge of these horses." He had asked Uncle Nick—it was just after the old gentleman had made the will—whether Townsend belonged to him or to Uncle Ralph. And the old gentleman had looked at him pretty sharply and said: "He is an Allard nigger, sir, brought here from Virginia by my mother and left to me at her death. Is there any other information that you desire about my private affairs?"

You never knew where you were with the old boy. He would fly off the handle about some inconsequential thing and then be sweet as honey when you expected the devil of a row. He had expected a row that morning when he had told his uncle that he meant to enlist in the cavalry. He had walked yesterday morning into the office where the old gentleman sat talking with Albert, the overseer, and Townsend. He had been all braced for the old boy to hit the ceiling. He had not even gone into the room. He had stood in the doorway, ready to turn on his heel at any minute. He would be

damned, he had told himself, if he would be dictated to by
an old curmudgeon with one foot in the grave. The old gentleman may have seen how it was—he himself thought that
the old boy knew more of what was going on around him
than people in general gave him credit for—at any rate he
hadn't turned a hair. He had even gotten up and set a chair
for him and had sent Albert and Townsend out of the room.

"Well, sir," he had said, "I suppose you want to join those
whippersnappers over at the camp. When do you reckon
you'll be going?"

"To-morrow," he had told him; "the regiment's leaving
for Hopkinsville to-night."

He had been pretty pleasant about that too, though it must
have been the last regiment that he wanted any of his folks
in—he knew, certainly, that Uncle Ralph had outfitted most
of the men. A thousand rifles and a number of horses he had
furnished, as well as money.

The most amusing part of the whole business had been
down at the stable that afternoon. Townsend had been on
his high horse, all day, grumbling because he didn't want
Flora to go off the place. "Which horse are you going to
take?" Charles had asked, and Robert had laughed mightily
and said, "It looks like Townsend is going to let him have
the pick of the mules." Then he and Robert had gone down
to the stable, and the old gentleman had walked in on Townsend, who was still grumbling. "Shut your mouth," he had
said—he had actually told Townsend to shut his mouth, there
before all of them!!! . . . "Shut your mouth, Townsend,
the boy'll take any horse he wants on the place. What about
that gray four-year-old? Bring him out and let's see how
Mister John likes him."

Townsend had grunted that the gray was in the pasture,
"whar he b'longs," he had added under his breath when his
face was turned away from Uncle Nick. He had sent a little

nigger out to round up the horses, though, and then had had them led past, one by one, four or five of them. Jed, the head stable-boy, had done that. Townsend had had a terrible attack of rheumatics about that time and had sat down on a pile of straw clutching his bad leg and grunting every now and then to show how much he was suffering. They had sat there on the straw all afternoon, in the cool, good-smelling stable, looking at the horses and talking.

When they walked back to the house, round five o'clock, Charles and Alice were still sitting on the bench, by the syringa bush, talking. Alice saw them coming and waved her hand, but Charles went on talking and did not even look up. Robert had wanted to go over and join them, but he had called him back. "Let him alone," he had said. "He's got to go in a few minutes."

Charles would have to be starting for Mayfield pretty soon, he had figured, to get there by supper time. Charles had had the whole afternoon with Alice, from two o'clock on. He hadn't minded then. He had been sure that Charles would go home that night. But Charles, to everybody's astonishment, had spent the night, the biggest part of it, that is, at Penhally.

Cousin Jessie, coming out on the porch, toward six o'clock, had told him that she thought he ought to be starting if he wanted to get home before dark. Charles had laughed and said that he'd like to stay there for supper if she didn't mind. When she asked him if he didn't think he ought to spend his last evening at home he had explained that he intended to get up at two or three o'clock and ride to Mayfield, arriving there, he said, in time to see his mother, who couldn't sleep in the morning and always got up early and walked in the garden for several hours. . . .

He saw suddenly jogging along, at his elbow, the white nose of the old man's horse.

"Come on," he said, "I think this must be the place."

They passed through a gap in the fence and, turning to the left, followed an old wagon road that slanted sidewise up a hill. It was narrow, grass-grown in the middle, but in the ruts there were the tracks of many wheels, and every now and then they came to a place where bushes on the side of the road had been trampled and slashed in order that two vehicles might pass each other. From the bluff above came a confused murmur of voices and the occasional shrill overtones of some musical instrument.

John rose in his stirrups.

"I see the tents," he said.

They rounded a bend in the road and came suddenly upon the camp: a dozen tents pitched on the bluff above the river, knots of people standing about in front of them talking. There were women in some of the groups. A girl in a white dress stood swinging a red parasol by a long black ribbon.

"There's Dick Elliott," Nicholas said in a low voice.

The big man who was riding toward them on a roan mare wore a new gray uniform, and he had on beautiful gauntlets of soft yellow leather. He drew one off as he leaned forward to shake hands. Straightening up he sat looking from Nicholas to John with eyes that had little dancing lights in them.

"You're Mr. Jeems Llewellyn's son, aren't you?" he asked. "Haven't you got a brother?"

"Bob's too young to join," Nicholas said. "Somebody's got to stay home with the women and the old men like me. It's all tomfoolishness anyhow."

"Well," Captain Elliott said, "if you want to have a good time, jine the cavalree. . . ." He looked at John again, laughing. His mustache and beard were bright brown, streaked with gold, his teeth very white against his full red lips. "Charley Llewellyn is around here somewhere," he said. "You want to go look for him?"

"I reckon I might as well," John said, and rode over to where on a bench outside the tent a lean boy in blue jeans lounged, picking a banjo. The cap that he had flung down on the ground in front of him had a squirrel's tail affixed to it. An old flintlock leaned against his right leg.

John reined in his mare. "That looks like a good gun you got there," he said, smiling.

The boy looked up. His yellow eyes were expressionless; his set lips made a straight bar across his tanned face. "You know old man Jack Hinson?" he asked. "He told me last night that he'd ruther have that ar rifle, that are old squirrel rifle, than any gun he ever seen."

"Is that so?" John said. "Well, I bet she's a good one. . . . You seen Charley Llewellyn anywhere around here?"

The boy shook his head. "You better ask the cap'n. I can't tell one of 'em from another."

He picked his banjo up. John rode down the white line of tents toward the river. The group in front of the last tent was breaking up. Half a dozen young men were advancing over the brown dead leaves that still covered most of the encampment. The old lady in the gray bonnet walked in front with two of them, but the girl in the white dress still stood on the edge of the bluff talking with a young man.

She was not tall; her hair was light and drawn into a knot low on her neck. She swung the parasol to and fro in front of her; he could not tell whether there were tiny white polka dots on the black ribbon that held it.

It could not be Alice. She couldn't possibly have gotten here. It was fifteen miles, at least, from here to Penhally. He and Uncle Nick, leaving immediately after breakfast, had been over two hours on the road. They had ridden slowly, of course, on account of the heat, and had stopped three times, twice to rest the horses and once to ask the way of the man down the road. . . .

Alice had not come down to breakfast. She must have been awake, though, when they left. She couldn't have slept through all the noise and confusion of their getting off. There had been a great deal of confusion, and toward the last shouting back and forth, between the stable and the house, the house and the Quarter. His father was not to be found anywhere when he went to tell them all good-by! There had been a big hullabaloo over that. Cousin Jessie was determined that the "poor boy" shouldn't go off to war without telling his father good-by. He couldn't see, himself, that it made any difference. His father would never know that he was gone. There was no use, really, in bothering him. But Cousin Jessie had insisted, so they had waited there for half an hour while little niggers ran in every direction, squalling "Marse Jeems!"

The old man had come sauntering toward the house by himself finally, reporting that he thought something must be wrong in the woods just above the swamp. "There are little darkies running all around the woods screaming. You had better send a man down there, Nick. Something may be after them."

The girl in the white dress had turned around. One of the Taylor girls from Gloversville. The young man was George Woodford, Ruffin's oldest brother.

After Ruffin's nigger had fiddled himself out last night they had all gone down to the Quarter to hear old Uncle Ben play. He had started back with Alice, but Charles had stepped up before they got halfway to the house. He had fallen back then, with Lucy and Kenneth. Charles and Alice had taken the path around the side of the house. Kenneth laughed when he saw them disappear in the lilac walk. "Miss Jessie won't get rid of that man to-night," he said. "Naw, suh, she won't get him off this place to-night!" But Charles and Alice had come up to the front porch only a little after the rest. They had stood a little apart from the others, talking, while good-bys were being said. He had had his back turned most of the time. He had not heard them say goodby, but he had seen Alice go upstairs with Lucy and Ellen. He had gone up himself a few minutes later. It must have been midnight then. He had not gone straight to his room, though. He and Robert and Ruffin had stayed in the hall upstairs a while, fooling around and talking. The whole house had been quiet when he finally got to his own room. But there had been voices under his window, in the lilac walk. . . . Didn't they *know* that that was his window? . . . Two persons talking. He had never been sure that one of them was a woman. . . .

The boy with the banjo was calling:

"Ain't that Charley Llewellyn? Hey. . . . Ain't that Charley Llewellyn?"

Charles was coming around the corner of the tent, with Ruffin. They had been in swimming. They were hatless and their hair was tousled and damp.

He swung off his horse. "Uncle Nick's over there with the captain," he said.

Ruffin was looking at him and laughing.

"You look pretty fresh," he said. "I had to take old Charley here in swimming to get him waked up."

Charles broke into a great laugh.

"You ought to have seen Ruff last night. I had a time getting him home, I tell you! Rode right into a tree and then bowed and said 'Ma'am?' as polite as you please. . . ."

"D'you go to Mayfield last night?" John asked. If Ruffin had gone to Mayfield he must have stayed around somewhere waiting for Charles after he went downstairs. He would know then who it was talking in the lilac walk after everybody else was in bed. . . .

"I see you got the mare," Charles was saying.

He nodded. "We better go on over there," he said; "the old man is getting ready to leave." He slung the bridle rein over his arm and walked behind the other two across the camp ground.

They moved still in the rhythm of last night's dancing. Charles hummed as he walked:

> "*Gone* again, skip to my Lou,
> *Gone* again, skip to my Lou,
> *Gone* again, skip to my Lou,
> Skip to my Lou, my da . . . arling!"

"You better hush," Ruffin said. "You'll have the old man down off that horse in a minute."

Charles laughed. "He cert'n'y was in high feather last night," he said. "I declare, I thought he was going to fall down right in the middle of the floor one time." He turned around to John. "Were you in there then?"

"I saw him through the window," John said. He hadn't, as a matter of fact. He hadn't even looked in the windows once. He hadn't cared what was going on in there. . . . Charles had a funny, excited look when he turned around then, and he laughed all the time to-day, as if he was pleased about something. He hadn't looked like that last night. He had been pretty glum then. He had actually caught himself feeling sorry for Charles last night. . . . Well, that was last night. . . .

He threw the reins over Flora's neck and moved forward to where the old gentleman and the captain still sat on their horses in the chequered shade of the trees. The captain was saying that the regiment would parade through the town that evening. Judge Hopkins and old Colonel Glover and Judge Martin would be in the reviewing stand in the balcony of the Arlington Hotel. There would be a band. Everybody in town would be there. . . . The captain's boots were an even,

dark tan, stiff and varnished as high as the knee, above that
soft, undressed leather. The thongs that laced them were a
lighter brown than the boots themselves, fawn color they
were. A good pair of boots. They must have cost him at
least fifteen dollars. . . . She might have stayed upstairs
because she wanted last night to be their good-by. . . . On
the other hand she might not have wanted to see him again.
. . . If that had been her voice that he had heard in the lilac
walk she very likely didn't want to see him again. . . . There
was no way he could find out, except to ask her. . . . He
would be damned if he would ask her. . . . If she wanted to
carry on with other men she could. . . . He would be damned
if he would ask her. . . . *"You know I love you . . ."*

He felt as if he were choking. He put his hand up to his
throat sharply. These shirts they made for him were all too
tight in the collar band. . . . The old gentleman was asking
him something, for the second time. . . . He wished to God
they would all quit shooting off their mouths so much. . . .

"You think I better stay, John?"

He had always thought the old man's eyes were black.
They were brown, really, the exact color of the dead leaves
under their feet. Dog's eyes. A dog that is begging for
something. And that confoundedly tight mouth of his. . . .
What in the devil was it that he wanted?

"Why, yes, sir," he said, "I wish you would."

10

August, 1861.

A fat woman in a blue dress took out her handkerchief for
the fourth time and wiped her red perspiring face.

"I declar," she said, "I jest wish Albert wasn't goin'."

A little black-eyed woman sighed. "You can't hope to do
nothin' with him," she said. "He's free, white and twenty-

one. You can't expect him to stay home when all the other boys is goin'."

"Albert ain't got no business goin' to war," the fat woman said. "He's got a weak stomach. They's days and days he cain't eat nothin' but batty cakes. Seems like everything he eats comes right up. . . . Mammy, you so small, you squeeze through thar now and see if they ain't comin'."

The old woman darted through an opening in the crowd. Nicholas drew back as she passed him and eyed her daughter defiantly. "I hope, madam," he said, "that that is not your foot I have just trod upon."

She shook her head, smiling. "You'd a heard from me if it had a been. I cain't stand no sort of pain."

Nicholas inclined his head in what he knew to be a courtly gesture and they remained for a moment companionably silent, until the woman observed, "You wouldn't think she was eighty-four years old now, would you? She's spryer than I am by a long sight."

"She's too old to be out in this sun," he said. "Why don't you take her upstairs? She could see just as well from the balcony."

The woman laughed. "Now you know they ain't no chance of us gettin' up on that gallery! They ain't room for a flea on that gallery."

"I'll take her up," Nicholas said. "You get hold of her and I'll take her up there."

The woman did not answer. She was staring over his head at the people on the balcony. "Thar's somebody callin' you now," she said. "They want you should come up thar. You needn't wait for Mammy. She ain't goin' to stir out of her tracks till them soldiers ride by."

He turned. Lucy was beckoning to him from the front row of onlookers. "Come up here, Uncle Nick," she called. "It's so much cooler."

"I'd go if I was you," the fat woman said. "Ain't no use in cookin' yourself jest for a parade."

"Parade?" Nicholas said irritably. "I ain't out here for a parade. . . ." But the woman had disappeared in the crowd. Her going had left an opening, through which, he saw, he could penetrate to the hotel steps. Over the heads of the people in the doorway he caught a glimpse of the darkened lobby. It looked cool after the dazzling light of the street. He forced his way up the steps and into the vestibule. Now that he was out of the sun he did not feel faint. He would go upstairs, after all, he decided. The balcony was crowded, but there was always room for one more, and he would be able to see whatever was going on.

In the upper hall little Ellen Crenfrew was hanging over the banisters. Her face lit up at his approach. Taking her in his arms he stepped over the window-sill and set her on the iron railing that ran around the balcony.

They had got there just in time. Captain Dick Elliott, at the head of his men, was just turning the corner of Second Street. They rode slowly, the men very erect and stiff in their saddles, the horses, grass fed some of them, fresh from the rocky pastures across the Cumberland, keeping only tolerable line. They were under the balcony now. Captain Elliott, riding very slowly, reached up and took the flag which Lucy knelt down to hand to him. The wind caught its folds and it fluttered prettily as the cavalcade passed on.

The band blared forth, louder than ever:

"Hurrah, hurrah, for freedom's rights, hurrah,
Hurrah for the bonny blue flag that bears a single star. . . ."

The child had clenched her little fist and was beating time on his back to the music. "There's John!" she cried. "Cousin Nick, look at John!"

He leaned over the railing. John, riding directly beneath

the balcony, was staring up shortsightedly. He had not seen them as yet; his eyes were all for Alice Blair, who was standing beside Lucy in the front row of onlookers. It occurred to him that he should have sent a nigger along to look after the boy. Tom was the man. He had as much judgment as Townsend, and he was more active. He took his handkerchief out and waved it wildly. "Tom!" he shouted. "Tom! You better take Tom! I'll start him to Hopkinsville to-morrow morning. You be lookin' out for him."

The young fool had seen them at last. He was shaking his head, and he had shouted back something. Was it "Don't want him"? He would start him up there to-morrow anyhow. He should have him whether he wanted him or not.

The child was moving restlessly in his arms. He could feel her little ribs straining outward in a long sigh. She was tired. The little thing ought to be home with her mother, but her mother was probably out there gaping after the soldiers, like all the rest of them. He made his way through the crowd back into the hall.

"You stay here," he said, "and wait for your mammy. I got some business to tend to."

He set her on her feet and walked down the cool dark steps into the lobby of the hotel. The last rays of afternoon sun beat through the open double doors and lay in a wide shaft on the chequered floor. He stepped across the sunshine toward the row of chairs that fronted the window. The clerk—an Edwards by his narrow face and close-set eyes—called to him:

"There were some ladies here looking for you, Mister Llewellyn, but I believe they've gone on up the street."

Nicholas nodded and sat down in the first chair. Cousin Jessie and some of the girls, probably. He ought to go over to the livery stable and see that the horses were hitched up properly. These town niggers didn't half know how to hitch

up a horse. That was how Berkeley Crenfrew had come by
his death. He had started home from town at night, with
the collar riding the horse's ears and maddening him until
he started running pell-mell down Allard's Hill and Berkeley
was thrown out to die of concussion of the brain.

He rested his head on the little cushion that was tied to
the high back of the rocking chair. From the street came
the confused murmur of many voices. The people were still
surging up and down out there. They were moving toward
the courthouse now. From a high knoll on the lawn Judge
Gavin harangued them. The Gavins all loved to talk. Handsome people, with rich, full voices, but no judgment. Martin was a well-meaning man, but he would never be as smart
as his father, the old judge. He could not hear what Martin was saying. The man in the next chair was leaning forward, a silly smile on his lips, humming:

"Hurrah, hurrah, for freedom's rights, hurrah . . ."

The refrain still beat lightly on the street under the flow
of indistinguishable words, and far away, down at the old
square, a band was playing the same tune. Old Colonel Glover had spoken there and from a platform erected in front
of Shelton's loose floor Judge Hopkins addressed another
crowd. They had asked Ralph to speak too, he had heard
somebody say, but Ralph had declined. He would leave the
speech-making to the public men, he had said, but he would
equip another company with arms and gear and would furnish a horse to any man who could not mount himself. He
would do it too. He would keep on pouring out money and
arms and horses until he had beggared himself. Beggar himself, he would, one way or another before he died. They
need not think he, Nicholas Llewellyn, would make a fool of
himself the same way.

Dark was falling. Old Nelson, the lamp lighter, had al-

ready started on his rounds. He had to shoulder his way
through the crowd to reach the big lamp that stood in front
of the hotel. The fools would not go home. They would
stand out there all night, arguing and singing while their sup-
pers grew cold. He wished now that he had not arranged
to spend the night in town. If he had started home with the
carriage he could have reached Penhally by dark.

He stood up, stiffly, and walked through the alleyway of
chairs out into the lobby. Three men were standing just inside of the doorway; one of them was burly and wore a
broad gray hat; they looked up when they saw him coming
and then went on talking. He would have passed them by,
but Colonel Glover, rotund and red-faced, put out a large
hand to detain him.

"Where you been keeping yourself?" he asked. "I been
thinking all day I'd run into you."

The burly man who was standing just behind the colonel
took a step forward. It was Ralph. Nicholas eyed him a
moment before he spoke.

"I been sitting in here watching these fools moil up and
down in the street," he said. "Looks like they going to stay
out there all night."

The colonel laughed and laid a hand on Nicholas' arm.
"Come over here," he said. "I want to talk to you."

Nicholas stood stock still, resisting the hand that was en-
deavoring to persuade him away from the circle. Let Ralph
turn tail and run. He was not that thin-skinned. He said,
looking scornfully past the colonel at his brother:

"What you want with me? Want me to give you a thousand dollars?"

The colonel laughed, the easy, rich laugh that was famous
at every speaking throughout the county.

"What about two thousand?" he asked. "Looks to me like
you ought to be good for two thousand."

Nicholas shook his head. "I got one young fool and a thoroughbred mare in the Confederate army now," he said. "And that's all they'll get out of me."

Colonel Glover was heaving his vast bulk into the semblance of a military posture. His hand went back to rest on an imaginary sword.

"Mister Llewellyn," he said, "the young men of this state and this country will never be found lacking when they are called upon to defend their hearthstones."

"Let 'em stay at home, then, and defend 'em," Nicholas said coolly. "They've got no call to go riding all over the country looking for trouble."

His eyes, darting irate glances at Colonel Glover, old Mister Atkins, and the tall, thin man whose name he could not call, rested obliquely from moment to moment upon Ralph. It had been twenty years at least since he had met his brother face to face, but Ralph's appearance was no shock to him. As his resentment toward Ralph grew he had felt the need of some bodily image upon which to focus it. He had built up, year after year, his picture of Ralph out of casual reports, stray sayings of members of the family. "They brought a picture of Uncle Aleck down out of the attic the other day," Cousin Thyra had said. "I declare you couldn't have told it from Ralph," and Nicholas had seen the thin features of the stripling Ralph slowly obscured by the heaviness that with middle age overtook all the Crenfrews. And once Cousin Thyra had contrasted his own dark locks with Ralph's rapidly graying ones. "It's strange now that he should be the first to turn and all of fifteen years younger than you . . ."

Ralph was gray. His head, uncovered in the light, was grizzled as a badger's, but his short, brown beard was only lightly touched with silver. He did not look old, though. He had the carriage of a young man, for all his portliness, and his eyes had exactly the same quizzical expression that they had had when he was a boy, blue eyes, flecked with yellow, and fringed with heavy dark lashes. It was those handsome, appealing eyes that got him his way wherever he went. He stood there now, with his head turned a little to the side, gazing out over the street, a half smile on his lips, as a man might stand and gaze and idly smile while his companions greeted persons unknown to him whom there was no reason for him ever to know. Damn his nonchalance! He stood there as if all that was going on was of no concern of his, when but for him John would be at this moment safe at Penhally. John would not have gone to war but for Charles' example. Charles riding up there every day on the best horse in the stables, in a spanking new uniform, a feather in his hat—no wonder the boy had been wild to go! Ralph had done that, and he had sent many another boy in the county off to war, with his offers of arms and gear and thoroughbred horses. . . .

Old Mr. Atkins was talking, in his quavering voice. "Something's got to be done. All I know is something's got to be done. They keep on runnin' these railroads all over the country. If they don't watch out they ain't goin' to be no river traffic pretty soon. A man can't keep up his boats and keep hirin' crews and sendin' 'em down the river if they ain't nothin' to take down the river."

"I loaded eighty thousand pounds of tobacco on a flatboat last fall for New Orleans," Nicholas told him, "and I reckon I'll send as much again this fall." The old skinflint must be ninety years old. Ninety-five years old. He would never die as long as there was a prospect of wringing a penny out of something. He was ready to go to war now to get the steamboat trade back. But the Yankees were not the only ones who were building railroads. The whole country was crazy about railroads. Colonel Glover here was part owner

of a railroad. He had tried to get him, Nicholas, to buy
shares. Came out to Penhally and talked to him about it all
one day last summer. The trouble with all of them, he reflected, was that they had no principles. Just let 'em know
that their fathers had believed in anything and they would
run the other way. The colonel wanted another war so he
could go around the country making speeches and waving his
old sword. He had never gotten over the Mexican War. It
was different when they had the Mexican War. The country
was younger then and rougher. It was all right for a lot of
young men to go down there raising a hullabaloo if they
didn't have anything better to do. But they had enough ter-
ritory now. Let 'em stay at home and tend to it. There were
fields in Ballard County where the sage grass was higher
than a man's head. But the land could be brought up to be as
good as any land around here. Let 'em get to work and
cultivate it. Then they wouldn't be worrying about the Yankees. The Yankees, likely, had enough trouble of their own
at home, if these politicians wouldn't keep stirring them up
all the time. That was the trouble on both sides, too many
politicians, eating their heads off on the people's money
and stirring up issues so they could have something to make
speeches about. Irresponsible, these new-fangled politicians,
landless men, with nothing to lose and everything to win.

He had suddenly a vision that had not come to him for
years, the Penhally clearing as he had first seen it when, as
a child of ten, he drove over the mountains with his father
and mother. They had come upon it at the end of a hard
day's travel, and were about to pitch tents and make camp
in the woods when he, peering down into the valley, had seen
the white glistening stumps of newly felled trees and had
raised a shout that brought them all to the side of the wagon.
They had known then that that must be the place of which
the old doctor had written, "a suitable site, sir, on which to

erect dwellings for your household, and not above five miles from my own habitation." His father had got out the letter and read the directions again. They had taken the rough trail that ran due north from a tree that they found marked according to the directions, for they would rest at the Crenfrews' that night, but he had turned in his high seat beside the overseer and had sat looking back at the white patch of stumps until they faded into the green of the woods.

Ralph had enclosed the forty acres that ran below his house for a deer park. When the deer occasionally jumped over the high cedar fence of the enclosure the people around the country shot them, pretending that they thought they were wild deer. But he could remember, as a little boy, having to run out a dozen times a day to frighten away the deer from the flowers that his mother had planted in the Penhally yard.

He said, clearing his throat:

"You gentlemen, and Ralph Llewellyn there, were born in this country, born with silver spoons in your mouths. But I came over the mountains with my father, from old Virginia. My father was a younger son. My grandfather Llewellyn had seven boys. We came west to get land. And now we've got it. Land is a responsibility. When a man's got land he isn't free to follow any fool uprising that comes along. He's got people dependent on him. Women and children. Niggers . . ." He stopped short, overcome with emotion. He imagined that the four men were looking at him pityingly. They thought he was an old fogey because he had voted for John Bell. He was an old-time Whig, as his father had been before him, and, by God, he would die one! He could whip the whole lot of 'em now, at seventy-seven. Shoot it out with 'em, he would, any day they named. The old duelling pistols were in the middle drawer of the secretary. He would ask Willy Crenfrew to be his second. . . .

But Willy was a fool. There was not a man in his whole connection that wasn't a fool, or too green and unformed, like
young John. . . . Not a man that you could ask to stand
up with you . . . on a matter of principle. . . .

Colonel Glover was speaking, slowly and with dignity.

"But there comes a time, sir, when a man must modify
his politics to suit his conscience. I could not refuse my
sword to my country. . . ."

Ralph moved forward, so that the light from the dim gas
lamp fell on his fresh florid face and silver hair.

"Gentlemen," he said, "we all know my brother's politics.
They do him credit. But they are not our politics. I think
there is no need to prolong this discussion."

"No," Nicholas said. "It's no use talking. Talking doesn't
do any good. You go your way and I'll go mine."

He turned back to the desk. The clerk was leaning forward to call to him.

"Will you have 24 this time, Mister Llewellyn, or 26? 26
is cooler. . . ."

Nicholas steadied himself with a hand on the counter. The
room, then, ceased to whirl about him. He drew a deep
breath. "There's one of my niggers hangin' around this hotel somewhere," he said. "You tell him to saddle Old Filly
and bring her around to the front. I've got to be gettin'
home."

11

April, 1862.

It was dead-still in the woods. But the twigs on the post
oaks kept trembling. The cannonading had not ceased, but
here among the trees it did not beat so against the ear
drums. For several minutes now he had been trying to figure out which road they had taken from Byrnesville. But
he was completely turned around. Shiloh Church was off
there to the right somewhere and the little creek was called

Owl—or was it Lick? They were not far, anyhow, from the Tennessee River.

The Yankee tent still stood on the edge of the field. Its ridge pole had fallen against a tree and so it could not go down. A dead man was lying there under the flap. The lower part of the body mutilated by a shell, the head fallen against the leather-cushioned campstool that they said belonged to a Yankee general. The shell had burst right in the opening of the tent. The ground all around was plowed up, deep. Like a ground-hog hole—or a fox's. . . . A man named Frazier, Company C, had been struck by a fragment of a shell, in the shoulder. He had not known at first what had hit him. They had taken him off to the rear somewhere, to a hospital. It was early in the day, when the shells first began screaming. . . .

He shielded his eyes with his hand. The sun, beating straight down, struck blinding light every now and then out of the arms of the men there on the field. A little man on a big horse was riding up and down in front of them, flourishing a sabre, preparing them for another charge. They wore blue, and they had been fired on earlier in the day by Confederates, but they were not Yankees. Louisianians. Colonel Mouton's regiment. The Eighteenth Louisiana Infantry, somebody had said. . . .

He repeated the name under his breath. The Irishman on his right must have seen his lips moving. He had leaned forward to speak to him. "Ye ain't rattled, boy?"

John shook his head. "You think we'll move soon now?" he whispered.

The Irishman nodded. He had torn a twig from a sassafras bush and was chewing it. The leaves hung down on either side of his mouth like a green mustache. When he was in a tight place he whipped his horse with his hat; he had had three quarrels on the march up from Corinth; with infantrymen who had been splashed with mud by his horse's hoofs. . . . He sat there now, not moving. Only his light eyes ranged back and forth in his weathered face. And he held his head a little to one side, as if he were listening. . . .

Ahead of them the lower boughs of dogwood and maple were a light veil over the dark wood. And below those boughs there was a thick growth of underbrush; that, too, already in leaf. The leaves everywhere still kept up that continual slight vibration. But the Federal skirmishers had vanished as completely as if the woods had swallowed them. . . .

The Irishman was clapping his legs into the barrel of his mare. And the man on the other side was gone, already, riding full tilt through the underbrush. The whole line was in motion. Flora, on the heels of Spencer Clayton's bay, was excitedly dodging the trees. He put spurs to her and she plunged forward again, straight through the woods at a gallop. But there was no enemy to be seen.

The trees in front of him were suddenly ablaze. Somewhere a horse was screaming. The Federal volley had leaped out, a solid sheet of fire, where a moment ago there had been only woods. . . . He put his hand to his face, then took it away quickly. Flora was rearing her full length. . . . The heap of dead boughs seemed very far below. With an effort he swung his leg free and she came down, panting, on her side.

He lay for a second, staring straight up over his head. There had been for several seconds a crackling sound there beside him. But it was gone now. Blood was flowing down over the lower part of his face and settling, stickily, inside his collar.

Staggering to his feet among the fallen boughs, he brought his elbow up over his face, clearing it of blood and broken twigs. There was no horse anywhere in sight. The crackling sound, then, had been Flora, making off through the under-brush. The cannonading must have ceased. He could hear all around him the quick thud of horses' feet, and above that the shouts of men. Confederate shouts. They had gone on straight through the Federal line! . . .

A young maple leaf had detached itself from the bough over his head and was sailing slowly to the ground. At the same moment the little dogwood tree at his right quivered and bent forward, its trunk split in half. He turned quickly and looked around. The Yankee marksman's cap had showed there for a second over the tops of those bushes. But he was gone now. . . .

He fell on his face behind the oak tree. The bullets were striking all around him. He could hear the soft rustle as each one spent itself in the leaves. He tore at the earth with his nails, pressed his face deeper into the dead leaves. It was not his head, though, that would be hit. It was his spine, his cold, unprotected spine. With his eyes closed he brought one hand slowly around and clapped it against the small of his back.

Wet earth was spattering into his face. He opened his eyes. The bullet had made a hole there in the ground beside his cheek. A small hole that shone wet in the sun. A curled, dried leaf that hung over it still trembled a little.

He got to his knees and crawled away through the under-brush. His mouth hung open. His nose had stopped bleed-ing but his lips were crusted with dirt and blood. When he released his breath it came in great, tearing sobs. They would hear him breathing, even if they didn't see the bushes shake.

Something was moving in the thicket just ahead. He closed his eyes and lay perfectly still, not breathing. The noise kept up. . . . But no bullets had come for a long time now. He opened his eyes. The horse was not a foot away. A sorrel

mare; sorrel and with a white streak down each forefoot.
Gunpowder's mark! . . . He caught hold of the stirrup and
crawled up into the saddle. The mare was quivering all over.
He whispered to her: "Steady, gal . . . steady!"

She had wheeled and was dashing through the thicket. The
ground in here was more open. Fallen timbers. Some of
them piled up on top of each other. She had taken that last
pile as neatly as ever she took the pasture bars at Penhally. . . . Townsend said that a saddler like Flora should
never be jumped. . . .

The trees were suddenly indistinct. A white cloud of smoke
was settling over the clearing. But the shouting seemed
louder. . . . There in the deep woods men were fighting.
With sabres. On foot, mostly. The riderless horse galloping
past had its saddle turned under its belly. . . .

The man behind the fallen tree was raising his arm . . .
slowly. . . . A fair-haired man. One side of his blue coat
was black with blood. . . . The rifle that had been stationary
for a second was sinking. It had disappeared below the level
of the tree trunk. . . . The man had seen him taking aim,
had heard him call out. He was walking out now from
around the tree, his gun trailing.

"All right, Johnny," he said, "but don't you touch my
shoulder!"

They went forward through the trees. The man was walking a little in front of Flora. John's Enfield was not an inch
from the bloody shoulder. He dropped it into the crook of
his arm. The Yankee was looking around, his eyes un-
naturally light in his powder-blackened face.

"You much hurt?" he asked.

John put his hand up and felt his face. "It ain't a thing
but nose-bleed," he said.

12

December, 1862.

"Nostalgia," the sergeant said. "Nostalgia." He moved his chair so that the firelight fell on the doctor's report smoothed out on his knee. "Y'all ever troubled with that?" he asked.

Charles laughed. "Lord, man; it's chronic with me! That feather bed over there has got me plumb demoralized. And here it's Johnny's turn to sleep on it the last night." He took a pair of dice out of his pocket. "Roll you for it, Johnny," he said.

John shook his head, smiling. Leaning back in his chair he allowed his eyes to rest with satisfaction on the elongated shadows that leaped on the far wall. The whole room was warm now, and brightly illuminated by the flames. It had been Mrs. Handley's bedroom until three days ago. Mrs. Handley had given up the room to the colonel, but she had left the immense four-poster bed with its high feather mattress there in its accustomed corner. She had been adamant about that. "Don't care if you are a soldier, you're going to sleep on a good feather bed as long as you're in my house. She and the colonel's wife had been schoolmates—at the convent in Bardstown. She fussed over him as if he were her own son. It was nice to be around a woman like that. They would all sleep warm one more night anyway. It was Kenneth's turn to lie beside the colonel, but he would stretch himself across the foot of the bed and sleep very comfortably. The colonel was a short man, thank God, and he had found that if he took a pin to bed with him and stuck Kenneth once or twice during the night he would keep his feet drawn up under him for hours. He would not shoot dice with Charles, though, for the night's sleep. Charles was too damn lucky. . . .

"What makes you think this is our last night here?" he asked.

Charles shrugged his shoulders. "This is too good to last," he said.

John studied his face in the light of the flames. That was a lie, of course. Charles knew more than that. He had been one of the colonel's escort to a conference at Morgan's headquarters the night before. He would have picked up whatever news was floating about. He was good at that, but he was canny, too, and close-mouthed, in his way. He talked all the time, but he rarely told you anything. He was a good officer. He had been mentioned twice in dispatches—for "conspicuous bravery in action." He would be a general if the war lasted long enough. He was standing now in the exact centre of the hearth, his legs spread far apart, his hands on his hips in an attitude of almost insolent ease. The new uniform—it was really only the jacket; he had had to content himself with his old trousers—his new jacket, duly embellished with gold braid, was a shade too light for him, though. There was a bulge over the left breast. He carried Alice's letters there, in the upper inside pocket. She must have written him eight or nine in the last few months. He tried to imagine what the letters she wrote Charles would be like. She was not very well educated, although she had spent four years at that convent. She spelled "regardless" with one "s." It was a word, too, that she was always using. Virginians always did. "Regyardless" and "It certainly is" they said, every other breath.

The sergeant was still shaking his head over the doctor's report. "That two-fisted Nace Perry that's out there now fiddlin' to them men, he's been lyin' out in the office all day, suffering from nostalgia. Yas, sir, he's been sufferin' right smart from his nostalgia and the doctor he couldn't do a thing for him."

John bent and examined the sheet over the sergeant's shoulder. Price Settle, Milton Payne, Ed Palmore, Robert Dockery, Nace Perry . . . Doctor Walker had written "Nostalgia" after the names of five men. Nostalgia. No other ailment. No wonder it drove the sergeant wild. It was queer that it should have descended on the men now when they were comparatively comfortable, in the snuggest quarters they had ever had, with for once enough cooking utensils. On the first march to Mud River they had had to bake their bread on their ramrods. Their ration of bacon they had eaten raw.

"I had a bird dog once that always got sick when you took him away from home," he said. "I remember one night he hollered so that I had to get up and ride fourteen miles with him. Stormy night, too, but he was quiet as a lamb soon as he knew we were on the road home."

The sergeant folded the report and stuck it in his pocket. "I look for 'em to be havin' blind staggers next," he said. "Yep, first thing we know they'll all be goin' down with the blind staggers."

John walked over to the doorway and stood looking out. From that side of the house a wide path ran through the snow to where half way down the slope the big tent was pitched. A fire burned brightly in front of the big tent. Thirty or forty men were grouped around it, on camp stools or fallen logs. On the highest pile of logs a man sat, picking a banjo. The mountaineer, Perry. He knew songs that were strange to these lowlanders. Old English or border ballads they were, mostly. Old Mister McLaughlin, the fiddler at Mayfield, sang a lot of them. Different versions, but the same songs.

The sergeant was stepping down onto the hard, trampled ground. John followed him. The ground around here was worn clear of snow by the feet of men and horses, but beyond

the big tent the fields sloped away, white, clear to the edge of
the woods. It would be through those woods that they would
ride to-morrow, if they moved, as the Irishman, O'Donnell,
predicted, toward Hartsville. O'Donnell had come back from
the Logan farm the other day primed with news. Four
thousand Yankees had come down the pike and were en-
camped at Hartsville. That meant two thousand, or more
likely fifteen hundred. O'Donnell usually doubled his figures.
Only eight hams left in the smoke house, he had reported
this morning, when as a matter of fact there were seventeen.
He had had that himself from Mrs. Handley, who *was* getting
a little worried about supplies. She would go on using them
up, though, as long as the colonel was there. She was going
to fatten him up, she said. The colonel—"Old Flintlock"
the men called him—sat his horse in the attitude of a sick
man bending over a fire, but he was not afraid of God, man
or devil. They had had coffee now, with sugar, for four days
running, and at supper last night there had been lemon foam,
with custard. Where in the world had she got lemons?

The sergeant, fortunately, was subduing his voice as they
approached the camp-fire. "That there Nace Perry is a
reg'lar varmint. Sleeps all day and comes out at night to
raise Cain." The sergeant hated mountaineers. He thought
they didn't make good soldiers.

The Irishman, Jerry O'Donnell, saw them coming and
moved over, smiling, to make room for them on his log.
John sat down beside him, but the sergeant walked over to
join a group of his own cronies. The sergeant despised the
Irishmen, too, for "furriners." The sergeant was a fool. A
duck-legged, bullet-headed fool from Barren County. There
was not a better fighting man in the whole squadron than
Jerry O'Donnell. His eye had the expression that one sees
in hawks and game cocks. He was clapping his hands now
and laughing wildly. "Will ye listen to him? Will ye listen
to the boy now?"

Nace Perry had discarded the banjo and was bent low over the fiddle somebody had handed up to him. He was fiddling as if for a wedding, sweeping the bow grandly over the strings, cracking his heels together and calling out shrilly from time to time as if the instrument did not suffice to discharge all the music that was in him. He had a strange face, thin and pointed like a fox's, with great hollows under the cheek bones. The mountaineers all had those long narrow faces and hollow cheeks. Malnutrition, the doctor said. He was fond of discoursing around the camp-fire on the different breeds of men. Three generations, sometimes only two, it took to make a new breed, he said. People who had been in Kentucky or Tennessee for two generations were as different from the Virginians as the Virginians were different from their ancestors across the water. . . . Alice was born a Virginian. All Virginia women had little tartnesses of speech, were peremptory in general. Aunt Jessie was. And Cousin Thyra's speech was like the dropping of some tart, ripe fruit—persimmons, no, damsons!—to the ground.

The music had stopped abruptly. Nace Perry was sliding down from his wood pile. He shook his head when they asked him to play again, and sat down on a log by the fire. John stared at him as he walked past. Nace Perry was a dead shot. He picked out the button he wanted on a man's coat when he fired. And a week ago he had come riding into camp, a brace of wild turkeys at his saddle bow. Three or four men had seen those black specks floating far above the valley and had not thought it worth while to shoot at them. Nace had barely checked his horse's stride to take aim. But he was not a particularly good horseman. The sergeant thought that that was what was the matter with him. He said that all the mountaineers were skeered of horses and that the first thing you knew they rolled off in the bushes some day and up a gulley and that was the last you heard of them. . . . This boy had been lying in bed for a week. The doctor couldn't find anything wrong with him. A lot of them were taken that way at first. But Perry had been in the army as long as he himself had. He remembered seeing him at Boone the day he enlisted—a lean boy, sitting under a tree, his flintlock behind him, picking a banjo. . . .

He turned away from the firelight. The moon looked cold and blue above the great leaping flames. This snow had been on the ground now for almost a week. O'Donnell was probably right. They would be moving toward Hartsville to-morrow. Morgan would never lose a chance like that. When he thought of Morgan he saw him always as he had dashed across the field at Shiloh, swarthy, black-mustached, standing in his stirrups to scream at his men in a voice that cut through the roar of the cannon. He could be kindly, though, and amiable, Charles said. They all worshipped him, Charles, Kenneth, Dan Taylor, every one of those fellows.

He himself had never been in his general's presence. He had talked with Albert Sidney Johnston, though; had shaken his hand. The general had sent for him, had received him in his tent over a glass of Tom and Jerry. It had been like the peace-time visit of one gentleman to another. The general had made him sit down, had called him Jack, and asked him about all the family; had even joked about the quarrel between his uncles Ralph and Nicholas. "Where do *you* live? Penhally? I'd like mighty well to make one more visit to old Penhally before I die. . . ." At the close of the interview he had walked to the tent flap and motioned to the shed where "Umpire," the horse that Uncle Ralph had given him, was stabled.

"Better stop and see your old friend, Fire Eater," he had said.

"We call him Umpire," John had stammered out un-thoughtedly.

But the general only laughed. "He's a war horse now," he said. "He's had to change his name along with his ways."

He had stopped at the shed. A skeleton of a stable it was, nothing but a few planks nailed on to uprights and roofed over with boughs. A rough sort of place for a Gunpowder colt. At Mayfield they lived luxuriously, in special stables, looked after by the more experienced grooms. And their blankets were of a brighter blue than those of the other horses, and specially marked. Fire Eater—he thought of him now always as Fire Eater—had whinnied as he approached. A beautiful piece of horseflesh he was, the best of all Gunpowder's get. He had found a curry comb sticking in the planks and had gone over him from head to foot and then had brought him some clover from the field.

General Johnston had been riding Fire Eater when he was killed. He had seen the horse afterward, just before they shipped him off. They had offered to return him to Uncle Ralph, but he had told them to sell him for the benefit of the Confederacy. Or perhaps he had wanted the money given to the general's widow. There would never be another leader like Sidney Johnston. No, as well say another Napoleon. But Morgan was a good man to follow. . . . Lieutenant John Llewellyn. . . . He had been a lieutenant now for four weeks. He had rather be elected lieutenant by the men themselves than get a commission the way Charles got his because his father had given so many horses, so much gear to the Confederacy. They did not know yet at home. He had sent the letter off Thursday a week ago. It couldn't have gotten there yet. He had written to Aunt Jessie. He had never written to Alice. She had never written to him. Charles had had three letters from her in the last month, and Kenneth two. Kenneth had read his letter aloud. She was staying at Mayfield now. She wanted to go home, to Virginia, but her father would not hear of it. He said she must stay there now till the war was over. They had a hard time getting enough to eat in Petersburg, where her people lived. They had nothing for dinner sometimes but cornfield peas, she had told Kenneth in her letter. The raiders fared better than that, but then they covered enough ground foraging. They would gallop up to a house sometimes to find nothing but fat meat sizzling in the skillet. But the next house might yield dessert, stewed dried peaches, sometimes even fried pies. If there were only once in a while some decent bread! It was hard to have to eat hoe cake day after day. "If you're hungry," Aunt Jessie used to say, "you're hungry enough to eat dry bread," but at Penhally you could always steal preserves out of the crock that Aunt Siny kept in the little entry, and butter from the spring-house. . . .

The fiddler, Nace Perry, had left the group around the fire and was walking down over the snow-covered slope toward the woods. The Irishman had turned around on his log to stare after him.

"Now where do you suppose that boy's going?"

John shook his head. O'Donnell was always running around after Perry. He had sat in the office with him all day when he was sick. It was because he admired Perry's marksmanship. O'Donnell himself was not a very good marksman. But he was a born fighter. He had set off down the slope after Perry now. John got up and strolled after them. The snow was a thin, brittle crust over the whole field. His feet crunched through it at every step. It would go in an hour if it turned warm. But the ground was hardly frozen. There would be mud then. Mud was worse than snow.

The two men before him were walking almost on a straight line. Beside his own there was one prodigiously long shadow that moved slantwise across the field. The Perry boy reached the edge of the woods and stopped. His right arm went up in a stiff, exaggerated gesture. The Irishman leaped

to his feet as the shot rang out and ran full speed across the
slope. John ran too. The hill before him was alive with the
racing shadows of men. They were all coming from around
the camp-fire. The Irishman was on his knees in the snow.
Perry's chest and the ground all around him was covered
with blood. The Irishman was saying something over and
over again in a low voice. John stooped and took hold of
the mountain boy's feet. Poor devil . . . poor devil. . . .

13

December, 1862.

It was dark in the woods now that the moon had gone
down, so dark that you could hardly see your hand before
you. They rode in close formation, one horse's nose brushing
the tail of the horse in front. The Irishman on John's left
had spoken only once in the last ten miles.

"The cavalry," he had said, "it was no place for him."

He was still thinking about the mountaineer, Nace Perry.
It was the claybank mare that kept him reminded. He had
fallen heir to her this morning. Certainly nobody would
have disputed his possession. He had not left the wounded
man's side from the moment they brought him into camp
until he died. He had died, conveniently enough, at half-
past nine that morning, just half an hour before they left
the crossroads. Four men had been detailed to effect the
hasty burial. They had carried him in a hurry up the slope
to the place on the edge of the woods where he had fallen
—Mrs. Handley had picked that spot for some reason. They
had not tried to argue her out of it. It was easier to send
the men on the double quick up the hill than to waste time
talking about it. The Irishman had wanted prayers said. He
had not minded so much the man's dying without receiving
extreme unction—Perry was doubtless a foot-washing Bap-

tist!—he had not minded that so much. There was a special provision, he said, for men who died in battle. Strange to die on the eve of a battle of a self-inflicted wound. How did a man get up nerve enough to shoot himself? But Perry had been a little off for some time. The Irishman was right. The cavalry was no place for him. He should have enlisted with the sharpshooters. "Pick your holes, boys!" That was all the orders they ever got. And their rations were the sandwiches they stuffed in their pockets before they scattered. In trees usually, or in holes in the side of a hill. . . . The Irishman had wanted prayers said. There had been tears in his fighting cock's eyes. Seeing them, he, John, had hastily rolled out some lines from the burial service for the dead:

"Behold I show you a mystery: we shall not all sleep, but we shall all be changed, in a moment, in the twinkling of an eye, at the last trump: for the trumpet shall sound, and the dead shall be raised incorruptible. . . . For this corruptible must put on incorruption, and this mortal shall have put on immortality. . . ."

Something—it might have been a man or it might have been merely a swaying limb—had leaped out suddenly from the underbrush. The Irishman had seen it too and was leaning sideways to peer down the line. . . . He could not remember what came after "this mortal shall put on immortality," and there was something about making beauty to consume away, "like to a moth fretting a garment." . . . When a man was killed you were sorry, but you were damn glad sometimes to get his boots or his gun or his horse. The claybank mare, though, was a poor mount for a raider. She showed up from a distance as if she were white.

The column ahead had halted. The shadow, then, had been a man. He smiled to himself in the dark. Young Clayton, feeling his way along, was identifying him, Lieutenant Llewellyn, by the top buckle on his right boot. They had all laughed at that buckle. Mr. Handley's blacksmith had made

it out of a big nail. He bent over until his ear was close to
the whispering mouth. The cavalry would detach itself immediately from the main body . . . to pass at a ford some
seven miles below. They would rejoin the main body of
troops at Hague's Shops on the other side of the river. . . .

He turned his head and gave the order. His voice did not
wake the echo in the woods. There was a trick about that.
You brought your tongue up against the roof of your mouth
instead of against your teeth. Then your voice stayed beneath the echo. He had heard commands given in a wood
ring out like pistol shots. . . . There was nothing to be heard
in the wood except the bookity-bookity-bookity of the horses'
hoofs. One stumbled every now and then and broke the
rhythm. They did not step along so briskly now. They
would have to go another fourteen miles anyway. Hartsville must be at least five miles beyond the ferry, and they
would have to go seven miles out of their way to get to that
damned ford. Charles and Kenneth were lucky to stay at the
ferry. They would have a devil of a time getting those guns
across. It was something, though, on a night like this, to
have a boat, even a one-horse affair, such as the ferry was
sure to be.

They emerged from the woods. In the centre of the clearing that sloped before them toward the river lay a cluster
of black buildings. There was no light to be seen but a door
had banged somewhere. There was the sound of feet on the
path. Two figures had sprung up at his stirrup. One of them
was Fred Woodard, or if not Fred, his brother Tom. The
guide they had picked up back there was not sure which
house came first. It did not matter. One would do as well
as another. You had to be careful, though, about these people
along the river. They were not all loyal.

He addressed the figures:

"You goin' with us?"

Fred—or Tom—was shaking his head and motioning to his companion. "My boy Ed'ard'll take you right there."

He came closer and laid his hand on Flora's neck. "I've got an uncle livin' at the ford. Name of Boulder. You let that boy off when you git to Boulder's."

John laughed. "Lawd, man, we don't want no boy with us when we get across that river."

He held out his stirrup and the boy climbed up behind him. They left the clearing and took the narrow trail that led to the river. It was as dark here as it had been in the woods. The sumac bushes that bent over the trail were as tall as trees. Their branches were still laden with snow. It brushed off continually against their clothes. They would be soaked to the waist before they got to the river. He put his hand back on the boy's jacket and found it wet.

"You better get in front," he said.

The boy clambered around obediently. A thin boy, not as old as Robert, but nearly as tall.

"How you like being in the army?"

"I could go acrost the ford with ye," the boy said hoarsely. "I could dry my clothes out at Uncle Tom's. He wouldn't never tell on me."

"No, pardner," John said, "you stay on this side." He unfastened the lower buttons of his cloak so that it would cover both of them. The warmth of the boy's body struck agreeably through the thin jacket, but his shoulders and back were beginning to feel numb. It had grown colder in the last hour. It was always colder before dawn.

The boy was saying that thar was a flat rock up thar in the bend of the river that looked right down on the Yankee's camp. He and Alick Glenn had clomb up thar one morning and watched 'em eating breakfast. Set right thar and watched 'em while they was eating their breakfast.

"Did you take a shot at 'em?"

"Didn't have no gun."

"Now if you had just had a couple of howitzers up there you could have cleaned the whole bunch out. Saved us a lot of trouble. Saved us this long ride."

"How far you come this day?" the boy asked.

"Forty miles, no, more like fifty. Lord sakes, boy, I ride so much I lose count o' the miles."

Charles considered that Alice was engaged to marry him. He had said so that morning, at three minutes after five, to be exact. It had been a hard night. The doctor had said that there was no chance for the Perry boy. He would contract pneumonia if his wound didn't kill him. They had put him on a cot in front of the fire. And the room had been full all night long of his great soughing breaths. Nobody had slept much, except the colonel, who had snored through it all. Toward dawn he himself had felt that he could not stand it any longer and had gone outdoors to find Charles pacing up and down in the snow. They had turned together and had walked aimlessly past the tents and up over the field until Charles, stopping short, had said irritably:

"God sakes! Can't we go some other way?"

He had been astonished to see Charles' face drawn and yellow in the gray light. He had had the worst of it all night, no doubt; his pallet was separated only by the width of the hearth from the dying man's cot. You would not have thought, though, that Charles would take this so hard. He had ordered out the squad for the execution of Tommy Ware and Slocomb and Edgoten last fall. He had walked down the woods road behind them, the three men astride the guns, their feet strapped down, their hands tied behind them. He had come back up the road smoking to raise Cain with the mess sergeant because breakfast was late. He had not seemed to mind that at all, or not much. It had been, perhaps, because there was an inevitability, a formality about it that made it part of the day's work. It had taken place in the curious unreal atmosphere of very early morning. Ware and Slocomb and Edgoten had been silent, composed, moving as mechanically as marionettes. But Nace Perry had walked out in the woods and shot himself, after fiddling. . . .

"God sakes!" Charles had said, "can't we go some other way?"

He had not spoken again until they were back on the path, when he had said abruptly:

"Did you know that Alice and I are going to get married?"

John had said: "Yes. She told me about it." She hadn't told him, but he had known what was in the letter Charles got the other night. Charles had read it there before the fire and then had gotten up quickly and walked around the room, laughing and joking with everybody as if he were excited about something that he couldn't mention. . . . He had told Charles that she had written him about it, but she hadn't. He had thought at the time that that lie was the last service, probably, that he would ever do her. She would be pleased, doubtless, to have things as straight as they could be made between herself and Charles. She would not care very much how it was done. A lie, one way or another, did not make much difference. Charles, however, had not quite believed him. He had felt it necessary to furnish details of the time and place of his engagement. "Last July . . . when we were all at Sycamore?" Or had he said Mayfield?

There had been two house parties that summer. One at Mayfield, the other, at Sycamore. He wished now that he had asked Charles to repeat what he had said. It did not make any difference, though, what he had said. . . .

The horses' feet crunched on gravel. The boy was slipping down. They were at the ford. The river was black and swollen with winter rains. Flora had quivered all over when the water struck her ankles, but she was moving steadily forward. A good mare. Her great-great-granddam was Gunpowder's filly out of Starlight. . . . When you bred to a Gunpowder stallion you got long, strong legs, powerful hindquarters, but weak eyes. She was a bad mount at night. She shied at every rock. A piece of paper blown into a fence corner would send her dancing. But she had the good long legs. She was swimming now, with short, resolute strokes. An easy motion, like Rock-a-bye-baby in the tree tops. . . . If you could forget that your legs were cased in ice. There *was* ice in the river. Little cakes went floating by every now and then, but this river never froze solid. . . . Unless it was in 1826. They had had snow in every month but one that year. . . . The water was as yet not above his knees, and they must be over the worst. That black bar ahead was the line of trees on the opposite bank. They *must* be in the middle of the river by this time. It was all right as long as only your legs were numb. If you went numb to the waist you might fall over in the saddle, face forward as like as not, and then you could drown, before anybody knew what had happened. A fine end for a raider! *Drowned, crossing a ford.* He put his hand in his pocket and took out the locket that had Alice's picture in it. She had given it to him that last night. She had known then, probably, that she was going to marry Charles! He cast the locket by its velvet ribbon into the water. Black, strongly flowing water was the place for such a keepsake. He would not send it back to her. It meant nothing, nothing to her and nothing to him. He would not send it back. . . .

The claybank mare was not making any headway. She skittered along sidewise and would not breast the current. He turned downstream and, catching hold of her bridle, brought her forward until they reached a place where the current was not so strong.

The Irishman was laughing softly in the dark.

"The little devil needs tachin, sir."

"Horses aren't all born knowing how to swim," John said. "Some of them have to learn. I had a horse . . . a bay gelding . . ."

Now that his legs were out of the water he felt loquacious, but the Irishman was not listening. His mare had gone to dancing again, though the water was not now over her fetlocks. The lean figure at the left must be Spencer Clayton. He continued the story of the bay gelding to Spencer as they splashed through the fifty feet of shallow water that lay between them and the bank. Spencer would remember the bay, as handsome a horse as you could find in the whole country. A good performer and not at all skittish—till you tried to make him cross a creek. Flora's full brother. No, he must have been her half brother. His dam had been Starlight, while Flora's was Old Gal. But the bay had had Ambassador for his sire. There had been three Ambassador colts that year. The bay, certainly, had been one of them. Did Spencer remember the name of the brood mare who had succeeded Old Effie?

"You're talking in your sleep, ain't you?" Spencer asked. "Look at those men . . ."

They were swarming up the bank in a disorderly mass, the orders that were undoubtedly being called out in front lost in the splashing of the horses' feet in water. He spurred past the straggler and came upon his own men. "All right, boys," he called, "we're almost there now!"

The column formed quickly. There was again the beating of horses' hoofs on the road behind him—a hard, flinty road that wound slightly uphill. They had left the river now. It was only a matter of a mile to the shops. He had a little more knowledge of this country than could be gotten from a map. He had been over across the river on a hunting trip once when he had spent Christmas vacation with Bob Anderson. They had shot a wild turkey on a hill that might have been this very hill. There had been anyhow the same line of trees skirting a triangular field that sloped down to the river and on the left a long wooded knoll. The trees lay like a cloud on the field. The field itself stretched away gray and undefined, but the whole country was beginning to stand out. Ahead of them the stake and rider fences were black against a sulphur-colored sky. It would be day now very soon.

They halted before a sleeping building. This was the shop, all right. Old Bill Atkins and his three old-maid daughters lived there. Old Bill was deaf as a post. The whole army of Tennessee might have assembled on that plain and Bill would not have turned over. But the old-maid daughters were probably fluttering around inside the house in their nightgowns, with their hair in curl papers. There was the sound of horses' hoofs on the road to the right. The rest of the cavalry was coming up. And not too soon. A pale yellow light was tingeing the horizon. You could make out the faces of the men now and even discern the ridge poles of the enemy's tents. The irregular gray mass toward which they were moving was the bivouac of the enemy. A thousand, the man from Gallatin had said. More like three thousand. The bivouac stretched across half the field, in one long, unbroken line of tents. They were turning white in the first rays of the sun. The round dark object there to the left might have been the projecting branch of a sassafras tree, but it had slipped out of sight just as that second shot rang out. They were finding the pickets and shooting them down. The shots had alarmed the Yankees. They were already falling in. The colonel's courier, who had been riding beside him for some moments, speaking hoarsely, had galloped on, to halt beside another officer. They were dismounting two regiments then. Chenault's men over there would oblique on the flank.

He called out the order, then leaping to the ground, gave Flora's bridle into a grasping hand, and ran, shouting, over the frozen field, toward the white line of the enemy's tents.

14

December, 1862.

Charles made his way slowly toward the house, with the last turn of the wood that he had been an hour chopping. He was still so weak that he had to stop at the horse block to rest. He sank down heavily, the wood across his knees. From where he sat he could look straight down the path that straggled past the cornfield and the scrap of a tobacco patch to the river. They had brought him up that path three weeks ago, old Burny Beard and the girl, old Burny swearing every step of the way, the girl saying nothing, only grunting from time to time. Strong as a little ox that girl. And pretty too, in a milk-maidish sort of way.

He was aware that she and the old woman were staring at him now from the window of the lean-to. They had been opposed to his going to the woodpile, but old Burny had been obdurate.

"Ef'n he's able to travel he's able to chop wood. . . . Yes, sir, I always say ef'n he's able to travel he's able to chop wood. . . ." The words went on and on in Charles' head in a dull sort of sing song. The old man had said them so often, that morning at breakfast and the day before and the day before that. It had been three days now since he had first thought of leaving Beard's. He would not make it to-day, though; the wind had been in the east since early morning. Lying awake just before dawn he had heard it rising in the woods that were separated only by a field from the cabin and had known that he would have to stay another day. If the old man would only lend him a horse—or sell him a horse—if he would only do that he could leave any day. He was strong enough now to sit a horse. He could last all day long if he only had a horse to ride. . . .

He got up and walked unsteadily toward the house. The chopping had not been so bad, but the effort of stooping to pick up the wood had thrown him, as it always did, into a perspiration. It was springing out now on his forehead and under his armpits. In a few minutes his whole body would be bathed in icy sweat. Entering the big room he dropped his turn of wood in the box at one side of the hearth and sat down in the nearest rocking chair. The room was still, except for the ticking of the clock that stood on the mantel between two china statuettes, Corydon and Phyllis, they were. Or Amaryllis. . . . What was it? Or sport with Amaryllis in the shade or in the tangles of Nærea's hair. . . . When he had been ill there on the pallet in the corner he had been wearied by the scraps of poetry that said themselves over and over in his head. But when he had been really delirious the whole room had seemed to float, a soft carpet covered with those tiny, star-shaped white flowers that you found sometimes in abandoned fields. He had floated on it, very soft and easy, just a little above the smells of sour grease and cabbage that were rank on the floor beneath.

The old man was looking up, a flicker in his bright, squirrel's eyes.

"Feelin' peart to-day, ain't ye?"

"Pretty good," Charles said.

Leaning back in his chair he resumed his contemplation of the events which had preceded his coming to the Beards' house. It had been three weeks since they had brought him up from the river. They had left the crossroads on the night of December 9. He remembered that part of it very well.

A moonlight night and the whole countryside white with snow. They must have ridden fifty miles that night. The horses had been badly winded when they reached the shop. The engagement itself had been short, so short that there had been something ludicrous about the whole affair. That Yankee captain shouting orders, in his drawers, with his teeth chattering! Somebody had run him through before they reached the crest of the hill. The warm work had been there. One of the Yankee shells had struck a Confederate caisson and had blown it into a thousand flinders. The Yankees had fought hard there on the side of the hill, but they had broken in a few minutes. It had been easy then to drive them to the cliff. The rest of the dismounted cavalry had come up, on the flanks and the rear. Young John had been in that charge, young John and the crazy Irishman, O'Donnell. He remembered observing them for a moment, with something like amusement. Young John fought like a berserker. He went insane, really, during a battle, and afterward he could never tell you anything that had happened. He always gave a good account of himself, but he would never make a good officer. In his berserker rages he forgot about his men. He himself was not as good a soldier, but he was a better officer. He knew that his mind functioned with peculiar clarity during a battle, and afterward he enjoyed taking out the pictures that it had registered, things sometimes that he was not aware at the moment of having seen. He could see this whole engagement now, from the time of the first advance to the moment when the Yankees fled to the cliff.

It was only a few minutes after that that the retreat across the river was ordered. He remembered seeing the river full of Confederates, breast deep it was along there. They were having a devil of a time with the wagons and guns they had captured. John or Kenneth he had not seen again, but they must have gotten away. There had been only three men on

the Yankees' side of the river when he went down. He
remembered clearly looking about and seeing only two men
beside himself, Spencer Clayton and Dan Gilley. Gilley's
horse had balked at the cliff—it must have been a good
twenty feet—he had abandoned it and had slid down the
bank, but Spencer's horse had taken the leap like a bird. It
was then that he himself had gone down, with a ball in his
shoulder—the Yankees were attacking hotly from the rear.
He had gone down in the muck among the reeds and had
lain there quietly, watching Spencer's horse swim after the
wagons. Then the Yankees had closed in. He had seen them
coming and had closed his eyes. He had felt that it was no
concern of his, the pain in his shoulder having started about
that time. He did not know to this day how they had missed
him. They had been gone a long while before the old man
and the girl came down to search among the reeds that bordered all that bank. The old man had not been actuated by
feelings of benevolence. He had found a ten-dollar gold-
piece on a battlefield once, and he was not likely to forget it.
He had been pretty well fooled that time, finding nothing but
a soldier, delirious and with a ball in his shoulder.

He drew his chair nearer to the fire. He hoped to God
that he didn't take cold from this sweat. If he did, he would
just walk out into the woods and lie down in the snow. He
would not lie another day on the filthy pallet they had made
him there in the corner. It was not the rags that made him
so sick, but the smell of stale grease that permeated that
whole side of the room. They had fed the dogs there until
they had elected to pitch his pallet in that corner. The dogs
had come snuffing around him when he lay there sick, and
once one of them had dug a bone out from under the roll of
rags that served as his pillow.

The old man was taking a twist of tobacco out of his
pocket.

"I'd best be plain with ye," he said. "Yes, I'd best be plain. Thar ain't ary horse on this place I could spare ye. Naw, thar ain't ary horse I could let go off with ye."

Charles said non-committally as he had said fifty times before:

"My father would give you a mighty good price for the horse. He'd send a nigger man over here with the money right away. I know that."

The old man laid the twist of tobacco on his knee and began painstakingly to smooth out the leaf. "I don't doubt but that your daddy's a right clever man, though I ain't ever heard tell of him. I don't doubt but that he'd do what was right; though, as I say, I don't know nobody in that country and ain't any manner of idea what kind of folks they air crost the river. I don't doubt but that it's all like you say. It'd take a right smart nigger, though, to find his way clear across this river, the country being onsettled like it is."

"Oh, he'd manage it," Charles said off-handedly. He was not going to be drawn into any argument this afternoon. They had had all that out last night. He had mentioned the name of every man of influence he could think of in the whole country, only to have the old devil smile and shake his head. "Judge Gavin? Naw, I been livin' round here all my life, but I never heard tell of *him*. . . . Colonel Glover? Thar was a Glover now used to live at Purcell's Ferry. . . ." He had even repudiated knowledge of old man Atkins, the steamboat owner, who must be known to every river rat in the whole country.

The girl was calling from the lean-to. Macon's boy had come again to say that that ar muley cow weren't no better. The old man was already rising to get his coonskin coat down from its peg behind the door. He would walk back with the boy, three miles through the snow, and spend the rest of the day doctoring the cow. Bring her through too, probably. He was a born horse doctor, cow doctor. Some people had a gift that way. His own father had it. Cows, horses, sheep, he could doctor anything on four legs. But he knew a little about everything. He could have made a good living at any one of a half-dozen trades if he had not inherited property. Half a dozen shops he had there on the place. The saddler's shop was the best of all. He took more interest in that than in any of them. He had trained the two young negroes that Uncle Ben had now as his assistants. Well, he himself loved the smell of new leather, the smell even of hides tanning. Women as a rule hated it. Alice had come near fainting one day when the shop door opened suddenly as they walked past. . . . Alice would never say that she liked Mayfield better than Penhally. She pretended that she felt more at home at Penhally because she was closer kin to the old gentleman than she was to his father. Her mother had been an Allard. So had the old gentleman's. But her grandfather was a Crenfrew. These relationships, crossed and recrossed as they were, were too complicated to keep in your mind. If you had anything else on your mind, that is. Old women like Miss Nannie could keep them all in their heads. She could give you the pedigree, right off the reel, of anybody in the whole county—of the gentry, that is. She never seemed to bother to keep in mind the connections of the plain people. . . .

The girl had come into the room and was kneeling on the hearth, replenishing the fire. A warm-blooded creature. He had seen her out in the stable lot at intervals all morning, without a cloak, and her thin dress of linsey woollen turned down at the neck. She was moving nearer to say something in a low voice:

"That ar gray mule's penned up in the stable."

He was on his feet almost before he comprehended the words.

"You mean I could have him?" he whispered.

She lifted three sticks of wood from the box and threw them noisily on the fire. "I'm going out thar now," she said. "You come on in a few minutes. Come the front way."

He took his coat down from its peg behind the door. One sleeve had ripped out of the armhole. The old lady had been promising to mend that for him. She would not do it now. He walked over to the window. The girl was entering the stable lot, walking daintily over the black-crusted ice that covered the whole enclosure. He waited until she disappeared in the runway of the stable, then buttoning his ragged coat about him he stepped out into the cold.

He walked slowly along the path that led past the wood pile, thrusting now and then with his stick at the dried sunflower stalks that grew all over that part of the yard. It would have been better if he had cut straight across the lot. There was still time for the old lady to come out of the back door, come to the stable to look for eggs, or to slop that infernal hog that grunted at him now from its pen. He gained the runway of the stable and stopped beside the gray mule's stall. The girl came forward and took his arm.

"You'll have to fasten that girth," she said. "He's done swelled up on me."

He put his foot against the bulging side and pulled until the mule grunted, then fastened the girth and got into the saddle. The saddle was new, of a good grade of leather, a high-pommelled McClellan saddle with fancy stitching on the skirts. Funny, to be stealing a man's saddle. Worse, somehow, than stealing his mule. He thrust his hands deep into his empty pockets. "I sure am sorry," he said. "I haven't got a thing. I haven't got a thing that I could give you."

Her eyes were very large and bright in her brown face. She laughed excitedly. "You wouldn't think it," she said, "but he's easy as a rocking chair. His mammy was a fine saddle mare."

He laughed too, partaking of her excitement. "Aren't you going to kiss me good-by?" he asked. "Looks like you ought to kiss me good-by after I been visitin' you all so long." She laughed again and coming close to the mule's side, stood on tiptoe to receive his kiss, then remained a moment in the curve of his arm, to point him the way he should take. "If you ride along the fence a little piece under those sassafras trees you can keep under cover the whole way. Dan Purcell at the ferry'll take you crost the river."

He lingered. "What'll that old man do about his mule?" he asked. "Will he beat you?"

"That old man? That old skinny man beat me?" She brought her hand down sharply on the mule's sleek rump. "G'long now," she said, "or Mammy'll be wonderin' where I am."

He nodded, and touching the mule lightly with his spur rode from the dark runway of the stable out on to the snow-covered trail that would take him to the river.

15

January, 1863.

Townsend had the tow sack that held the rabbit tobacco slung around his neck by a piece of twine. Every time Alice got an apron full she had to walk over and dump it in his sack. He would rear back on his hunkers and stare at her out of bleared, purplish-brown eyes as if he had not known till this minute that she was in the field.

"Dass a help," he would mutter. "Yas'm, dass sholy is a help."

She had offered to assist him in gathering rabbit tobacco to make a brew for Aunt Siny, who was ailing. There was nothing the matter with Aunt Siny, Doctor Latham said, except senile indigestion, but Townsend was convinced that the

tea he made from the herb would cure anything, so he went
stooping about over the field like a great coon, a white-headed coon. The tails of his absurd tight coat—it had been black
originally, but was weathered now to an extraordinary bottle-
green—waved behind him over the brown grasses. The
sleeves left his gnarled wrists bare and were fantastically
tattered. When he stood up and waved his arms, as he did
every now and then, "to get the kinks out of his rheumatics,"
he resembled nothing so much as a scarecrow. She imagined
that the blackbirds that kept flying low over the grass eyed
him respectfully.

The bottom of the sack was covered, but he would not
quit. When she suggested a few minutes ago that they had
gathered enough he muttered sententiously:

"Some folks gives up at de first trial . . . while others
keeps on . . ." and then went off into the recital of some
ancient quarrel. . . . "You say thass so . . . I ain't sayin'
it ain't . . . I'm tellin' you, though . . . I'm tellin' you. . . .
I been in this world a long time. . . . A long, long time I
been in this world. . . ."

If he went on muttering like that much longer she
would go crazy . . . raving crazy. She straightened up and
stretched her arms high above her head. . . . From this
high, sloping field she could look down on the house, the
stable lot, the gardens, and even catch a glimpse of the big
pond. At this moment a spare black-clad figure was crossing
the road to disappear in the shrubbery of the lower yard:
the old gentleman returning from his constitutional. He kept
up his customary routine, no matter what happened. An hour
after breakfast he spent in conference with Townsend and
the young negro who had acted as overseer since Albert, the
white overseer, had enlisted. What they found to discuss
during this hour Alice couldn't imagine. Not a third of the
land was in cultivation, Cousin Jessie had told her, and she

knew herself that every colt in the pasture was unbroken. There were four-year-olds on the place who had never been saddled; the Yankees were much less likely to take them if they were unbroken. The hour after the conference the old gentleman spent walking about the place, no matter what the weather was, up into the pasture to stand looking at the horses, who were already beginning to put on their winter coats—it would be a hard winter, everybody said—or down along the branch, or sometimes across the road to circle round and round the big pond. The hour's walk, then dinner, which consumed just as much time as it ever had, though they sat down often to nothing but corn pone and black-eyed peas. After dinner he slept an hour, then took a turn around the yard and came back to his big chair in the chimney corner and his toddy. He would have his toddy every afternoon if Cousin Jess had to go down into the still-house herself after it.

It was something to have a routine as inflexible as that. She would be better off herself, she knew, if she had one. But what could she do except knit and plait straw hats? She was plaiting a hat now out of straw that she had picked up at the straw stack. Cousin Jessie had showed her how to dye it and plait it into a cone-shaped affair that she trusted would become her when it was molded into some sort of shape, and Josephine had written her directions for making a trimming out of white chicken feathers that she said all the girls in Petersburg were using.

She had felt a little guilty at first to be making a hat when she could be knitting, but she had thought, after she finished her fiftieth pair of socks, that she would go raving crazy if she made another one. Mrs. Robert E. Lee and her daughters had presented Posey's brigade with one hundred and ninety-six pairs of socks. But Mrs. Lee was the best woman in the world, everybody said. It was easy to sit still

knitting sock after sock when you were naturally saintly and
an invalid besides. She had met Mrs. Lee once at the Carys'.
A gray-haired woman with a gentle smile, who limped a little. Her daughters probably took after her in saintliness. Josephine said that the girls in Petersburg were cutting up old
silk stockings, unravelling them, and crocheting them into
mitts. And Mrs. Rogers had crocheted an entire suit—a silk
suit!—for Mr. Rogers.

It was remarkable how the tone of Josephine's letters had
changed since the war came on. She wrote every few weeks
now, often at length. Her letters were vivacious, though the
things she told about were grim enough in all conscience.
Pen Latham had lost a leg, and one of the Peyton twins was
blind, and poor, handsome Alec Leigh had been dead now for
over a year. They had parties, though, in Richmond and in
Petersburg in spite of all that. The boys stayed in town all
night sometimes, at dances, and then galloped back to camp
at dawn. And Josephine had attended two of Mrs. Davis'
receptions. Somebody said that Mr. Davis had suggested
that the people of Richmond might have to eat rats. They
were as good as squirrels, he said, when properly fattened.
. . . Josephine, her mother, none of them ever mentioned her
coming home. It was a comfort, they said, to know that she
was safe out in Kentucky, with enough to eat. . . .

Townsend must be down in the ravine. She could not
see him anywhere, but she could still hear him singing, dole-
fully:

> "De buzzards *an'* de flies
> Keep a-pickin' at his eyes,
> Po' lil black sheep,
> *Cyahn* come home . . ."

She got up and walked to the house. As she entered the
hall Mally, the yellow house girl, was just going into the
big room. Through the half-open door the old gentleman

could be seen asleep in his chair before the fire. After Mally had swept the hearth she bent over and laid a stick or two of wood on the fire, casting a discreet glance at him over her shoulder. It was his particular pride to keep up the fire himself; he would make a big fuss if anybody else tampered with it, but he was always going to sleep and letting it die down. Without the flames the great room was given over already to the shadows of evening. She could hardly make out the articles of furniture in the remote corners: the tall chest of drawers between the west windows, the dull gilt frame of some old portrait above the old cherry desk, the secretary made of rosewood that had belonged to Ellen Laurie. Mally was tiptoeing past his chair now, taking away his empty glass; she would bring it back in a minute full of good hot toddy. He was horribly spoiled, really, with all those women hanging around him. Cousin Jessie, Cousin Virginia, Cousin Thyra—if it was something that didn't involve cards—none of them ever thought of anything but his comfort. No wonder he had never married. If he had married he would have had only one woman to wait on him, whereas as an old bachelor he had half a dozen. She had never heard of his wanting to marry anybody. Too conceited, probably. Could never forget that he was Mister Nicholas Llewellyn, of Penhally. She smiled at the yellow girl as she went past, wondering if she were Nicholas' daughter. She was very light, certainly. She leaned forward to study fiercely the lean profile that jutted out from the high back of the chair. Mally had a negro mouth and negro eyes, but her chin was shaped just like his, and her hands were like the hands clasped on the head of his cane, slender hands, with very long fingers. Mally had always been around the house, from the time she was a very little girl. Perhaps Cousin Jessie knew all about it and had seen to it that she was kept around the house where work was easy and light.

Her mother was Violet, the enormous, heavy old negro woman who had died not so many years ago. Oh, how could
Uncle Nick, how could he? Still, men did, she knew. If
John . . . or Charles . . . if she ever so much as *suspected*
either of them. . . .

She turned back into the hall. The things you thought
about when you stayed by yourself all day in an old house
like this! She might as well be alone in the house. The old
gentleman never listened to anything you said. . . . He
talked to himself, almost as much as Townsend did. . . . And
Cousin Jessie was getting almost as bad. She had always
nowadays a perplexed absent frown. She hardly seemed
the same person: she actually looked different. Her skin,
that had been as smooth and soft as a baby's, was covered
now with tiny, crisscross lines. They came from worrying.
She was always worrying, about whether they would be able
to get another barrel of sugar, about whether Miss Nannie
was getting enough to eat—she was convinced that the old
woman was on the verge of starvation and either went herself every afternoon or sent a negro across the fields with a
basket at noon—about whether any more of the servants
would run away. . . . There was absolutely no end to the
things you could worry about, once you got started. It
might be easier, actually, to be in the situation her own family had been in for more than a year, down to the very bottom, with nothing to worry about except where the next
meal was coming from. . . . They would never hear to
her coming home until the war was over. People in Petersburg thought, no doubt, that anybody who was in the country, in Kentucky, was pretty lucky. . . . Well, they did have
enough to eat in Penhally. Miss Jessie saw to that. . . .

It was several degrees warmer on the porch than it had
been in the hall. All these old houses had a graveyard chill
in winter. They lived, really, only in the summer time when

the doors and windows were wide open and life flowed on
easily and pleasantly. The thing to do was to stay outdoors
as much as you could, even in winter.

She wrapped her cloak closely about her and went down
the steps and through the little gate into the rose garden.
There were some late roses blooming there. It would be better to gather them and take them into the house. A cold snap
was coming, Townsend said. He was probably still infalli-
ble on weather signs, even if he was losing his mind. . . .
A comfort, at least, to know that you are safe out there. . . .
Safe enough. Gathering rabbit tobacco all afternoon in a
dead field with a crazy old negro. . . . Josephine had been
under shell fire . . . for six months. She wouldn't care
how much danger there was. She would brave anything—
death, mutilation, that must be worse, the sight of others'
suffering. . . . Jenny Lowe, who had always been a perfect
cry baby, was assisting surgeons in a hospital in Richmond.
. . . She could stand *anything* if only she were there where
things happened instead of way off here in this lonely country house. It would be better next week when Cousin Thyra
came, but that would mean playing cards all day long and
half the night. . . .

There were two bushes with roses on them, but she had
forgotten her scissors, and it was hard to tear the roses from
their stems. She plucked six, and then walked around the
long bed that held the centre of the garden to the bench that
was built around the willow tree. It was really very pleasant
out here. There was warmth in the sunshine. She could feel
it through her coat. And it was astonishing how many things
were still green: the rose bushes and the violets that bordered all the beds, and the honeysuckle. There were actually
blooms on the honeysuckle. It was only when you raised
your eyes to the house itself that you felt that it was winter.
The Virginia creeper that covered one whole side was dead-

brown everywhere, and the house itself looked gray and cold, as old houses do in winter.

This was the bench she had sat on with John the evening before he went away, while the music and the dancing went on in the parlor. Ruffin Woodford had ridden over from Fairfields that evening, with his tall, coal-black smiling negro fiddler. They had rolled the rugs up and taken all the chairs out of the parlor except a row of rockers along one side for the older people. Ruffin had set his fiddler down in the biggest chair he could find, in the doorway that led into the little hall. "He's snaggle-toothed," he said, "and double-jinted. You have to give him lots of room." The negro seemed, indeed, to be double-jointed, tying himself into the most ridiculous knots, and ending up finally by holding the fiddle high above his head while he sang and beat time with his enormously long feet. Now and then Ruffin could be heard urging him on: "Come on now, Pace! You want to show these Penhally niggers what fiddling is. They ain't nobody on this place can fiddle with you and you know it. It's a downright shame, that's what it is, you and me havin' to ride fourteen long miles just to show these Penhally folks what fiddling is. . . ." He had gone on like that until there was a fringe of dark faces at each of the six windows on that side of the house, and there had arisen finally from the Quarter the thin wailing of an ancient fiddle—Uncle Ben, the oldest negro on the place, fiddling on the porch of his cabin! Cousin Jessie had made them all walk down to the Quarter to listen to him. They had stood in a row under the dark trees while the white-headed, trembling old negro scraped away at "The Arkansas Traveller." When the volume of sound was too thin—Uncle Ben was so palsied that he could hardly hold the bow steady—the old gentleman and Charles—they were both pretty mellow by that time—had helped him out by singing the words. And at the conclusion of Uncle Ben's performance the "tall, stylish nigger," as Mally called him, had bowed low before his nonogenarian rival, observing handsomely: "You is what I'd call a fiddlin' man, Uncle Ben. You sholy is!"

She had started back to the house with John, but Charles came up after they had walked a few steps, and John at once fell back with Lucy and Kenneth. John and Charles seemed to have an understanding. They allowed each other just so much time with her. When the time was up the one whose turn came next presented himself and the other one got up and left with no ceremony. Charles had been very angry. He pretended that she was letting him go away without saying good-by. "Oh, I suppose you'll kiss me there before all of them. It's all right to kiss your cousin." She had slipped down the back stairs to meet him in the lilac walk after all the company had gone home. A light rain had started falling by the time she got downstairs. They had stood there, beside the slumbering gray house, a long time, while the rain beat down through the leaves. She could see now, when she closed her eyes, the slippery black trunks of the lilac bushes and, against them, Charles' face, white and distorted with anger. "Am I the one you love?" He had stood still in the middle of the walk to ask that over and over again. She could not ever remember afterward just what she had said in her attempts to soothe him. She had been frantic, fearing that somebody in the house would hear him and come down to see what was the matter. There had been for a little while a light burning in the window just above them. She had been cold and faint when at last she got upstairs to bed. She had lain there wakeful a long time after the hoofbeats of Charles' horse had died away down the road. . . . Toward the last he had been repentant and tender. She stood there like stone, hardly feeling his arms about her, thinking only that in a few more minutes she could go upstairs. . . . She had slept a

little before dawn, but was awake when John and the old
gentleman rode away just after breakfast. She had been
awake in plenty of time to dress and go downstairs, but she
had not gone. . . .

John had never written. In seven months he had never
written. She had been at Sycamore once when he was home
on leave. Another time at Mayfield. A morning's ride either
place. He had not come. . . .

Feet were shuffling in the leaves that covered all the garden paths. The latch of the little gate had clicked. She got
up and walked around the syringa bush. A man was standing at the head of the garden steps, grinning at her, a beard-
ed man in a ragged suit of butternut jeans. She ran toward
him over the dead leaves, her hands outstretched.

"Charles!" she cried. "Oh, *Charles!*"

16

January, 1863.

Cousin Thyra slapped a card smartly on the table. "Send
a boy to mill, would you?" she said with a short laugh. The
old gentleman looked down at her twelve of clubs grimly
and did not answer. He rarely spoke when he played whist,
whereas Cousin Thyra kept up an indignant gasconnade all
the time. Charles, in the big chair by the window, yawned
and stretched himself, and felt tenderly of his side just under
the last rib. Semi-invalidism, such as he had enjoyed for
the past month, had its advantages. But for it he would be
playing cards with the group there by the fire. As it was,
he had only to look undecided when the table was drawn up
and Uncle Nick would say testily: "Oh, let the boy alone,
Thyra. Can't you see he doesn't feel good?"

He stood up. The trees crowded close on this side of the
house. Their bare branches tapped continually against the

panes. The chamber, even at this time of day, was lighter now than it was at full noon in summer. When you stood at this window in summer you saw nothing but green, layer upon layer of deep green. He tried to recall how the place looked in summer. The branches of the juniper and the sugar tree swept the ground. The earth under them was always dark with moisture, and cool to the touch on the hottest day. . . . He had been thinking that it was a long time since summer. But they had had summer—two summers—since he went away to war. They had gone unmarked because they had brought with them none of the joys that belong to summer. It was as if it had been winter for years!

He saw suddenly, as something that he had known for a long time, the house that he had meant to build for Alice. A square, white house set in the heart of a thick grove. It would never be as gloomy as this house, though. The trees were mostly oak and their branches grew too high to cast a very deep shade. He knew which trees he would cut down and which he would leave. He had walked around in there all one morning, marking with his pocket knife the trees that he intended to have felled. The grove had been a pleasant place that morning, with the new leaves just come out big enough to cast their full shadow. . . . June of '61 it had been, a month or two before he and Kenneth joined the army. . . .

They had all been here at Penhally a week later, John, Kenneth, Ruffin Woodford, the Crenfrew girls, all the young people in the neighborhood. He and Kenneth had left for Camp Boone in August. John had followed a few weeks later. John's young brother, Robert, had been the only boy left at Penhally. The old gentleman had refused to let him go. He had run away finally to enlist under Breckinridge. . . .

It was funny that nobody had heard from John. Over a month it had been, Cousin Jessie said, since they had had a letter. He had had an idea before he came that the boy still wrote to Alice, but she had not received any letter from John since he had been at Penhally. He was certain of that. The boy had been in love with her, all right, when he went away in August, but perhaps he had gotten over it. When they were all together there at the Handleys', he hardly ever mentioned her, rarely mentioned any of the Penhally folks, in fact. Still he himself had had at the back of his mind for some months the conviction that John *was* infatuated with Alice. He had actually remonstrated with her once for leading the boy on. The same feeling had made him tell John—it had been the night that the crazy mountaineer had shot himself— that he and Alice expected to be married as soon as the war was over. He had asked her if she would promise that. Her letter had come that day saying that she would. And something had impelled him to break the news to John. They had been walking together in front of the tents. Snow all over the ground and the day just breaking. The boy had stood there looking at him a second and then had said something— he couldn't remember just what—to the effect that he already knew it. He had never been able to make out whether he had looked the way he had because of the news or because he was thinking of something else. He had been pretty badly cut up about Perry . . . and nobody had slept much that night. . . .

He had no right, perhaps, to ask Alice to marry him, a refugee who did not even know that he would be able to rejoin his own regiment. He had thought then—it was only two months ago—that the war would be over in another six months, eight months, a year at most. He did not think so now. The Yankees had been in possession of this country for almost a year. A great many of the negroes had already gone north. How would people live if the Yankees won the war and all the negroes left the country? Somebody said that Alf, the overseer at Mayfield, had gone—suddenly in the night, without a word to any one. His father would be cut up over that. He had picked Alf out when he was ten years old as the likeliest pickaninny on the place and had trained him himself for his duties as overseer. He had heard his father boast that if he cared to he could leave his plantation for as much as six months at a time. Alf would see to it that nothing was neglected. He was, certainly, an intelligent and competent negro, and of a fine character. If Alf left, you could not expect any of the negroes to stay. They were, perhaps, like rats, whose instinct told them to desert a sinking ship. . . .

It would not be easy to get through the Yankee lines. He had an idea that Morgan's men were somewhere over in the Blue Grass. News of a skirmish near there had come through the other day. He would, at any rate, head in that direction when he left. . . . The cold snap might be over by that time. It broke, often, the last of January. . . . He ought to go, any day now. . . . They thought that he was not able to travel yet. He would not argue the point, just get up and leave some night. That would be the easiest way. But Alice cried whenever he mentioned leaving. . . .

The group at the card table had not stirred. They played cards like that every afternoon, Cousin Thyra, the old gentleman, and the two Crenfrew girls. They had been sitting there at that table since right after dinner and it was almost time to light the candles now. . . . Ellen Crenfrew was looking tired, though. She would be wanting Alice to take her place after dinner. . . .

He moved nearer the window. Beyond the black branches the big field stretched away, a bare expanse of brown grass patched here and there with snow. It had not been in cultivation last year. The first time he could remember when that field had not been in cultivation. The old gentleman was raising quantities of sorghum and corn in the bottom and the usual amount of wheat on the uplands. He had succeeded pretty well in feeding his people, better than almost anybody around there. . . . In the middle of the field two figures were black against a gray sky: Cousin Jessie and Alice, returning from a visit to Miss Nannie Whitcomb. But where was the negro girl whom they had taken along to carry the basket of provisions? They had started out right after dinner. Cousin Jess had insisted on going this afternoon, although it was so cold. Miss Nannie was scraping the flour barrel when she was there three days ago, she said. She was afraid that they would find her with literally nothing to eat in the house. The war was hard on people like Miss Nannie. What *did* she live on? Of course everybody in the neighborhood gave her things. Still, there was not much to spare these days and you could not get for love or money the things she needed, coffee, sugar, quinine to break the intermittent fever that she had had since early fall. Her nephew, Joe, whom she had raised, had sent her part of his pay for a while, but he had not sent any money for three or four months now. That was not to be wondered at. The poor devil probably hadn't had a square meal himself for weeks. Eleven dollars a month didn't go very far. They *could* not live on the rations, and when they bought food they paid exorbitant prices. He himself remembered giving a dollar and a half for two sweet potatoes. . . . And the quinine pills that the Hartsville doctor had prescribed had been a dollar a piece. Seventy-five cents for a sweet potato and a dollar for a quinine pill. What was the world coming to?

He could have walked with them to Miss Nannie's as easily as not. Once you got across the big field the road went through the woods all the rest of the way. Cousin Jessie had seemed so frightened at the idea, though, that he had abandoned it. . . . Miss Nannie lived in a little house on the edge of a clearing, like an old woman in a fairy tale. He had heard his father tell how old man Whitcomb had cleared one field and then had sat down on his porch to rest, declaring that he warn't no hog, and had sat there the rest of his life fiddling and drinking whiskey. But his grandson, Joe Whitcomb, had cleared some more land just before he joined the army. Uncle Nick insisted that it was that stumpy new ground that had sent Joe to war. A Whitcomb, he said, would do anything to get out of work. . . . Joe was a teamster with the Second Kentucky, a good, steady fellow too, a fine hand with horses and mules. . . .

The door opened. But it was only a negro boy bringing in wood. The back log was burned in two. He replaced it and then kneeling on the hearth blew on the embers and piled smaller logs against the new back log. Charles walked over and stood in front of the fire while the flames mounted. He could hear in the room above his head the rattling of fire dogs and the falling of logs into the wood box. Jube, his own body servant, was up there making a fire. It would be roaring by the time he went upstairs. Jube would be there to wait on him. His mother had heard, somehow, that he had gotten as far as Penhally, almost as soon as he arrived. She had sent Jube up the next day, with a note begging that he would not on any account try to come home. He had never had any intention of trying to reach Mayfield. They said that a detail from the fort rode out the pike every day. . . . They wanted him to take Jube with him when he went away again. Jube could cook as well as Spencer Clayton's Russell that they all thought so much of. A nigger who was any good at foraging could feed himself and you too. . . . Nobody ever knew exactly where Russell got the things he cooked. . . .

The quilts that were piled on the box before the window had slipped to the floor. He replaced them carefully. The long wooden box, like a coffin, covered with quilts and on top of them an enormous split basket filled with women's work, had been put there for him to hide in. He had practised getting into it last night for the amusement of the family. Cousin Thyra, wearing his cloak, had impersonated the Yankee officer who was expected to turn up on the doorstep any minute. Alice and Ellen and Sarah, stomping in the hall, had been her escort. They had all laughed a great deal over the questions that Cousin Thyra rolled out in her deep bass voice. . . . Cousin Jess, though, probably got more pain than pleasure out of his being there. She was perpetually on the *qui vive* for fear he'd be caught. She had had up some sort of scare yesterday and had made him sit in Aunt Siny's cabin all afternoon. There was a loose plank in the floor under Aunt Siny's bed. He was to pop in there if he heard anybody coming. . . . Alice had stayed with him. They had sat there before the fire all afternoon. Alice wanted him not to leave. She said that she couldn't stand it here without him. She talked about going home, to her family in Petersburg. He had tried to show her that it was unreasonable, finally that it was impossible. She had not listened, though, to anything he said, just sat staring into the fire and twisting her hands the way she did, saying every now and then, "You won't go away? . . ."

There was a rush of wind from the passage as the door opened and Alice entered. She had not even looked toward him. She had gone straight over to where the old gentleman still sat at the card table and was saying something to him in a low voice.

There was all at once an outcry about the table: the Crenfrew girls and Cousin Thyra murmuring. The old gentleman was pushing his chair back, fumblingly, as if he were very tired. The firelight played on his brown, saturnine features. The skin of his face seemed suddenly tighter and more like parchment. He said:

"Joe . . . you mean that Reeves boy that Miss Nannie raised?"

Alice had walked around the table and was sitting down on one of the high wooden seats by the fire. The cold air still hovered in her garments. The fingers that were unfastening her cloak were bare and reddened by the wind. She looked up at Ellen Crenfrew, who had risen and was standing in the centre of the hearth.

"We were just getting ready to leave," she said, "and the little Proctor boy came in with the letter. . . ."

Cousin Thyra got up heavily out of her chair. "I'm mighty sorry to hear it," she said. "That boy was all the dependence Nannie had."

Sarah Crenfrew was fumbling with her handkerchief. "It may be a mistake. They thought Will Foss was killed . . all summer . . . and then he came home on leave. . . ."

"The letter was from Richmond," Alice said.

He sat down on the wooden seat beside her and began chafing her fingers. "You didn't wear any gloves," he said.

She did not look up. "They haven't any fingers. It's really warmer without them."

George was in the room, setting fresh candles in the two big candlesticks that stood at either end of the high mantel shelf. Cousin Thyra motioned to him peremptorily. "Don't be lighting those candles, boy, right at supper time. Don't you know tallow's scarce?"

They were going out of the room, the old gentleman first with Cousin Thyra. Ellen Crenfrew had left the door a little ajar. He walked over and shut it, then started back. Alice had risen and was coming toward him. The hands she put up to his shoulder were trembling.

"Not to-morrow," she said. "Please . . . you won't go to-morrow. . . ."

"No," he said, "I won't go to-morrow."

17

January, 1863.

They had brought Nicholas' great armchair from across the hall and had set it beside the east window in the dining room, in order that he might command a view of that part of the stable lot where the Yankee soldiers moved about loading wagons with corn. They had come in at the gate half an hour ago, thirty or forty mounted men, headed by a slim blue-coated officer on a gray horse, army wagons lumbering behind. He had sat there on the front porch, watching them come up the drive. The young springald of an officer had said coolly that he would be obliged if Mister Llewellyn would direct him to the granary. He would like to get a load of grain, several, in fact. They were short of provisions at the fort.

He had felt uprushing in his throat the great, gusty breaths that with him preceded overpowering anger. Simultaneously he had heard in the hall quick footsteps, the rattling of spurs on a bare floor, and had known that Charles was making his escape through the back way. He had had to sit silent, eyeing the young coxcomb until he heard the back door close, when he had said slowly:

"Corn? You want to load up *my* corn and take it away from here?"

For answer the officer had proffered an order, written and duly signed by Colonel Bruce, authorizing him to take from the granaries of William Llewellyn, Nicholas Llewellyn, and Orrock Crenfrew, corn or other grain amounting to seven army-wagon loads.

"Young man," he had said as he got to his feet, "I suppose you know that you are a thief? You and your whole damned army. . . ." But even then he had not been able to let his anger have full play. His mind followed Charles, down the flagged path that led past the spring, past the graveyard and down to the bank of the creek where, ever since the last bunch of Yankees came, Powhatan, saddled and bridled, was kept hidden in a clump of elder bushes. It should not have taken Charles two minutes to get to him. He had kept talking, though, for several minutes, rolling the words out and glaring at the lieutenant under drawn brows. He had told him what he thought of people who stole other people's corn, what he thought of the Yankee army and the Yankee nation in general, ending by saying that a boy who was not yet dry behind the ears would be better off at home with his mother than engaged in such practices. The lieutenant had listened respectfully, a very faint smile on his lips, his hand going up now and then to finger his downy mustache. They had told him down the road that old Nick Llewellyn would be a hard nut to crack. The boy was thinking that he was not getting any worse than he had bargained for.

There had been nothing to do after that but give the keys of the granary over to the thieves. He had even had some enjoyment out of that part of the business. He had walked beside the young scoundrel, out into the stable lot where Townsend sat on his bench before the carriage house oiling harness. He had enjoyed Townsend's start of surprise. He had called to him loudly:

"Townsend! Hey, Townsend! These Yankees have come to steal my corn. Give 'em the keys and let 'em have it."

Then he had turned and walked back into the house. He had not felt that he could stay there to watch them plunder. In the hall he had met Cousin Jessie and Alice. Alice was perfectly composed, though she must have just told Charley good-by, or perhaps he had not had time to tell her good-by. She would not care much, either way. A cold proposition, that girl. Exactly like her mother. Cousin Jessie was crying. The little lace bow that she wore on top of her hair had slipped to one side, giving her a strangely freakish appearance. Tears kept running down her face. She had not even tried to wipe them away. It had given him quite a turn. He could not remember in his whole life having seen Cousin Jessie cry. It had upset him more than the Yankees' coming to steal his corn. He might have expected that. They had all been expecting it, in fact, for some time.

He had taken her arm and had whispered to her: "It's all right. I *know* he's all right. None of 'em saw him."

He had looked up to find Alice smiling a little. "Cousin Jess isn't crying about Charles," she had said. "It's Horace."

He had not known till that minute that Horace, the saddle-colored middle-aged man whom Cousin Jessie used as intermediary between herself and the other servants, had been missing since early morning, and that none of the other negroes could give any account of his whereabouts. He felt that he could. Horace was on his way to the Yankee lines, and travelling with him was that slew-footed scoundrel, the negro preacher whom they called Ben Duck. He had known now, for almost a week, that Ben was holding meetings of the Penhally negroes, at the far end of the place, sometimes in the abandoned ginhouse, oftener in the swampy stretch of woods beyond the Big Pond. He had walked there and had found evidences of where twenty or thirty of them had squatted in the bushes to hear him. He had intended to go over there to-night and break up the meeting. There was no use in letting a rascal like Ben Duck fill their minds full of nonsense. Ben was a Sycamore negro, Willy's foreman for years, until the morning when he went north without a by-your-leave to any one. Letters and messages had drifted back from him at intervals. He was in Philadelphia, preaching to white people. He was a big man in some sort of abolition society, and then one day he had appeared at Sycamore, full of tales of hardship and outwardly repentant.

Willy, like a fool, had taken him back, though he, Nicholas, had warned him that it was bound to make trouble. Willy had even allowed him to hold meetings—ostensibly purely religious—among his negroes. It had not taken Ben long to make monkeys of *them,* and now he had slunk over here to corrupt the Penhally negroes. Horace, for all he was such a white folks' negro, had been the first to fall. They had not told *him* about it at first because they thought it would upset him. As if the loss of a nigger more or less could upset him when the Yankees were at his very door plundering! He could see from where he sat an army wagon being driven up to the door of the corn crib to be loaded with corn, *his* corn! They had come to him first, of course. It was well known in the country that he always had a good corn crop. Some years he had enough corn to give away to his neighbors. He had never thought to have it taken away from him!

He averted his gaze from the scene. It struck him suddenly that the room he was sitting in was in a state of extraordinary confusion. There was actually a tumbler half full of stale wine under his very nose and crumpled napkins lay here and there on the polished surface of the long table. That meant that that scamp Horace had known he was leaving last night. It was his job to set the dining room to rights. He himself did not care, though, about losing Horace. He had never liked him. One of those annoying, officious negroes, always wanting to know if you weren't too hot or too cold. If a fly settled on your face while you were asleep he would wake you up killing him. And it was Horace who had rigged up that infernal arrangement of rods and papers and pulleys that served now to keep off the flies instead of the good old-fashioned way of putting a little nigger with a bush in his hand at each end of the table. But Miss Jessie regarded Horace as her right-hand man. She could not turn a wheel without him. She was lying upstairs now, in a darkened room, a cold compress on her forehead and a bottle of smelling salts in her hand. Virginia women talked very brash, but when anything came up they went to pieces. Like Aunt Sophia Allard, who, when her children were sick, could only walk the floor and wring her hands. A queer streak in all of them. Well, God knows, enough of them had married into the family. His lips curved in a smile at a remembered witticism of his own. He had told Willy Crenfrew—or had it been old Doctor Allard?—that you had only to go to the state line and blow a horn and every unmarried woman in Virginia would come trooping over into Kentucky to get her a husband. Ellen and Polly Allard, Sarah Crenfrew, the twins, Fanny and Dolly, five Virginia girls, had been married to young men of the family in that very parlor across the hall. Six, counting Alice Blair. She had been in the neighborhood so long that he had almost forgotten that she had a mother and father in Virginia. Not much of a father. He remembered Spencer Blair very well. A boiled shirt every day and his feet on the veranda railing, while his mother and grandmother hustled to make things go around. If he had been like that with them he likely didn't do much better for his wife. Ellen was not the woman to make anything out of him, though she would marry the girls off to the best advantage. It was not for him to say that Alice hadn't married well. Charles was doubtless regarded as a good catch, though how any girl in her senses could prefer him to John he could not see. It was not that the girl really preferred him to John. But Charles was the better love-maker. While John was standing around wondering if they really liked him, Charles jumped in and made love to 'em. Made love to all of 'em whether he cared anything about 'em or not. It would have been a good joke on him if some of those plain girls he had proposed to had taken him up. But he was smooth. Knew how to get away before they even knew what he was after. He had heard him out on the porch one night picking a quarrel with that long-nosed Woodford girl. He had convinced her that she had said she wouldn't have him when everybody knew that the girl was dead in love with him. He had had her almost crying by the time he got up and walked away. Well, he would have his hands full with Alice Blair. Spoiled little hussy and deceitful, too, like all her mother's people. She didn't really care a snap about either of them. Just liked to receive attention.

The door behind him had opened. George, the half-grown negro boy whom the cook used to run errands, was advancing toward him. He motioned him backward peremptorily. They ought to know better than to come running in here all hours of the day. But the boy stood his ground.

"Marstuh," he said, "them soldiers done told Aunt Siny dey want dey dinner."

Nicholas started up out of his chair. "God damn my soul!" he said. "Have I got to feed the whole Yankee army?"

"Dem soldiers say dey gwine mek her feed 'em. Dey say dey gwine mek her cook dey dinner."

Nicholas struck at the boy with his cane. The blow missed him and fell athwart a great porcelain bowl that stood on the sideboard. It shivered into thin pieces that fell tinkling on the floor. He struck at the boy again, more feebly. He could not see him now for the black mist that danced before his eyes. He steadied himself with a hand on the table.

"Git out of here!" he shouted. "You git out of here before I take all the hide off you!"

The boy was moving sidewise toward the door. He called him back.

"You been to those meetin's?" he cried hoarsely. "You been to any of those meetin's down at the old gin?"

The boy was trembling. "Naw, sir," he said. "Mammy don't let me go nowhar after dark."

"Don't you lie to me," Nicholas cried. "I know what you been up to. All of you. I know what that nigger preacher's been tellin' you. I know that Ben Duck. I know how slick he is. I'm goin' to have that nigger beat within an inch of his life if he ever sets foot on this place again. I'm goin' to make that nigger wish he'd never been born. . . ."

The boy's black eyes were shifting away from his, toward the window. Nicholas turned and saw three soldiers walking along the path that led from the woodpile to the hen house. He screamed with rage and lunged at the boy again.

"G'long!" he shouted. "G'long, I tell you. G'long out of here!"

When the boy had gone he sat down heavily in his chair. A thin stream of tobacco juice had trickled from one side of his mouth down over his chin. He wiped it away and sat for a few minutes, leaning forward, his finger tips pressed hard against his eyeballs. He was trembling all over, so hard that he had finally to hold himself steady with a hand on either arm of his chair. He felt weak and sick. That was because he had had to swallow so much anger in the last half hour. It was bad to repress anger that way. It always made you sick.

The Yankees had finished loading the corn. Three wagon loads. A few of them were still working, piling corn on the wagons. The rest were strolling around, talking and laughing. A woman was just entering the stable lot from the path that led to the spring: Anna Bracy, the fat, middle-aged wife of the overseer. A good woman, who kept to herself and made no trouble on the place, the granddaughter of old man Tarbot, the miller. She was halting now at the entrance to the lot. Her mouth was open. There was a dazed expression in her weak blue eyes.

The Yankee officer approached and greeted her. He was motioning to the great iron pot that stood in that corner of the lot for the scalding of hogs. Two little negroes were already laying a fire under it. They would have Anna Bracy make some sort of stew in it. They would have to cook all over the place if they fed thirty or forty men at such short notice. . . . He withdrew his gaze from the window and bent it on the darkened room, finding something akin to pleasure in its disorder. The chairs still ranged the table in an irregular line, just as people had pushed them back to drink the bride's health. They had drunk her health in Burgundy—Dick's Burgundy, it was called—because Dick Allard, his great-uncle, no, his great-great-uncle, had brought it back with him from Europe and laid it down in the cellar with his own hands for just such occasions. They hardly ever had it up except when there was a wedding or an infare of some kind. He himself did not care greatly for wines. A mint julep in summer, a hot toddy in winter—that was good enough for any man. But the young fry and the women liked wine. The bride had looked very handsome. She had worn his own mother's wedding veil which Cousin Jessie had had laid away somewhere, and the women had pieced a white dress together for her. They had worked on it for days, chittering and chattering, and had complained a good deal about not having this or that thing that they considered necessary, but he, for one, had not been able to see anything amiss when they had finished. She had looked just like any other bride to him. Still, it had been a queer affair, with the blinds all down and everybody speaking in whispers and looking over their shoulders. There had been very few of the kin present, just the Sycamore folks and the folks from Fairfields. He had sent a boy on a horse to Mayfield to say that he hoped Maria would come to see her son married—he had told Cousin Jessie that he would be damned if he would invite Ralph. Maria had not come, but she had sent back blessings for the young people and a civil message to the effect that she and Charles' father were glad that they were having the wedding at Penhally and that he was on no account to come to Mayfield; it was too close to the fort.

Charles had had a hard time getting the little vixen to make up her mind. She was in love with John. That was what was the matter with her. You could see that with half an eye. Still, every one to his taste. If Charles wanted to take another man's sweetheart for his wife, sleep with her one night, and sneak out of the back door, it was nothing to him. It did not make much difference to him what they did. There was a queer numbness now in his left leg all the time. He was dying, probably, by inches. When the numbness stole up over his whole body, when it reached his heart, he would be dead. But the Yankees would have taken the place by that time. Some people said that if we lost the war they would come down here and take all our land, that that was what they had wanted all along. Well, they had had this whole country in their power now . . . for seven, no, eight, months. . . .

He raised his eyes from the disordered table to the deer's antlers that were fixed above the door that led into the hall. He had shot that deer when he was a boy of sixteen, on a hunting trip to Arkansas, with his father. They had gone down one fall to visit Cousin Ned Allard. Cousin Ned was a great one to hunt. He had had them up before daybreak every morning, to surprise the deer at their drinking place, a pool of living water in the heart of a swamp. That whole country was full of swamps then. He had heard that it was somewhat changed now. The old muzzle-loading shot gun that rested in the prongs of the deer's antlers had belonged to Edward Gilmer, the grandson of that George Gilmer who was said to have been the first man to set foot in Kentucky. He and his son-in-law had bought six million acres of land from the Indians. Paid 'em in glass beads and whiskey, but taking possession of it had been another thing. Land crazy, all those people. . . .

He leaned forward and peered through the knotted branches of the wistaria vine out into the lot. The soldiers had abandoned all pretense of work now. They were sitting around on the fence rails or the wood pile, talking and laughing. They were laughing at the Bracy woman. Each time she stirred the mixture in the pot she had to step over their feet. She did it nervously, lifting her skirts to display enormous swollen ankles. One of the soldiers, a thin, black-eyed fellow, leaned forward every now and then and made a play at grabbing her ankle. . . . Back in the kitchen the niggers, his own niggers, were working like dogs to feed these swine! They should have thought of this, old man Atkins, Colonel Glover, all of them, before they got the country into war. They had stirred these Yankees up and now they were loose over the land. There would not be a sprig of grass or a sheaf of wheat left in the whole country by the time they were through.

The Bracy woman had taken one of the great smokehouse ladles to stir the pot. She was bending forward, her back to the soldiers. Her fat buttocks were revealed, wabbling under her voluminous skirts. The man who had been pretending to grab her ankle prodded her once or twice, airily, with his bayonet. She was turning around. Her red, fat face was streaked with tears. Her pendulous cheeks were quivering.

He rose and took the shot gun down from its place above the doorway. In the hall he paused before the old walnut secretary, then his hand went to the upper right-hand pigeon-hole, where, ever since he could remember, a bag of buckshot had lain. The powder-horn was hanging on a hook under the stairs. He took it down and poured a charge into the muzzle of the gun. He hesitated a second, then ripped a corner off his neckerchief and rammed the wad home. He dropped a

handful of buckshot into the gun, tore off another wad and
rammed it home, then walked out into the stable lot, the gun
in his hand. The soldiers saw him coming and looked up.
He was aware that the young officer was beside him, a hand
on his arm. He brushed him aside. The lean, black-eyed
soldier had not moved from his seat on the woodpile. He
called to him before he fired:

"You there, that's been tormentin' that woman. . . ."

The soldier had fallen face forward over the great iron
pot. The Bracy woman was scrabbling around, trying to
get his face out of the steam. He spoke to her before he
turned back into the house:

"The hog's dead. Don't hurt if he does scald."

18

July, 1863.

The last soldier had filed past, a burly man, poorly mounted and cumbered with his loot. His figure at the distance
of a few paces took on a strange, mediæval appearance, the
bolt of calico swinging out on either side of the saddle, the
trapping of a war horse, the canary cage that the idiot had
slung over his shoulders a warrior's high casque. John,
standing beside the shattered street lamp, watched him until
he disappeared into the dark, then swung himself on his
horse and rode slowly after the column. The squat houses
that lined the Cincinnati street were gray blurs to either side
of him. There was otherwise no break in the dark. He might
have been riding alone except for the muffled clop-clop-clop
of the horses' feet. He sat up straighter in the saddle, opening his heavy eyes as wide as he could. Now that the exer-
tion of the last halt was over he felt descending on him again
an immense, overwhelming weariness. Aware of it con-
sciously for the first time he reflected a little upon its nature.
It was different from the fatigue of the first part of the

march. That had been an ache that rose sometimes to pain, the natural sharp exhaustion consequent upon twenty-one continuous hours in the saddle, a fatigue that might have been cured by one or at most two good nights' sleep. But this present fatigue engulfed the whole being. He imagined that every perception of sight and sound was colored by it as objects seen through water appear wavering and distorted. It was better, after all, to be one of the men. They could sleep in the saddle.

It was this blackness that made the advance so difficult. You could not see your hand before you. He could, indeed, make out only with difficulty the faces of the men riding past him. And he could not identify any one. . . . His horse, blundering too near the coping, had stumbled. He pulled him up and spoke to him in a voice that he made mechanically soothing. He had not gotten used to being without Flora yet. To ride another horse was continually irritating. Flora had anticipated his movements. She knew what he was going to do before he was ready to do it. This poor beast had been on the march only two days and he was already on the point of giving out. A slow-witted animal, fit only for farm work. He should have been left to crop the grass in that tidy, small enclosure to the right of the white farmhouse. But he had picked him out at night, in the pitch dark. . . . It had been pitch dark when they got to Summansville. He had known when he rode up to the house that Flora was on her last legs. She had sunk to the ground the minute he dismounted and he had not been able to get her up again. That stable had been full of oats, and corn. . . . But she could not eat. He had known •then that she could not live and had contemplated shooting her. Somebody must have told the colonel. He had stopped to say kindly that Captain Llewellyn would hesitate before wasting any ammunition. Some men were down to fifteen rounds now. . . .

A dead Yankee is a Yankee dead. But Flora deserved the mercy of a bullet. It is one thing to see horses killed and wounded in battle. It is another to see them starve day after day. . . . The trees at that winter camp had had their bark peeled off . . . as high as a man's head. . . .   .

He had left Flora in the stable yard and had walked on up the trim gravel path—did these people *ever* do anything but trim and prune and sickle about their tight, squat houses?— he had walked up the path in the bright shaft of light that was thrown from the open door to find officers and men crowded about a blazing fire. The inhabitants of that house had left hastily, but they had left it well provisioned. . . . A dozen fresh-baked pies on a table in a back entry. The men had been afraid to eat them at first, thinking they were poisoned! After they had had a square meal they amused themselves by pitching china cups at a spot marked on the wall. The wanton plundering of that house had seemed to refresh and exhilarate them. There *was* a satisfaction in wanton plundering. It had been a satisfaction to him—before he knew that Flora could not eat—to sink his hands deep in that fellow's oats. It was no doubt the same feeling, carried to an extreme, that led the men to plunder, senselessly slinging half a dozen pairs of ice skates about their necks or cumbering themselves on a long march with canary cages.

Quirk said that people fifty miles away from the line of march were hiding all night in ditches and in the woods. . . . He saw Morgan's march, a bright sabre through the dark countryside . . . like their own flexible battleline whose wings sometimes curved back one upon the other. They would get an engagement to-morrow, certainly, with the militia if not with the regular soldiery—if they ever got out of the suburbs into the level, strangely monotonous, countryside. They would even then be four or five days' march from West Virginia.

If General Morgan did not succeed in cutting his way through to Lee he would lose his command. The squadron, even, might be disbanded. They would set the men to doing picket duty for Bragg's army . . . on foot as like as not. . . . The men knew that. They were already asking questions about the geography of the country, and yesterday he had seen a man making a map in the dust with a stick, a long line for the Ohio River, a still longer line for the route that would take them through West Virginia to Lee's army.

But the raid had been made, the war carried into the enemy's country, no matter how things turned out. . . . They knew now what it was to flee from your home in the dead of night, to fear for your property, your life. . . . Those white, frightened faces that had peered out of a thicket at Xenia! . . . An old man, a middle-aged man and a woman, two small children huddled in front of them. . . . Strange how many able-bodied men were still to be seen in this country. . . .

He thought suddenly, with a pain that pierced even weariness, of Penhally in the hands of the enemy. . . . The yard had been swarming with blue coats when Charles got away . . . on Powhatan, the gray gelding—the same horse that Alice had ridden through the creek that day. . . . Charles and Alice had been married at night, with the blinds drawn, only two candles b' rning in the whole house. . . . The Yankees had come the next day, at ten o'clock in the morning. . . . *"You know I love you!"* She had been crying. Her lips were salt. . . . It was late when she made him leave her, in one of the garden walks. The house that had been so brightly illuminated was dark by that time, except for a candle here and there at the upper windows. He had stopped at the gate to watch her slip past the box hedge and the shrubbery. When he could not see her any more he had gone around to the front of the house and upstairs. . . . And then there had been the voices under his window . . . until **nearly dawn . . .**

The column ahead was wavering. Cluke's regiment had lost the way again. If they had had sense enough to put a few guides in the rear instead of keeping them all up front! He dismounted stiffly and felt for the bundle of splinters that was thrust through his sash. Around him men leaned forward, wearily, waiting. The light caught the outer splinters and flared high. He fell on one knee in the middle of the crossroads, the torch thrust straight out before him. The dust particles hung motionless in the air for a little, then settled slowly to the ground, eddying, he noted, to the right. He got up and walked a few steps along the right-hand road, throwing the light of the torch from side to side. This must be the way. The dust hung thick and the roadside bushes and weeds were flecked here and there with slaver.

He mounted his horse. The torch was still flaring. He held it high over his head. "This way," he called, "this way, men!"

There was a murmur all along the line, then the trampling of horses' feet began again. He wheeled and beat the torch's light out against the grass. The advancing column was an irregular black mass, distinguishable from the shrubbery only by the fact that it was in motion. He rode down the line, putting his hand out now and then to touch an elbow or jostle a horse into a smarter pace. Through his weariness he could hear his own voice calling, loudly, cheerful, but as if from a distance, "Get along! Get along! Nearly out of Cincinnati now."

There was suddenly above the slow passage of the cavalcade the sharp rattle of hoofs. A dozen men had come up from the rear. Their leader was pulling up beside him. Charles' voice came out of the dark:

"Johnny . . . is this the way to Glendale?"

He could not see Charles' face. He could make out, though, the gelding's forward pricked ears and the long line

of his body. The smell of sweat, mixed with horseflesh, came
sharply up to him. He ran his hand over the horse's side.
The ribs were already standing out. Well, Charles had ridden him clear across Kentucky to join them at the river. . . .

"Damned if I know," he said. He lowered his voice. "You
let 'em get scattered on you once, and it's hell to pay. I lost
half a dozen men at that last crossroads. . . . Where you
taking these boys?"

"We're going up the road a little piece," Charles said.
"Want to find out how good a guide you are."

John reflected that Major Steele was being sent in the extreme advance to drive pickets and scouts, presuming that
there were any, off the road. Charles and his men were
doubtless on the way to join them. It would be a picked
body of men. They would execute the mission in fine
style. . . .

Charles had come closer and was laying his hand on his
shoulder, in the elder-brother way he sometimes affected.
"I'll see you at Glendale, maybe," he said.

"It'll more likely be Williamsburg," John told him. "You'll
make Williamsburg before day."

The horses' hoofs rattled off down the road. There was no
sound now except the slow passage of the cavalcade. The
Ohio farm horse had fallen back into his dejected walk.

They would make Williamsburg by day. It couldn't be
more than thirty miles away, off somewhere to the west.
They had ridden fifty miles through the snow after night fell,
to the battle of Hartsville, but they had had Kentucky horses
then. Their bones were harder; they could endure more. It
was said that General Morgan, himself born an Alabaman,
would rather recruit Kentuckians than men from any other
state. Hard bones, too, in the men? His own bones felt
like water, water that flowed away through black night into
some great void. He could remember when he had ached

for endeavor. And bivouacked at Nashville he had cried because he had not been sent on a scouting party to Gallatin! Lying on the cold autumn leaves that rustled with every movement of his grief . . . Charles had asked, no doubt, to be sent on that scout. He was fresh still and had something of the old spirit. He looked now more like a soldier than any man in Morgan's command. In a new gray uniform. A new hat too. And a good long cloak that had an embroidered collar. . . . Charles was a good man to send on such an expedition as that of to-night. The best rider in Cluke's regiment and the men would stick with him as long as their horses could move. He himself could have gone, if he had asked to go. . . . But he could not have left his men. It did not make much difference now what you were doing . . . as long as the bright sabre kept curving its way through the dark countryside. . . . There was on the lower lawn at Penhally a small flowering tree. Some foreign friend had sent it to his father. Five-petalled white flowers, that might have been cut out of paper, so exact they were, set so sharply against the dark-green leaves . . . as stars might have been set in this black sky. . . .

The man opposite him was reeling in the saddle. He caught hold of his arm and shook it. "Wake up," he said and cursed him. The man did not answer. His face was a gray blur sliding past John's shoulder. John struck at it with the flat of his hand. The man grunted and fell face forward across the pommel of John's saddle. John drew both horses off to one side of the road. His knee that had been brushing against bushes touched suddenly nothing. There was, then, a gap in the fence. Pasture bars, perhaps, down. He rode off the hard turnpike over a little declivity. The led horse stopped as his hoofs struck turf. The man was already sliding from the saddle. John leaned over and eased his body to the ground. The horse was standing perfectly still.

His hard breathing could be heard above the man's long
snoring breaths. Winded. He could not have gone another
mile even if the man had been able to stay in the saddle.

Back on the road there was a commotion. Shouts and
cries. He was not sure that he had not heard shots. Strag-
glers from the regiments ahead surged against his own men.
Officers tearing back through the dark whipped them into line.
They were moving forward steadily again, perhaps into an
ambuscade. Plenty of cover on both sides of the road. But
it was strange that there were no more shots. . . . Well, if
they were going to have a battle it would be fought, thank
God, in the light, unless the enemy set on them in the next
few minutes. The sky that had been black was gray now,
and one small point of light was showing above the horizon.
The air, too, was fresher, as it always is toward dawn. The
men were feeling it already, sitting straighter in their saddles. Somewhere down the line a man was actually humming.

What he had thought was the low hanging branch of a
tree was moving. A man who had been sitting under the
tree by the side of the road had gotten up and was coming
toward him. Palmore, Cluke's regiment. Charles had covered up his desertion once. Went home, the poor devil had,
to plant his corn, because his wife had never worked in the
field. . . . A horse's head showed just over his shoulder. A
gray horse, with intelligent, forward-pricked ears. Back
there under the oak tree something lay sprawled. A discarded great-coat . . . or the body of a fallen man? The trooper
was saluting. "Cap'n Llewellyn, J. O.?" he asked.

John nodded and getting down off his horse pushed past
the man. Charles lay face downward, one arm outstretched.
His long cloak that had bright embroidery on the collar had
composed itself about him as he fell, so that he might have
been thought to lie at rest . . . except for the black stain.

Palmore was leaning forward, lifting the cloak. "Right through here," he said, and, straightening up, laid his hand on his own breast. "I saw him go down. Warn't more than a minute ago he was riding along here."

John threw the reins over his own horse's neck and mounted the gelding. Palmore was lifting Charles' body from the ground. The gelding side-stepped as the weight fell across his withers. John stroked his neck. "Steady, boy . . . steady," he said. They rode forward at a slow pace. The horse was straining under his burden. It would not do to let him get down. . . . The point of light had grown to a long spear. John watched it pierce the bank of gray clouds. As soon as it was light he would stop, with Palmore, long enough to dig the grave.

Penhally

Part II

1

Autumn, 1900.

The doorway of the cabin was so low that John had to stoop as he went in. The boy, Chance, who was barely five feet, strode through upright, bearing the basket of food that Lucy had packed for them. As soon as he had set it down they both turned to the bed where the sick man lay. John spoke to him:

"O'Donnell! . . . We've come to sit with you. . . . O'Donnell!"

The muscles of the face did not stir, but the lids lifted, disclosing enormous gray Irish eyes. Their gaze, in spite of the man's eighty years and his desperate illness, was bright. He would have smiled if he could. John took the gnarled, dry wrist in his fingers.

"I've brought you a little dram," he said. "Want it now?"

O'Donnell's eyes had fallen shut again. His face was immobile. Only his light, rasping breaths showed that he was alive. One of the daughters had come up and was standing at the foot of the bed.

"We can't git it down him, Mister John," she said. "Doctor told us the other day it'd be good for him, but we can't git it down him."

John set the bottle of whiskey down under the bed. "Maybe he'll feel like taking some before I go," he said. He left the bed and stood for a few minutes on the hearth where a good fire was blazing. It felt good on his back and on his leg that was already having a few twinges of rheumatism. He lowered himself carefully into the big split-bottomed rocker and stretched his rheumatic leg out to the flames. Up at the house they had bricked up all the fireplaces except the

ones in the dining room and the family living room, but the
fireplace in this cabin was the old-fashioned kind, big enough
to accommodate the enormous back logs that old Jerry always had stacked up against the side of the hill. A terrible
man for wood, old Jerry. But white tenants nearly always
used twice as much as negroes. That was one thing they
weren't too lazy to do, cut wood, where a negro would sit
and let his heels freeze. Still, they didn't have much in their
lives, and a good fire was one of the pleasantest things in life.
It was already illuminating the whole room, to the farthest
corner of the whitewashed walls. He measured the room
with his eye. Twenty-two by twenty-two, at least. Under
the whitewash the logs were chinked with lime and sand,
the old-fashioned way. Big logs, hewed and squared with a
broadaxe. The lean-to at the back was a flimsy affair, built in
the last thirty years, but this great square room would be here
when he and old Jerry both were gone. The puncheon floor
that must have been here a hundred years—he had heard his
uncle say that they had built the cabin for Mammy Julia, who
died before he was born—was good for another fifty.

The room, itself, with its high feather bed, its tall mantel
clock (an old one, discarded from the house twenty years
ago), was not much changed in its appearance from the days
when Molly O'Donnell was alive. The interior of O'Donnell's
cabin had always been a little different from those of other
white tenants on the place. He had brought a few old-coun-
try ways with him and had taught them to his wife. Jim
Latham had reported once, with apparent horror, that "them
Irish folks is keeping hawgs in the house now," and it was a
fact that Molly O'Donnell (Molly Bracy she had been, the
miller's granddaughter) had put some clean straw down beside the hearth one winter night for the old sow to farrow in.

O'Donnell had married well. The Bracys were good people
and Molly's grandfather, old Mr. Tarbot, had had the respect

of the whole neighborhood. One of the girls, the one who married a Gaither, looked exactly like her mother. The other, the one who hadn't married, was the spit of old Jerry, red vigorous face, sparkling gray eyes and, as they said, the map of Ireland spread all over her face. She was standing at his elbow now, the sparkling eyes dull, the broad Irish features fixed in grief.

"All right, Anna," he said. "You go right along and get some sleep. Chance and I'll stay here, till daybreak anyhow."

She walked back into the lean-to. He could hear the bed creak as she lay down heavily upon it. There was no sound in the room now except the sick man's light breathing.

The boy, Chance, had dropped down on the hearth in front of the fire. His gray eyes were fixed on the flames.

"That back log's beech," he said, "and the one just in front of it is persimmon. What's the little bitty log in front, Grandpa?"

"Hornbeam," his grandfather said. " 'Tain't good for anything but firewood. Grows too twisty."

The boy, Chance, liked to learn the different kinds of timber. He rarely passed a tree without identifying its wood. He was slower than his brother Nick, but methodical. Remarkably methodical for a boy his age. John had seen a memorandum once in his cramped, eight-year-old scrawl: "They are seventeen trees in the little triangle field seven red oaks and three white oaks and seven sweet gums. . . ."

Lucy had disapproved of the boy's coming down here to the cabin to-night. "It isn't right," she had said, "taking a boy where there's death. He'll see enough of it."

He had felt impelled to go against her, however. And indeed it was almost impossible to resist the boy's pleading. He knew, too, that it would please old Jerry to see the boy again. Probably nothing in his life had ever pleased him more than this boy's devotion. They had been inseparable until the old

man's illness, beginning six weeks ago, had confined him to
his bed.

Lucy liked old Jerry. And it was not that O'Donnell had
gotten around her with his Irish blarney. She genuinely re-
spected him. And indeed, he thought, he was the ablest and
most estimable man of his class in that whole neighborhood,
but perhaps that was because he had come here from the old
country. The tenantry were a shiftless lot nowadays. It was
a fact that they did wanton damage to the houses they lived in,
that they seemed bent, whenever possible, on exhausting the
land, that they cared for nothing on God's earth but the money
they got out of their tobacco crop, and that never lasted them
from one Christmas to another. But it was not *their* land.
There was no reason why they should help preserve its fertility. Those instincts had never been built up in them. The
system prevented it. It was a bad system. It was better, perhaps, when people had slaves and directed their efforts. Or
perhaps it was not the system. Perhaps it was that land-
owners did not feel their responsibilities in the way they once
had . . . responsibilities to the land or to the people who
lived on it . . . but you could not manage white people the
way you did negroes. You had to let them go their own
way. . . .

A rustling in the corner of the room made him turn around.
The sick man was looking at him out of luminous, feverish
eyes.

"Jawn," he said, his voice low but perfectly clear, "Jawn,
do you remember that old lady in Woodstock?"

John laughed. "I sure do," he said.

The old woman had come out into the bright sunlight of a
May day . . . in a cavernous slat sun-bonnet. The men who
were feeding their horses with hay out of her barn had not
known she was standing there until her deep voice had
boomed:

"You're a gang of rascally, thieving Kentuckians, that's what you are . . . afraid to go home. . . . All our boys have surrendered long ago and you're still pillaging around the country."

The boy, Chance, was sitting up, his hands locked around his knees. "Where was that, Grandpa?" he asked.

"In Georgia," John said. "Jerry here stole a horse from that old lady. Stole him out of the end stall in that stable while she was fussing at the men in front. That's how he happened to come to live here."

"But you said that was in Georgia. . . ."

"Well, he couldn't a walked here, could he?" John asked drily.

The boy did not answer. He was not much interested in stories of the Civil War unless there was violent action in them. John had ransacked his memory long ago for these. There was the story of how Jerry, assailed by a Yankee with a bowie knife, had seen another Yankee levelling a gun at him, John, and had stopped long enough to shoot the man with the gun before killing his own assailant. He liked that. And the story of how they had swum the Ohio River after the fight at Buffington. Sergeant O'Donnell, he realized suddenly, figured in most of his stories. . . . Yes, Jerry O'Donnell as a youth had been possessed of the highest courage he had ever seen in any man. Fighting had seemed his native element. He was listless, and a great nuisance to his superiors when there was nothing going on. . . . His mind went back to the stolen horse and that day in Georgia. . . .

The men had been paid, at the Savannah River, with part of the money that Micajah Clark had brought from Richmond. Twenty-six to thirty dollars for every enlisted man. It was at Washington, Georgia, that the President set off in his attempt at escape. . . . Some Yankee soldiers had set afloat the rumor that he had been wearing his wife's clothes when he was captured! . . . General Breckinridge had taken his men off in the opposite direction, hoping to divert pursuit, but it had not done any good. . . . Ferguson's brigade had marched to Macon . . . to surrender. There had been breaking up all along the line. . . .

Duke's brigade had marched to Woodstock the next morning. . . . Some of those men had walked all the way from Virginia, more than three hundred miles. . . . Breckinridge had not been there to meet them. . . . They did not know that he had been captured, preparing to charge with forty-five men a battalion of Federal cavalry! . . . The men had ranged up and down the dusty village street, in the white-hot May sunshine . . . for hours while they waited for the order that must come from Breckinridge. . . . It had been hard keeping them in order. They were crazy for horses, mostly, horses to get back home. He remembered that he had kept an eye off and on during that long day on O'Donnell. He had been afraid that the man, deprived of the stimulant of battle, might go to pieces entirely. When O'Donnell had located the stable full of hay, on a side street at the edge of the village, he had not been able to refuse him permission to forage. Horses had to be fed. He had followed the men down the lane and up to the stable and had stood concealed behind an enormous spreading holly bush during the old lady's tirade. Out of the corner of his eye he had watched O'Donnell slip silently around the corner of the building. And he had been relieved when he saw him emerge from the back of the stable on a gaunt four-year-old chestnut. . . . The old lady had run screaming out into the sunlight and had hovered around the edges of the soldiery all day like an indignant hen. He remembered soothing her several times: "A Kentuckian, you say . . . tall, but sort of thick set? . . . Yes, ma'am, I expect I can find him for you. . . ."

He had been thinking that it was strange how the pacifying of old ladies, the looking after men and horses, all the familiar routine, went on when there was not to be any more fighting. . . .

It was late in the day when Colonel Breckinridge had come riding into town with the general's message. The men had formed there in the road for him to address them. . . . The chosen, sonorous words had rolled down the village street. . . . "Immediate surrender . . . folly . . . to risk further the lives of men . . . brave men. . . ." One fool who had got hold of a woollen blouse that last winter and had worn it all through a Georgia spring had kept up a continual harsh scratching . . . through all the words. He remembered the man's face afterward, the dazed blue eyes and the loose mouth agape at a changed world.

He himself had not known what to do, for five, ten minutes. He had caught himself considering what must be done next. . . . Half his men had no horses . . . and then he had realized that they were no longer his men. . . . He had put his hand in his pocket and had found no tobacco. The search for that had taken up ten minutes. Coming out on the edge of a group of men he realized suddenly that it would be the devil of a job to get home. The horse he was riding was jaded now . . . and it would be harder now to impress horses from the citizenry. . . . The realization of his difficulties was stimulating, like a plunge into cold water. Seeing Spencer Clayton walking uncertainly about he called to him:

"Well, Spencer, when we going home?"

Spencer had turned quickly, with an air of relief. They walked across the street to where a man was holding their horses, mounted and rode slowly through the eddying crowd. Their departure had started a general exodus. A dozen or more men of their regiment had ridden with them out of town . . . slowly along the red road . . . men stopping

every now and then to exchange good-bys and last words.
. . . One man had stayed behind in a heated argument with
a comrade over a tin bucket that they had owned in common. Spencer had called back to them:

"You don't need it now. Plenty of buckets at home."

But they had stood there arguing, the hot sun beating down
on their perspiring faces. A little farther along O'Donnell
had emerged warily from a side road on the gaunt chestnut
colt.

They had halloed him wildly, joking him about the danger
of being locked up in the local constabulary. He had sat
there, glancing about him, his light eyes sparkling in his red
weathered face.

"Well," he said, "I'm a thievin' Kentuckian. I reckon I
better get back to Kentucky as soon as I can."

It had taken them nearly three weeks to make their way up
from Georgia. They had started in May—the last of May.
Clayton and O'Donnell had had good horses—they could
have made it in much less time, but they had accommodated
themselves to the pace of the others. The Irishman, it turned
out, was going through Gloversville to Elkton. The only
kinsman that he had in this country lived there. John had
told the man that he should ride along with him in that case.
He could spend the night at Penhally.

"Your uncle'll be glad to see you," he had said.

"He's me mother's brother from Donegal," the Irishman
had returned with dignity.

It had been well into June when they rode into Gloversville on the Nashville Pike. Old Mr. Shelton had been out
in his yard when they were passing and had made them come
in to dinner: English peas and lamb and a few late straw-
berries. They had started on soon after dinner. A mile out
of town they had parted from Spencer and then had cut
across town to the Red River bridge and out to the Russell-

ville Pike. The gray had given out just after they passed
McBride's. They had left him with old Uncle Tom Sims
and meeting nobody on the road had gone on riding and
walking alternately. They had reached Penhally in the late
afternoon. Nobody was expecting them. The house was
there, gray in the sunshine, the old gentleman asleep in his
chair under the poplar tree. As they started up the walk a
little negro came around the corner of the house bearing a
tray with upon it a solitary julep glass. He set the tray down
on a stump and ran pellmell to the Quarter so that the shrill
cries of the half-dozen negroes who came running had waked
the old gentleman up from his nap.

He had opened his eyes upon them standing before him,
and had gazed at them a second before he said, "John . . ."
uncertainly as if he did not know whether he was really
awake. Then he had sent a negro boy running to tell Cousin
Jessie and had raised a great clatter with his cane on the
gong that was set at the base of the millstone table. Everybody had come out in the yard and they had sat there under
the poplar tree talking until it was dark. He remembered
looking up once, to see above the hedge that separated the
yard from the stable lot the chestnut colt's gaunt head and
shoulders proceeding slowly toward the stable, the little negro
who was leading him looking back every now and then . . .
as if he feared the colt might fall on him.

The Irishman had slept that night at the office, he himself
in his old room upstairs in the wing. And after breakfast
the next morning he had talked to the ladies for a half hour
or so before going back into the little dark office that was
tucked away between the chamber and the dining room. It
was very much the same, that room, the same oblongs of
morning sunshine on the same dusty account books piled on
the old walnut desk. He had sat down at once without invi-
tation . . . in the chair that had usually been occupied at

those conferences by Albert Owens, the overseer. Albert, he recalled with a sharp inward shiver, had been killed over two years ago, at Stone's River . . . the top of his head blown off, somebody had said. They had never found his body, at any rate. . . . And he himself was here, sound in wind and limb. . . .

The old gentleman was turning pages in a yellow-leafed book. He kept endless sheets of accounts in a handwriting that was illegible to any other human being. . . . He was looking up, shrewdly. . . . He was not very much changed. He used a cane now to get around with and he did not talk as much as he once did. He had sat humped over and silent for hours last night, but when he did speak it was with the same vigor, and he was fully as irascible as of yore. . . . No, he was not much changed by the war. . . .

But at Mayfield everything was different. He had learned that in his few minutes' conversation with Cousin Thyra on the porch. Ralph Llewellyn was very ill, dying, most people thought, and God knew what would become of that family. . . . Ralph, Cousin Thyra said, had just about beggared himself . . . as Cousin Nick had prophesied. . . . He had maintained a hospital for wounded Confederate soldiers for over a year. He had actually sold off a piece of land, a hundred acres of river bottom, to keep that hospital going! . . . Very few of his fine horses were left. . . . Still there had been even in the last year or so a considerable sum of money left, but he had not, he would not, turn that into gold as Nicholas had done . . . so that now they were left with nothing but Confederate money . . . and of course the land. But with Charles dead there would be nobody to take charge of affairs. . . .

He had asked if Kenneth and Lucy were not going to be married. Cousin Thyra had looked at him with good-humored scorn. "Did you ever hear of a McNance marrying

where there wasn't property?" she had inquired. He had reflected that she probably knew them better than he did. They
were her kin, not his. He had heard his mother say once,
when she was asked if somebody or other were not related
to her, that there was not a drop of McNance blood in her
or in her children.

A curious thing had come out in that conversation with
Cousin Thyra. Ralph Llewellyn, in his anxiety to obtain
money, "to squander," Cousin Thyra said, on the Confederacy, had done something his personal necessities would
never have forced him to do. He had actually borrowed
money from his brother. He had not, of course, gone to him
in person. But the men he had asked to attend to the matter
for him had gone straight to Uncle Nick. There was nobody
else in the neighborhood who had been prudent enough, almost, he thought, *rascally* enough, to turn his paper money
into gold. . . . Nicholas Llewellyn had, of course, taken out
a mortgage on the land. Nobody, not even Aunt Maria,
knew for how much. . . . Uncle Ralph had been for some
months now incapable of transacting business. He suffered,
Cousin Thyra said, from the delusion that he was still a rich
man . . . an afternoon caller was as likely as not to go away
with a cheque for a thousand dollars in his pocket. . . . He
had asked if Alice Blair were still at Mayfield. . . . She
was, but she probably wouldn't be there long. She would
have to go back to her kin in Virginia . . . unless she married that Louisville man. . . .

Uncle Nick was saying that they would have a hard time
getting through the winter. It was the meat that was the
difficulty. Old Colonel Bruce had held those Yankee soldiers in check pretty well, but they had ranged just far
enough to clean the country of hogs. There would be little
or no meat to furnish the niggers. Still, this was a rabbit
year and they could do as they used to do in the old days,

shoot enough wild turkeys in the fall to last well into the winter. He remembered that his mother had started off one fall with sixty-five wild turkeys hanging up in the smoke-house. . . . People would have to go back to a lot of old-fashioned ways, spin more, use every available food supply. . . . These niggers here had gotten so lazy that they would not even gather wild greens. . . . There was nothing better than the wild turnip sallet that still grew in profusion on that sandy bluff land, and tender pokeberry shoots were as good any day as asparagus. He had learned during the war that sorghum was a good thing to raise. It was hard on the land, but it came as near carrying the niggers through the winter as anything could. . . . He had thought that they might, perhaps, put in as much as twenty acres . . . that second bottom would be a good place. . . .

He had been looking out of the window while the old man was talking. A negro boy was leading a horse around to the block . . . a rough-looking bay that nevertheless stepped well . . . and was saddled and bridled. . . .

He rose. "I've got to see the folks at Mayfield," he said. "I believe I'll go down there now."

The old gentleman was protesting as he left the room. The vehement, protesting voice had followed him . . . all through the front hall and down the steps. . . . He had been aware that it was going on, but he had not really listened. He had not felt that he had the time to listen.

2

A little negro boy was on his knees grubbing up the blades of grass that thrust through the interstices of the brick walk. The bushel basket beside him was filled with grass and the blown fallen seed pods of the sugar trees. Another larger boy was sweeping the front porch, moving about slowly over that part of it that was covered with sunshine. He remembered that he had felt a faint surprise at seeing all the familiar routine going on.

The boy on the porch had told him that Miss Alice was in the front parlor. He had gone in through the hall into the dim room. A negro man was mounted on a step ladder in the centre of the room, his arms reaching up to the enormous cut-glass chandeliers, mumbling to himself in a soft, complaining voice. . . . She stood a little way off, beside one of the windows. . . . In a dark tight-fitting dress, a lace bow at her throat.

Her eyes were upon him as soon as the door opened. "John . . ." she said, and came forward and gave him her hand. He stood there a moment holding her cool fingers in his before they moved over to the window. She kept looking back to the negro man, calling directions to him every now and then. His own eyes when he was not looking at her had roved about the room. He had been all the while puzzled by its changed appearance. He had not realized until afterward that that had been because there was no furniture in it, except the pier glass that had always been there between the windows and before it a small sofa of some dark wood that, they said, had come years ago from Scotland.

Her face was thinner than he had ever seen it before, and almost without color. Its triangular shape was accentuated by the way she wore her hair, drawn up into a knot on top of her head, instead of in the smooth bands that she had used to wear. . . . But her eyes were the same. . . .

The negro man was leaving the room in search of something. Her low voice went on . . . about the chandeliers. They were taking them all down, those in the back parlor and in the dining room too. Cousin Maria naturally wanted to keep them if she could. . . . He had wondered who would be taking the furniture and chandeliers from Mayfield? . . .

They had been bridal presents to her grandmother . . . from Mr. William FitzHugh of Chatham. He had heard, doubtless, of Mr. William FitzHugh of Chatham. The families had always been very intimate. One of her own great-uncles was named for him. . . .

"Let's go outdoors," he said, and as if he were talking to some stranger, "it's cooler outdoors than in on a day like this. Don't you think so?"

She would walk in the yard with him after the chandeliers were down, she said. She had promised Cousin Maria to overlook the whole proceedings very carefully. The chandeliers were, of course, rather valuable, aside from the sentiment attached.

The negro man was coming back into the room with a screw driver, looking carefully at nothing. A bandy-legged negro with smoky eyes, he had some association with him . . . possum hunting, probably. The averted gaze meant that his feelings were hurt at not being recognized. But he could not remember his name. He was mounting the ladder again.

He called to him peremptorily: "Have you got any of those fastenings out? No . . .? Well, come on down. You can finish this some other time."

The negro was coming down the ladder, faster than he had gone up. As he passed he said in his soft voice that he wished Marse John would tell ol' Miss about them chan'lers. She told him to be sure and get them down this morning. John shut the door behind him and went back to Alice.

"I didn't come down here to help you take those chandeliers down," he said, and laughed a little.

They had walked in silence through the hall and out on to the porch. The larger negro boy was down in the yard now, sweeping the trash and grass off the walk into the smaller boy's basket. He had not noticed until this moment that the leaves were out full . . . sugar-tree leaves, mostly. Their shadows were sharp and black on the level lawn. . . . The little negroes knew without looking around that they were coming. Their chatter and shrill laughter was dying away.

"I never saw anything like the niggers around here this morning," he said. "You can't move without stepping on one."

"Let's go down in the garden," she said.

He assented, first casting a glance over his shoulder to make sure that the garden walks were out of sight of the house.

In the garden they had sat down on a bench that was fixed between two gum trees. In the centre of the garden. The clean white gravel paths curved away from it toward the gate, borders of new green all along the sides. Halfway to the gate some shrub trailed great wreaths of bloom, long sprays set with miniature white roses. Beyond that the tall Japanese quince bushes formed a green wall around all the garden.

Her hand hung between them, white against the folds of her dark skirt. There was a thin gold band on the ring finger and the great emerald that had been Aunt Maria's. . . . It occurred to him that he was the last member of the family, the last person almost, to see Charles alive. Charles had gone off down the road laughing and rallying his men. The colonel riding up a few minutes later had commented on the fact that Captain Llewellyn was always gay, an inspiration to the men he had said. He had replied that it would in his opinion have been better to leave a few guides in the rear, instead of putting them all up front with General Morgan. The colonel had received the suggestion so amiably that he had been emboldened to add that it was the Goddamnedest foolery he had ever heard of. It was well known that General Morgan had an instinct for the lay of a country, but you could not say the same thing for the men—or officers—

of Colonel Cluke's regiment. They would get lost if they had
to stick their heads in the mud. The colonel had patted him
on the shoulder and had said that he—and Charles Llewellyn
too—would have gone far by this time if they had been in
any other command. But it was well known that you laid
personal ambition aside when you rode with Morgan. . . .
He ought to tell her that about Charles. People liked to
hear about their loved ones' last moments. . . . *Loved* ones?
He did not know that she had ever loved Charles. They had
been there together at Penhally, the only young people in the
neighborhood . . . for nearly two months. Charles would
have been urging her all that time to marry him. . . .

That was a strange place where Charles was buried—a
square plot of ground enclosed by a thick wall of some dark,
straight-growing evergreen—cedars, probably. He had been
too dazed with fatigue to notice. But the woman at the
house had been kind. She had led them up over the hill to
the graveyard and had stood there, putting her apron to her
eyes once or twice. . . . It was because she had come from
Kentucky with her father and mother as a little girl. He had
not known it at the time, but later somebody had told him
that that section of Ohio was full of copperheads. . . . If
he could only know *why* she had married Charles. . . .

She was saying that the garden had been prettier last
week when the snapdragons were in bloom . . . and the
bleeding hearts. That round bed in front of them there had
been one crimson mass of bleeding hearts. . . .

He brushed the smooth, meaningless words aside. "Did
you miss me while I was gone?" he asked. "Did you think of
me at all?"

Her gray eyes seemed to light her whole face. "Miss
you?" she said.

Suddenly his arms were about her. They were whispering
together: "There at Penhally I used to think about you . . .

all the time. I used to think that I couldn't stand it . . . that you would *have* to come home. . . ."

"I thought about you, too . . . all that first year . . . but mostly when we were riding. . . . We used to ride all night . . . and I would be thinking of you. . . ."

She had put her face down on his shoulder. The tremor still ran through both their bodies. He touched her hair. "Alice . . ." he said. "Alice. . . ."

She had risen and was standing in front of him. "You didn't write," she said. "Why didn't you ever write?"

He sat there looking straight before him. The garden was flooded with sunlight and still except for the light chatter of the little negroes' voices. In the flower bed in front of him a June bug was lighting on a snapdragon stalk. It bent almost to the ground, then righted itself only to bend again, but the fellow clung on. . . . He was aware that he was blinking a little as if he had come out of a dark room into blinding light. He thought suddenly that he was very tired. His mind wanted to veer away from what she was saying. He brought it back with an effort. "I don't know," he said. "Does it make any difference now? . . ."

Her hands clasped in front of her were shaking. "My mother is sewing by the day," she said, "for the wives of Yankee officers. . . . She walks six miles to one woman's house. Six miles and back. . . ."

He got up and stood beside her. "Couldn't she come out here and live?" he asked.

"Oh," she said desperately. "You haven't even talked to your uncle. I *know* you haven't!"

He said slowly: "It wasn't in the bond. When he willed his property to me I didn't promise to ask him who I should marry."

She had begun to speak again, agitatedly, with gestures of the hands. He was not able afterward to remember anything that she said, except that her sister, Josephine, sat down each morning and made herself shoes, out of scraps of silk and cotton. They wore out during the day and each morning she had to make a fresh pair. . . . Soldiers used tow sacks, which lasted longer, but of course a fine young lady could not do that.

She was badly frightened. It was natural that she should be, living as she had so long on the edge of nothing, and now seeing everything going to pieces about her. . . . It came to him that it is a terrible thing to be separated from the beloved. The long days and nights, the continuous, irresistible flow of time and always the sharp, bewildered straining of the mind. . . . If she would let him comfort her! . . . People who had never endured much imagined that the earth would fall away from beneath them if they had to do without certain things, and then after the earth had fallen away they went on. She had never really endured any suffering, except in anticipation, a little privation maybe; not much of that. It was mostly fright. . . . But it was stronger in her now than anything else.

"I'm not dependent on Uncle Nick," he said. "My father has some land . . . in Arkansas. We can go there."

It was then that Nicholas had come around the rampart of the quince bushes and out on to the white gravel walk, slowly, leaning on his cane. He walked past them without speaking and sat down on the bench, his head bent a little forward, his hands clasped on the knob of his cane.

John said: "Good morning, sir." When the old man did not speak he continued to address Alice: "It's wild land, but so was this country once. . . . We could build a log cabin. . . ."

She was not listening to him. Her eyes were fixed on the old man. As he stopped speaking she took a step toward Nicholas. She was panting a little and there was a light beading of sweat on her forehead.

"Tell him," she said. "You *don't* like me. . . . You never
have. . . ."

Nicholas raised his head. His eyes that had been the color
of a dead leaf were milky brown now with age. His hands,
that were spread out to the sunshine as if it had been a fire,
were shaking as the hands of old men do, but he spoke with
composure, looking past the girl at John: "I haven't got anything against her personally. . . . It's her blood. . . . I
don't want my property to go to any of her blood. . . ."

There was silence after that. In the stable lot below a
negro boy was leading a horse round and round the silver
dollar that was the pond. A shining sorrel horse who tossed
his head and stepped with the delicate precision that is in-
duced by a bitting rig. For some seconds now there had
been a light swishing sound over the gravel. She was walking away, toward the house. He watched her pass the white
blooming bush and disappear around the quince bushes.

Nicholas was getting to his feet, slowly, manœuvring in
the loose gravel with his cane. An extravagantly thin old man
whose skull showed through his parchment-brown skin. He
ought to have some young man's arm to lean on. His voice
though, was still resonant: "Well, I reckon I better be starting
home."

John nodded, but did not speak. When the old man had
gone he sat down heavily on the bench. The June bug was still
zooning persistently about the flowers. His ears registered
the sound, but he did not lift his eyes from the walk. He
thought, with something like relief, that between them they
had made everything very plain—the whole thing as sharp,
as exact, as the noon shadow of the beech leaves on the
gravel.

3

It was three days after that that Ralph Llewellyn died.
Died raving about the glories of the Confederacy and the

fruits of victory . . . or he would congratulate himself on his own achievements. He had never neglected his affairs, he said, and had added to his patrimony. Charles would have as handsome an inheritance as any young man in the family. His daughter, Lucinda, too, was well provided for. She was to have five hundred acres of land and the choice of any four negro men on the place. She would have to arrange with her mother about the women. But certainly two of the younger dining-room servants could go with her to her new home. He would recommend them to build in that grove of silver poplars. He had stopped there many a time and had observed that there was always a breeze, on the hottest day. Then the tenor of his thoughts would change. He would say over and over in his delirium that he had done wrong. He had allowed his brother, Nicholas, to defraud him of his patrimony. His children would suffer. The wrong must be righted before it was too late . . . and he would start up out of his bed. . . . The two negro men that they kept sitting there in the shadow of the headboard would have to hold him down until the paroxysm had passed.

They buried him at Penhally. Aunt Maria settled that with quiet bitterness. He would want, she said, to be buried on his own land—but all the land he had ever owned belonged now to his brother. She would like, when her time came, to lie beside her husband . . . and there was no other place. All her people were buried in that same graveyard.

Robert—and Ruffin Woodford and the Crenfrew boys—came home in June, Robert lean and bronzed and with three fingers gone from his right hand. He married Barbara Crenfrew and they set up housekeeping at Mayfield. The old gentleman had that year given Mayfield to Robert, or rather he had entailed it on his heirs.

Alice had left Mayfield before the breaking up, to visit some of her mother's family in Louisville. She had married

while she was there, a tobacconist named Parrish. He had
business connections in France; they were said to have gone
abroad immediately after the wedding. He had not heard
of her marriage, though, till late in the summer. Cousin
Thyra told him. He had observed without rancor her little
pig's eyes twinkling. He had felt no emotion at the news.
There was, even, a kind of relief in thinking of Alice. Four
years . . . no, ever since he had known her he had been
occupied with wondering if she loved him. Well, he knew
about that now. . . . He contemplated the fact sometimes
when he was alone. . . . But he was not alone much that
summer. The house was full of people. There had been a
great deal of going back and forth between the various
places, a sort of excited gayety hanging over the whole
neighborhood. Back of it you felt an anxiety to establish all
the old ties. People who could not afford to buy thread to
mend their clothes had dinings and invited all the kin. When
the ladies from Penhally drove out he rode often beside the
carriage. He came at some time during the summer—he
could not say when or how—to consider himself as Lucy's
cavalier. . . .

The Irishman, O'Donnell, had been installed in the office.
After a few days he moved down there with him. He was
at that time training a setter and it was more convenient to
have him down there. He had liked, too, being with O'Donnell. And he had liked being away from the bustle of the
house. The office was secluded, the privet hedge, untrimmed
now for several years, shut it off from the rest of the grounds
and a thicket of young poplar trees had sprung up all around
it. The back porch overlooked the creek. They would sit
sometimes on the porch, watching the boys' white bodies
flash in and out of the swimming hole, talking about some
old camp character or speculating about the fate of this or
that comrade. Or he would lie through the heat of the

afternoon on the bed just inside the door, watching the play of shadows on the whitewashed wall, O'Donnell, on his bench outside, whittling or calling out from time to time to the boys in the swimming hole. . . . The shadows of the leaves would be on the ceiling. Sometimes a sheet of quivering, luminous light would spread over the whole wall. Lying there, watching the play of the shadows, he would think of Alice, but not with any dumb longing such as he had known before. It was just that pictures of her would come up in his mind, sharp sometimes, sometimes flowing in so gradually that the whole picture would be there before he even knew that he was thinking of her. . . .

It was in July that Aunt Maria, with Cousin Cave Maynor and Lucy, came to live at Penhally. He remembered the day they left Mayfield, Edmund driving the carriage, he and O'Donnell riding alongside. The wagon that rumbled behind was piled high with household goods. A stout, split-bottomed chair had been fixed in the centre of the pile. The old negro woman who sat in it held clutched in her arms a portrait: a lady in a crimson ball gown, an ivory fan pressed against her lips.

Arriving at Penhally Aunt Maria took up her abode in the west wing. If you walked in that part of the grounds you saw her sitting at the window, with bent head, her hands that were badly swollen with rheumatism moving painfully over her needlework. After a while she did not leave her room, even for meals. You forgot gradually that she was there.

But Lucy, from the first, took a part in the life of the house. Cousin Jessie was even then on the brink of her last illness and was obliged some days to keep to her bed. Lucy carried the keys and gave out the provisions. She rode, sometimes, with him and Ruffin, through the woods to Sycamore, sometimes as far as Gloversville. In the evenings after supper she walked with them on the lawn. At such times she did most of the talking, commenting on the doings of this one or that one in short, ironic sentences that seemed to burst from her. Or she would stop and look at them, her eyes very blue, under high, arched lids.

There was about her in those days an air of unbounded energy. The old gentleman, who liked to see things going on, would comment approvingly on her energy. Lucy, he said, had not a lazy bone in her body; she would soon get the place in order. The housekeeping did not seem to exhaust her energies. She would go out and weed the salsify beds, hatless, in the heat of the afternoon. By the end of the summer her face was as deeply tanned as any poor white woman's. When some of the older ladies remonstrated with her she laughed her short, hard laugh. "Well, I am a poor white woman, ain't I?" She would say things like that and laugh. But she seemed to have no resentment against Uncle Nick, who was, more than anybody else, responsible for the breaking up of her home. They were, if anything, companionable. More companionable than he and the old gentleman had ever been. Uncle Nick sat every afternoon in the same place under the poplar tree to watch the sun go down behind the row of cedars that bordered the graveyard. She would bring her work out after four o'clock and sit down beside him. The two of them would sit there, never speaking, staring at the dying sun. . . . One night when the office was so hot he could not sleep he had gone out and lain down under one of the trees. The moon had been bright. He could see a woman's shadow passing and repassing one of the upstairs windows and knew that it was Lucy, sleepless and walking to and fro. . . .

There was a good deal of speculation all that summer about Kenneth Llewellyn. Cousin Thyra, who kept up a correspondence with the Silvania ladies, was the only one who seemed to know anything about him. Old Cousin Richard was dead, she said, and Tom and Orrock had been killed in the war, the one at Seven Pines, the other in a skirmish at Trevilian's station. The three boys that were left were living at the old house and farming the land. The old-maid sister who lived with them sold violets in Charlottesville. They were all dog poor, of course. . . .

Lucy never mentioned Kenneth's name. There was much speculation about that, too. They had been engaged, certainly, when he went away to war. Had she refused him or had he jilted her when he found out that she was not, after all, an heiress? Cousin Thyra had a great deal to say about McNance blood. According to her you might as well expect water to run uphill as for a McNance to marry where there wasn't property.

Lucy kept her head high and faced them all. With her eyes, blue like ice, in her tanned face she looked these days like a boy. An angry boy. She had had typhoid fever in the very early spring and they had cut her hair off, short. It was only now beginning to curl around her face. She said that she would not leave the place until it was long enough to do up. . . . But she went with them to Ruffin's and Mary's house warming.

He drove her and Cousin Thyra over in the buggy. At the last minute Cousin Thyra decided to spend the night, so he and Lucy drove back alone. It was late, or rather early in the morning, when they left. They had danced as they used to dance in the old times—till the fiddlers gave out. Ruffin had kept calling to them and urging them on in just the way that he used to do, and when the guests finally began to leave, after the fiddlers had taken up their fiddles and gone back to the Quarter, he followed them out on the lawn.

John and Lucy driving off along the river road could look back and see the light dresses of the ladies glimmering through the trees and could hear long after they had turned into the woods road the chorus of gay voices:

"Don't leave. . . . Don't leave. . . . Why don't you spend the night? . . . You come to see *us* . . ."

It had been like old times.

She sat erect in her corner of the buggy, muffled in her cape. The mare stepped out freely on the winding road. It had just turned toward day. Cold air arose from the hollows. There was already a stirring of birds in the branches that overhung the road. They had both been a little fey with dancing when they got into the buggy, but the chill air of dawn was like cold water dashed in the face. He was aware of Lucy's shoulder just touching his. Once, absorbed in conversation, he failed to see a mud hole that covered one side of the road. The soft, flying mud had splashed Lucy's cheek. She put her hand on his and guided the mare to the opposite side. "Don't you know how to drive a horse?" she said, laughing.

He turned to look at her. She was looking at him . . . the kind of look she had given him once or twice before. He kissed her. Her lips were soft and clinging. He pressed her body passionately against his, murmuring her name over and over. He felt excited, almost happy. The black weariness was slipping away. He had come alive again. . . .

It was the next day that she came to him. In the late afternoon. He had just ridden in from the field and was unsaddling his horse at the stile blocks between the stable lot and the yard when he saw her moving toward him through the shrubbery. She had stood there silently beside the stile while he lifted the saddle off the horse's back and gave him the slap on the rump that would send him to the stable. He could not see her face plainly in the dusk but he knew the expression that her eyes would have. He stepped slowly up on the stile, looking down at her. Her gray dress melted into the dark japonica bushes, but back of her the whole wall of shrubbery was irradiated; every leaf seemed to stand out distinctly in the light that streamed from the dining-room windows. In there negroes moved to and fro, setting the table for supper. . . . The anger that was rising in him was the tight, hard core of his being. In a moment now it would have entire possession of him. . . . He stepped down off the stile. Her face, uplifted, was a white blur in the falling dark. He touched her cheek. She was crying. He stepped closer, pressing her back into the japonica boughs. "Lucy," he said, "Lucy . . ."

4

They were married in August, a hard, bright day when the dust was thick on all the roadside bushes. Guests, taking off their dusters in the hall, left a light layer of dust particles on the floor that had been newly polished for the festivities. The doors and most of the windows had been closed since early morning so that the house would be cool. But the heat beat in gradually during the day. By four o'clock, when the ceremony was said, it was a quivering band stretched tight around the house, pressing in a little at the windows. The dark faces of the negroes who stood at the four long parlor windows had seemed to swim in it.

They had stood in the exact centre of the floor for the ceremony, people ranged about three and four deep on every side. Lucy's dress, of some thin, silky material, was the color of crushed raspberries. The black velvet tabs that ornamented the bodice and the tight sleeves were pointed, like the diamond spot on cards. She had made the dress herself and she had plaited the straw for her bonnet, but the wreath of artificial roses that trimmed it she had bought from a milliner in Gloversville.

After the ceremony they had a glass of wine with the others in the dining room. When the women had done kissing Lucy they went out through the crowd to the side porch where Banty Blue stood at the sorrel mare's head. They drove in the cool of the evening along the river road to Gloversville and then on to Springfield. A full moon and the whole countryside as light as day, with that chill that comes with August nights over everything. They slept that night in Springfield at the hotel that was kept by Tom Jarrell. Mrs. Jarrell said that they must consider the vine-shaded porch that faced toward the east their parlor, so they idled the day away there, going in to dinner only after the other guests had finished and eating a light collation on a little table on the porch before they started on their journey again, around four o'clock. It had rained a little during the night and turned off much cooler. The mare travelled well. They had reached Nashville before midnight. They had stayed all that week at the Maxwell House. In the evenings, after supper, they went to the Vendome Theatre. Once or twice old General Harding sent his carriage in and they journeyed out to Belle Mead to spend the day.

When they got back to Penhally the house was emptied of guests. Old Cousin Jessie, who had over-exerted herself the week before the wedding, had had a slight stroke and was in bed. Lucy had to take over the housekeeping. Winter came with surprising swiftness that year. A short, rainy fall and then the cold weather had set in. Everything was different after that. Melancholy invaded the house with winter as mice creep in from the fields at the first touch of frost.

That first winter was the hardest. The Yankee soldiers had ranged just far enough from the fort to clean the country of hogs. There was not half enough meat to carry the people on the place through the winter. The niggers shot quantities of rabbits, but of cured meat there was very little. Robert made two or three trips to Arkansas and brought back venison each time. That had helped out a good deal. But it seemed almost impossible to get enough food to go around—and the negroes would not work on empty stomachs!

A man who owned a farm near the Red River bridge had advertised in the paper for four negro men, under thirty, to make a crop on his place. He would carry them through the winter, he said, provide meat, salt, meal and would give them a third of the crop. He had taken three of the likeliest young negroes on the place over and had made the trade for them. They had eaten that man's meat and meal all winter and had showed up at Penhally with the first spring days! He sent them back again, but they would not stay. The Llewellyn niggers—Ellen they came finally to call themselves—had gotten a reputation for being trifling, that had come down to this day. He remembered sitting one day in Doyle's livery stable waiting for his horse to be brought around while Doyle interrogated a young negro who wanted a job feeding. "George Ellen," the boy said his name was.

"Allen or Ellen?" the stable man had asked. And when the boy said Ellen he told him he couldn't use him. Coming back to his seat in the row of chairs tilted along the stable wall he had remarked to a crony that he never hired a Llewellyn nigger if he knew it; none of them were worth killing.

But right after the war they had been even less worth killing. They would not leave and they would not work! . . . And Ben Duck, the nigger preacher, was still going around among them, making trouble. He had told them that the farms were to be divided up among them, so much land and so much money to every negro man.

Uncle Nick, in the third year of the war, had hidden ten thousand dollars in gold in the woods. Robert and old Uncle Townsend had carried the money in a steel box out in the dead of night and had buried it, in a place not more than a quarter of a mile from the big spring, beside a peculiarly shaped rock. They had notched the letter H on twin saplings that grew near the spot and had not thought of having any difficulty in locating the money. But the saplings, when they came to look for them, were gone. At least no twin saplings marked with H were ever found in the woods. Old Uncle Townsend, dying, had confided all that he knew about the hiding place to his son, Banty Blue. When they went into the woods again and again to look for the money, at first at night and finally often by broad daylight, they found fresh earth upturned and the marks of tramping feet, and knew that the negroes were searching too.

Lucy had had the idea finally that the saplings might have been cut down and the rock so covered with vines as to be unrecognizable. They had gone through the woods then tearing vines off every rock until they found the money.

It was at night. Lucy had rigged up a lantern that they used in their digging. It had a shade made of half a dozen thicknesses of burlap so arranged that it could be slid around the globe to shoot forth one solitary ray of light. He had been standing there holding the lantern in the curve of his arm while Robert dug. When Robert threw his pick down and, stooping, lifted the box from the earth, he turned with the lantern still in the crook of his elbow. The light, shooting out over the leaves, flickered on the yellow eyeballs of a negro man. Simultaneously there had come to his ears a light stirring of leaves.

He had spoken to Robert, quietly, and then had picked his gun up from where it lay among the vines. The stirring in the bushes was louder now; he could hear the negroes breathe, could pick out a face here and there in the dim light.

He stepped out from beside Robert and, bending, traced a line with his finger in the wet mould.

"I'll shoot the first man who steps over that line," he said, "and I'll shoot Ben Duck on sight. Any time he sets foot on this place again I'll shoot him . . . and no questions asked . . ."

There was a sharp rustle in the bushes and then the sound of scurrying feet. They calculated, walking back through the dark woods, that there must have been twenty or thirty negroes. He had speculated for a long time after that as to just which negroes had been in the party. He could name the ring leaders, of course, but he could never be sure of their followers. Sometimes, catching a negro's eyes fixed on him enigmatically or detecting an unusual undertone of guile in a voice, he would say to himself that that man had probably been one of them. It had not bothered him much.

But Lucy came gradually to hate the negroes. . . . She came to hate them! It was not so much that night's business as the long strain of trying to provide for them. She said finally that they ought to be run off the place. If he refused to feed them, to help them in any way, they would *have* to go.

"They will starve us all," she said. "They are bleeding us to death now!"

Coming to the house one afternoon for a drink of water, he found her pouring buttermilk on the ground. The picture stayed with him for a long time: Lucy, her face flushed, gasping a little as she strained to tilt the heavy stone jar farther forward. And beside the syringa bush a negro woman, standing quite still, a child in her arms, another child tugging at her skirts, her face expressionless, except for the eyes that kept following the white trail of the milk over the hard ground.

It was in the fall of the next year that the old gentleman died, quietly, toward the end of a rainy day. Ralph Llewellyn had raved for weeks before his death, but Nicholas passed quietly. Toward the very end he rambled a little, talking of horses, hobbled, that made off through the woods, of wolves that howled at night, and once of a coon that would not be shaken down from its tree. Cousin Thyra, who sat a day and a night by his bedside, said that he fancied himself a little boy again, driving with his parents over the old Wilderness Trail.

In his will were found minute instructions for his burial. In that part of the graveyard where were buried Francis Llewellyn, his three wives, his infant daughter, Georgina, and his son, Ralph. Nicholas had written a paragraph into his will after Ralph's death: "He said that he would never set foot on Penhally land again, but we will both lie in it with our father, he beside his mother, I beside mine."

The day of his death was chill and rainy, but the next day, the day of his funeral, was clear and hot with a burning September sun. Neighbors began coming in the early morning, bringing flowers from their gardens. All the tables and chairs that could be found were taken out into the yard. People sat around under the trees, partaking of cold meats and salads. Where the shade was thickest negroes stirred iced drinks in zinc tubs or tall buckets. The table in the long dining room was stretched to its longest to accommodate the close kin. . . . While they sat there at dinner they could hear the continuous shuffling of feet: the procession of those who wished to view the corpse forming on the side porch and moving in through the side hall past the dining-room door to where the coffin stood in the parlor between the west windows.

Cousin Thyra and Ellen Crenfrew had had to do the honors of the house on that day. Lucy stayed in her room, viewing the funeral procession from her window, which gave on the graveyard. She would not go out among the company because she was expecting her child any day.

The boy, Frank, had been born that night. He *came* into the world on the heels of death! The baked meats from the old man's funeral not cold, old Cousin Jessie, who had been bedridden for almost a year, dying in the bedroom downstairs all the while Lucy was in labor. The doctor, still flushed from the funeral potations, had gone panting up and down the stairs to attend first one and then the other. Leaning over the banisters to say "A fine boy!" he had called out in the next breath, "Is she gone?"

There had been other funerals that year, too. Old people dropping off all around them like leaves from the tree. When he saw the boy as a baby he was being dandled on black satin laps . . . or making in his nurse's arms one of a procession to the graveyard. . . . Why was it that these things had stuck in the mind?

5

It was when the boy, Frank, was three years old that Lucy turned against him—as quietly and as surely as the bough that you have drawn aside swings back into place. He knew the very day, the hour, the minute even. A rainy day in early April. Coming by the wood pile in the late afternoon he had filled a basket with chips and kindling and had taken them into the chamber, intending to make a blaze on the hearth. Lucy was there, the child in her arms. A cold gray light, filtered through dripping boughs, filled the room. Kneeling on the hearth, arranging his kindling, he had anticipated the way the blaze would in a minute start up and light all the room. Something, the way she moved her chair back or drew her skirts aside, made him look up at her. He knew before she spoke what her voice would be like, low and hard and perfectly expressionless. She said something—he could not remember what. He answered without looking up again. When the fire was burning he got up and went outdoors, and in the half hour that was left before supper walked around and around in the yard.

He had known what it was—he had known from that very moment what the rest of his life would be like—but the top

part of his mind had busied itself with finding—with invent-
ing—plausible explanations for the change that had come
over her. He told himself finally that it was because she was
going to have another child. She had just discovered it, or just
been made certain of it, and he came upon her in that moment of certainty.

But they had never had another child. They had rarely
after that lain together. For many years now they had not
even occupied the same bed. The bedroom that had been old
Cousin Jessie's was still formally hers. She kept her clothes
hanging up in the closet and she sat in the daytime to sew
or read in the little low rocking chair by the window, but she
had had the little missy bed brought down from the attic and
placed between the two south windows. She was nervous,
she said; her turning and twisting would disturb him. She
lay down at night in that little bed, but he knew that if he
went in the dark half an hour later to run his hand over the
covers he would find them empty. And if he went out through
the house in search of her he would find her on the latticed
porch or in the kitchen, attending to some belated task. If
he questioned her she would look at him calmly, saying that
she had forgotten to make out her rolls or that she had just
remembered that the milk had not been set in fresh water,
and he would go back through the black hall into the bedroom. If she came into that room again it would be just
before dawn. But she rarely came. Waking with the first
light he would look over and see that her bed was still empty.
He would hear her sometimes in the very early morning,
moving about in the rooms upstairs. He did not know *where*
in that great, empty house she slept.

During those years—it was a long time now—he had
seemed to move in an infinite leisure. Things had come up
in his mind, things unremarked or hardly noticed at the time.
Gradually Lucy, the young Lucy, whom he seemed hardly

to have known, took form before him. He could see her as a very young girl: the wild rose color in the cheeks, the bright, curling brown hair and the blue eyes. . . . She had worked hatless day after day in the broiling sun, and when the ladies of the family remonstrated with her she had laughed. . . . She had taken pleasure in ruining the complexion that was her chief beauty! He knew, too, that she had tried to wear herself out with ceaseless activity, and finally she had come to him with a question. . . . She had had it in her mind to ask a question that night! . . . He had read somewhere that the desire of a man is for a woman, and the desire of a woman is to be desired. . . . And Lucy was inordinately proud. Nobody had ever heard Kenneth Llewellyn's name pass her lips. . . . She had perhaps thought of herself as twice betrayed . . . by love. . . . He could weigh and consider all these things now, but he could not do it then. . . . The tired horses of the Second Kentucky in their last charge had been able only to breast the fences, not to clear them. He had been like those horses then, and for a long time afterward. . . . To this day he could not sit down to a table without observing with a glow of satisfaction that all the necessaries were upon it. . . . And there was always somewhere in his mind a deep, a very deep pool of weariness. Certain exertions that he had undergone had left it there. To even think back on those exertions made all other fatigues seem casual. . . .

He was then too tired at that time in his life to make any decision, even to think about anything very clearly. But he had for the rest of his life to abide by the consequences of that fatigue!

His mind, freeing itself gradually from consideration of his own affairs, busied itself in a contemplation of his times. He saw his own personal misfortunes monstrously shadowed in those of the nation. It had been a time of debauchery and carnival. He had followed in the newspapers the trial

of a president of the United States for treason—Beast Butler
had recommended that it proceed like that of any ordinary
horse thief! . . . One of the Frazier negroes had gone to
the state legislature in the identical blue broadcloth coat with
the brass buttons that his master had worn in that assembly!
He took a grim relish in observing and commenting on these
things. He must have talked of them more than he realized
. . . at the table, whenever he was in company. . . . And
Lucy, at the foot of the table, seeming to say by her with-
drawn and brooding gaze that these things that he was holding up as monstrosities were, after all, negligible. . . . It had
been a gloomy atmosphere for a child to grow up in!

But perhaps things like that didn't make any difference to
children. His own father had been mad as a hatter, but he
could not remember having been much concerned about it.
He had been painfully embarrassed once or twice in his life
by the old gentleman's eccentric appearance in company, but
that was after he was a grown boy and had started calling
on the girls. Perhaps children—the roistering age, anyhow
—didn't care what their parents were like, as long as they
had other children to play with. . . .

The boy had had young companions! He could hear them
now, shrieking boisterously around the house: Tom and
Aleck Woodford, the three young Crenfrews, Robert's two
boys. There had always been half a dozen of them there off and
on during the summer. He could see the boy moving among
them, lean and dark and, yes, not as talkative as the others.
But if he had seemed sombre compared to them, it was because he was dark while they were all so fair. He had a
Llewellyn face, lean, with brown eyes like old Uncle Nick's
set under heavy black brows. Such a face does not light up
easily, or if it does, it is like the sun coming out on a stormy
day. And a shy boy when he begins to grow up nearly always
takes on that air of gloomy dignity. . . . He remembered

going down to the creek once when they were all in swimming. Frank, lounging on the bank, heard him coming and
turned to look around . . . mirthfully. . . . He could see
him plainly as he had been at that moment: the flash of white
teeth against the brown skin and the sudden lightening that
had had come into the dark eyes. . . .

No, the house had not been altogether gloomy. People
had liked to come to Penhally. It was still the place to
which they came when there were too many of them at home
or when their affairs did not prosper. . . . There had been
something in the old man's will about offering asylum to infirm kinsmen. . . . Well, he had done that: old Cousin Cave
Maynor, Ellen Crenfrew . . . and dependents. . . . That
was how the girl, Faneuil, had come to them!

Her mother was one of old Cousin Jessie's nieces, a widow
with five girls and one delicate boy, on a poor Virginia farm.
It had seemed proper to write, inviting her to come. There
had been, in fact, no question about it, either in his mind or
in Lucy's.

It was strange. . . . He could remember the day the girl
had come. A gusty day in early February. He had idled in
conversation at the livery stable until the train whistled for
the station. She was already standing on the platform when
he got there. A small figure in a tight-fitting coat that was
made up of enormous black and white checks. And she must
have had glossy curls down her back. He remembered tuck-
ing the lap robe over the black and white checks. He even
remembered snatches of the conversation that they had had
on the way home. She had asked him if there were any
young people her age in the neighborhood. He had told her
there were plenty, and had said that now there was a young
lady in the house they would have to give a ball. . . . But he
could not remember very clearly her face, or at least he could
not remember it as it had looked then.

He had not thought of her as a young lady, but she must have been seventeen then! Seventeen to Frank's eighteen or nineteen. His own mother had been eighteen when he was born and he had been a lieutenant in the Confederate army when he was nineteen. But he had not thought of that. He had not really thought about the girl at all. Hearing her light, chittering voice about the house and observing the muscles around Lucy's mouth twitching once or twice at something the girl said, he had told himself that those two were, perhaps, not going to get on well and had wondered cloudily what was to be done if Lucy turned out actually to dislike the girl, but that was as far as he had gone . . . until that night. . . .

She had come to them in February. And Frank had come back from the university in June. It was, then, toward the end of that month that it happened.

May had been wet and chilly, but good weather came with the change of moon. The fair, cloudless weather had continued all through June. There had been a good deal of gayety among the young people. They had been dancing that very night at one of the houses in the neighborhood. Coming home from the dance they had talked awhile on the porch and then had gone upstairs to bed. He had heard them on the stairs: Faneuil and Frank and one of Robert's boys, who had come home with them. The house had become very quiet. He had turned a page of his book, considering whether he should read a little more or go to bed. . . . And then Lucy had come into the room with another lamp. She had set it down on the marble-topped table before she spoke.

"Frank is in that girl's room," she said and walked over and sat down on the edge of the bed. He had remained silent, staring at her hands that kept plucking at the counterpane. When she raised her head finally and looked at him he got up and went up the stairs to the door of the girl's room.

There was no sound within. He put his hand on the door knob and then took it off again. The moonlight made the place as light as day. He called: "Fan . . . Fan . . ." in a low voice until finally the girl came to the door. In some sort of white wrapper, her cloudy black hair hanging about her shoulders.

He had stood there staring at her. . . . It was as if he were seeing her face for the first time. The enormous dark eyes in the soft, rather thin face and that dark hair hanging all about. He remembered thinking that the eyes were *too* large, too dark. . . . She put her hand up nervously to the door frame. "Cousin John . . ." He could not remember now what she had said.

He pushed past her into the room. Everything was perfectly still for a minute and then the boy stepped out from the shadows of the embrasure in which the bed stood. . . . The last time he had seen the boy alive. . . . He could not even remember looking at him. He had been occupied with thinking that it was possible to go from this room into a lumber room which gave on the back porch and so down the back stairs. He had been agonized, too, trying to remember whether the back door which commanded a view of those stairs was open. . . . All the time he had been aware of Lucy downstairs in the bedroom.

He had spoken to the girl:

"Put your clothes on. Don't try to take anything. I'll send your clothes to you . . ."

She had put her hands up to her face and was crying, a low, soft wailing that filled all the room. The boy had his arms around her and was trying to comfort her. He looked up at that.

"If she goes away from here, I go too," he said.

John made a gesture of annoyance. He remembered that he had felt a vast impatience at their slowness, at their *youth*.

His mind had been racing on ahead, down the back stairs, out to the stable, half way already to Gloversville. He brought it back, speaking slowly and plainly, as if he were giving them directions for finding a road.

"Your mother is in the bedroom. You'd better go down the back stairs. Take the gray colt or Rory, if you'd rather have him. That preacher at the station'll marry you. He'll be in bed but you get him up." Putting his hand in his pocket he had found only a dollar bill and some change. "Make him get you some money," he said. "He can go somewhere in town and get you some money. Tell him I'll settle with him to-morrow."

The boy had said that he didn't want his money. He had reminded him that he had money of his own in the bank. The legacy that old Cousin Jessie had left him before he was born was still untouched. If there was any difficulty about his getting it, not being of age, he would be glad to lend him some money until he did come of age. He added that he would be glad if they would write to him as soon as they had located somewhere.

They had talked quietly there together about the money while the girl moved around in the other end of the room. When she had finished dressing she came and stood beside them. The boy put his arm around her. He held open for them the door that led into the shuttered lumber room. They went through it and out to the back stairs. It had all seemed a very long time, but it had taken only a few minutes. He had stood there, holding the door open until the soft sound of their feet on the stairs had died away. Then he had gone over to the window. He had not been able to see them crossing the lawn or entering the stable—the shrubbery was thick all around that side of the house—but he had stood there looking out until he heard the clop-clop-clop of a horse's feet on the dirt road.

Lucy was not in the chamber when he went downstairs. He found her in one of the other rooms, stretched out face downward on the bed. She would not look at him or speak to him. She had just lain there beating her hands up and down on the coverlet and making every now and then a queer, strangled noise in her throat.

He could not say at this date how they had come to know all that they eventually knew about the girl. Frank had written to them, of course. They had been at no time completely cut off from him, but his letters were laconic, businesslike. He told merely what they were doing, what they planned to do next. They had lived one year in Louisville, another year in Memphis. Then the letter came announcing their removal to a small town in Arkansas. Old Judge Sinclair—Faneuil's father had been his artillery captain—had offered to take Frank in as his law partner. They had lived there three, no, four years. The letters had continued to come at fairly regular intervals. The practice that Frank had inherited from the old judge had increased until he was making a very good living. . . . Nick was seven years old yesterday and going to school, to Miss Betty Lane. The baby, Chance, was so lonesome at home by himself that they had let him go too. Miss Betty insisted that he was no trouble. He played out in the yard by himself while the other children were saying their lessons and he enjoyed playing with them so at recess. . . .

The house would have been empty all day long, both children at school and Frank at his office. . . . That woman would have had plenty of time for her amours. . . .

He could not remember just which of her escapades was the first to reach their ears. Robert's oldest daughter had visited in Osceola. She must have brought back a pretty complete report. There was, even then, a man . . . "a common drummer" Lucy said fiercely the only time that she brought herself to discuss the matter with him. . . . But the man Faneuil had run away with, two weeks after Frank's death, had been a ne'er-do-well cousin of the Sinclairs. . . .

It was strange. . . . It was that girl, Faneuil, who suffered . . . all the things that women suffer when they burn their bridges behind them in that particular way. Edgar Sinclair was not only dissolute and incapable but morally irresponsible. The Sinclairs had written pretty plainly about that. They left no question of what, in their opinion, that girl's life would be like. Reading their letters, he had had always a curious delusion. It was Frank, not the girl, who was wandering over the face of the earth. . . . He seemed to see him on dark, interminable slopes, or walking down street after street of some city, rain falling. . . . He would have to remind himself that the boy was dead . . . was under ground. . . .

Twenty-eight years old he would have been that fall . . . and it had happened on the twenty-eighth of October. A fair day, but with a rain blowing up from the south. They had been bringing the wagons up to the granary to divide the corn. He was sitting in the shade along the fence row watching the clouds pile up and wondering if they would get through before the rain. The little boy who brought the telegram had come walking slowly across the enclosure following with his eyes the motions of the men and the mules. He had taken the slip of paper in one hand as he turned to give some order. . . . It was the sound of the ears of corn falling and falling on the granary floor that roused him finally to go to the house. . . .

Lucy was weeding in the little flower bed before the window. She had looked up at him with eyes dark with surprise and then had fallen down sidewise among her flowers. Her hand had kept clutching at her side. "I knew it," she said over and over. . . . He had not thought then to ask her what she meant by that.

As once before when she had said bitterly that the boy was dead to her, she lay for two days and nights in a darkened chamber, cold compresses steeped in vinegar over her eyes. . . . And she would not look at the boy when they brought him home. . . .

He had sat beside him that night, and walking to the graveyard he had kept his hand all the way on the casket. . . . Once, when the room was empty of people, he went to the window to look out at the graveyard. It had not seemed possible that they would in a few minutes consign him to that earth. . . .

The young man, Dick Applegate, who had brought him up from Arkansas, a fair young man with blue eyes that gazed at you agonizedly, he must have tortured that man! He had had an intolerable desire—perhaps people always have it—to know everything about the last minutes his son had been alive. He had made Dick Applegate tell him exactly how it happened, until gradually the scene had taken shape in his mind. It had come finally to seem something that he himself had witnessed: the two young men in the early morning, walking out over the fields, the dogs moving before them through the high, sere grass. The fence that divided one field from another would have been grown up in trees and bushes. . . And one or the other of them had crossed over into that field. That was how they had gotten separated. Dick Applegate's dog would have made a point on that side of the fence and he would have fired. . . .

His hand closed down on the arm of his chair. He got to his feet. The boy, Chance, had rolled off his quilt and lay on his back, breathing heavily in the hard sleep of childhood. He stood looking down at him.

The picture, then, was not as he had seen it all these years. Dick Applegate on his side of the fence had not fired. It was Frank who fired. . . . He had shot himself! . . . Oh, the poor boy . . . the poor boy. . . .

He took a turn around the room, moving with quick, uneasy steps. The windows that had been black were gray now. The whole room was filling with gray, cold light. He walked over to the bed. O'Donnell had fallen sidewise on his pillows. His eyes, open, stared at the opposite wall, his upper lip was drawn tightly across his gums. . . .

Anna had heard him moving around and had come in from the other room. She was beside the bed now, drawing the covers up over the inert form. As he watched she leaned over and laid her hand for a moment against the pale cheek. Straightening up she crossed herself, looking at him out of startled eyes.

"He's dead," she said, "Holy Mother!"

He laid his hand on her shoulder. "Yes," he said, "he's dead."

Penhally

Part III

1

The room was long and narrow; whatever light came into it was admitted through curtains of some filmy green material that, hanging in light, straight folds, were like nothing so much as clear green water. The effect on this unseasonably hot day was agreeable, Chance thought, as if sunlight had been filtered through running water. There was a bowl of jonquils on a little table and on a low bracket that had been fixed in front of an old-fashioned portrait at the far end of the room another deep glass bowl held a profusion of some white lace-like flower whose name he could not call. The lady in the portrait had on a crimson velvet dress. The frail cups of the white flowers glimmered against its hem—as if somebody had thrown down flowers at her feet. Phyllis had chosen that portrait out of the Penhally parlor for the red dress.

He caught sight of his own reflection in the pier glass that was placed half way down the room between two windows: a burly man in rough corduroys, a battered felt hat swinging from his right hand. He looked out of place in the delicately colored room. Mud was undoubtedly crumbling at this moment from his boots onto the pale-gray carpet. He tip-toed to the nearest chair and sank into it.

His sister-in-law, Phyllis, was still drifting about the room. She had been on the point of going out when he arrived, but she wouldn't go now until Nick came. She was hoping that she could persuade Nick not to go on that nigger's bond.

He sank back into the deep arm chair, half closing his eyes. He was very tired, not tired so much as exhausted from lack of sleep. It had been after one o'clock when he

got in last night and it had been fully an hour after that
when he had gotten out of his bed to see what all the shouting was about. He had anticipated that the ruckus, whatever
it was, would be in Russ' cabin. He had known for some
time that there was bad blood between Russ and Major. But
he had not been prepared for the sight that met his eyes.

Major lay dead on the ground in front of Russell's cabin,
one arm flung wide, the other cradling his head. Blood was
oozing from an enormous hole in his chest to form a pool on
the hard ground. The bullet had drilled a hole clean through
him. "Shot his heart out," one nigger murmured in an awed
whisper.

Averting his eyes involuntarily from the sight, he had
caught sight of a shadowy figure moving about in the cabin.
He left the circle and stepped up on the rickety porch.

"Russ," he called sharply, "Russ, come here!"

Russ had come out after only a moment's hesitation. They
had stood there together, the negro silent, he talking reasonably. "Now, Russ, here's half a dozen folks saw you shoot
this man down. . . . You better come along with me. . . .
That's the best thing you can do. . . . You come along with
me. . . ."

It had been appalling to see one expression succeed another on the negro's face. Panic had given way to complete
composure. He surrendered with a soft sigh.

"All right, Mister Chance, I know you goin' to do the best
you kin for me," he said as they went over the lawn toward
the black house. They had gone in tiptoe so as not to wake the
old ladies. He had had a devil of a time getting the operator,
of course, and the sheriff was not to be located anywhere.
He had finally left word at the jail that he was bringing the
negro in.

All the way to town he had had to listen to a recapitulation
of the affair as Russ chose to view it; the unseemly epithets

that Major had applied to him; the things that he, in his turn, had said about Major; the things they had said to each other; the threats that Major had made against his, Russ' life, ending with the sinister elevation of the elbow that had made him grab his gun quick. . . . On and on through the interminable windings of the affair, never touching, of course, on the core of the quarrel, which was that Russ' wife, a buxom twenty to his thirty-eight, just naturally preferred sleeping with Major to Russ.

He had seen this quarrel shaping up as far as three months back and could have foretold then that it would end in a shooting. Still, it never did any good to mix in niggers' affairs. You just had to let things run their course. It was strange, though, the way it was always the good, reliable niggers who got into scrapes like this. You could almost set it down that a white folks' nigger was mean to his own race. That girl wouldn't have encouraged Major the way she had if Russ hadn't tyrannized over her. . . .

Leaving Russ at the jail he had put his hand in his pocket and had found only a two-dollar bill—and two cigars. The bill, reposing in Russ' pockets, wouldn't be much good, but the cigars could be bandied about, to show that his white folks were standing by him. Russ had been pathetically grateful. He was already estimating what the amount of his bond would be: a thousand, no, more like five hundred; after all, he might be said to have shot in self-defense. . . . There was no question in his mind as to whether the Llewellyn brothers would make his bond. . . . It would be a blow to Russ, if he knew that he, Chance, didn't have as much as five hundred dollars in the bank! . . .

Phyllis had sat down in a chair near the window and was lighting a cigarette. "What I can't see," she said, "is why you don't let the law take its course. He shot the man down in cold blood, didn't he?"

"Well, no," he said, "there was provocation. The other nigger had been tampering with his wife."

She made a slight gesture of irritation. "Oh, their *wives!*" she said. "If they're single, they're out every night slashing somebody with a razor, and if they're married, somebody is always fooling with their wives. . . ." She began telling him about the derelictions of her boy, George, old Aunt Miny's youngest son, and, like all of Aunt Miny's children, a perfect joy around the house. . . . But he was always cutting somebody with a razor. It had gotten so now that Nick tried to stay at home on Saturday night in case George wanted him. . . . She was about ready to give him up. . . . It was just too much of a nuisance. . . .

He eyed her reflectively. He didn't believe George was as bad as all that. A woman like Phyllis was apt to be funny about negroes. She regarded them evidently as machines. They were all right as long as they worked smoothly but she had no use for them when they broke down. He wondered what she would say if he put the case to her bluntly. "Look here, this nigger, Russ, is your husband's . . ." What kin was Russ to him and Nick? He was old Aunt Dora's grandson and everybody knew who *her* father was. . . . You couldn't go shouting things like that around, but you couldn't put them clean out of your mind, either. Russ actually had more of a claim on Nick than he had on him. He was Nick's foster brother. They had sent Darthula down to Arkansas to nurse Nick when he was an ailing baby. Nick had thriven on Darthula's milk, but poor old Russ had had malaria as a result of the change of climate. . . . He had better not mention that, though. She was rabid on the subject of negro nurses for children. She had one for her own, but the negro was washed and sterilized every morning. Actually getting pale, Nick said; Phyllis was washing all the nigger out of her.

He wondered where she had gotten that mania for cleanliness. Certainly not from the Fosters! He remembered Phyllis' grandfather, old man Foster, very well. He had kept a feed store on Market Street for years. A bent old man —Miss Lucy always called him "Mister Pumblechook"—the reddish-brown beard that encircled his face looked as if it had been composed of some of his own hay. Red top—it had looked exactly like red-top! You couldn't say that that old man was distinguished for cleanliness. His son, Phyllis' father, was a different sort of fellow. He had run a bucket shop and somehow, nobody ever knew quite how, had made a fortune in wheat. The oldest girl, Susan, hadn't married so well. The old man made his money too late to do her any good, but it had come along just in time to launch Phyllis on the crest of the wave.

He remembered her as she had been ten, twelve years ago—small, but she had even then been verging on plumpness—with very fair hair and big brown eyes, usually in the shadow of an enormous floppy hat. Her clothes must have been remarkable; at any rate, the women all talked about them a lot. The Fosters had kept her at expensive schools abroad for several years, and the year after she came home she married Nick. . . .

They had a big wedding, with the bishop and ten bridesmaids, and the ices from Miss Jennie Benedict's in Louisville. He remembered coming home from school for the occasion. His train had been late or something. Anyway he had not had time to dress. He had come right on up from the station just as he was. Phyllis' aunt, who was running the show, took one look at him and then shoved him off in a corner with some old ladies, instead of putting him at the table with the wedding party. Nick had kept looking around, saying the train must be late, when all the time he was off in that corner gorging himself on scalloped oysters and caramel

cake. He had not been sore about it, being pleasantly occupied, but the memory still rankled in Phyllis' bosom. She
thought that he considered that, being Chance Llewellyn, he
was privileged to do as he pleased, even to ruining her
wedding. She *had* been severely tried that day. Old Cousin
Alfred, septuagenarian, eccentric and very wealthy, had attended in khaki trousers, flannel shirt and the dairymen's
boots that he bought from Sears, Roebuck, and had spat
tobacco juice, noisily, three times during the ceremony. They
had had to put up with him because he was so rich. Cousin
Alfred had not exhibited much patience with *them*. To one of
Phyllis' Chattanooga cousins who had inquired curiously what
business he was in, he replied irascibly: "Gre't God, feller,
what do you think I am?" But all that was family legend
now. . . .

He wondered whether Nick had married the girl for her
money or whether he had actually been attracted to her. . . . It
was impossible, of course, to know the sexual attraction that
any woman had for any man. She had good features, a fair
complexion, fine hair. He supposed that she would be considered beautiful. It was a beauty that did not appeal to him
—his own sweetheart, Emily Kinloe, was thin and dark, with a
nervous way of flinging her hands about. . . . Certainly he and
Nick had very different taste in women. He didn't care so
much what a woman looked like as long as her personality had
a certain flavor. He thought of it as being somewhat the
same quality that distinguishes a thoroughbred horse, a certain quickness of movement, nervousness, even, in gestures,
that he characterized in his thought as being "spirited."
Phyllis had none of that. She was always placid, unless she
was irritated, as she was now about this negro. . . .

The front door had slammed. There were quick steps in
the hall. The lean, fair-haired young man who had come in
stood smiling at them good-humoredly as he drew off his
gloves.

Phyllis half rose from her chair, then sank back. "Where *have* you been?" she said. "I've been telephoning all over town for you."

Nick laughed. "I've been in conference," he said, "with Mister Russell Llewellyn, at the jail."

Phyllis had taken a pack of cards from the table behind her and was shuffling them idly in and out of the case. "I imagine it was a pretty expensive conference," she said.

"Bond was a thousand," Nick said. Advancing into the room he looked past her, at Chance. "Sheriff wants to see you," he said.

Chance nodded. "Russ'll stick around," he said. "He'll be afraid to leave the place."

Phyllis laughed. "He'll be afraid to get that far away from you and Nick," she said. "He thinks you and Nick keep the law in your pockets. He thinks he can do anything he wants to and you-all will get him out. . . . He'll probably shoot somebody else before he comes to trial. . . ." She got up and left the room. They could hear her light, uneven footsteps in the hall for a moment and her voice giving an order to some servant and then the house became quiet. . . .

Nick sat down opposite Chance. "Lord," he said, "I'm tired!"

"How's Mister Llewellyn bearing up?" Chance asked.

"Oh, fine. He informed me that he knew everything would be all right as soon as I got there." He grinned. "Seemed to think you had done as well as could be expected . . . under the circumstances. . . ."

"I suppose he thinks the whole business is finished now," Chance said.

Nick nodded. "I tried to sort of prepare him for the idea of doing ten or fifteen years, but he couldn't take it in."

"Well, I sure will hate to give him up," Chance said. "He's just about the smartest nigger on the place."

"Every one of those niggers is smart," Nick said, "and every one of 'em is high-tempered. This George we got here is just like Russ. I look for 'em to take him up any night. . . ."

The door opened and a negro man came in, bearing a tray. Ice tinkled in its pitcher as he drew a little table up between them. Chance nodded at him and took in silence the glass that he proffered.

"Country toddy!" he said, when he had lifted the glass to his lips.

Nick smiled. "George makes 'em good, doesn't he?" he said.

The two brothers fell companionably silent. Nick had turned his chair so that it faced a little toward the window and was staring absently out on the street, his lean body relaxed and motionless, as weary apparently as if it had been he, and not Chance, who had been up half the night. As he turned his head slightly to take up his glass, Chance saw that the very fair hair that glistened on his temples was actually silver gray. The discovery shocked him. He remembered that Nick had come in on this mild spring day wearing an overcoat. Well, a man's blood was apt to get thin if he stayed indoors as much as Nick did. Twelve years now he had been in that bank. . . . He had, of course, something to show for it. He had started in as a common clerk and now at thirty-two he was president of the bank and of the Valley Trust Company, and God knew how many other concerns he had a finger in. He had made enough money, anyhow, to build his wife a fine house. When he, Chance, got married, as he hoped to do in the fall, he would have to bring his bride to the old house. Nick's house it was, really. He had sometimes to stop and remind himself of that. Penhally always seemed to belong to him so much more than it did to Nick.

It was Nick's, though. Every acre of it. It had been entailed on him before he was born. Their old great-uncle, Nicholas Llewellyn, when he chose his foster brother's children for his heirs, had entailed most of the property on the eldest son. *Their* father, Frank, had died when he was still a young man and so had never come into his inheritance. Their grandfather, John Llewellyn, had followed the old uncle's example. It had probably never occurred to him that he had a right to do anything else! It had been apparent, though, from the time Nick was a small boy, that he was not cut out for farming. It had been understood all along that he, Chance, would run the place. He could not remember when he had not looked forward to some day farming that land!

Nick, leaning over to refill his glass, was asking if he had sold any tobacco.

"I sold some on the loose floor yesterday morning," Chance said.

"What'd you get for it?" Nick asked.

"Oh, around nine cents," Chance told him.

"Nine cents . . ." Nick said. "That's a hell of a price for prime leaf!"

His brother nodded absent-mindedly. He was thinking that he would be better off if Nick did not insist on carrying his confounded business methods into farming. He had wanted to farm Penhally on shares, giving Nick as owner of the land one-third of whatever he made. But Nick wanted things on a business basis, so they were a firm: Llewellyn & Llewellyn. It had been a piece of generosity on Nick's part, or at least Nick had been influenced by generous motives, when he made the suggestion. But he, Chance, would have done better as an ordinary share cropper. As it was, he had been losing money for three, four years now. . . .

He stood up. "Well," he said, "I reckon I better go see about my nigger."

Nick pulled out his watch. "Good Lord," he said, "I had an appointment with Sabin at twelve and it's ten past now."

"You better run along then," Chance said.

"Well," Nick said, "he'll keep. . . ." He looked at Chance vaguely, as if he could not remember what it was that he had had on his mind. As Chance went out into the hall he walked beside him. "Any lambs yet?" he asked.

"Six last night," Chance said, "only one set of twins so far."

"And Miss Lucy has got the odd one up at the house, I reckon?" Nick said.

"Yes, damn it!" Chance said. "She hooked my bathrobe to wrap him in."

They had arrived before a rack that was placed in the back hall for the accommodation of wraps. Nick was fumbling among the various garments for his overcoat. "George," he called, "George . . . for God's sake!" The negro had come swiftly from the entry and was already detaching the coat from its peg. Nick spoke, irritably, to Chance. "You can't lay a thing down here two minutes or it'll get away from you."

Chance laughed, exchanging glances with the negro. "Well," he said, "you haven't got anybody but Phyllis and George here hiding things from you. Suppose you had Miss Ellen and Miss Lucy both working on you."

They went out of the door and down the steps. The pavement was white in the spring sunshine. In a few minutes now the sun would be on the other side of the street and the day would have turned. Chance walked slowly, matching his steps to Nick's. He felt an impulse to detain his brother beside him as long as he could. It occurred to him that he very seldom saw Nick these days, and when they did meet it was usually in a crowd of people. . . .

Nick was talking about a new Japanese clover that he had heard of. He had gotten a few pounds of the seed and wanted to try it. He would get out to Penhally in a day or two; they could decide then where they'd put it.

"Come out Sunday," Chance said, "I want you to take a look at those Herefords. If you get out early enough we could ride over to the north end, too."

"All right," Nick said, "I'll be out." He stopped short. "No, I can't," he said, "I've got an engagement to lunch with Sabin."

Chance did not answer. He told himself that he would not live as Nick lived for any amount of money. The fellow couldn't even get out on Sunday to look over his own land!

Nick was still standing there, frowning. "Hell!" he said, "I'll come. I'll tell Sabin he'll have to make it some other day."

"All right," Chance said, "I'll be looking for you."

2

After leaving Nick, Chance turned off Market Street into North Second. It had occurred to him that he might go by and see Emily a few minutes. The chances were that he would find her at home this time of day. North Second, at this early hour of the afternoon, was deserted except for a few children on their way back to school and a negro here and there spading up flower beds in somebody's yard. He walked slowly, breathing in the spring air. He always enjoyed walking along Second Street. It was parallel to the river, but higher than First Street, so high that he could catch every now and then between neat grass plots glimpses of the shining water. It was strange the way the town turned its back on the river these days. Time was when North Second was *the* street of Gloversville simply because it was on the bluff above the river. All the old houses like the Pryors' and the Rodman place fronted the river. Those old houses

were pleasant, with their long lawns that stretched sometimes clean down through what was now First Street and
River Street to the water's edge. And of course in the old
days everybody had had his own wharf. Then when the town
was picking up in reconstruction days old Mr. Bade Watson
had built a string of tobacco warehouses all along the river
front, and everybody who lived along there had been out of
luck; that was all. A good many people had solved the problem by simply turning their backs on the river, making the
backs of their houses the fronts. That had led to some ridiculous complications. The outbuildings, kitchens and all
had been right in people's front yards. Some people had
torn them down and rebuilt them in what were now their back
yards, but most people had just moved away.

The last of those old landmarks had been the old Pryor
house, which was still standing when he was a child. His
grandmother, when she came to town, had always left him
there to spend the day with Robert Pryor, who was about
his age. They had run wild in the grounds which then covered this whole block. The garden must have been laid out
formally at one time. He remembered that running about
in there, playing hide and seek, you came sometimes upon
statues with behind them dark, curving walls of box. But
the whole place had been a tangle of honeysuckle and trumpet
vine even in those days. Now you could pass by here and
not find a sign that it had ever existed, though he believed
that Phyllis said that the ivy that covered her walls was from
roots that she had found on the grounds. Tudor Heights
the place was called now. And it was once again a very
fashionable place to live, with all sorts of restrictions, which
he understood operated to make it extremely desirable. If
you wanted to build a house, for instance, in that section, it
had to be of Tudor architecture, whatever that was. It was,
for one thing, money in Charley Foster's pocket, for Charley,

as Nick said, was the only architect in town who knew Tudor from a hole in the ground. He had done very well last year, what with the Latham house and the Radnors' and the house he had built for those South American tobacco people. . . .

He emerged from the green walks of Tudor Heights. The Kinloe house loomed up before him: an immense pile of yellowish-gray brick, with three turrets and a fretwork of iron balconies across its front. He had heard Emily say that it was without doubt the ugliest house in Gloversville. He had not thought about its exterior before she said that, but he saw what she meant. It was the turrets. Old Mr. Kinloe, Emily's grandfather, had built it when he first began to make money in the tobacco business. Alfred Robbins, the rival tobacconist, had had two turrets on his house, so Mr. Kinloe had put three on his. It was a good, well-built house, though, with room in it to turn around.

He went up the brick walk that was bordered on either side with double clumps of jonquils and pulled on the old-fashioned bell. The negro woman who let him into the house told him that Miss Emily hadn't come downstairs yet, but she reckoned she must be up by this time.

Chance smiled at her as he gave her his hat. "What kind of wife you reckon she's going to make for a farmer, Matty?" he inquired.

Matty showed beautiful white teeth in a broad smile.

"She'll be all right if you can just git her up in the mornings," she said.

She ushered him into the family sitting room. Some china and an electric percolator were laid out on the table that stood before the east windows. Emily evidently intended to have her breakfast in here. He sat down in a chair beside the table. A parallelogram of bright sunshine fell across the grayish-brown carpet that had woven in it immense faded yellow flowers. The other half of the room was in gloom.

There was never enough light in here, but it didn't do any good to open the front windows. The ash tree outside completely obstructed them. A damn nuisance, but Emily's mother would not have it cut down because somebody had brought it as a seedling from Longfellow's home. There were two portraits in oval frames hanging between those windows, a choleric-looking young man and a young woman with a dark, oval face and a lot of white transparent stuff billowing off her shoulders. The chiffon or whatever it was shone in the dim room, but the face was dark, foreign-looking. He had always thought that the girl looked like Emily. One of her French grandmothers, probably. She had French blood not very far back, on her mother's side. . . .

She was coming into the room. A slim, dark girl in a green dress. She kissed him, then sat down at the table and began pouring coffee from the electric contraption. He drew his chair up beside hers and she pushed a cup of coffee negligently toward him. "Did you have a hard morning, darling?" she asked.

He decided that he would not tell her about the shooting.

"I was over at the loose floor most of the morning," he said.

"And it made you sick?"

"It's enough to make anybody sick," he said.

She fed herself toast with one hand while the other caressed his cheek. "It'd been nice if you'd got a shave," she said. "Oh, darling, I went to the Parrishes' . . . last night after you didn't come in . . . with Nick and Phyllis. . . ."

"Parrishes' . . .?" he said.

"You know . . . those terribly rich people that the Offenbachs have under their wing."

"Are they tobacco buyers?" Chance asked.

"No. . . . I met them a year or two ago . . . in Munich. They seem to have been everywhere in the world since then. . . . But they're going to live here. . . ."

"I don't know what all those foreigners are moving in here for if they aren't tobacco buyers . . ." Chance said. He was thinking of the first time he had met Emily, or at least he always thought of it as their first meeting. He had known her all his life, of course. She had visited at Penhally a lot when she was a little girl. Her mother was, somehow, in the connection; at least you called her "Cousin." . . . But Emily had been away at school for eight or ten years. He had not seen her after she was grown—until the day when she came riding out of the woods on to the road that ran through the farm. He was out in the field, watching the negroes set tobacco. She came up to him to ask the way back to the pike and just as he was giving her the directions he would have given a stranger she turned in her saddle to look back at the house just visible through the trees. "Don't tell me that's Penhally!" she said.

Something in the quick turning of her head, the inflection of her voice, had brought back to his mind the eight-year-old child who had tagged him and Nick over the place for three summers. "Little Em!" he ejaculated, remembering how she had always detested that name and she had cried out "Chance!" in the same breath. He had described to her what a nuisance she had been. She asked him if he recalled how brutal, tyrannical and generally overbearing he had been. They had quarrelled there, lively, in the shade a whole morning. He had called upon her that night. Two weeks later they were engaged to be married. . . .

She had finished her coffee and was coming around to sit on the arm of his chair. "They're not foreigners," she said, "they're kin to us. At least they're kin to you. . . ."

"Parrish . . ." Chance said. He added that he knew who the man was now. His mother was one of those Virginia Blairs. She *was* pretty close kin, closer through his mother's side than his father's. . . .

"Don't start on one of those Llewellyn-Crenfrew connections," Emily said, "my head aches. . . . Well, anyhow, they have scads of money . . . *scads*. . . . You feel it in the air. . . . What I can't understand is why they're fooling with Gloversville."

Chance said that he had observed that anybody who had any connection with Gloversville usually came back to spend their last days here. He added that he expected that Parrish was a pretty sharp business man. His grandmother always said that anybody with McNance blood in 'em would skin you out of your eyeteeth before you knew they were looking in your mouth.

"Your grandmother," Emily said, laughing, "thinks of people as if they were a sort of cocktail. . . . Half and half Llewellyn is best, of course. . . . Mixed . . . by God? No, she would think the devil had more to do with *that* . . ."

Her voice went on brightly . . . in the dark old room where there was nothing else bright or colored except for the glass bowl of some sort of purple flowers . . . on a low table that she had drawn up level with their knees. She had finished her coffee and was lighting a cigarette. He watched her white hands manipulate the lighter that he had given her last Christmas while she gave him an account of the rest of the evening at the Parrishes'. Phyllis had been terribly impressed by the Parrishes. She had said *"been"* all evening. Nick and Mr. Parrish had seemed to get on awfully well. She had heard him asking a lot of questions about Penhally and the old neighborhood. He wanted to go out there some day. . . .

He listened with half his mind to what she was saying. There was very little chance, he thought, of his paying out that year, even if he got a good price for his tobacco. But they would get married in the fall, anyhow. She had set the first of October once as a tentative date. He would hold her to it. She was still talking about the Parrishes. . . . He caught one of her moving hands in his. "Did you like 'em?" he asked. "Did they seem to be nice people?"

His ring sparkled as she gestured with her free hand. "All right," she said, "a little overpowering. . . . You can just *feel* money all over the place. But the woman is perfectly beautiful, Chance . . . *perfectly beautiful!*"

3

The house was gray in the fading light and silent, except for the sound of negro voices back in the L. Aunt Dony, moving heavily about getting supper, was having her usual evening round with her grandson, Price—he never would get his coal up before dark! She had set a lamp on the table before the kitchen window. The light streamed far out over the grass and fell across the black trunk of the enormous old silver poplar that stood at the corner of the wing. Chance, sitting on the bench that was wedged between two of the great roots, looked up into the splotched branches that shone white even in this half dark. The old tree would be going soon. Already most of the top limbs were dead. He would have to send a man up there to saw them off. The tree was a menace, growing as close to the house as it did. The first March wind would send some of those rotten branches down to cave in the roof. The thing to do, of course, was to cut the tree down. But Miss Lucy would never stand for that. She was sentimental about this particular tree. Her grandfather Llewellyn, she said, always sat under it in summer to read. It would have been a good thing if the old gentleman had gotten up enough energy to walk a little farther down the slope. For as long as he could remember the boughs of that old poplar had been overhanging the roof, choking the gutters with its leaves so that by fall the cistern water was bitter

as garbroth. Miss Lucy herself remarked on it every year
and as regularly refused to let the tree be cut down. . . .

The supper bell pealed out from somewhere in the rear of
the house, faint at first, then more insistent. Chance stayed
the hand that had been about to roll a cigarette and sat, not
moving, while the sound grew. Presently Price came into
view around the corner of the house, reeling in spirals, the
arm that held the bell thrust out rigidly before him. Chance
waited until he had twirled himself into the calacanthus bush
before he picked him up and set him on his feet. The very
old spare man who had been pacing up and down in the
shrubbery came over and stood looking down at the little
negro. "Boy," he said, "are you ringing that bell or is it
ringing you?"

Chance laughed. "Come on, Cousin Cave," he said, "we
better go in."

They walked past the wing toward the house. Chance,
seeing a scraggy root protruding in the path, kicked at it and
found that it came away easily from the loose earth. An old
lilac root, no doubt. This part of the grounds was still called
"the lilac walk," but no lilacs had grown there since he could
remember. There was an old picture in the upstairs hall,
though: half a dozen young men and women in funny, old-
fashioned costumes, standing here at the side of the house
and the lilac bushes behind them with great, twisted trunks
as large as trees. Those old-fashioned shrubs, lilac, althea,
Japanese quince, died out that way. A place would be full
of them and then suddenly in a few years they would all be
gone. They said that lilacs would not die if you took the seed
pods off the bush every year, but of course nobody ever
thought to do that.

Ahead of him Cousin Cave paced, in his familiar attitude,
attenuated body bent a little forward, gnarled hands clasped
behind his back. But for his posture you might have taken

him for a young man. His figure moved agilely enough along the path. A crazy kind of lightness, but different from the usual shambling movements of the aged. Well, Cousin Cave took pains to keep himself young. He exercised every morning, winter and summer, before an open window and he could stand up and flick his extended palm with his toe, something he, Chance, could not do to save his neck.

They passed through the hall that still had the chill of winter in it, though the doors stayed open now all day long and turned into the dining room. Miss Lucy and Cousin Ellen were already at supper. The old lady looked up, her blue eyes fresh and alert in her weathered face.

"Chance," she said, "was there a circus in town to-day?"

Chance said that as far as he could see there was nobody in town but a lot of people trying to give away their tobacco. Looking at his grandmother he thought he had never seen her so cocky. It was the spring working in her. . . . She had been down at the big gate nailing up the sign that said "No passing through this place." Quarrelling, no doubt, with the Howards. She was saying now that they had come through —Virgil, Amalia, Cleo, every one of them—pretending they were going to the doctor. . . . Doctor nothing! There was a carnival in town, or at least a free medicine show. . . .

She called them Howards and they answered to the name, but they were not really Howards at all. The last male Howard was serving twenty years in the penitentiary for shooting Ben Folkestone. He himself had had a letter from him not long ago, saying that he thought it was about time something was done to get him out. Joe Howard was behind the times. He thought that because the Llewellyns still owned a lot of land they had influence with the governor, when as a matter of fact any merchant in Gloversville could have done as much for him. . . . Those people whom his grandmother called Howard were named Shutt. The Howard farm had been sold a half dozen times since he was grown. The people stayed a couple of years but they never could make their payments on the place, so the bank had to take it back. The people before the Shutts had been Stewart county folks, Gaithers, and before that there had been the Tarbots, and God knows how many others. But it didn't make any difference to her. She called them all Howard. . . . He wondered how she had had the vigor to prosecute the quarrel so long. The Howard farm had been cleared a little later than Penhally and the Howards—or their successors—had been taking the short cut through Penhally to the pike ever since. There had been no reason in the old days why they shouldn't. The original Howards had been clever people and had never abused the privilege. The people who lived there now were not as good people as the Howards. Still, they were not bad neighbors. It was not they themselves that were a nuisance. It was their company, people who drove out from town in hordes on Sunday and never stopped to shut a gate. . . .

She was through with the poor white folks now and was starting on the niggers. She didn't believe those new niggers were going to be any account. The woman had been up at the house this afternoon. She had a bad wrist and couldn't churn. She didn't see why some of those little niggers couldn't churn. There were at least a dozen of them.

Chance replied that Ed had six children. Four of them, boys, were old enough to work in the field. The two little girls were too young to be any use around the house. . . .

Mammy never could realize that niggers were free. She thought they ought to be glad to work for you for nothing. She would make them do it, too. Step out to the fence if she saw a strange nigger passing through the place: "You one of Uncle Henry Blake's grandchildren? . . . Well, just step over the fence and cut Dony some stovewood. . . ."

And the nigger would step every time. They fooled her,
though, by making a long circuit around the house. Kept his
fences worn down at two places just so they could get by
without her seeing them.

The only quarrel he had ever had with her had been about
negroes, years ago, when he first took over the management
of the farm. She had insisted in those days on passing on
the tenants. There had been innumerable rows, of course.
The Angel Gabriel couldn't have pleased her if he had remained white, and as for negroes it came down to it that the
only ones she could get along with were descendants of old
Penhally slaves. And there was not one of *them* that was
worth a damn. Well-dispositioned negroes, often with a
good deal of judgment, possessed, every one of them, of the
secret of handling Miss Lucy, but dead set against work.
Chester had missed paying out by two or three hundred dollars
for years. He had told him finally that he had better hunt another home. Chester had received the news in dignified silence and had found it convenient to call at the house during
the afternoon. The old lady had come right out to the field,
as mad as a wet hen! He would have given in, no doubt, if
she hadn't jumped him so quick. But something had risen
up in him at her first words. He had shouted at her—the
words had seemed to hang there in the air between them for
days afterward! Looking at her wrinkled, working face and
fiery eyes he had shouted:

"You think those niggers can't do any wrong because
they've got Llewellyn blood in them. . . . Their white blood
just makes 'em no-'count, I tell you. . . ."

She had turned around and was walking back toward the
house before he quit shouting. The reference to the white
blood took her right off her feet. She couldn't—even in a
rage—bring herself to admit that a negro could have white
blood, much less argue about it. He had taken an unfair

advantage of her. . . . He had been mighty young and in-
experienced then or he would never have gone at her like
that. It had been a good thing, though, to let her know
from the start just how things stood. She had actually
seemed to realize after that that she must limit herself a bit.
It hadn't been that way when his grandfather was alive. She
hadn't hesitated then to interfere with things out on the
farm. Once when he was a small boy she had come storming
out into the field and halted one of the binders, declaring that
the wheat wasn't ready to cut. His grandfather, kneeling in
the shade of a tree, engaged in repairing some part of another binder, had gone silently on with his work. Uncle
Isom, the foreman, had sat glancing from one to the other.
When the silence grew oppressive John Llewellyn had looked
up. "You better take out, Ise," he had said, "Miss Lucy here
thinks the wheat ain't ready to cut." He had not seemed distressed. There was actually a twinkle in his eye, though he
spoke gravely. He seemed to regard her most of the time
with a sort of grave humor. Sometimes at the table he would
lay his knife and fork down to sit staring at her abstractedly,
as if he were trying to figure out what it was all about. There
was some sort of compulsion on him that made him do her
least bidding . . . without argument. It was almost, Chance
thought, as if she had something on the man! The idea
amused him. His grandfather, he thought, was probably as
good a man, as really *good* a man as had ever lived in that
country. Brave, too—he had been a dashing raider—and
daring in his thought, for those days. A free thinker, he
called himself! Always reading Carlyle and Huxley and
Robert G. Ingersoll. Fiery, too, on occasion. Once, ruffled
by something a backwoods preacher had said, he got up and
left a church in the middle of the service, his wife on his
arm. The preacher had leaned over the pulpit to yell: "There
goes John Llewellyn and his wife—straight to hell!" The

old man had turned around to say "That's a damn lie" before he walked out of the church.

Strange what life the memory of those old times had in them! Some of those old codgers were as well known to him as if he had seen them walking around in the yard, as they had walked many a night: his own great-grandfather, Jeems, who wore his long white hair floating to his shoulders and was thought to be a bit touched in the head because he had spent his whole life perfecting a formula for fertilizer; Cousin Thyra, a well-connected old maid, who owned nothing but her carpet bag and silver snuff box and travelled about the neighborhood, staying as long at each place as it suited her; old Cousin Jessie, who had been the housekeeper here during old Uncle Nick's lifetime—he knew them all, as well as he knew any of the people who lived in the neighborhood now.

But an old house like this comes finally to have a life of its own. In its unstirring air jokes and sayings vibrate long after the people who uttered them are dead. His grandmother still reproved unruly children in the words of Aunt Phœbe, an old dining-room servant. Three admonitions she had had, each accompanied by a sharp dig of the elbow: "Whar you come frum?" "Ain't you never seen vittles before?" and "Ain't you white folks? Well, 'have like white folks then. . . ." An old lady, like his grandmother, utterly cynical as she seemed always to have been, could tell you a lot of interesting things about the old days, that is, if you were interested in hearing about your ancestors. . . .

. . . His grandmother was not interested in *her* ancestors. Life, for her, seemed to have stopped with the Civil War. She could not conceive of places more magnificent than Mayfield or Penhally in their palmy days, of a gentleman finer than her own father. Old Uncle Nick she had it in for, because he had gypped her father out of his property, but the mantle of those days had even begun to descend on his

shoulders. If you asked her questions about people farther
back than those days she said impatiently, "Oh, I d'know,"
and the thought in her mind was that it made no difference.
. . . She was prouder of her "blood," as she called it, than
any human being he had ever known. And of her name. If
a dog belonging to a Llewellyn ran through the yard of a
woman in the family way, the child, she said, was sure to be
called Llewellyn! . . . Llewellyn was the name of an ancient Welsh king. Llewellyns would tell you that they were
Welsh. Old Cousin Edward Woodford, who was a genealo-
gist, said that that was all nonsense. They were English.
"Beef," he would say—he had a French great-grandmother
—"beef, from brisket to heel!" Well, one Llewellyn *was*
very much like another, commonplace, of no interest to anybody except for the three hundred and fifty to a thousand
acres of land that they managed always to have. But holding
on to your land was, in this day and time, something of an
achievement! . . . The Penhally tract was as large as it
was because his old great-uncle Nicholas had been fanatical
about keeping the property together. He had believed in
primogeniture, entailment of property and all those old-fashioned ideas that had died out, even in Virginia, whence his
people had come long, before they died out in Kentucky.
The old gentleman, as a matter of fact, had stolen most of
his younger brother's inheritance, claiming that he, as the
elder son, was due to inherit all the land when younger
sons even in those days were inheriting an equal share of
their father's estates! Ralph Mayfield, as they called him,
had preferred to act the nobler part and had never done anything about it, and during the war Uncle Nick had somehow
gotten a mortgage on the rest of his land. . . . That very
probably was why a match had been made between Miss
Lucy and her cousin, his own grandfather. They were great
on property marrying property in those days, and indeed

Ralph Llewellyn's heirs might have gone to law about the matter. . . .

People in town thought that it was absurd that all the land should be entailed on Nick, who was not and never would be a farmer. Nick himself thought so. He persisted in regarding him, Chance, as half owner of Penhally. He did not care to have it that way, however. He could not go back and disentangle all those quarrels, and if the property was left to Nick it was left to Nick and that was all there was to it. It was unfortunate, though, that it was he and not Nick that had the love of the land. . . .

There was something about entailing property. It made a man feel that he was not really the owner, or at least that he had heavy obligations to his successor. He had noticed that about his own grandfather. He was sure that the old fellow—and he was the best man of the whole caboodle—had never regarded himself as owning a stick or stone. When he made any changes on the place, cut down a piece of timber or anything like that, he would say, 'I *think* that will be all right," reflectively, as if he were appealing to the verdict of somebody else. And he had made his son, Chance's father, entail the property on his eldest son as soon as he came of age. . . .

Cousin Cave was speaking in his deep, reverberating voice:

"Ye swains, invoke the powers who rule the sky,
For a moist summer and a winter dry. . . ."

Chance shook his head. "No," he said, "what we need now is a season. I want to start stripping tobacco this week." Cousin Cave thought that a farmer ought to have a knowledge of the classics. He was always quoting something at you, "Works and Days," or the Eclogues—Nick said that he thanked God the ancients had never written much about banking! Cousin Cave talked a lot about the constellations, too, Arcturus, the Pleiades, Orion—stormy Orion—and the Hyades. He followed a sort of cycle in his quotations. One about gelding the boar he came forth with at about the same time every spring. Emily said that Cousin Cave was really a very fine classical scholar. Certainly he had a vast amount of learning that would never be any good to anybody. He was supposed to have deranged his mind through over-application to his studies when he was a very young man. He was thought harmless, however, so he had never been confined in any institution. They had set him instead to teaching the young men of the neighborhood! Everybody agreed that he had been in his day a very fine teacher, in spite of his being what they called "eccentric." He had, as a matter of fact, been clean off his head all through the Civil War. When he came to himself, ten or fifteen years later, he was living at Penhally instead of Mayfield. It didn't make any difference to him where he lived, though, as long as he had his books. He had started only this spring on what he called the enterprise of his life: the translation of "The Bride of Lammermoor" into blank verse! Probably concocting some of the verses now. Sitting there staring at vacancy; exactly like a dog in a dead set. His "beautiful detachment" Emily called it. The old fellow had never had anything to detach himself from. Life had just gone on past him, without his knowing it was there. . . .

He tried to imagine Emily at Penhally, moving quick and light about the dark rooms. He had tried to give her some idea of what it would be like, painting everything in its darkest colors. She would not be permitted to have any hand in the housekeeping. She could not do over rooms or even rearrange furniture the way women liked to do. She would just have to live there, stepping around the old lady the way he and Cousin Ellen and Cousin Cave did. Emily had laughed at him. She loathed housekeeping, she said. She could not see why they wouldn't all get along beautifully. She was going to read Greek in the mornings with Cousin Cave, and in the afternoon she would ride over the place with Chance. She would even play euchre in the evenings with the old ladies if they wanted her to. . . . And they were not going to see anybody in Gloversville for at least four years. She was tired to death of everybody she knew there. . . .

They were getting up to leave the table. Cousin Cave had paced on ahead, through the hall and out on to the porch. He would be back in a minute reporting what stars were out. Chance followed the ladies down the long hall into the chamber—his grandmother's bedroom was still used in the old-fashioned way as the family sitting room. Dee had made the fire up brightly. The big lamp stood, wick turned down, on the little table that was the centre of the ring of rocking chairs. The old lady was arranging her chair as near the table as she could get it. Her eyes were failing, but she could still see to read every word in *The Courier-Journal*. The newspaper rustled crisply as she unfolded it. In a minute she would be reading the editorials aloud. . . .

4

The barn was full of people. Every hand on the place, man and woman, white and black, was stripping tobacco. The negroes sat up front, warming themselves in the frail spring sunshine. The half a dozen white families were gathered in the rear. Chance, making his way through the bulks, paused and took a leaf from the hands of a white child and drew it slowly through his fingers. "Your tobacco's in right good order, Pearl," he said, smiling.

The child's father, Mort Sully, looked up at the square of bright blue sky framed in the wide doorway. "A little more rain would put this tobacco in *fine* order," he said.

"Yes," Chance said, "we could stand a little more rain."

He stood, staring abstractedly at the whitewashed stone foundation that came up as high as his head. This barn—the old barn it was called, because it was the first barn built on the place—was the only one that had a stone foundation. They had built them like that very often in the old days. The tobacco cured in this barn was usually the best on the place—the rocks kept an even temperature. He climbed up on one of the logs that jutted out above the heads of the strippers and taking a twist of tobacco out of his pocket crumbled the leaf into his palm. The corncob pipe that he had thought lost was stuck there between the rocks. He poured the crumbled leaf into it and lit it. All around him there was a clatter of talk and the occasional high laughter of women and children. Sully and the other white tenants had brought their whole families to help strip. The women idled away a good deal of time gossiping. They rarely made more than seventy-five cents a day; but some of the young girls did better than that. Rob Boulder's fourteen-year-old daughter, whose thin, dirty hands moved steadily there below him, always made as much as a dollar a day.

The new white man, Charley Graves, kept talking. He was asking now if they had ever had a barn burned on this place. He had been living at Mister Clint Stokes' place when his barn burned. Bran-new sixty-acre barn, full of tobacco. They had just started firing. He himself had been in town and was starting home late at night when he caught sight of the blaze from the top of Spring Creek hill. Man, it was a sight! Looked like the whole country was going up in flames. He had run his mules all the way from Spring Creek to the church and when he got there that barn was nothing but a big ball of fire. Old Mister Stokes just kept walking around and crying: "All my tobacco! . . . All my tobacco!"

He spat into the sawdust. "But it warn't all his tobacco," he said with a sly smile. "I had fifteen hundred pounds of tobacco in that barn and my brother Jim and his boys had two thousand. It was just before the war, too, when tobacco was way up yonder."

Chance said that he remembered the fire very well. They had stood on the upstairs porch at Penhally to watch the flames shoot up over the woods. There warn't any sense in barns burning up full of tobacco. Ninety-nine times out of a hundred it was just pure carelessness. His grandfather, old Mister Jack Llewellyn, hardly ever came around the house when he was firing tobacco. No matter how many men he had on the place or how much judgment they had, he stayed right at the barns. He remembered once when he was a kid they had had fires going in six barns. His grandfather and an old white man that he had for overseer had gone the rounds from barn to barn all night, for going on five weeks.

Charley said that it didn't look like people fired tobacco as long as they used to. Forty days, his old daddy used to say, forty days or you might just as well never put no fire to it. . . . He launched into a story of the goings on of the night riders in Trigg County. They had set fire to four barns right there in one neighborhood. No telling how many plant beds they had scraped. The man that had been the captain was still living right there on the same place. Everybody knew who he was. . . .

The monologue flowed on slowly. Under the man's lean, clever fingers the pile of tobacco stalks had grown, as high now as his shoulders. He caught up a tobacco stick and thrust the sticks to right and left, then fell to stripping again. A beam of sunlight penetrating through some aperture in the roof fell slanting across the levelled pile of brown stalks. Chance watched the dust motes dancing in it and realized, oddly stirred, that that was one of the first memories he had

in life: an arrow of golden light falling across piled brown
tobacco stalks and himself watching the whirling parti-col-
ored motes, in this same barn. He must have been a very
small child. He had had hold of somebody's hand. His
grandfather's, no doubt. . . .

It would have been when he first came up here to live, just
after his father's death. . . . He remembered perfectly the
day his father was killed. He and Nick had been playing in
the yard when the men drove up to the door, a countryman
driving, the other two men sitting in the bed of the spring
wagon. Both children had known at once that something had
happened. He remembered standing still in the yard while
there went through him the sharp thrill of pleasure with
which children greet any catastrophe. Nick had gone running to the house, calling "Mama!" His mother had sat
down on the side of the bed, saying, "Frank!" with a kind of
groan.

Later, he had tried to recall that morning. In the late fall
it had been because the two friends had driven far out into
the country to shoot birds . . . but he had no very clear
memory of the day or of his father, except that he was a tall
man—he must have been thin, too—and spoke always teas-
ingly to children. But he could see now the face of his father's friend, Dick Applegate: a sandy-haired man, with a
drooping moustache, his face fixed and hard, against the light
from the window. His eyes had been on the soft felt hat
that went round and round in his hands, while he said that
he didn't know how it had happened, that he had handled
fire arms all his life. . . . He had said that over and over
to somebody who had not answered. An old negro woman
had grunted in a corner. . . .

His father had shot himself! . . . He did not know why
he had not realized it before. . . . And poor Dick Applegate had agonized, trying to make everybody believe that he

had held his gun carelessly getting over a fence. He had
perhaps succeeded at the time. A whole countryside will
connive for a while at some pretense like that, and then little
by little over a stretch of years the truth will seep out, like
water rising in marshy ground, until finally people having
no need of the pretense abandon it. . . . Old Mr. Laban
who had been shot by one of the slaves he had mistreated had
had the biggest funeral ever seen in the county, but his son
when he showed signs of following in his father's footsteps
had been ridden over Spring Creek hill one night on a
rail. . . .

A negro man was at his elbow, saying that he had just
been down to the new barn. The tobacco warn't in order yet
by any manner of means.

"All right," Chance said, "I expect we'll get a rain now in
a day or two. . . ."

He wondered why his father had shot himself. An only
child, heir to what was even in those bad times a handsome
inheritance, happily married—his father and mother had run
off to get married; they must have been devoted lovers—it
would seem that he had every incentive to live. More incentive, for instance, than *his* father, Chance's grandfather. A
Confederate soldier coming home from the war had had a
devil of a time. It would seem that they had little to live for,
in public or private life. People had felt themselves more
a part of the whole country then, or at least they were more
politically minded. His grandfather, he knew, had felt a
keen humiliation at being deprived of his civil rights. The
East Tennesseean, Parson Brownlow, had said in a public
speech that he would concede to ex-Confederates only two
rights: one to be hung in this world, the other to be damned
in the next. His grandfather used to quote that, with fire
in his eye. It had pretty near killed the old fellow not to be
allowed to vote. In his later years he had referred humor-

ously to that period of his life as "the time when Uncle Isom
was doing my voting. . . ." He wondered if his grandfather
would care so much about voting if he were alive to-day.
. . . He himself would not give a damn if they took his
vote away from him for the rest of his enduring life. He
was twenty-seven years old and had voted only once, the
straight Democratic ticket, of course. . . .

He leaned his head back against the planking and half
closed his eyes. His head felt heavy—and no wonder! It
had been well after two o'clock when he got home last night.
They had gone to Nick's and Phyllis' for dinner. He had
expected a party, but there had been nobody there but himself and Emily and the Parrishes.

It was strange how you could never form any conclusion
from what women said. It was not that they did not know
what they were talking about, but you never drew the right
conclusions. Emily had told him the Parrish woman was
beautiful. "Perfectly beautiful," she had said and had added
something about an overpowering display of wealth. He was
sure she had used the word "overpowering." His imagination had therefore pictured Mrs. Parrish as some voluptuous
creature; as floridly handsome, say, as Mrs. Offenbach, the
wife of the German tobacconist. He had even pictured the
old Miller house as it must have been transformed under her
hands; full of Oriental rugs and Italian refectory tables. He
knew a woman in Memphis who had had the whole dining
room, tapestries, wood work and all, ripped out of some mon-
astery in Italy and inserted in her new house. But the Parrish woman had turned out not to be like that. A quiet woman, rather tall, with a pale face and pale-brown hair. Not
much color about her anywhere, except in her eyes, which
were golden—like a setter dog's.

It turned out that Parrish didn't play bridge, so after dinner they had just sat around talking. The talk had fallen on

cities and places that he did not know and had no interest
in, and he had taken no part in it. Sitting there beside Emily
and yet not able to touch her, even to take her hand, he had
deliberately forced his thoughts into another channel. He
had come out of his absorption to find that Douglas Parrish
had moved over and sat down beside him. A low-voiced man,
Parrish, around fifty, rather handsome and wholly agreeable.
He had asked a great many questions about this or that cousin, displaying a knowledge of the family connection that
was surprising. He had wondered how the man happened
to have all that stuff in his head. He himself, through long
association with older members of the family, had a rough
outline of the Llewellyn-Crenfrew-Allard connection in his
mind. But he had acquired it bit by bit as occasion arose. If
you wondered, for instance, how a certain cousin came to be
in possession of his land, you asked your grandmother whom
Cousin Tom Allard had married. You were then told, not
only of the marriage of Cousin Tom, but of the marriages
of his six brothers and four sisters and, as they said, their
issue. And some of it stuck in your head, so that you found
yourself on occasion correcting people who were not quite
sure whether their own great-grandmother was a Crenfrew
or an Allard.

He had had a little run in with Phyllis during the evening.
Parrish had been asking about the old graveyard and some of
the people who were buried there. That graveyard was a
sore subject with Phyllis. She resented the fact that almost
all of the members of the enormous family connection kept
on burying their dead there, just as they had done in the
old times, while the upkeep of the whole thing fell on Nick
as the owner of Penhally. She had actually tried to get Nick
to send out a circular letter once asking them to subscribe
so much a head for their dead! Nick had had too much
sense to do that. Last night he, Chance, had suddenly found

himself pointing out to her that Nick wasn't losing money
on that graveyard; he had advised her to look up the will.
Old Uncle Nick had left John Llewellyn more money than
he had left Robert as a consideration for keeping up the family graveyard. Considering that a good part of that money
had been stolen—there was really no other way to look at it
—from Ralph Llewellyn and his heirs, Nick might well afford to keep the graveyard up, to salve his conscience, if
nothing else!

Phyllis had been rather taken aback. Nick had laughed
heartily. It was a fact, he said. He had had occasion to go
over the will a few years ago. It was all set down there.
There was also something about offering asylum to infirm
and dependent kinsmen and kinswomen. . . . Giles Llewellyn now, who made the big road his home and was subject to
epileptic fits—weren't they obliged morally—if not legally
—to take him in? Phyllis had shrieked out at the idea.

The talk had fallen then on pioneer times in Tennessee
and Kentucky. Parrish seemed to be a good deal of an
antiquarian. He had been engaged for years, he said, on a
history of the Cherokee nation. He hoped to have leisure
to finish it now that he had retired from business. Toward
eleven o'clock they had all gone over to the old Miller place to
see some books and things that Parrish had.

They had had to halt the cars at the foot of the hill and
go up to the house the side way. The Parrishes had bought
up the little negro settlement—Vinegar Bottom it was called
—that had fringed all that side of the hill. They had razed
the cabins and were going to level the whole thing with road
machines, but at present you couldn't get over it in a car.

There was a lot of shrubbery higher up on the slope and
the grounds around the house were laid out formally, but
they hadn't done much to the house inside. And there were
no refectory tables or tapestries—a lot of plain old furniture,

instead, that they might have bought around here. And in one of the big rooms upstairs Parrish had a collection of miscellaneous articles from pioneer times. None of them seemed very remarkable: a set of gourd dippers and a set of gourd dishes, carved and stained with pokeberry juice; old smoke-house keys; the flat rock, even, from some South Carolina smoke house. He had told the man that he ought to come out to Penhally. The rock that they built their smoke-house fires on had been there ever since the house itself was built, 'way back yonder. He could just as easy get another one from the field and Parrish could have that gem for his collection.

Parrish had laughed and said that he would like to come out some time soon. He had never seen Penhally, but he had heard about it all his life. All the stories his mother used to tell him when he was a little boy centred about Penhally—or Mayfield. Chance had been surprised to find that Parrish was closer kin than he had thought he was. Parrish's mother, Alice Blair, had been second cousin to both his grandmother and his grandfather. She had also been his grandmother's sister-in-law. His grandmother had told him that, rather tersely, when he was asking where these people came in the connection. This Alice Blair seemed to have been a great belle in ante-bellum days. He seemed to have heard that his own grandfather had been in love with her. . . . Perhaps that was why Miss Lucy had not expressed any wish to see Alice Blair's son!

He had caught himself feeling rather sorry for Parrish. The fellow was evidently tired out, wanting only to settle down among his Indian relics and hominy mortars, with the pretense of writing a book to keep him occupied. But he had married a young and beautiful woman. He wouldn't get to settle down anywhere very long.

In the car going home Phyllis had raved about Joan Parrish, her looks, the way she walked, the dress she had on.

"Patou," Emily said shortly. She had suddenly grown very angry. "They have no business to do that," she said. "No business in the world. . . ."

"Do what?" Nick asked.

Emily had sat up very tense and straight. "Turn our niggers out of their house and home," she said.

Nick said that the niggers didn't have to sell and that he couldn't see what they had to complain of if the Parrishes had given them a good price for their property.

Emily, who was by that time very angry, said that he didn't know what he was talking about. It turned out that she had been all week trying to comfort their washwoman, Keziah. Keziah, a woman of fifty, had foolishly given her son a deed to her cabin and two acres. He had sold the place over her head. She had had to go to live in a house on Baseball Hill, but she sat in the Kinloe kitchen for two or three hours every day, talking about a peach tree that she had had in her back yard—a "Stump of the World." It had been for years the wonder of all Vinegar Bottom, but had disappeared now under the machines that were levelling all that ground. . . .

5

Chance had let the screen door swing to behind him. The old pointer had not been able to get into the hall, so he was lying propped against the door, cocking an eye open occasionally to see if it wasn't time for Chance to come back.

Emily stooped down beside him and ran her hand over his ribs. "Dog . . ." she said. "Dog . . . you like to live here, dog?"

The dog groaned softly and turning over pawed at the air. Emily buried her hand in the loose folds of his throat and stared over his body into the dark hall. A ray of sunlight from the open doorway fell on the steel engraving that hung just inside the parlor door: Lee and Jackson, composed, heroic, their chargers' tails rippling, looking courteously past each other into the night. And from above the parlor mantel a pale-faced woman in a lace cap stared steadily at *them*. She had thought when she was a child, brought here to visit, that that woman in life must have had some quarrel with the Confederate generals! But she had been born a hundred years before the Civil War and had never seen America. A Scotchwoman who had married one of Chance's great-grand-fathers and had died at sea. The devoted widower had had the portrait painted from a miniature . . . a few months before marrying his second wife. . . .

She gave the dog a little push and getting to her feet walked to the edge of the porch. The poplar branches were everywhere black about the house, but beyond them there was a shimmer of bright green: wheat or oats or something in those fields that went away from here to the river. There were six of those fields and every one had a name: the hedge field, because of the Osage orange hedge that ran along two sides of it; the track field where the old race track had been, and one that had been called simply the big field, ever since anybody could remember. Chance had told her the names of all of them one time. He had shown her, too, how beauti-fully the land lay in those fields, sloping away ever so slightly from the slight eminence on which the house stood. They had built the house on this little rise because it was the best they could do on this level land for a hill, and old-fash-ioned people liked to build their houses high, so they could sit on the front porch and look over their land. You could not see two feet from this porch in the summer time, when the leaves closed the house in, but now with the branches bare the whole west end of the farm was spread out before you: all those fields, flat as a checker board, the broad patches of green alternating with the red brown of freshly plowed earth until you came to the dark line of trees that marked the river. . . .

That day last summer when he had stood there beside her, pointing out the different fields, she had understood, for the first time, really how he felt about this place. He had no sentimental feeling about the house, or about the fact that his people had lived here for several generations. It was the land he loved, the very particles of the red clay. It was some special kind of red clay—she could not even remember the name now. Only two per cent of the earth's surface was like that, Chance said. He was proud of the fact that the Llewellyns had their share of it! Once, driving to town along the Ridge road, he had pointed out to her where the geological formation changed, where the good land gave out and the bad land began. You could see—even *she* could see —that the land was different. On one side of that invisible line red clay and on the other a lighter clay with little pieces of rock crusted in it. Conglomerate, he had called it . . . scornfully.

The murmur of voices that had been in the hall had died away. Chance and Mrs. Parrish had come out of the dining room and were going now out on to the back porch. That thudding sound was Chance lifting the double doors that covered the cellar stairs. He would take her down into the cellar and show her where they had hidden the horses during the Civil War and the little square, boarded-up room where old Uncle Nick had kept sixteen shot guns hanging on pegs, ready for the visit of the James boys. His preparations had all been useless. They had found him alone in the house one night and had taken him out and strung him up to a tree on the lawn. But the old man had loved his money better than his life; he had protested with what he must have thought was his last breath that the money was in a bank in Louisville, when all the time it was buried in the woods two or three miles from the house. Chance's uncle and an old negro man had buried it at night, without even a lantern to light them by, and somebody going through the woods had cut down the twin saplings that they had picked to mark the place. They had had to dig all over that timber land before they found the money! . . . Chance would be telling Mrs. Parrish all this. It would take him several more minutes yet, because she wouldn't know who the James boys were. He would explain that too, with grave patience. All the time she would be looking at him out of golden, expressionless eyes. . . .

When they had come up to the barn a few minutes ago, Chance had apologized because the ladies of the family were not at home. Mrs. Parrish, with one of her indolent smiles, had said:

"We want to see the house. . . ."

Chance had been rather taken aback by that. He had given her, Emily, a startled glance. She kept her face perfectly expressionless, and after a second he turned like an obedient little boy and led them through the orchard and on up to the house. He took Mrs. Parrish at her word! He was showing her the entire house, even opening the door of one of the cuddies! Parrish had brightened at the sight of those cuddies. He wanted dreadfully to get in there and rummage about among the old newspapers and all the other oddments, but Mrs. Parrish said, "Oh, Douglas, . . . some other time, . . ." and he reluctantly let the door swing to.

Going down the hall he confided to Emily that it was a mistake not to go over things like that. It was astounding the way people would stick things around . . . in old shoes, bundles of old newspapers, old rags. . . . He had found an important letter regarding the lost state of Franklin in an old shoe in North Carolina. . . . An old *shoe!* . . . Time, too, was valuable in these matters. Once, driving to Mississippi from New York on the trail of some old letters, he had gotten very tired and had stopped to spend the night at a hotel instead of reaching the destination that he had planned to reach that night. When he got there early the next morning the smoke of those letters was still in the air. The smoke! The wife of the man who owned them had had a fancy that morning to go over all the old trunks in her attic. She had hay fever badly and the dust had been too much for her, so she just burned them all up. . . . Of course, the friend who put him on the trail of the letters had not told the woman that they were valuable. You had to be wary about those things . . . extremely wary. . . . But if he had only not stopped that night in Corinth!

She had thought that it was perhaps best for him not to dwell on that too long, so she had pointed out to him in the upper hall a case of old books. He stiffened at the sight of them, like a dog making a point, and then went fumbling along the shelves, flicking the pages of one book and then putting it up to take down another. She had spoken to him once or twice, but he had not seemed to hear her. After a little she came on downstairs and out into the sunshine. . . .

The voices had come back into the hall again. The curve of the stairway hid Chance and Mrs. Parrish from her sight, but she knew where they stood. She even knew what they were looking at; a curiosity that had stopped in this dark corner under the stairs on its way to the attic: a pyramid formed of miniature tobacco hogsheads, the whole enclosed in a bell glass and resting on a little rosewood stand. It represented eighty thousand pounds of tobacco that some horse had won in a race. The horse's picture hung on the wall above: Anne of Geierstein, or was it Rowena? The old gentleman here had named his horses out of Scott's novels, while old General Harding, in Nashville, had claimed the

Greek alphabet for his. The picture had an inscription on it: "Too fleet for the fast and too stout for the strong," and something else, about falling outside the distance. Somebody—the eccentric old uncle, no doubt—had worn mourning for the mare when she died. . . .

Joan Parrish was crazy about horses. It was amusing, riding out from town to see that aloof, disinterested look slide occasionally from her face, usually at the sight of some colts in a pasture. She would be disappointed in the colts, but she would stop to look at them every time. Emily had told her that she need not expect to find any good horses in this part of the country now. The horse that she herself was riding was as good a saddle horse as you could find in the county, five-gaited, smooth enough, and well made, but nothing extra in the way of breeding. Joan thought this a shocking state of affairs. She spoke—with something like animation—for five, ten, minutes on how this could all be remedied. The importation of a few good sires and so on. It was unfortunate, too, that there was no hunt club. She missed the riding. . . .

Emily wondered why she stayed in Gloversville. Still, she had to be somewhere, and it was perhaps difficult to choose a place to go to when you had all the world before you. And Parrish had his Cherokees or Chickasaws. . . . She was energetic under all that languor. She had completely made over the old Miller place, in three weeks. People in Gloversville were still talking about that, in an awed way, and they would drive out there just to see what all she had done. "Well, well, and who would think this was the old Miller place!" . . . There was something in the air of the South that stimulated Eastern women! If she stayed here long enough she would have to do something about Gloversville at large . . . organize a hunt club, perhaps. . . . Well, no matter what she did, they would all follow her like sheep.

. . . And Phyllis Llewellyn would be the first sheep over the
fence. . . .

Phyllis had gotten her into bringing these people out here,
making an engagement to ride out with them, and then going
to bed at the last minute with one of her headaches. She
had not been able to think quickly enough to get out of it.
She and Joan had started out right after lunch, riding along the
river road. Parrish, who was never known to mount a horse,
had followed an hour later in the car, and had passed them at
the top of Church Hill. She had hallooed him back to show
him the grave of Alex Wald, a free trapper who had been
killed by his Chickasaws. Standing there by the big rock
that was supposed to mark the grave, he had made them
quite a little speech on the Chickasaws, their habits in the
council house and on the warpath, the very great differences
between them and the Cherokees, the even greater differences between them and the Shawnees. She rather liked
listening to him. . . .

He had come down the stairs and was stepping out on to
the porch now, a slight, gray-haired man in summer flannels,
three calf-bound volumes under his arms, a mouldy green
one sticking out of his pocket. He was having for a moment
difficulty in remembering who she was and was deciding that
it didn't matter.

"I have no doubt Chauncey will lend me these books," he
said. "Remind me to speak to him about it."

She nodded. He ought, really, to have his secretary attached to him when he went abroad, as ants—or is it butter-
flies that have antennæ? He was rather like an elderly butterfly, mauve, say, hovering from flower to flower. Rubbing
his thinning hair now, he said that he would like to see the
graveyard.

"I have seen the graveyard in the Northern Neck and the
one in King and Queen, and now I would like to see this one
here in the west."

"The west," he called it as if he were an eighteenth-century man contemplating the continent from the banks of the James! He ought to have been born in the latter half of the eighteenth century. He would have had enough adventure in him to come to Virginia—under adequate patronage —and would have spent his days in remote corners of some colonial house, instructing young boys in the classics, and enlivening dull family dinners with tales of Oxford or Cambridge—no, it would be Edinboro that he came from. He was a sort of reincarnation of that old Parson Douglas whom the king had sent out to the colonies. Old Parson Douglas had been poor as a dog. Marrying into the family he had left the Llewellyns nothing but Douglas for a middle name. . . . But this man was many times a millionaire, with his nicotine plants and his button factories or whatever they were. They said he could not possibly spend his income, no matter how hard he tried. That, no doubt, was what gave Joan Parrish those faint, hard lines about the mouth. It hadn't affected Parrish that way. He was rich enough to delegate responsibility, and in his personal life he had escaped into a world where important letters were found in old shoes, or obscure Indian tribes made treaties with all the dignity of nations. But it was harder on the woman. She had, one way or another, to live with the money. . . .

She turned her head and called into the dark hall, "Chance . . . we want to see the graveyard. . . ."

They were coming down the hall. Chance, striding along beside Mrs. Parrish, was still telling ancient anecdotes of the turf, how a Penhally jockey, accused by Andrew Jackson of riding foul, had spat tobacco juice into the general's eye. The wind had been blowing hard; the general had accepted the apology of all concerned, but Charles Llewellyn had given the little negro a new suit of clothes when he got him home—the Llewellyns all detested Andrew Jackson. Banty

Ed that nigger had been called, a pigmy; he had lived to be
nearly a hundred years old. Some of his dwarfish descendants were still here on the place. . . . Chance was chuck-
ling over his own story. Mrs. Parrish's lashes, drooping,
made the usual shadowy line across her cheek; there was a
very faint set smile on her mouth. If she raised her lids
now, her eyes would be perfectly expressionless. She was
as blank-eyed as any Greek statue, but the Greeks had
never introduced eyes of pure gold into marble faces.

They had come out from the dark hall into the sunlight
that lay in frail wavering bars on the gray floor. "The graveyard . . ." Chance said and motioned them to the path
around the west side of the house. Ragged clumps of box
were all about here, the remains of what had once been a
labyrinth of winding walks. They would never restore the
walks, but they would never cut the ragged shrubbery down
either. She laid her hand on Chance's arm.

"Chance, show 'em where old Uncle Nick shot the Yankee
soldier."

He had gone a little way down the slope and was stepping
off feet from some imaginary landmark. "It was right here,"
he said, "just about here. The old fence ran along here and
they said it was right in the corner of that fence. . . ."

Emily's own laugh sounded unpleasantly in her ears. "He
fell face forward," she said, "into a pot of boiling water."

Mrs. Parrish's perfectly shaped brows drew together
faintly. "But that was terrible!"

"Well," Emily said, "the soldier was insulting the overseer's wife, and the old gentleman was very irascible. And
he had had to sit there all morning watching them haul his
corn off. It was really a good thing. They behaved beauti-
fully after that. The officer at the fort sent old Uncle Nick
his compliments and said that if any more of them acted like
that he hoped he'd shoot them too."

Parrish asked if the soldier were buried in the graveyard.

"No," Emily said before Chance could answer. "They wouldn't bury him here. He was just a Yankee."

The other two had gone on ahead. Chance was holding the gate open, his eyes fixed on hers in a sort of wonderment.

She said between her teeth: "I *detest* rich people!"

The gate had swung to, with a little clanking of the iron weight that held it in place. Chance was walking on, silently. He couldn't understand why she had said a thing like that. Well, she didn't know herself. Except that she couldn't stand these people. She really couldn't *stand* them! . . .

Very old people—people who had been living while the war was going on—did not feel as she did. They said that the war was over and we were all one country now! But she had always been fiercely Confederate. They had left her too much in the library when she was a little girl, with her grandfather. He had two enormous calf-bound volumes of the "Rise and Fall of the Confederate Government" that he read and read. . . . There was a steel engraving on the wall just above his arm chair: "The fall of the Gallant Pelham." . . . And on the street just back of the house Father Ryan had written "The Conquered Banner." "The gall*ant* hosts," her grandfather said when he read it to her, "the gall*ant* hosts are shattered, over *whom* it floated high. . . ." His voice would break when he came to that and she would cry, too, sitting on an ottoman beside him. . . . They had left her with him so much because her mother had headaches and the cook didn't like children. . . . But you cannot let a little girl spend all her time reciting Father Ryan with Confederate veterans without having her turn out a little queer. . . .

Once, in a book-collector's apartment on the rue Delambre she had found an anthology of Civil War verse and had sat down and read all those poems. A man who wrote had come and sat on the arm of her chair, explaining how bad each one was. She had said she reckoned they were rotten, all right, but still they made you have that catch in the throat. He had said that they didn't affect him that way. It was because she was one of the defeated. They cried easily. . . .

It was probably that. But she couldn't stand these people. She really couldn't stand them! In another minute she would scream something insulting at that horrible woman, or bash Parrish's sedate gray hat over his eyes. . . . *We want to see the house!* . . . Chance didn't even know that they were patronizing him! But Chance was really much more arrogant than she was, in his old-fashioned country way. He was nice to everybody, the whole world, out of an immense condescension. All those thousands of people who couldn't possibly be Chance Llewellyn—he had to make it up to them some way! Oh, he was darling . . . darling. . . . She adored him!

They had come out from the narrow path into the centre of the enclosure. The graveyard was smaller than she had remembered it, the gravestones sunk lower in the ground and darker with mould. That big, round rock in the middle was the horse block that the old Virginia grandfather had had placed there for his monument. He had caused a weeping-willow tree to be planted, too, for a double reminder. It dominated the whole graveyard with its ragged trunk and airy, drooping branches that were already putting out pale yellow feathers of leaves. The periwinkle was as yet only dark tendrils over the young grass. By summer it would be a thick mass. You would not venture in here so lightly then: what negroes called a snaky place. Periwinkle must feed well on the dead. You found it always in old graveyards.

She walked a little way off the path, and sitting down on the grass lit a cigarette. The three others had progressed to the centre of the graveyard. Parrish was stooping along, pushing the vines from off one of the flat sunken stones.

Joan, standing beside him, let her eyes rest for a second on
the inscription that he was uncovering and then glanced away.
Her right hand, going into her pocket, brought out a cigarette
case. Chance struck a match on the stone and lighted her
cigarette. She thanked him with a faint smile.

Parrish was reading the inscription that was carved into
the horse block.

"Your great-great-grandfather," he said, looking at Chance.

"I reckon so," Chance said. "It's the one they called
Frank of Orange."

They had called him Frank of Orange to distinguish him
from another Frank Llewellyn. His portrait hung in the
lower hall. A dark face, lean, but full-lipped, and with a
curious light in the eyes. He had been sixty years old when
he died, but he had been a young man when he set out from
Virginia, with his wife—his second wife—his slaves, and his
two children. The baby had travelled in a wagon in its
nurse's arms; the little boy had ridden beside the white
overseer—she had heard Chance say that the Owenses in
Gloversville were descendants of that man—but the man and
the woman had ridden horseback ahead of their train. The
Church Hill road that ran through this place was part of the
old Wilderness Trail. They would have come along that on
their way to the old Crenfrew place. The fields all around,
even the hill on which this house stood, would have been deep
woods: hickory and elm and oak and gum and maple. They
would not have known where their land was until they got to
the Crenfrew place, but they would have turned in their
saddles to look back at this hill, not knowing that it was here
that they would live and some day be buried. . . .

It was strange how little people left for reminders of
themselves when they died, or if anything survived over a
long period, it was accidentally. Francis Llewellyn, choosing
his horse block for his monument, had perpetuated only the

fact that he was eccentric—or ostentatiously simple in his tastes. And there was somewhere about the house the powder horn that he had worn slung about him on the trip out from Virginia. There was even in an old desk a letter that he had written when he was a student at the University of Edinboro, saying that a young fellow named Napoleon was kicking up quite a fuss in this part of the world, but that most people thought he wouldn't amount to much. . . . But these things, surviving accidentally, told you little of the man. The face in the picture was arrogant, with that glint in the dark eyes. A younger son, with no patrimony, he had gone off into the wilderness in search of the land he had not inherited, and all the people who had lived and died and been buried on this hill had come into being through the stirrings of this one man's pride. . . .

They had finished with the tombstones on the other side and were coming back to the path, Parrish carefully putting back in his pocket the notebook in which he had noted down whatever dates and facts that were not stored in his extraordinary memory. Chance was walking beside Joan. She was flicking with her crop at the grass that grew beside the path. An extraordinarily beautiful woman, longer legged in riding breeches than you would have thought, but graceful in every movement. She was bending ever so little toward Chance as he talked, a delicate flattery she did not accord every man, but there was still that air about her of having the cosmos to choose from. The sun, declining, sent their shadows monstrously before them over the grass. The gigantic woman's hand might have been swinging out to uproot the big sugar tree, or demolish that whole row of ragged cedars. . . .

6

The telephone bell had stopped ringing. Oscar had at last come from the recesses of the back porch to answer it. He stood in the doorway now, bending a little forward from the hips, to give the impression of arrested flight.

"Miz Llewellyn calling," he said. "She want to know if you and Mister Pa'ish kin come out to the club."

Joan glanced at her husband. "Do you want to go?" she asked.

He had put his pencil down and was looking from her to Oscar, abstractedly. "The club . . .?" he said.

"It's Phyllis Llewellyn," she told him, "and Nick. They're out at the country club . . . playing bridge. That Mrs. Fosbie is with them, probably. . . . And a very drunk young man."

"A drunk young man . . ." he repeated.

"They change him every time," she said, "but they always have at least one."

He seemed to think the matter was settled. He had taken his pencil up and was writing again. Oscar was still standing there, looking at her. His eyeballs, that were yellow and smokily veined, gleamed in the light as he turned his head from side to side. He wanted to get back to the vine-shaded porch of the servants' house, where he was no doubt engaged in the seduction of that pretty yellow maid that she had gotten from Mrs. Robbins. Phyllis Llewellyn said that if you once got used to negro servants, you couldn't bear to have any other kind around you. But she didn't believe that she would ever get used to Oscar. His attention, when he gave you any attention, was too insistent. She could recall having had in the course of her whole life only one servant with a personality as obtrusive—a thin-faced Irishman who had landed finally in the penitentiary.

She made a sharp gesture of dismissal.

"Tell them that I'm ill," she said. "In bed. With a headache. Mr. Parrish doesn't think he'd better leave me."

Oscar's footsteps died away softly in the hall. He *was*

nearly noiseless, if he was dilatory. Douglas had closed his notebook and was spreading his map out on the table: a map of this country when it was inhabited by the Indians, a rather pretty thing, with criss-crosses and tiny, flying wings to mark the places where cane and wild turkeys had been abundant, and Indian signs for running water. He had had it made in Louisville. They had stayed there a whole month while the young artist was finishing it. Douglas had sat beside him most of the time, saying over names of places. Some of them had been beautiful, some merely strange: Tumbling Run, King and Queen Bluff, Sequatchie, Skillet Fork. . . .

She got up and began walking about the room. She was glad he had refused to go. She really couldn't have stood that place to-night. Saturday night. It would be full of people . . . with high, insistent Southern voices. They were really doing something to her nerves, those voices. . . . She must not see quite so much of these people for a while . . . or have some other people down. The Crosleighs would come if she asked them. But perhaps she had better not. Dan Crosleigh would begin being wearisome again. She had an idea—it seemed absurd—but she really fancied that it annoyed Douglas to see him mooning about the place the way he invariably did. It would be a godsend to Mona, of course, to have him off her hands a little, but she had to think of Douglas first. She had promised him this year— this whole year—among his Tumbling Runs and King and Queen Bluffs and she would stick it out. . . . But she had been seeing too many people lately. Nick Llewellyn wasn't so bad, or that dark nervous girl, and she quite liked the young farmer, but Mrs. Llewellyn, striving so earnestly to be *mondaine,* was wearisome . . . wearisome. . . . The wo- man's face had actually been coming before her at night when she couldn't sleep: the small, tilted nose, the big brown eyes set too close together and all that blond hair wound about her head. . . . *Why* did they all do their hair exactly the same way? . . . *Pour tout le monde, non . . . mais pour Madame . . . AhhHH!* Charles would say and press your head ever so gently between his long, supple fingers. His face came before her sometimes at night, too, and the face of that chauffeur they had borrowed from the Reynoldses, the one who stole two fur coats and all of Douglas' razors . . . faces and faces of quite unremarkable people—half the time she couldn't even call their names. . . .

She walked through the hall and out on to the porch. The light from the tall windows fell before her, over the wide terrace. The magnolia leaves shone in it, stiffly, as if they had been varnished, and beneath them the minute flowers of some trailing shrub glimmered palely. She walked to the end of the terrace. From here she could look down over the long slope of lawn, across the little valley that they called "Vinegar Bottom" to where on the opposite slope the lights of the town were sprinkled. It made a pleasing vista at night, but in the daylight the eye was arrested at the end of the drive by a broad band of red clay. They were dragging that ground now with some sort of road machine that the young contractor had hired from the county. And to-morrow they would start the trucks out into the country for turf. By the end of the week that whole expanse would be green sod. The place would be much improved. There would be nothing then to break the really lovely line of that long slope. A few more trees would have to be set out: a flowering almond or pink dogwood, or if they were too exotic—the tone of the whole thing *was* rather grave—the white dogwoods might be the thing. Something, anyhow, that seen from the river road would heighten just a little the sombre effect of those massed trees. She would drive up there to-morrow and try a few things in her mind's eye. . . . But when she got it all

done, what would it be? Another house—an unremarkable
house in an obscure Southern town. It wearied her—it had
wearied her now for some time to even think of all the
houses she had in her time to do with. . . .

Douglas said that all the really good houses in this section had not been built but had evolved—from the double
log cabin with the dog run down its middle. It was true that
the houses built before 1830 had more character. That old
place where they had been yesterday . . . T-shaped it was,
with the detached wings on either side and the L running
back from the centre, the whole perfectly balanced, and
somehow quite *right*. She had commented at the time on its
beauty. Coming home, Douglas had pointed out an old log
granary that had exactly the same lines: two cribs of hewn
logs with an open runway down the middle. The settler, he
said, hurrying to build a second log crib on to his one-room
cabin, often built a better house than the rich tobacco planter
of the '30's and '40's. It was doubtless true. That old house,
Penhally, had evidently been built that way, a wing added
here to meet the needs of a growing family, an L stuck on
there, merely because it was the most convenient place to
put it . . . yet the whole thing had a line and a character
that the more pretentious houses did not have. Tiresome,
those houses, with their Corinthian columns and double parlors and fantastic balconies of wrought iron. The Penhally
house was really the best house she had seen in this section.
A good thing that those people had never had the money to
remodel it!

That boy—the one who ran the farm—did have a touch
of the grand manner. Where could he have gotten it? She
had asked Douglas who the Llewellyns were. He had told
her, reciting dates, and names—counties, doubtless, in Virginia. She had not been able to listen after the first paragraph. Douglas was like that. You pushed a button and out

came facts, about Latin law, the habits of Lucretius, the
exact position of the troops at Gettysburg, or Austerlitz.
You never knew what he hadn't gone into. But then he had
been reading all his life. That immense, book-lined room in
the old house on Servandoni! She could see it now when
she shut her eyes. Square, high-ceilinged, gray in the spring
twilight, with green branches from the court pushing in at
the tall windows, Douglas' mother and two other old ladies
sitting there in the gloom, drinking tea, Marcelle handing
around the *petits fours* from Pons. Names would keep coming up in their talk: Silvania, The Brackets, Pleasant Grove
—those places would seem to spread themselves out around
you in the gray light until you would think you were in
Virginia, not Paris. Douglas' father had kept going back to
America, for his business—he had died at sea, his sixty-fifth
crossing!—but Douglas' mother had never been back since
the Civil War. She had just sat there in that gray room,
receiving calls from people like the Fauquiers or the Fauntleroys.

Natalie had been rather going in for those people that
year. That was how she had met Douglas Parrish. At the
Fauquiers' . . . or the Fauntleroys'? Another high-ceilinged
room, certainly, with green pressing in at the windows and
old ladies drinking tea and talking about Virginia. . . .
They kept talking about Virginia! All the time she had been
seeing that place in the Kinloch woods. . . . The little negro
had come around the curve of the path, whistling. The
branches had made splotches across the paper as she spread
the note out on her knee. She had read it twice before she
fell forward into the grass, her hands flung out in front of
her. Some frail, climbing weed had covered all that bank.
For a long time, whenever she shut her eyes, she could see
those pale green leaves and feel the frail stalks breaking in
her fingers. . . . When she opened her eyes, the little negro
was still standing there, staring. . . .

She had had to talk that day at the Fauquiers'. She had talked about that place. When she called it by name, Douglas said that it had belonged to his great-grandfather. He had been quite excited about that. . . . He was at that time planning his first visit to the United States.

But he had followed them to Cannes and later to Scotland. It was when they were back in Paris that Natalie had come into her room, late at night, in pajamas—people were just beginning then to wear pajamas—and with her hair all disarrayed. She had talked and talked, about Cecily and Gertrude coming on. But it was her own two girls she was thinking of. Eleven and nine years old they were then, and with their teeth still being straightened, and, of course, Grandma Brown was going to die the next spring but she couldn't know that. Her hair would keep coming uncoiled and she would screw it up quickly and then shake her head to make it come down again. "A married man," she kept saying, "and I can't see what you are thinking of. . . ."

"My God," she had said, "weren't you ever in love?"

"In love!" Natalie screamed and ran out of the room. . . .

That had been eighteen years ago. In two more years she would be forty. Forty! It was, then, middle age that she felt coming on her. She did not look her age, by five, ten years. She could see that in the mirror. Still, everything was more of an effort lately. But that was because she so rarely slept well.

But when she had been young, seventeen, eighteen, she had slept like a person drugged . . . in the old house in Baltimore. Her bedroom had overlooked the back premises. Her father would be up and dressed by six o'clock, and walking around in the garden. Hearing his voice, she would bury her face in the pillows, aching for a few more minutes' sleep. If she did not come at the second or third call, he would be up the stairs to pull her out of bed. They would breakfast in the arbor and would be on the road to the farm before seven. The boys would still be feeding when they reached the stables, whistling as they moved about, clouds of steam rising from buckets of warm mash and over everything the clean horse smell. Her father and Ed Terry would sit on a pile of blankets, talking absorbedly, yet following with their eyes the movements of some stringy colt that was just being turned into the pasture. It had been a happy time. . . .

7

There had been silence in the little room for several minutes. Nick had dropped the window cord he had been fooling with and sat now staring out on the street as if he had no interest in what was going on. The banker, Proctor Sabin, sighed and, leaning back in his chair, clasped his hands behind his head. His voice took on a kindly tone:

"I know how you feel. The hardest day in my life was when we sold our old place. . . ."

Chance lifted his head and stared into the man's eyes. "I don't see why," he said. "It won't bring four bushels of wheat to the acre, will it?"

Hearing his own words ring out brutally he was stimulated. It occurred to him that the other two were seated while he had all this time been half standing, half leaning against the small table that flanked Sabin's desk. Like a menial. Exactly like a trusty menial come to get his orders! Well, he *was* there to receive Nick's orders. . . . If Nick would only speak out and say what he was going to do!

He sat down, heavily, on the ornate bench opposite the window. Mr. Sabin had lowered his eyes to the photograph of his daughter, Katherine, that stood in the centre of the broad desk, before the brass penholder and mounted inkwell. In a leather frame that had delicately tooled edges. A

silly girl to be the daughter of such a shrewd father. She
had married a man from Montgomery, Alabama. . . . The
old man was still blinking and a flush showed in his gray
cheeks. Well, no man—not even a Sabin—liked to have his
land aspersed! But it was crawfishy, the whole five hundred
acres, part of that ridge that ran through this county and
the next, and on up through Kentucky. . . . Robert Pryor
had been a fool to pay forty dollars an acre for it. His eyes
still lowered, Mr. Sabin was speaking . . . in his bank di-
rector's voice:

He would not presume, of course, to advise either brother.
Still, he could not but be interested. They knew—bankers
as well as farmers knew—what the agricultural depression
had been. There was old Bob Haynes had refused a hundred
and fifty dollars an acre for his fine wheat land ten years ago.
He knew that for a fact; he himself had advised Bob to
refuse the offer. He was not ashamed to admit it now; any
other banker in the country would have told him the same
thing. . . . But when they sold old Bob out the other day
they didn't get more than fifty cents on the dollar. That was
the way things were and you might as well face it. They
might even have to face a greater depreciation of land values.
He didn't think so. . . . He didn't really think so, but it was
possible. He did think, though, that it would be a long time
before land was up again. . . . The sale at such an advan-
tageous price of such a large acreage as the Penhally tract
would doubtless have a beneficial effect on land values all
over the county. There was that to be considered. He was
not sure that the brothers, as public-spirited citizens, had a
right to refuse an offer that would mean so much to the
whole community. . . .

Nick had taken up the window cord again and was swinging
it this way and that, making little circles of shadows on the
black-and-white-checkered floor. Leaning forward, the cord

dangling between his spread knees, his face turned toward
Mr. Sabin, he had the remote, disinterested air of a man attending a public lecture. He had rather taken that attitude
through the whole thing. The first time, even, when he
brought that woman out to Penhally to see what Chance
thought of the offer. It was her idea, evidently. Parrish
would do anything she said, buy anything on God's earth that
she wanted. She had run hotfoot to Nick as soon as the idea
struck her. Then the two of them had come out to Penhally.
He had seen them coming and had started down the walk.
She called out to him before he reached the gate: "Mr. Llewellyn . . . Mr. Llewellyn . . . I want to buy your farm!"
Gaily, and with a little fluttering of her hands, as if neither of
them could be so unchivalrous as to refuse. Six thousand
acres of the best land in the state turned over to the whim of
an idle woman! No, twenty thousand at least. She had
talked Jim Crenfrew and Edward and the Sycamore people
into selling before she even tackled him. With the two Crenfrew places and Mayfield and Sycamore they would have a
solid block of land extending from the outskirts of Gloversville to the border of the next county. . . . The Llewellyns
had once had the grant of a county from the king. She
ought to have bought up the whole family while she was
about it. They would have sold. Every God-damned one of
them would have sold, except old Cousin Alfred, and he was
crazy. . . .

She would even do away with the names of the places.
Cloverlands Foundation she wanted to call it. It was to be
a sort of glorified hunt club. She had the whole thing worked
out on paper. The land was to be put down in grass. Penhally and Mayfield were to be turned into club houses.
Steeple chasing. And fox hunting, of course. "Revive the
sports of the old South!" He had told her bluntly that Tennesseeans did not ride to hounds. Virginians used to. Still

did, though it was mostly northern millionaires who did the hunting there these days. . . . His mother's grandfather, old Judge Blair, had had the best pack of hounds in eastern Virginia. Old Mag and Old Whiskey and their pups. Every pup had a white ring around his neck and four white feet, and anybody the length and breadth of the county who saw a dog marked like that knew he was Quentin Blair's hound and could run like a shadow. . . . He had heard about them many a time. . . . The people in upper Kentucky rode to hounds. Like the devil. Through brush and over precipices. . . . But Tennesseeans went out of nights and made them a fire and sat there drinking and talking while they listened to the music of the hounds. . . . But all the fool women in Gloversville—and half the men—were enamoured of the idea of getting themselves up in pink coats. . . .

They were already looking at each other wondering who would make the grade socially. It would all be money in old Proctor's pocket. Five thousand dollars they had decided on for the initiation fee. A lot of them would have to borrow the money from the bank. The bank would lend it to them, too. And that meant that they would come down on the farmers, who would need it worse than ever this year. Half of them hadn't sold their tobacco yet. . . .

The news had gotten out, he didn't know just how. Everybody knew that it depended to some extent on him. . . . Mrs. Estlin had stopped him on the street the other day to shake hands with a secret, elated air. The Llewellyn family had always meant a great deal to the community, she said. She was proud of them and she was proud of Gloversville for being so progressive. . . . He had turned on his heel and left her talking. . . .

Standing there on the walk that first day Nick had come out to the farm with the woman, he had had a queer feeling go all over him. He had known from the first how it would turn out. Nick, though he talked non-committally, was in reality swept off his feet by her magnificent plans. The big thing about it, he said, would be the contacts. . . . Contacts with Eastern capital was what he meant. He supposed that was the way business—big business—was done. In club rooms, on golf courses. . . . Then, of course, there was the money. . . .

They had talked it all over for the hundredth time, walking around in the yard at Penhally last night. He had said that it was all right with him for the woman to organize a hunt club, or do any other fool thing that came into her head. But why couldn't she amuse herself with poor land? It was just as good to ride over. Foxes ran just as well over it. The people that she would get down here from the cities wouldn't know one kind of land from another. Why didn't she buy some of that wild land across the river? Why in the name of God did she have to turn twenty thousand acres of the best land in the state into a picnic park?

Nick had told him that he was behind the times. It wasn't land that counted, it was location. The woman was offering a big price for the land because it was located where she wanted it. That land across the river wouldn't do at all for her purposes. . . . He had spoken then, wildly, out of a deep inner confusion:

"Well, by God, I'd hang on to it if it was mine."

Nick had laughed. "I'm a business man," he said.

Going out to get into his car he said coolly that he had told the woman that he wouldn't take a cent under one hundred thousand. She had come up five thousand dollars already. He had an idea that she would reach his figure by Monday. . . . She must have come to it, or they wouldn't be here now. . . .

A hundred thousand dollars sounded like a lot of money. Nick said that they could never hope to have such an offer again, even if land doubled its present value. He supposed not. And if Nick was ever going to sell, this was the time. It was strange, but it had never occurred to him—until this came up—that Nick would ever consider selling the farm! He had never even thought of such a possibility until that day, when, looking from one to the other of their flushed faces he had known that this woman would sooner or later have the land . . . to do what she pleased with. . . .

Nick, walking up and down there under the trees, had had a good deal to say about what the money would mean to the family, to their grandmother, to old Cousin Ellen. Phyllis had already found an apartment in town that she thought would suit them. Mrs. Rollins would let them have the whole upper floor of her house. It had a back gallery that looked out on a garden. Two acres in the whole enclosure. There was even room for a little vegetable garden. Miss Lucy could go on raising her English peas if she wanted to. . . . It would be all right, he supposed, for Cousin Ellen. And it didn't make any difference as far as his grandmother was concerned. She would be dead before the year was out; it made her sick now to spend a night off the place. . . . That was what they couldn't understand. They thought that "conveniences" ought to make anybody happy. But Miss Lucy liked to run out to the back-house, and she boasted that she could keep as clean as any of her grandchildren in a quart of water a day. . . .

He put his hand up and wiped the sweat from his forehead. He had just remembered that he was to have seen Robert Pryor yesterday. About a place for Mort Sully next year. Mort was almost crazy, wanting to know what they were going to do. His wife had been sick over a year now and he was behind on his doctor's bill. He *had* to get a home quick. The other white men on the place could make out all right. Rod Burnham was going to make a crop somewhere up near Russellville and Charley Graves had enough provisions to run him a year. But he didn't know who in the name of God would give Uncle Russell or old Uncle Stephen a home. . . . None of those niggers were any 'count. . . .

Mr. Sabin was saying that a hundred thousand dollars was a good deal of money . . . a good deal of money. . . . Still, he didn't want to advise. . . .

Nick left the window and walked out into the centre of the room. His face was impassive, but the cigarette that he was rolling between his thumb and forefinger trembled. "I reckon we better take a little more time to think this over," he said.

"Yes," Mr. Sabin said, "there's plenty of time." Rising, he, too, seemed to put the matter from him. He pushed the box of cigars that stood open on his desk toward the two young men. "Well, Chance," he asked, "you sold any tobacco?"

"You know damn well I haven't," Chance said. He took a step toward Nick.

"What's the use of fooling around?" he said. "I know what you're going to do. . . . But I'll tell you one thing. If you do keep that land you'll have to get somebody else to farm it. No hand of mine'll ever put a plow in it again. . . . I'll tell you that right now. . . ."

Nick had flung his head up and was looking at him. His eyes were bright, his mouth made a straight line across his pallid face. The cigarette kept going round and round between his thumb and forefinger. Mr. Sabin, fumbling among the papers on his desk, was making a clucking sound, like a disturbed hen. But neither man spoke. They had not spoken by the time Chance found his way to the front door of the building and plunged out into the white sunshine of the street.

8

Across the hall they were dancing. In both parlors. But in this room you could hardly hear the music for the talking. People were standing about in groups of twos and threes, talking, or walking about looking at things. The stout, red-faced woman who for some minutes now had been walking beside Chance was pausing before a portrait that hung on the west wall. Her lorgnette clicked against the frame as she bent forward. She was reading the inscription aloud:

Nicholas Allard Llewellyn
1784–1866

Chance contemplated the brown eyes that looked out from under straight brows as black and heavy as his own. The old boy had scowled even when he was having his picture taken. Well, they said he had been a right mean old fellow in his day. Set on having his own way, at least. If he had not been so hell bent on entailing property and all that business, this red-faced woman would not be walking around in here now. He wished he could remember her name. Something with a hyphen. That meant she was divorced—or English. Something funny, he couldn't remember just what. They seemed to have been together a long time. Just walking around, looking at things. It had been rather a relief. The one he had been with before had talked very rapidly, in a peculiar way. He hadn't been able to understand anything much that she said. . . . He wondered why Nick had given that portrait to the club. It ought, by rights, to go to little Nick. Still, he didn't suppose little Nick would care anything about it, unless he changed a lot after he was grown. He was a peculiar kid. He had gotten to talking in that funny, quick way, too, since they had sent him east to school. Or perhaps it was English. They said that those schools were all run on

the English plan and all the masters were English. They
evidently took a lot of pains with the way the boys talked.
He had heard little Nick say things the Southern way and
then correct himself. He wondered what old Sandy Ware
would have done to a boy who talked like little Nick. Flailed
the living lights out of him, probably. . . . Old Sandy in-
toned Latin verse just the way Cousin Cave did, his chin lifted, his eyes half closed, his voice rising every now and then
to a high quaver. He could spit tobacco juice out of the side
of his mouth without losing a beat. Into a big brass spittoon
that stood always beside his chair. The boys weren't allowed
to spit into that; they had to twist themselves little cups out
of paper. . . .

The stout woman, having made the circle of the room, was
coming to rest on a sofa. She had let her lorgnette fall on
her bosom and sat there now, not trying to see anything,
humming under her breath. As if she were alone. Her face
was a network of spreading purplish veins. The white curly
hair that stood straight up above her forehead was like the
wool of a very old negro. He stood there uncertainly beside
her for a second. This would be a good time to get away.

Mrs. Sabin was beckoning to him now. He left the sofa
and made his way through the crowd of women to where she
sat. She put her plump hand on his arm. "Chauncey," she
said, "who is that one you were talking to?"

"I didn't catch her name," he said, "some sporting woman
from up north."

He had said "spo'ting." When negroes said "a spo'ting
woman" they meant a whore or keeper of a whore house.
But this would be a woman who had her picture in the roto-
gravures. The Nashville *Tennesseean* rotogravure . . . that
was where he had seen this woman's face, the broad, good-
humored face, framed by a horse's forward pricked ears, shot
at you like the projectile from a cannon: Lady Somebody on

Play Boy. The picture had been taken right here, in the hedge field. That cedar tree that showed over the woman's shoulder was one he had left standing, for years, because he liked the looks of it. They said a tree drew fertility out of the soil for sixty feet on every side. He had thought of that every year when they were plowing. . . . Mrs. Sabin kept talking and plucking at his arm. She was trying to pick out all the celebrities. There were half a dozen but he did not know one from the other. There was somewhere about the place a Russian prince. The Sabins had gotten him for dinner, but Phyllis, he had heard Emily say, had done better than that. She had captured the baronet for the evening. He would have thought that a prince was better than a plain baronet. . . .

From where he stood he could see Nick. In a remote corner of the room, talking to a dark, Jewish-looking man, young Rodney. His father had bought the old Blair place in Virginia, almost a generation ago. The spare, blue-eyed man beside them was the English rider all the girls were crazy about. . . . Nick looked thinner than usual, a little drawn about the mouth. This business had probably taken it out of him. . . . Perhaps Nick wasn't thinner than usual; perhaps it was merely that he hadn't seen him in some time. It had been two months now since he had talked to Nick and Sabin there in the bank. Nick had called up out home once or twice. He had not gone to the telephone. He had given them all to understand that he had said his say to Nick and that was all there was to it. He had seen Nick only once since then, in the drug store. Nick had raised his hat curtly, but with no light of recognition in his eye. He had stared blankly and had gone on talking to Leslie Pryor.

Emily was dancing past the door again, with Edward Wickersham; the time before that with a very blond, foreign-looking young man: the Russian prince, probably. They said that Russian aristocrats were washing dishes in restaurants in New York. Well, they couldn't be any harder up than old man Wickersham. He couldn't get credit anywhere in town for a nickel's worth of groceries. They must have let some of these birds in free. . . .

He himself had had no idea of coming until an hour ago. He had never decided not to come. It had just not entered his head, one way or the other. He had been sitting there in the apartment waiting for supper when the bell downstairs had rung, so violently that he had thought it must be a Western Union messenger, or a man to read the meter. When he got out in the hall Emily was already coming up the steps. In a black, low-cut dress, her white cloak slipping off her shoulders. Standing on the step below him she had said, "Chance . . . I'm sorry . . . but you'll have to go to-night. . . ."

He had gone right on up the steps and had set about dressing. The pistol was in the dresser drawer. He had taken it out and put it in his pocket. . . . All the time he could hear her walking around restlessly in the living room. Her car was standing at the curb. They had taken the river road. They had seemed to get here in a very few minutes. He had not even asked Emily why she had decided at the last minute that they must come. She would have what she considered a good reason, or she would not have used that tone. . . . It didn't make any difference. . . .

Mrs. Sabin was turning around to talk to somebody else. If he slid away now she would never know he was gone. It was too hot in here anyhow, the room too full of people. But the hall was empty. Nobody there, that is, but Mrs. Parrish and one man, a short man with a reddish Vandyck beard. He, too, had the air of being somebody. In love with Mrs. Parrish, probably. He kept bending toward her as he talked. She had her head thrown back, a veiled, bright look on her face. She was the kind of woman to set a man crazy all right, but she had the air of being above that sort of thing; probably had had all the men in love with her that she wanted. So now she was taking up horses. . . . Her arms showed up against the white of her dress. Where that stout woman in there burned red she only turned a light biscuit brown. . . . He wondered how long her interest in this hunt club would last. They said she was out every day riding over the land. Once when he passed on the road on the way to Mayfield—what used to be Mayfield!—he had seen her on that big roan, taking a fence. She rode well, and she knew horses. . . . But he wouldn't trust her to pick out a saddle horse for him . . . but that was because eastern people had queer ideas about saddle horses. That last filly of Maggie's, five gaited, but choppy; he had been about to sell her to a negro when Ruffin persuaded him to send her east with some horses he was shipping. Some fool in New Jersey had paid seven hundred and fifty dollars for her!

The man in the funny-looking trousers was turning around. Cousin Alfred! No chance to get away. He was coming straight forward. His fox's face was breaking into a thousand wrinkles. His pale blue child's eyes were bright. He patted his shirt bosom.

"I told 'em I wouldn't come if it was going to cost me anything, so Ruffin he lent me this suit . . . and they gave me a free ticket." His lean hand still clutched Chance's arm. "Look here, boy, you ain't throwing away money on this foolishness?"

"No, sir," Chance said; "they gave me a free ticket, too."

They turned off into the room on the right: Miss Lucy's bedroom it had been. They were using it as a sort of ante-room to the dining room. At any rate this was where the drinks were; the young crowd was congregating: Tom Sidney, the Wickershams, all that set. . . . In the corner by the window some girl was turning handsprings, her white legs flashing up and past a row of black shoulders. She had evidently come prepared for the act; her legs were encased as neatly as any circus performer's in close-fitting satin bloomers. . . . All the bored people from the hall were drifting in to watch her. . . . The Englishwoman with the red face was giving him a smile as she turned away. . . .

Cousin Alfred had stopped in the middle of the floor and was looking up at a picture over the mantel. A plump, brown-haired woman in a tight-waisted black dress, old Cousin Jessie Blair, who had kept house here in the old days. . . . But why had Nick given her picture to a hunt club? Oh, to match the old gentleman, of course; everything correct, even symmetrical. They had kept the picture in here to indicate that if she were still alive she would be dispensing hospitality over a long table that was banked with red roses and glittering with silver and glass.

Cousin Alfred was trying to figure out what kin she was:

". . . Her mother was an Allard and his mother was an Allard and her grandfather was old Cousin Dick Blair that married your great-grandfather's sister. . . . Now, what kin'd that make 'em?"

"God knows," Chance said.

He wasn't up to figuring things like that out to-night. Besides, what difference did it make? The old gentleman had rotted long ago in the old graveyard back there, and so had old Cousin Jessie. . . . His own grandmother was the only person left who even remembered the old days and she would never again set foot in this house.

God knows they had had a hard enough time getting her out of it. Three weeks packing up and the dust rising out of those old cuddies till you couldn't get your breath anywhere in the house. Cousin Ellen kept clawing around on top of wardrobes looking for old letters and things. "I *know* your grandpa's parole is in that black box on top of the wardrobe in your room and now you've gone and done something with it. You reckon you burnt it up with that trash?"

"Now look here. I told you six times already I never saw that damn box. What time have I got to be reading old letters? I never looked on top of that wardrobe in my life and, what's more, I'm not going to do it now. You get down off that step-ladder or I'll pull you down. . . ."

She had collapsed on the bed, crying, and then had called up Nick and told him they couldn't get off that day. None of the furniture wrapped yet, and that man from the transfer company must have lost his way, because he hadn't come back yet, and Miss Lucy wanted to know if he or Phyllis or any of them had ever taken a little hair bracelet out of a box in the bottom drawer of her wash stand.

Standing in the hall, you could hear Nick's voice as plain as if you were in the next room, soothing at first and then getting higher and higher as she kept on nagging at him. "Oh, all right . . . all *right!* Just quit worrying now and everything will be done. I'm starting some more men out there right away. . . ."

He had walked out into the hall and, taking the ear piece away from her, spoke into the black receiver:

"Now, listen. . . . You send one more of those damn fools out here and by God, I'll put a bullet in him. There's six of 'em standing around here now and the sideboard stuck in the front door half an hour. . . ."

Nick had not answered for a moment, then he laughed. "Oh, all right," he said, "if that's the way you feel."

"That's the way I feel," Chance said. . . . That had been about twelve o'clock. They had gotten off around three o'clock in the afternoon. Cousin Ellen had made herself sick with all her going on and they had to stop at Miss Lena Carter's and let her lie down a few minutes. The old lady wouldn't get out of the car. Just sat there, stiff as a ramrod. And she wouldn't even talk to Miss Lena when she came out to the fence and kept asking about where Uncle Stephen and his family had gone, and what they had done with all the Jersey cows, and how she was going to like living in town, and all the questions that a silly fool of an old maid could ask about what wasn't any of her damned business.

When they got to town the old lady took two or three turns around that apartment and then settled down at the window.

She seemed to have been sitting there ever since. Every time you looked up you seemed to see her beaked old nose against the light, like a fierce old hawk that you had caught and put in a cage; the same dead look in the eye. Cousin Ellen fussed around in the kitchen—God knows she didn't know anything about housekeeping; the old lady had never even let her take up the butter. But she was doing the best she could. They had had to let Aunt Dony go. She had quarrelled and gone on until they were all nearly crazy. Cousin Ellen had been upset, but the old lady had hardly turned around from her window.

"That kitchen ain't big enough for Dony," she said. "Tell her to g'long."

The old lady was meaner'n garbroth; couldn't anybody get along with her unless there was plenty of elbow room. Cousin Ellen would try to adjust herself. She would go scrambling around the rest of her life, trying to make the best of things, but the old lady was too old for that and she knew it. . . .

If you couldn't live in a place you couldn't live in it. Then if they put you forcibly to live in such a place it was the same as putting you to death . . . for one hundred thousand dollars. . . . But anybody would say that an old lady, eighty-five years old, had no right to keep her grandchildren from making one hundred thousand dollars . . . because she liked to live in a certain house better than any other house in the world. She had liked to live in that house—it did not seem the same house now—because it was, in a sense, *her* house. She would go calling in the afternoon and then come home and say that it was strange how much cooler the Penhally house was than any other house in the neighborhood. And the flies never bothered you when you sat on the front porch the way they did other places—it was because the niggers kept such a mess around the back door that the flies never had to forage!—but it was in her mind that the Penhally flies were smarter than other people's flies . . . and he had heard her swear up and down that *her* cows wouldn't touch onions! . . .

They had had to send old Cousin Cave over to the Kinloes'. He had a habit of pacing the floor and reciting poetry half the night. You never noticed it at Penhally because he stayed off in the wing, but the woman next door had sent a note over yesterday to say that she would have nervous prostration if she had to listen to it one more night, so Emily just bundled him up and took him over to her house. . . .

A waiter was rearranging the bottles at one end of the long table, crowding them back under the drooping roses to make room for the bowls of ice. He motioned to the man to pour out two drinks. Cousin Alfred received his abstractedly. He couldn't take his eyes off the other end of the room. Everybody seemed to have left except Chloe Ryman and the Wickersham boy.

Chloe was sitting on the arm of a chair, powdering her face. The Wickersham boy kept catching at her and pushing her backward. . . . If he was so hell bent on making the girl, why didn't he take her out on the porch or in somebody's car? He was sprawling on his knees now, his face buried in the chair seat. She was evidently trying to catch somebody's eye; she kept looking around distressedly, but with a kind of smile. It served her right. She had no busi-

ness to go flashing her legs around like that among all these
strangers. It was bad enough when she pulled that sort of
thing over at the club.

Cousin Alfred drew a long breath. *"Well!"* he said, "he's
cert'n'y goin' after her, ain't he?"

"They're both of 'em tight," Chance said.

He moved forward. The Wickersham boy was getting to
his feet. His face was redder than Chloe's; you could hear
him breathing all over the place. Chance took him by the arm.

"Come on," he said, "let's get some air."

The boy was hanging back, looking at Chloe. Chance
closed down on his arm and propelled him through the hall
and out on to the front porch. When the front door had
closed behind them he heaved the boy up by the scruff of his
neck and shot him forward over the shrubbery on to the
grass. He loosed one long hiccough as he fell and then lay
still, his arm curved up over his face.

Chance stepped down from the porch. They had taken up
all the old brick walks around here and made new beds of
gravel. They glimmered away in a dozen different directions.
Right here was where the old poplar tree had been. Nothing
now but smooth turf. It must have been a job to get all
those roots out. They couldn't blast this near the house.

He stopped under the juniper tree. It was too dark to see
anything now. When it was day time you could look out
from here over the whole farm, all the fields, spread out before you. Sixty acres in the hedge field, sixty in the track
field, the big field more like a hundred. . . . He was going
to have a farm. Cousin Sally had given Emily the deed to
the old Kinloe place. Two hundred and fifty acres. None of
it any good, except one creek bottom. . . . "Yes, you can
build 'em up, clays you can build up, any good subsoil . . .
but when land's crawfishy . . ." Emily had cried, sitting
there in the grass.

He went back up the walk. The Wickersham boy had turned over and was lying on his back, but with his eyes shut. He walked past him and up the steps into the hall. The music was still going. Emily was standing near the door with Ruffin Woodford. He went up to her and took hold of her arm.

"My dance," he said.

She laughed. "I should think it was time."

They moved off. The orchestra was playing "Happy Days." You could hear Tom Sims shouting over everything. She had her head tilted back and was looking up at him. He could see the lights of the room reflected in her eyes, and people's faces.

"Have you danced with your hostess?" she asked.

"No," he said.

"Are you going to?"

"No."

She looked away and then back again. *"My God!"* she said, "it's horrible, isn't it?"

He tightened his arm about her shoulders, drew his right hand in to press it against her breast. She held it there for a second, then swung both their hands out again.

"Darling . . ." she said, "did you hate coming very much?"

"It didn't make any difference," he said.

Somebody was cutting in: Ruffin. He was saying something about engaged people dancing together all evening. The music had started again. They were gone. He walked down the hall and back into the room where the liquor was.

Some people were still standing around in there. Three or four men and one woman. He could see her pale-colored dress shimmering on down past the black legs, but he could not see her face.

He poured himself a glass half full of whiskey and drank it off quickly. The whiskey warmed him as it went down, then settled coldly at the pit of his stomach. That was because he hadn't eaten. He hadn't eaten any lunch, and Emily had come just before dinner time. . . . But he must have had breakfast. He could see a heap of cakes, buttered, on a plate . . . but that might have been yesterday. . . .

The group in front of him was breaking up. One of the men was leaning across the table to signal a waiter. *"Garçon, est ce que vous avez . . ."* he broke off, snapping his fingers. "Hell!" he said, "I'll do that every time. . . ."

The woman in the pale dress had stopped and was speaking.

"Chance,. . . . where've you been?"

He stood there looking at her.

"I was just saying I couldn't imagine . . ." The color had receded from her face, leaving it perfectly white except for the spot of rouge high on either cheek bone. . . . "I was just saying. . . ." A man's black shoulder was thrusting past her. Nick's face was suddenly where hers had been.

"Chance isn't dancing much to-night. . . ." He was not looking at the woman. "Chance . . . isn't dancing. He doesn't like the company. . . ."

Chance took a step toward him. "The hell I don't!" he said. He dropped his right hand into his coat pocket. Nick had not moved. The hard, bright look was still in his eyes. His lips, opening, seemed about to speak again. Chance raised his hand with the pistol in it and fired. Nick swayed sidewise against the rattling table, then fell to the floor.

The woman in the pale dress had run out into the hall screaming. The floor was empty for a moment, then people were crowding in from the porch and the halls. There was the black heap in the middle of the floor and above it the white faces. The thin, gray-haired man kneeling beside the body was Parrish. He kept looking from face to face. In the hall a woman was still screaming.

Chance put the pistol on the table behind him, then stepped over and laid his hand on the man's arm.

"You better call the sheriff," he said, "Tom Beaumont. You can get him at the jail . . . or Frank Ebberly's cigar store. . . ."